Summer Rain

Center Point
Large Print

Also by Barbara Freethy and available from Center Point Large Print:

The Lightning Strikes Trilogy
Beautiful Storm
Lightning Lingers

This Large Print Book carries the Seal of Approval of N.A.V.H.

Summer Rain

A LIGHTNING STRIKES NOVEL
BOOK #3

BARBARA FREETHY

CENTER POINT LARGE PRINT
THORNDIKE, MAINE

This Center Point Large Print edition
is published in the year 2017 by arrangement with
Fog City Publishing, LLC.

The text of this Large Print edition is unabridged.
In other aspects, this book may vary
from the original edition.
Printed in the United States of America
on permanent paper.
Set in 16-point Times New Roman type.

ISBN: 978-1-68324-227-7

Library of Congress Cataloging-in-Publication Data

Names: Freethy, Barbara, author.
Title: Summer rain / Barbara Freethy.
Description: Center Point Large Print edition. | Thorndike, Maine :
Center Point Large Print, 2017. | Series: Lightning strikes ; #3
Identifiers: LCCN 2016044595 | ISBN 9781683242277
    (hardcover : alk. paper)
Subjects: LCSH: Large type books. | GSAFD: Romantic suspense
fiction.
Classification: LCC PS3562.O4474 S857 2017 | DDC 813/.54—dc23
LC record available at https://lccn.loc.gov/2016044595

PROLOGUE

She hit the water hard, a relentless force dragging her deep into the sea. She fought with all her strength to get back to the surface, but she wasn't sure she would make it. Her lungs were bursting. Her head was spinning. She could barely think. She needed air desperately.

Kicking and pulling at the water, she finally began to come up. When she burst through the surface, she gasped, sucking in air as quickly as she could. She was yards away from the flaming remnants of the boat, which had been completely shattered by the explosion. How quickly things had changed.

Thunder crashed over her head; lightning flashed across the sky. She swam through the darkness, using the lightning strikes to find her way. She'd never believed in the power of lightning, but now she could feel the electricity charging the air and the water around her.

You will find the last piece of the puzzle. You will know the truth. Her great-grandmother's words rang through her head.

Dani hadn't understood the prophecy.

She hadn't believed her sister when Alicia had said the lightning would show her what she needed to see.

And she'd been doubtful that her brother Jake had actually seen a vision of their dead father right before his plane crashed in the Mexican jungle.

For months, she'd maintained they were all a little crazy, that there was no conspiracy, no mystery to solve.

Now she was a believer. But had she taken too long to see the truth?

The lightning vanished. Darkness surrounded her. The rain poured down on her head, a steamy shower on a hot summer night.

She couldn't see a foot in front of her. But she had to keep going. Lives were at stake, including her own.

She swam harder, then she bumped into something hard and heavy—a body.

Her heart stopped.

Terror ran through her.

Oh, God! Was she too late?

ONE

Eight days earlier

T he storm clouds had been moving through the Texas sky all afternoon, getting darker and thicker by the minute. Dani Monroe had grown up in the southern Texas city of Corpus Christi, and she was used to summer storms, but she'd hoped that today would be dry, that the wedding of her younger sister would be filled only with sunshine and happiness.

Not that Alicia would care that a storm was coming, she thought, as she stared out the window of the childhood bedroom she'd once shared with Alicia. Her sister had been chasing lightning for years, taking award-winning photographs of dramatic electrical storms, hoping always to find a clue to their father's disappearance in the flashes of light.

Lightning was Alicia's gateway to the truth, or so she believed. Dani was not convinced, but she had to admit the events of the past six months were difficult to explain and rationalize away. And it wasn't just Alicia who had started to believe in the lightning legends of their ancestors; it was also her brother Jake. Right before he'd crashed his plane into the Mexican jungle, he'd

7

told her that he'd seen their father in a burst of light. It had happened again days later when he'd been fighting to save the life of the woman he loved.

Both Alicia and Jake were convinced that there was a mystery surrounding their father's death in a stormy plane crash ten years ago. They'd found some clues to support their theory in the last year, but still had no definitive proof, which left them all in what felt like an even worse limbo than they'd been in before.

She wanted it all to go away. She felt almost desperate with that desire. But she couldn't seem to escape the past, no matter how much she wanted to.

She let out a sigh. Damn the storm clouds for making her think about lightning again. Today was supposed to be happy and joyous. She didn't want to feel sad. But it wasn't just the weather making her nostalgic and wistful. Her father's absence on this day was pronounced.

Wyatt Monroe wasn't going to walk Alicia down the aisle for her wedding. He wouldn't be there to give Alicia's groom Michael Cordero a slap on the back and tell him to take care of his little girl. He wouldn't argue with his wife Joanna or stand next to his oldest son Jake in the wedding photos.

And he wouldn't be there to tell her, his middle child, not to worry about being left behind, not to feel bad that both Jake and Alicia had found love before she did. Her father, more than her mother, had always seen the insecurity she tried to hide, a result of middle child syndrome. She wasn't the oldest or the youngest, so she had to be the best. The need still drove her, and she tried to embrace that part of herself, because it did make her try harder, work more, strive for greatness.

On the other hand, she didn't need her dad to tell her anything. She wasn't looking for love. She had a career in Washington DC, working as a legislative assistant for the United States senator from Texas, Ray Dillon. It was a lifelong dream that had finally come true.

She'd started out in Dillon's Corpus Christi office seven years ago, and now she was working at the Capitol with legislators and lobbyists for one of the most important men in the Senate, someone tagged for a presidential run in the not-so-distant future. Her life was crazy but good, and tomorrow she'd be heading back to that life, thoughts of her Texas past forgotten.

The bedroom door opened behind her, and she turned around as Alicia entered the room. Her sister wore a short pink floral bathrobe. Her long, dark hair had been pulled back in a stylish but loose bun at her neck, and her wedding makeup enhanced her thick black lashes, dark eyes, and glowing olive complexion. Alicia took after their father's side of the family with her Latin looks, while Dani had inherited their mother's fair skin, green eyes and dark-blonde hair.

They looked like night and day and their personalities were just as different, but there was still a strong bond of sisterly love between them.

"You look beautiful, Alicia." She felt a knot of emotion come into her throat. "And you don't even have your wedding dress on yet."

"Thanks. I could say the same for you. What do you think of your bridesmaid's dress?"

She glanced in the full-length mirror on the closet door as Alicia walked over next to her. "I like the dress. I might actually wear it again." The silky teal-colored, spaghetti-strapped dress fit her like a glove, and the mini-length made it feel more like a cocktail dress than a bridesmaid's gown.

"I had to fight Mom on it," Alicia said. "She wanted a more traditional gown. You owe me, Dani."

She grinned. "Fine. When I get married, I'll let you pick out your own dress, too." She turned to face her younger sister. "I thought Katherine would be here by now," she added, referring to Jake's girlfriend and the other member of the small bridal party.

"She's downstairs. She'll be up in a second. Mom says the limo will be here in thirty minutes to take us to the church. She wants everything to go according to schedule."

"I'm sure it will," Dani said with a smile, seeing

the stress in Alicia's eyes. "Today will be perfect."

"I hope so. It feels like it's been a lot of work so far."

"Now starts the fun part."

Alicia nodded. "I'm definitely looking forward to the honeymoon."

"Are Jake and Katherine making wedding plans yet?" she asked.

"Not that I've heard. While they're officially engaged and living together, they don't seem to be in a big hurry to set a date. They're just lucky Mom has been consumed with my wedding. As soon as it's over, she'll be pushing them to pick a church and a reception location. I heard Katherine say something about next spring, but we'll see. She's settling into her job at the hospital, and it took her so many years of study to become a doctor that I think she wants to make her career a priority for a while."

"That makes sense."

Alicia wandered over to the window and gazed out at the gray sky. "It looks like rain is coming."

"I think it will hold off until after you tie the knot, but I'm glad you didn't choose to get married outside."

"Me, too. I thought about it, but if it weren't raining, we'd probably all be sweltering in the heat. Summer in Texas is never cool."

"Very true. I just wish it was a sunny day for all the photos." She paused. "But maybe this kind of weather is perfect for my little lightning chaser."

Alicia laughed as she turned back around. "I'd actually prefer to skip the lightning today. It usually brings chaos and change with it."

"Is that the lightning or you?" she teased.

"Maybe both." Alicia paused, her expression turning serious. "I'm so glad you came, Dani. I know you're super busy at work."

"Not too busy for your wedding. I would never miss your special day. But to be completely honest, I am mixing in a little work this weekend. Senator Dillon needs me to represent him at an event in town tomorrow. It's a ribbon-cutting at a new park in honor of a congresswoman who died awhile back in a plane crash."

"I remember that," Alicia said with a nod. "It happened about two years after Dad died, and the circumstances reminded me of that horrible night that we all had to live through. Every time I hear about another crash, I feel the panic and uncertainty of those first few days when we thought a miracle might happen, but the miracle never came."

"I know." She was sorry she'd brought it up. "Let's not talk about any of that today. And I don't want you to worry about me running off before the wedding reception is over. The park event is not until four o'clock tomorrow afternoon. You and Michael will be on your honeymoon by then."

"I'm not worried."

"Good, because Mom made a snotty comment about how I always find a way to do business even during important family events."

"It's fine, Dani. I think it's wonderful that you're passionate about your job. I've always admired your ambition. I certainly don't have the same drive as you do. You're going to change the world—I know it," she added with a smile.

"I'm not sure about the whole world, but I'd like to make some small changes somewhere. Anyway, that's a conversation for another day. I have something else I want to discuss with you." She pulled a dark-purple velvet pouch out of her handbag and took out a gold band. "The wedding ring that our great-grandmother gave me—I think you should have it. You should wear it today. It will bring you luck."

Alicia immediately put up her hand in protest. "No way. Mamich gave that to you. It's your luck, not mine."

"You know I don't believe in Mayan magic. But you do, so the ring means more to you." What she didn't tell Alicia was that the ring had been weighing on her mind ever since Jake had brought it back from Mexico and given it to her. She didn't know why, but having it made her feel strange—it connected her to something she didn't understand and didn't want to learn more about.

"I'm sorry, Dani, but I can't take it," Alicia said with a definitive shake of her head. "That's the wedding ring our great-grandfather put on our great-grandmother's hand. It was her wish for you to have it. She said it would give you strength. That you would need it."

"It's not magic, Alicia."

Alicia's steady gaze met hers. "Why does it bother you to have it, Dani?"

"It's not very attractive."

"That's not the reason," Alicia said with a dismissive wave of her hand.

"I wasn't close to Mamich or that side of the family. I don't believe in lightning gods and other worlds and all that stuff. I just don't. I have too much of Mom in me, I guess. I'm realistic and pragmatic and I believe in what I can see, what's real."

"None of that matters, Dani. Mamich wanted you to have the ring. So, it's yours."

She sighed. "Fine, but it would have been a nice *something old* to wear today."

"Mom already gave me the necklace she got from her mother for my *something old,* so I'm covered. Why don't you put the ring on, Dani? I'd love for you to wear it during the ceremony. It would make it feel like Mamich was here with us."

Alicia's pleading gaze made it impossible to say no. And she was just being silly. She could wear the ring. It didn't have actual magic powers. She slipped it on the third finger of her right hand and then immediately wanted to take it off, but she resisted. If she really believed the ring had no power, then it shouldn't bother her to wear it.

Needing a distraction, she said, "Shall we get you into your dress?"

Before Alicia could reply, the door opened, and Katherine Barrett walked in.

Wearing the same bridesmaid's dress that Dani had on, Katherine's golden-blonde hair was pulled back in a French braid, and her blue eyes were sparkling with happiness.

"How's the bride?" she asked, giving Alicia a hug.

"I'm great, and you look so pretty," Alicia replied. "The color of the dress brings out your eyes."

"Thanks. Any nerves?"

"Not about marrying Michael. About this whole wedding hoopla—a few. I really wanted a simple ceremony and a small gathering, but somehow Mom invited half the neighborhood, and all of Michael's relatives from Miami made the trip, even though we're going to have a dinner there in a few weeks to celebrate. I just wasn't expecting this to turn into such a huge affair."

"You need to breathe," Dani said with a laugh as Alicia ran out of breath. "It's all going to be good. Mom will make sure of that."

"She's also the reason I'm nervous. If I mess up her perfect wedding—"

"You won't. You couldn't." She walked over to the gown hanging in front of the closet. "You need to get in your dress now. It's almost time."

With Katherine's help, she got Alicia into a stunning off-the-shoulder, white lace gown.

"Gorgeous," she murmured, truly impressed by the vision that was her tomboy sister. "You clean up nicer than I imagined."

Alicia laughed. "It took a village to get me to this point." She paused. "But seriously . . . I want to thank both of you for being here, for standing by me. Over the past few months, we've come so close to losing each other that I want you to know how grateful and blessed I am that we're all together."

"We are lucky," Katherine agreed. "There were a few moments in Mexico when I wasn't sure Jake and I would make it back to Texas."

"And a few moments for me and Michael in Miami that made me realize how tenuous a hold we all have on life," Alicia said. "I just wish . . ."

"That Dad was here," Dani finished.

Alicia's troubled gaze met hers. "That, too, of course. I'm going to miss him walking me down the aisle. But I was going to say that I wish we had all the answers and that I could feel like the danger was over, but I don't."

"Alicia, stop," she said. "Not today. You shouldn't be thinking about anything besides marrying Michael."

"I know, but I can't help myself. Dad has been on my mind a lot the last year, and even more because he isn't here today, and he should be. There are still so many unanswered questions about his death, Dani."

"You're not going to answer those questions today—maybe you never will. Sometimes you have to let go and just accept reality."

"I can't do that," Alicia said, shaking her head. "Dad's death ties into what's been happening at MDT, the leak of classified data, the stolen weapons—it's all linked together in some way. And Mamich told Jake that you're going to find the last piece of the puzzle, that you'll be the one to find the truth, Dani."

A shiver ran down her spine at her sister's words. "Mamich always spoke like she was delivering the last line in a tragic play. She was living in a tiny village in Mexico at the time of her death. How could she possibly know anything?" As she finished speaking, thunder rumbled through the air, sending another shiver down her spine.

"I feel like you just woke someone up," Katherine murmured, an uneasy gleam in her blue eyes.

She frowned at her soon-to-be sister-in-law. Katherine was a doctor, a woman of science. "Woke up who?"

"I don't know—angry lightning spirits?"

17

"Come on, Katherine. I know you don't believe in any of this."

"I didn't believe before I went to Mexico with Jake, but that trip and meeting your great-grandmother changed my perspective. Things happened there that I can't explain, and they all seem to be tied to lightning."

"Okay, enough," she said firmly. "We are not going to talk about all that now. Today is for you and Michael, Alicia. It's to celebrate your love and your promise to stay together for the rest of your lives. Let's concentrate on that. The unanswered questions have to wait. I want you to have a happy day."

"Fine," Alicia said. "I will shut up for now. But when I get back from my honeymoon, and I'm finally done with all this wedding mania, we are going to talk again."

"Deal."

"It's time," her mother announced from the doorway, interrupting their conversation. "Is everyone ready?" As Joanna Monroe walked into the room, her gaze fell on her youngest daughter and her eyes grew teary. "Oh, Alicia, you look so pretty."

"Don't cry, Mom," Alicia said warningly. "Or I'm going to start."

"Me, too," Dani said with a little sniff. She wasn't usually sentimental, but today she felt overwhelmed with emotion.

18

"I'll try not to cry, but I make no promises," her mother said, dabbing at her eyes. "The limo is downstairs. It's time to go."

An hour later, Dani watched Alicia and Michael exchange their vows. The look of love on both of their faces was so powerful and intense that Dani felt a huge tug on her heart. She also saw Jake and Katherine exchanging the same kind of adoring looks from across the aisle. Her siblings were on their way to forming their own families.

She was happy for them, but she felt a little alone, a little wistful. Which was silly, because she had a great life. She just needed to get through the reception, and tomorrow's ribbon-cutting, and then she could be on her way back to her life in DC.

After the ceremony, as Michael and Alicia paused for photos on the steps of the church, Jake caught up with her in between pictures of the entire bridal party.

"How are you, Dani?" he asked. "I haven't had a chance to talk to you since you got here."

"It's been a whirlwind," she replied. "It looks like you and Katherine are doing well."

He grinned. "Better than well. She's the love of my life."

"I think I always knew that. Even in high school, you two had a special kind of something. I'm glad you found your way back to each other."

"With a little help from some lightning," he said dryly.

She sighed. "You're not going to start in on me, too, are you? It wasn't so long ago that you were on my side, and we both thought Alicia was crazy."

"Good point. Now I'm as crazy as she is." He paused, his humor dimming. "I just want you to be careful, Dani. I don't think this is over. And I feel like you're going to be the one to finish it. That makes me worry."

Nervous goose bumps ran down her bare arms. "I don't know what *it* is."

"Neither do I. So watch your back."

"Dani, Jake," Alicia called, waving them over. "We want one more family shot."

"Coming," she said, following her brother up the steps.

As they posed together, she was once again very aware of her father's absence.

In the distance, she could hear the buzzing of a small airplane, another reminder of Wyatt Monroe, the man who had spent so much of his life up in the sky.

The clouds parted for just a moment, a sliver of blue shining through. She hoped that was a good sign. But as quickly as it had come, it disappeared.

Maybe Jake was right. Maybe the storm wasn't over yet.

TWO

I t looks good. They'll never forget her now," Patrick Kane told his father, Harris Kane, as they surveyed the newly-landscaped children's playground and park.

The placard at the entrance of the park commemorated his mother, Jackie Kane. His mom had been a congresswoman and a tireless advocate for the poor in her years as a public servant. It had been her dream to turn what had once been a drug and violence-riddled park into a place where children could play safely, where mothers could watch their kids without being afraid of who was watching them. That dream was coming true today, and he couldn't quite believe it. Ever since his mother's death eight years ago, his father had worked on the idea of creating something lasting in her honor, and today it was done.

As he glanced at his father, he saw the stress in his dad's blue eyes. Since becoming a widow, his father's hair had gone from salt-and-pepper to gray and finally to white as he passed his sixty-sixth year. Building this playground and park had kept his dad going through the grief and anger, giving him something positive to think about in the wake of the tragic accident that had taken Jackie's life along with four others. Patrick just hoped that the culmination of his father's vision to honor his mother would be fulfilling for him, and that he wouldn't suffer a huge let-down when it was over.

"I hope the rain holds off," Harris continued, looking up at the sky. "I thought the storm would pass last night, but there is thunder and lightning in tonight's forecast, too. If we have to cancel this—"

"We won't. The rain isn't expected for another hour or two. And you know it won't last long. It's summer in Texas. It will shower, and then it will be done."

"I hope you're right. I want this to be perfect."

He hoped he was right, too, but while it was a little before four in the afternoon, it was dark as night, huge black storm clouds blocking out the sun. It wasn't cold, though. The temperature was in the low eighties, and he was sweating through the dress shirt and tie he'd put on for the occasion.

His father's gaze turned back to him. "I want to thank you, Patrick. This project has taken up a lot of my time over the years, and perhaps there were occasions when I didn't give you as much attention as I should have."

"Not at all, Dad. I wanted this as much as you did. It was Mom's dream, and you made it happen." He'd been twenty-two years old when his mom had died. Sometimes it felt like a lifetime ago, and sometimes it felt like yesterday. "I just wish she could have done it herself."

"We all do, son," Harris said with a heavy sigh. "But it was God's will."

"Was it?" The question came out before he could stop it, and he mentally kicked himself as he saw the change come over his father's expression.

"Patrick, we've talked about this—"

"And I'm sorry I brought it up today," he said, quickly backpedaling. "But the more research I do on the events of that day, the more I wonder if we really know the truth about the plane crash."

"It was an accident, Patrick. Do you really think law enforcement didn't do everything they could to find out what was behind the crash that took the lives of a US congresswoman, a US senator, two staffers and a pilot? You just have to accept that some tragedies are unexplainable accidents. I know it's difficult. I've gone over the same kinds of questions in my head. And I've wasted a lot of time doing that. I don't want to see you make the same mistake, and frankly, I don't understand why you're suddenly so interested. It's been eight years. What's changed?"

He couldn't tell his father what had triggered his renewed interest in the crash, not unless he knew it was true, because the last thing he wanted to do was paint his mother as someone other than the saint everyone believed she'd been, including himself. But since he'd reached out to some of the family members of the people killed in the crash to invite them to the ceremony, he'd heard some comments that made him uneasy. He'd always followed his instincts, especially when it came to mysteries. It was what made him a good investigative journalist.

But this wasn't just a story; this was his mother's life and her legacy, and he was conflicted about how far he wanted to go. He just knew he wasn't quite ready to put all his questions away.

Seeing his father's speculative gaze, he realized his dad was still waiting for an answer. "You're right, today is not the day to discuss the past. I want this afternoon to be only about Mom."

"Good. Your mother wouldn't like you stirring up trouble."

He wasn't so sure about that. While his father hated conflict, his mother had never shied away from a fight. He just hoped her courage to do battle wasn't why she'd lost her life.

"There's Jill," his dad said, waving his hand toward the parking lots. "Let's say hello."

He followed his father down the path. His mother's younger sister, Jill Conroy, a short, curvy brunette who looked a lot like his mom, gave him a hug. Next to her was his uncle Wallace, a tall, thin man with bookish glasses that always seemed to slide down his nose, and on the other side was his cousin Marcus, who'd inherited his brown hair and stocky, football player physique from his mother's side of the family. Marcus was a year younger than him and since they were both only children, they'd been more like brothers than cousins.

"How's it going?" Marcus asked, as their parents moved away to greet friends and relatives.

"Good. It looks like we will have a big crowd for the opening."

The small parking lot was now lined with cars, and the streets surrounding the park were also showing heavy traffic, with more people walking in from the surrounding neighborhood. In an area that was not known for its beauty, the two-acre park with its children's playground, basketball court, and newly planted rose garden was an oasis of beauty in an otherwise blighted block of crowded, dingy apartment buildings and run-down homes.

"The park looks great," Marcus said. "Your mother would be happy."

"I think so, too. Hopefully, it will stay the way it looks now."

"You and your dad have done all you can; the rest is up to the community."

"Yeah, I know." His gaze moved to a very tall man dressed in a black suit. A former NBA player, Congressman Davis Parker had taken his mother's congressional seat after her death, and he had been very supportive of his father's efforts to build the park.

"Is that Davis Parker?" Marcus murmured, a note of awe in his voice.

Patrick smiled. "I suppose you want to meet him."

"Hell, yes, I want to meet him. He took the Lakers to two NBA finals."

"About fifteen years ago."

"Still, he's a legend. Introduce me."

"After the ceremony," he said, as Davis and his father joined the mayor.

"Fine, but don't forget."

"I doubt you'll let me."

"Have you talked to him about the plane crash?" Marcus asked.

"He's been unavailable. Same with Senator Dillon. No one wants to talk to me."

"I can't imagine why," Marcus said dryly. "You just shook up the entire pharmaceutical industry with your book about counterfeit drugs. Your story has singlehandedly launched about three dozen lawsuits and sent at least six people to jail."

"I hit a home run with that one," he acknowledged. "But the only people who should be nervous around me are people who have something to hide."

His cousin shook his head, giving him a worried look. "I know I can't tell you what to do . . ."

"But you're still going to try."

"There are a lot of controversies that could serve as the subject of your next article or book.

Digging into your mom's crash is going to be painful, and who knows what you'll find out? You've already heard one disturbing comment about your mother. Do you really want to hear more?"

"Maybe I just want to know if it's true," he said evenly. "If it's not, I want to make sure that her reputation stays intact."

"You should just leave it alone. Don't let one rumor change the way you think about her. Let her rest in peace."

"You sound like my father, but the truth is I think my mother would want me to go after the truth. She always told me to trust my gut. She said that's what she did. So far, my gut hasn't let me down. If there's something to know, I want to know what it is."

"Fine. I'm too smart to argue with someone as stubborn as you."

"You argue in court every single day with people far more stubborn than me."

"Yeah, but they're attorneys. I know what makes them tick—how to find their weakness. You are not that easy." Marcus paused, his gaze moving toward the sidewalk. "Whoa, who do we have here?"

Patrick's gut tightened as he saw the beautiful blonde walking toward the park. An intense attraction immediately ran through him. The woman was like a beacon of sunlight on a dark day, her blonde hair shiny in the dim light as it swirled in waves around her face and shoulders. Wearing a form-fitting black skirt, a silky blue blouse, and high heels, she walked with confidence and purpose, the kind of woman who knew how to get attention without looking like she was trying. She literally stole his breath away.

The woman paused, and her gaze suddenly met his. Even from a dozen feet away, he could feel the heat of her look, and his chest grew tight. He felt a little like he'd been sucker-punched. He couldn't remember the last time he felt such an incredibly strong pull to a woman.

And then she looked away from him as Congressman Parker approached her and gave her a friendly hug.

So she knew the congressman. That was interesting. Parker was married with three kids, and had at least ten years on this woman . . . not that that meant anything. They could be involved—or not. He shouldn't care one way or the other.

"Patrick?"

Marcus's voice drew his attention back to him. "What?"

"Who's the woman?"

"I have no idea. She could be anyone."

"Maybe you should find out."

"Why?"

Marcus laughed. "Because I haven't seen that

kind of yearning look on your face since you asked Amy Rogers to the prom."

"I have no particular look on my face," he denied.

"She's hot. You should go talk to her."

He wanted to talk to her, not just because she was beautiful and sexy and really intriguing, but also because she knew Congressman Parker. Unfortunately, his father was waving him over.

"That will have to wait. It's show time."

The ceremony was more personal and touching than Dani had expected. She'd thought it would be a simple ribbon cutting, a few short speeches by community leaders and that would be that, but Harris Kane, a handsome and eloquent man, spoke at length about his wife Jackie, her love of family and friends, and her devotion to the people in her community and the state of Texas.

The stories about Jackie's life were inspiring. Like Jackie, Dani wanted a political career. It wasn't going to be enough for her to be someone's staffer; she wanted to be more. And it wasn't just the title of congresswoman or senator that she wanted, although that would be great; it was the idea of being able to do something that mattered. She wanted to make a difference in the world, the way Jackie Kane had made a difference.

When Harris finished speaking, his son Patrick stepped behind the podium.

Her stomach clenched as she realized Patrick Kane was the man she'd caught staring at her when she first arrived. She'd felt his gaze on her even before their eyes had met. And the look that had passed between them had been unsettling— intense, deep, a little dark—as if some important, meaningful moment had just occurred. But that was a crazy thought.

Patrick was a very attractive man. He was over six feet tall, with broad shoulders and an athletic grace. His dark hair was thick and wavy, and his compelling brown eyes demanded attention. He spoke in a smooth, husky male tone that made her nerves tingle and thoughts of hearing that voice in the dark of the night, his lips inches away from hers, sent an unexpected wave of desire through her.

She wanted to look away. In fact, there was a part of her that felt like she should walk away, get as far from this unsettling feeling as she could.

She had a plan for her life, one that was all about career goals and milestones. It had taken her a long time to get to DC. She wasn't going to let anyone or anything distract her.

She blew out a breath, wishing for a cool breeze, something to wash away the heat, but the humidity, the threatening clouds, showed her no mercy. She just had to hope that Patrick's speech would end soon.

In the meantime, she forced herself to look away

from him, her gaze moving to her hands, where she'd been subconsciously playing with the gold ring on her finger—the wedding band that had belonged to her great-grandmother, the ring she'd worn at Alicia's insistence, the piece of jewelry she couldn't seem to take off. Last night, the band had felt too small for her finger. She'd tugged at it, but it hadn't budged, so she'd left it alone. Now, the ring seemed looser, moving easily around her finger, feeling almost as if it could slip off at any moment.

Why, oh why, had her great-grandmother given her the most personal piece of jewelry she owned? And why had Mamich thought that it would bring her strength that she would need one day? *Just more superstitious mumbo-jumbo,* she told herself. Alicia and even Jake might be convinced that her great-grandmother had been imbued with some sacred magical powers from her Mayan ancestors, but she just couldn't go there. She didn't believe in magic or the universe or fate. Those just seemed like too-easy explanations for random events or chance meetings.

Life was made up of coincidences. They didn't always have to mean anything.

The crowd broke into applause, and she looked up, realizing that Patrick's speech was over. Congressman Parker said a few words and then turned the microphone over to the mayor, who also spoke. Finally, the ribbon in front of the

31

park entrance was cut. A crowd of children ran immediately into the playground, followed more slowly by their parents.

Dani waited for her opportunity to speak to the Kanes on behalf of Senator Dillon, but the line was long and never-ending, so she decided to take a walk around the park. Two basketball courts and the kids' playground took up most of the front end of the park, then a small incline led up to a barbecue and picnic area and new restrooms. Behind that building was a beautiful flower garden with grassy areas and benches placed in between the flowers, giving the area a serene and peaceful look.

Not many people had made it to this part of the park, and as she wandered along the path, inhaling the thick, floral scents, she started to relax. The past few days had been so busy. First, she'd had to work overtime to finish up projects before the weekend. Then the wedding chaos had consumed every second of her time. Finally, she had a chance to breathe, and it felt good.

She paused by a rose bush and leaned forward to see a perfect yellow rose. She gently fingered the petals, wondering how the flower was doing so well in the Texas heat. She'd always found it a little hard to bloom here in Corpus Christi. She'd tried, but she'd felt trapped, not just by the limitations of the job but also by the past. She didn't like to own up to the fact that her father's death still weighed on her mind, but it was the truth. In Corpus Christi, she couldn't get away from the memories, so she'd been thrilled when the job in DC had come along.

She'd finally felt like she had the opportunity to live her own life, to find her own way, whatever that way would be.

A chorus of voices drew her head up. She let go of the rose as three young girls approached. She gave them a smile and then made her way back to the front of the park. The line for Patrick and his father was down to one person. *Thank goodness.* She could pay her respects and go.

When the elderly woman in front of her finished her conversation with Harris, Dani stepped forward.

"Hello. I'm Danielle Monroe," she said, shaking Harris's hand. "I'm here on behalf of Senator Dillon. He asked me to give you his regards and tell you how happy he is to have the park finally open. He knows how much it meant to your wife."

Harris nodded, his eyes gleaming with gratitude. "I appreciate the support the senator has given us over the years. Please let him know that."

"I will. He told me that Jackie was an amazing woman, and he admired her very much."

"She was one-of-a-kind," Harris said. As he finished speaking, a female reporter from the local paper interrupted them.

"I'm sorry to bother you," the woman said. "But the paper wants to get a few more photos with you by the placard if that's all right, Mr. Kane."

"Yes, of course." He smiled at Dani. "Thanks again for coming. Please excuse me."

As Harris left, she gave Patrick a tentative, wary smile. "Your speech was very moving, Mr. Kane."

"Call me Patrick. My father is Mr. Kane. And it wasn't easy to follow my dad's speech. As a teacher, he's used to inspiring people with his words."

"He was very articulate," she agreed. "He painted a wonderful picture of your mother."

"They were madly in love for twenty-five years. He still misses her every day."

"You said he's a teacher?"

"A professor of English at Texas A&M."

"My alma mater. Did you go there as well?"

"No, I went to Northwestern in Chicago. At the time, I was eager to go to college somewhere other than Texas. Now, I sometimes wish I'd stayed home, that I'd been around those last few years of my mother's life."

She could see the pain in his eyes, and her heart went out to him. She knew how he felt. While she hadn't left home, she'd been living in an apartment near the university when her father's plane had gone down. So she hadn't spent that much time with her dad in the weeks preceding his death.

"So you work for Senator Dillon?" Patrick asked.

"Yes, I'm a legislative assistant in his DC office."

"I'm surprised he didn't send one of his local staffers."

"I used to be one of his local staffers, and I was in town for my sister's wedding. I know he wishes he could have come himself, but his schedule is extremely busy."

"Perhaps that's why he hasn't returned any of my calls."

"You've been calling him?"

"I have. I've left several messages with his chief of staff and also her assistant."

"His call-back list is a mile long," she said, automatically going on the defensive. "Was your question about this event?"

"No, it wasn't. It was about my mother's death. I have some questions about the plane crash that took her life, and I think he might be able to help me."

His words shocked her. "Why would Senator Dillon know anything about that? He wasn't in office then."

"But he was very good friends with Senator Owen Stuart, who died alongside my mother. Senator Dillon and Senator Stuart went to college together. I'm sure your boss followed the investigation very closely."

"Oh. I suppose that would be true," she said,

feeling a little unsettled by the conversation. She felt like she needed to be on her guard, but she wasn't sure why.

"How long have you worked for him?"

"Seven years. I came on board shortly after he won the seat."

"Would you be able to help me get a meeting with him?"

"I would be happy to pass along the request, but if you've already spoken to his chief of staff, there's not much I can do."

"I'm not trying to cause him any problems, but I lost my mother, and some information has recently come to light that's made me question what I know about her death. I really won't take up much of his time."

His words resonated deep within her. Not only because she'd lost her father, but because she'd also been given information in the past year that had brought back all the pain of her father's death. They'd both lost parents in plane crashes, and apparently Patrick had unanswered questions, too. It was an odd connection they had.

"Sometimes there are no answers—or at least no good answers," she said, talking as much about her own situation as his. "The truth doesn't always set you free. It's a nice sentiment for a card, but it's not reality."

"That's a cynical point of view."

"I'd prefer to think of it as realistic. I know what it's like to lose a parent. I lost my dad in a plane crash, too, and they never found his body. We've spent years looking for answers and there just aren't any. I've seen my sister, and most recently my brother, get completely caught up in a search for a reason that just doesn't exist."

His eyes blazed at that piece of information. "Who was your father? When did he die? Where did the crash happen?"

She frowned at the rapid fire of questions. "His name was Wyatt Monroe. You wouldn't know him. He wasn't anyone important. He flew small planes for a charter service, and he was in one of those planes when he got caught in a monster storm over the Gulf of Mexico."

"Did he make a distress call?"

"No, he didn't."

"There was no call from the plane my mother was on, either. When did he die?"

"Ten years ago. Two years before your mom. You're making it sound like there's a link between their deaths, but there isn't one."

"Probably not."

"No *probably* about it." She frowned, deciding she'd had enough of the conversation. "I should go. It was nice to meet you."

"I'd really like to talk to Senator Dillon. Can you give me some tips on how to get through?"

"Not really. I can tell him what you've told me,

but it's up to him on whether or not he wants to return your call."

"I can be very persistent."

She shrugged. "That's not really relevant."

A gleam entered Patrick's eyes. "You don't know anything about me, do you?"

"I know you're Jackie Kane's son. Beyond that, no. Why? What should I know?"

"It doesn't matter. Let's just say I'm good at getting to the truth, no matter how many people want to cover it up."

"Is someone covering up the truth?" she challenged.

"I'm not sure yet." Patrick paused as his father called his name.

"Looks like you have to go," she said.

"I do, but we should talk again, Ms. Monroe." He held out his hand.

As his fingers wrapped around hers, sharp, nervous, worrisome tingles ran through her body. The man was potent—no doubt about it. She was really happy she was getting on a plane to DC in a few hours. She needed to put some distance between herself and Patrick Kane.

Their hands clung together far too long. She didn't know why she felt like she couldn't let go—or why he was still hanging on to her. But finally she pulled her hand free.

As Patrick went over to join his father, she walked quickly out of the park, her heart beating way too fast. Fortunately, her car was parked a half mile away, so by the time she slipped behind the wheel, her pulse was heading back to normal. She needed to get out of Texas so she could get back on her game.

She grabbed the bottle of water she'd stashed in the console and took a sip. It was hot, but she didn't care. She needed something to wet her dry lips.

As she set the bottle down, her phone buzzed. It was the senator's private number. That pumped her heart back up again. She rarely spoke to the senator directly these days. Since he'd replaced his old chief of staff six months ago with Erica Hunt, all staff members were requested to go through Erica for things they used to take directly to the senator.

"Hello?"

"Dani, how are things going? Did you speak to the Kanes?"

"Yes. I gave Mr. Kane and his son Patrick your regards. The park is beautiful. It's going to be really good for the community."

"How was the turnout?"

"At least a hundred people or so."

"Excellent. Happy to hear that. Was Davis Parker there?"

"He was."

"I bet he was posing for a lot of pictures," the senator said dryly. While he and Congressman

Parker worked on some local issues together, they weren't friends.

"He's never seen a camera he doesn't like," she said.

"That's true. What did the Kanes have to say?"

"Harris Kane said he was grateful for the support you'd given him."

"It was a worthy cause. And his son?"

Was there something behind the senator's question? Or was she imagining things?

"Patrick told me that he's been trying to get in touch with you. He has some questions about his mother's death, the investigation of her plane crash. He thinks you may be able to help him."

"I wondered why he was calling me so frequently."

"Yes. He's very determined to connect with you."

"I sympathize with his pain. I lost a good friend on that plane. Owen was in my wedding. We were as close as brothers, but I can't get bogged down in that old story. Patrick is looking for dirt and controversy, and that's the last thing I need."

"Is there any dirt to find?" she asked tentatively. "I thought the crash was caused by mechanical failure."

"That was the conclusion, but Patrick Kane is making a name for himself digging into what he considers cover-ups. He's a troublemaker. I like his father, and I was a big admirer of his mother, but my support for the family ends there. I helped them get the park to completion. That's all I can do."

"I understand."

"I hope so. I've spent the last few months dealing with the fallout from the problems at MDT. I don't need another distraction. I want to move ahead with new legislation, not old problems. If you see him again—"

"I won't. I'm leaving the park now."

"Good. All right then. Thank you, Dani. I appreciate you taking the time. How was the wedding?"

"It was wonderful. It went off without a hitch."

"I'm happy to hear that. I'll see you when you get back to DC."

"Yes." She let out a breath as she ended the call, a little disturbed by the conversation.

It was clear that the senator wasn't just too busy to call Patrick back; he was definitely avoiding him. But what had he meant by saying Patrick was making a name for himself digging up cover-ups?

She clicked on the Internet icon on her phone and searched for Patrick's name. A dozen results came up, and she felt like an idiot.

How had she not realized that Patrick Kane was the author of the bestselling book *Medical Roulette*? His exposé on the rapidly growing counterfeit drug industry was now being made into a movie. She hadn't read the book, but she'd definitely heard about it. She just hadn't paid attention to the author's name. But now she understood why the senator was wary of speaking to Patrick.

She set the phone down on the console as thunder rumbled through the air. She suddenly became aware of the first drops of rain hitting her windshield. The storm had arrived. Time to go.

As she started the car, her gaze fell on her right hand, and her jaw dropped open in shock.

The ring was gone. Her great-grandmother's ring was no longer on her finger. What the hell?

She looked around the car and saw nothing. She searched her bag. Then she got out and checked underneath the seat and on the pavement. The ring was nowhere to be seen.

Where had she lost it?

It could have been anywhere. She'd walked through the entire park.

And then she remembered the roses. Had the ring come off when she'd touched the petals of that perfect rose? Or had it come off when she'd had a hard time letting go of Patrick's hand?

She stood next to the car, debating what to do. She didn't like the ring. She'd wanted to get rid of it ever since she'd received it. But she couldn't lose it like this. It felt wrong. Alicia would kill her if she didn't at least try to find it.

She grabbed her keys and handbag and walked back down the street.

By the time she reached the park, the lot had

emptied out and people were headed back to their homes and out of the rain. She searched the area where she'd shaken hands with Patrick and found nothing. Then she walked up the hill.

Thunder cracked the air and her nerves tensed.

She didn't care about lightning and thunder, she told herself. It was just a storm, not an omen. She wasn't Alicia. She didn't think the lightning was trying to show her something. Unless, of course, it illuminated where her ring was. That would be helpful.

As she walked behind the restrooms, the sky grew even darker. She had a feeling a downpour was coming, something worse than the random drops hitting her head now. She walked more quickly, entering the flower garden. As she turned from one path to the next, a jagged bolt of lightning ran down the sky, spotlighting the area in front of her.

She'd thought she was alone. But she wasn't. There were two men in the garden, and they were fighting each other with intensity and purpose.

She was shocked to realize one of those men was Patrick.

The other was unrecognizable, wearing dark jeans and a navy-blue hooded sweatshirt.

Lightning flashed again. It hit something metal. There was a knife in the hands of the man attacking Patrick.

Oh, God!

43

Her breath caught in her chest. She felt paralyzed with fear. She needed to help or run or do something.

Patrick swung a fist into the man's face. The other man took the blow but came back with a deadlier punch, knocking Patrick to the ground.

As a stunned Patrick struggled to get up, the man raised the knife. He lunged forward. Patrick tried to move, but the knife slashed his shirt. He put a hand to his chest as he lurched to his feet, and she saw blood covering his shirt.

Thunder ran through her, echoing the pounding of her heart.

The man raised the knife again.

Patrick was trying to get away, but it was clear he was too hurt to move fast.

Instinct propelled her forward. She had her keys and on the ring was a container of pepper spray. A *one-two punch* she thought, remembering what a self-defense instructor had once told her. *Use what you have and don't hesitate.* She didn't have much, but she had surprise on her side.

She ran forward as lightning struck again, giving her a good look at her target. She swung her large, heavy handbag at the back of the attacker's head.

He went down on his knees, the knife flying out of his hand.

She hit him again as he tried to reach for it.

He scrambled a few feet away, then got back on

his feet. He turned toward her, and she aimed the pepper spray at his eyes.

He screamed and put his hands to his face.

She hit him again with her bag as Patrick grabbed the knife from the ground.

The attacker hesitated for one second, then turned and ran.

She let out a breath in relief. Once he was gone, she turned to Patrick, who had one hand pressed against his chest, blood dripping from his fingers. "Are you all right?"

He stared at her in confusion. "I . . . I . . . Why did you come back?"

"That's not important. We need to get you to the hospital." She could see he was dazed and probably on his way to losing consciousness. She had to get him out of the park as fast as possible. She put her arm around him and helped him down the path.

As they passed the rose bushes, lightning flashed again, blinding them with a bright light. She stopped for a second to get her bearings. That's when she saw the glint of gold on the ground.

"Hang on," she said, letting go of him for just a second. Her ring was on the ground, right under the perfect yellow rose she'd admired earlier in the day.

She slipped it onto her finger, shivering as she realized the ring had brought her back to Patrick.

It was supposed to bring her luck, but tonight it had brought Patrick luck. *If she hadn't come back for the ring . . .*

She couldn't go there—at least not right now.

She helped Patrick down the street to her car. It seemed to take forever to get there. On her way to the hospital, she called 911 to report what had happened. The dispatcher told her that officers would meet her in the ER.

As she ended the call, she gave Patrick a worried look. He was slumped in his seat, but his eyes were still open, and his gaze was on her.

"You saved my life," he said heavily. "Why were you there?"

"I was looking for my ring."

"But why didn't you run?"

"I don't know. I should have," she murmured. "What happened? Who was that man?"

"I have no idea."

"Why were you alone? Why did you stay behind?"

"I wanted to spend time in the park after everyone left. The guy jumped me from behind."

"Did he want money?"

"He didn't ask for anything; he just started pounding me."

"It was random?"

He shrugged as if he didn't know, but she had a feeling he knew a lot more than he was saying.

THREE

When they reached the hospital, Patrick was whisked away to an examining room, leaving Dani to wait in the lobby of the Emergency Department for the police. Now that the crisis was over, she felt a little lightheaded. She stumbled over to the nearest chair and sat down. It was then she saw the blood on her blouse—Patrick's blood.

Drawing in several deep breaths, she tried to calm her racing pulse, but images from the last half hour spun through her head on a dizzying carousel. One minute she'd been sitting in her car, talking to her boss, and the next minute she'd been attacking a knife-wielding man with her handbag, and it was all because of the damn ring.

She looked at her hand. The gold ring was back in its place, but there was blood on her fingers.

The sight of it made her stomach roll. She had to fight not to throw up. The realization that she could have been killed tonight was starting to sink in. It was a staggering, unbelievable thought.

"Dani?"

The surprised female voice brought her head up. "Katherine," she said, relieved to see a familiar and friendly face. Her soon-to-be sister-in-law wore blue doctor scrubs, her blonde hair pulled back into a ponytail, her blue eyes worried.

"Are you sick? Are you hurt? What's wrong? I couldn't believe it when I saw you sitting here, and you have blood on your hands."

"I'm not hurt. It's not my blood." She started to get to her feet, then swayed.

Katherine pushed her back into the chair and sat down next to her. "What happened? Is it your mom, someone else in the family? I didn't even know you were still in town."

"It isn't my mom or anyone you know. I had to go to an event for Senator Dillon." She took another deep breath. "It was at a new park in a bad neighborhood. I went back to look for this damn ring." She held up her hand. "It had fallen off my finger, and I knew Alicia would kill me if I lost it, so I went to look for it. Everyone was gone. The storm had hit, and the park was empty, or so I thought. I suddenly found myself in the middle of a fight."

"Oh, my God! What did you do?"

"I knew one of the men. His father had built the park in honor of his mother. I knew he was a good guy, but the other man had a knife, and Patrick was in trouble. I didn't think. I just jumped into the middle of the fight. I swung my bag at the guy's head as hard as I could and then I pepper sprayed him. By that time, Patrick had gotten to the knife and his attacker ran away."

"I can't believe you did that," Katherine said in amazement. "Where are the police?"

"On their way. I called from the car. I didn't want to wait at the park for help so I brought Patrick in. I really hope he's all right. His shirt was covered in blood. I know he was stabbed at least once. Can you check on him?"

"Of course. But I can assure you that he's being well taken care of; I'm more concerned about you right now, Dani."

"I'm okay. I'm just a little shaken up, but I'll be fine."

"You were so lucky. I'm glad the person didn't have a gun."

"Me, too."

"Have you called your mother?"

"No," she said quickly. "And you can't tell her. She'll be down here in a quick minute, and I don't need that. I'm supposed to be flying back to DC tonight." She glanced down at her watch and realized her flight was leaving in forty minutes. "Damn, I'll never make my flight now."

"So go in the morning."

"I have to be at work tomorrow. I'll see if there's another one later tonight." She pulled out her phone, but before she could go shopping for flights, a man and a woman approached her. Both wore suits and badges from the police department.

"Miss Monroe?" the man asked.

"Yes." She got to her feet, happy to feel a little more stable now.

"I'm Detective Hobbs," he replied. "And this is Detective Rodriguez. We'd like to talk to you about what happened in the park. You reported an assault?"

"Yes. The man who was attacked is Patrick Kane. His family opened the new park on Freeborne Street this afternoon."

The two detectives exchanged a quick look, then the man said, "Tell us exactly what happened."

"I will. I don't know much, though. Mr. Kane might be able to tell you more."

"I'll check on him," Katherine said.

"Thanks," she said. "I appreciate it."

"No problem. I'm going to call Jake, too."

"I don't need my older brother."

"We'll see." Katherine left before Dani could offer another protest.

She turned her attention back to the detectives. She told them exactly what had happened in the park and gave as clear of a description of the man as she could, acknowledging that she didn't get a good look at the attacker's face, and it was possible that she wouldn't recognize him if she saw him again.

It bothered her that the man could probably recognize her, though. It made her feel vulnerable. But she told herself there was no reason to worry.

In a few hours, she'd be back in DC and several states away.

Jake came in as she was finishing up with the detectives. He had obviously rushed right over as soon as Katherine called him. As she gave him a hug, Katherine came back and told the detectives they could speak to Mr. Kane.

After the officers left, Dani sought a more detailed answer from Katherine. "How is he doing?"

"He's going to be fine. The knife wound wasn't deep and missed vital organs. He's been stitched up, and he's eager to be on his way. He did ask if you'd wait for him. He'd like to speak to you when he's done."

She frowned. "I don't know if I can. I still need to see if I can catch another flight tonight."

"Why don't you stay?" Jake asked. "If you don't want to go back to Mom's, we've got a nice couch you can sleep on."

"It's a great offer, and I might take you up on it if I can't get on a plane in the next few hours."

"Katherine told me you broke up a fight," he added. "What the hell were you thinking, Dani?" There was both annoyance and admiration in his tone.

"I wasn't thinking; it was instinct." She held up her hand. "And this stupid ring. Right now, it feels like it won't come off no matter how hard I try to slide it over my knuckle. Earlier today, it was slipping around like it was way too big. In fact, I lost it in the park. I went back to look for it, and that's how I ended up in the middle of the fight."

Jake stared back at her, a gleam in his eyes. "Well, that's interesting."

"It's not a magic ring, Jake."

"Are you sure? There was a lot of lightning tonight. It was rattling my nerves. I had the feeling something bad was happening, but I told myself you were on your way home and Alicia was on her honeymoon, and so far no one had called in with problems. Then the phone rang, and Katherine said you were in the ER, and I knew it was connected. I think something is starting again."

A shiver ran down her spine at his eerie words. "Nothing is connected. Nothing is starting. If anything, it's ending. I'm going home tonight. I'm not going to see Patrick Kane again. And as soon as I can get this damn ring off my finger, I'm putting it away and never wearing it again."

"Who is Patrick Kane?" Jake asked. "What's his story? How do you know him?"

"I don't know him. His mother was a congress-woman. She died in a plane crash eight years ago with some other political officials."

"I remember that crash. Senator Stuart was also on board. Why did you go to this event?"

"Because Senator Dillon asked me to. He wanted me to pay his respects since I was already going to be here for Alicia's wedding. Don't make more of this than it is."

"After what happened to Alicia, and then to me and Katherine, it's not crazy for us to think that something could happen to you, too, Dani. Mamich said it wasn't over, that you were the last piece of the puzzle. Now this happens."

"Stop," she protested wearily. "I can't get into all that tonight. I'm going to drive to the airport and get on the next flight out of here. Once I'm home, I'll be safe." She hugged Katherine, then tried to hug Jake, but his body was stiff as a board.

"I don't like you leaving like this," Jake said tensely, as she let him go. "And I don't know that changing locations will automatically make you safe. I feel like you should stay."

"I'll be fine. Don't worry and don't you dare tell Alicia any of this. I don't want her to be upset on her honeymoon."

"I won't tell Alicia," he promised. "But you should tell Mom. She'll hear about it somehow."

"I don't know how she would unless you tell her. So don't do that, okay?"

"Are you sure you won't at least wait and talk to Patrick Kane?" Katherine asked. "He really wanted to see you."

"No, it's better this way."

"Let me at least walk you to your car," Jake said. "Fine."

They walked out of the hospital, and her brother

53

didn't say another word until they reached her rental car. Then he said, "I know exactly what you're thinking, Dani, because I didn't believe in any of this until I crash-landed in Mexico six months ago. You don't have to believe in something for it to be true. It just is."

She didn't want his words to bother her, but they did. "I can't imagine what danger I could be in."

"Which is another reason for me to worry. You're so stubborn. Do you ever consider the fact that you might be wrong?"

She had considered it; she just didn't want to believe it. "I'm a big girl. I can handle myself."

"You'll call me if anything else happens?"

"Nothing else is going to happen." She got into her car and shut the door. As she drove out of the hospital parking lot, she told herself everything would be fine once she got the hell out of Texas.

His father, aunt, and cousin were in the waiting room when Patrick was finally released. It was after ten, and a quick glance revealed no sign of his rescuer, the beautiful and surprising Dani Monroe. A wave of disappointment ran through him.

But why would she have waited all this time? She'd already done more than most people would have done. She'd saved his life.

He still couldn't believe she'd come to his aid the way she had. She'd been courageous and determined, and she was quite likely the reason he was still breathing.

His attacker hadn't been after money; he'd been after him.

He just didn't know why.

His gut churned as a few thoughts ran through his head, but all seemed fairly ridiculous.

Maybe he was imagining things. Perhaps it had just been random; a crazy, violent person who happened to cross his path at the wrong time.

"Patrick," his father said, relief moving through his worried eyes. "Are you all right? The police said you were stabbed."

"It was a flesh wound. They put in a few stitches. It's not a big deal." He got up from the wheelchair the nurse had wheeled him out in.

"Not a big deal?" his father echoed. "There's a lot of blood on your shirt."

"It looks worse than it is."

"What happened?" his aunt asked, putting a concerned hand on his arm. "I thought you left the park with all of us when it started to thunder."

"I wanted to walk around by myself for a minute, so I hung back."

His father gave him an understanding look. "I thought about spending a few minutes there alone, too, but it was about to rain. I thought I'd come back another day. I wish now I'd stayed."

"You still haven't told us what happened," Marcus said.

"Some guy jumped me. I was looking at a text on my phone when it happened. He came up behind me. The next thing I knew, he was punching me in the face and the ribs, and then he pulled out a knife."

His aunt put a hand to her mouth. "No. I can't believe it."

"I'm all right. It's over now."

"The police said some woman rescued you," Marcus put in.

"Yes." He met his cousin's gaze. "It was the woman you told me I should meet; the one at the park."

Surprise filled Marcus's eyes. "No way. The hot blonde?"

He nodded. "She actually works for Senator Dillon. She'd lost her ring in the rose garden, and she came back to look for it. When the guy went after me with the knife, she hit him with her purse and then pepper-sprayed him. By that time, I was able to grab the knife, and he took off."

"Thank God she was there," his father said.

"And that she knew what to do," his aunt added.

"And that she was willing to do it," Marcus put in. "A lot of people would have just called for help or run away."

"I can't believe this happened in the park. It was supposed to be a safe oasis," his dad said, disappointment in his eyes. "I wonder if the neighborhood will ever feel safe there now. All the work we did, and someone does this."

"I know. I'm sorry."

"It's not your fault," his dad said quickly. "We should get you home. You'll stay with me tonight."

"My condo will be fine."

"You shouldn't be alone," his aunt protested.

"I'll stay with him," Marcus said. He gave Patrick a pointed look. "Just in case you need something. Don't argue."

He supposed having his cousin at his home was better than spending the night at his dad's house. "All right. My car is still at the park, and I don't know where my keys are."

"We'll get your car tomorrow," Marcus said. "And I have keys to your place."

"I'll see you in the morning," his father said, as they walked out to the parking lot. "Call me if you need anything."

"Don't worry about me."

"Easy to say, harder to do," his father said with a tight smile, as he and his aunt headed to their car.

He got into Marcus's car, wincing a little at the pain in his chest as he settled into his seat. The knife wound wasn't that bad, but he also had some bruised ribs from the beat-down he'd gotten. He was pissed that he hadn't had a chance to inflict the same kind of damage on his attacker. If he hadn't been taken by surprise, he would have done just that.

"So what's the real story?" Marcus asked as he started the car.

"I told you."

"That this was a random attack? I'm not buying it. You've pissed off people in recent months, like the entire pharmaceutical industry, some of whom have companies right here in Corpus Christi."

He'd thought about that fact, too, but it had been months since his book had come out. "I don't think this was connected to that story."

"Then what is it connected to? Your renewed interest in your mother's plane crash?"

"Maybe. It seems unlikely. I've asked a few questions, but that's about it. And most people I've tried to talk to have successfully avoided me."

"But not all."

"Not all," he agreed, keeping his answer vague. He'd told Marcus that he'd heard some rumors about his mom having a more than business relationship with Senator Stuart, but he hadn't gotten into any details. Nor had he told him how many more questions he had after reading the public accounts of the accident. Marcus was very close to his mother, who was his mom's sister, and the last thing he wanted to do was make his aunt unhappy or uncomfortable. So until he had some definitive information, he was going to try to keep the family out of it.

58

"You can't discount scare tactics. It was a low-tech assault," Marcus commented. "There was no gun, no hint that it was anything more than a mugging unless, of course, that was the way it was meant to look."

"It's possible."

"Or maybe it wasn't about your mom at all; perhaps it was about the park. There were people in the neighborhood who didn't want that park to get built. It cut into their drug territory. There has been gang violence in that area for decades. They could have been waiting for someone to linger behind after the ceremony and then make a statement. You were just the unfortunate one."

"The detective said the same thing to me," Patrick admitted. "He suggested someone wanted to give notice that the park wasn't going to be a safe place to hang out in."

"Well, hopefully the police will find your attacker."

"I don't have a lot of hope. I couldn't come up with a great description, but we'll see."

"So, let's get back to your beautiful rescuer . . . it's amazing that she would be the one to come to your aid."

It was amazing but it didn't feel that random to him. From the first second he'd seen Dani in the park, he'd had the strange feeling that she was important in some way. That feeling had intensified when he'd taken her hand and held on way too long.

"Do you think you'll see her again?" Marcus asked.

"I'm going to make sure of it."

FOUR

Dani arrived in DC after midnight. She was only able to grab about four hours of sleep before her alarm went off at six on Monday morning. Despite being exhausted from the weekend, she was happy to get back into her usual routine. She put on a sleeveless sheath dress since DC was also experiencing a heat wave and then headed out for coffee and a muffin at her favorite coffeehouse.

After picking up both, she walked down the street, feeling very much in her element with the other workers on their way to jobs in the nation's Capitol. This was her city. This was her life. She could almost forget about everything that had happened back in Texas—almost.

Patrick kept coming back into her head. She really hoped he would be all right and that whoever attacked him would be caught and punished. But as far as she was concerned, that was the end of it. She was never going to see him again. So it would be a really good thing if she could stop thinking about him.

A few minutes later, she entered the Russell Senate Office Building. Senator Dillon's suite of offices was located on the third floor. An intern greeted her from the reception desk. She smiled and said hello, then proceeded down the hall to the legislative center.

She'd been promoted from a staff assistant to a legislative assistant when she'd come to DC, and while she still had high hopes of having an impact on policy changes, so far she'd spent most of her time doing research and writing policy papers that only a few people read—make that skimmed.

The government was so bogged down with politics, it felt as if they were moving backward instead of forward most days. The staff still worked hard to influence positive changes for the constituents at home, but it was difficult to be satisfied with the effort when what she really wanted was results. But she had to be patient, work her way up. She was making valuable contacts, and for now that was enough.

"You're back," Erica Hunt said, stopping her in the hallway.

A stunningly sophisticated brunette of thirty-eight, Erica had been the senator's chief of staff for the last six months, and she was very good at her job. She was smart, savvy and a bulldog when it came to protecting the senator's interests.

"How was the ribbon cutting?" Erica asked.

"It was good," she said, not really wanting to get into it. "I let the Kanes know the senator sent his regards."

"Excellent. Let's go into my office," Erica said, leading the way down the hall.

Erica's corner office had a view of the White House that Dani hoped would one day be hers, but that day was probably years away.

"Shut the door behind you," Erica said.

"All right." Dani did as requested and then took a seat in front of Erica's desk.

"What happened yesterday?" Erica asked.

"I'm not sure what you mean."

"I mean—why were you involved in a mugging at the park where the ribbon cutting was held?"

She hadn't meant to keep it a secret, but she was shocked that Erica had already heard about the incident. "How do you know about that?"

"I have a friend in the Corpus Christi Police Department. He saw that you're a member of the senator's staff, and he gave me a heads-up. He said you were a witness to an assault. Is that correct?"

"Yes. It was after the ceremony. Everyone was gone. I realized that I'd lost my ring at the park, and I went back to look for it. I stumbled upon an attack in progress, and I helped scare the person away."

Erica gave her a thoughtful look. "I saw the report. You actually got in the middle of a knife fight. Why didn't you just call 911?"

"I acted on instinct. Patrick—Mr. Kane was in trouble."

"Patrick? The son of the congresswoman who died?" Erica asked with an arch of her eyebrow.

"Yes."

"Mr. Kane has been trying to get an appointment with the senator. Did you know that?"

"He told me that when I met him yesterday. He has some questions about his mother's plane crash. Since Senator Dillon and Senator Stuart were close friends, Patrick thought the senator might have some insight."

"The senator can't get involved in that old incident—not now—not with so many other things going on," Erica said shortly.

"I know his schedule is packed, but maybe he could carve out a few moments." She didn't want to get on Erica's bad side, but she felt she had to try to get Patrick a call back.

"He can't do that, Dani, and it's not just because he doesn't have time. Mr. Kane loves controversy, as evidenced by his recent bestseller. The last thing the senator needs is to become embroiled in some old mystery. He has more important things to do."

"I didn't think there was a mystery," she said.

"It sounds like Mr. Kane wants to make it that."

She frowned. "I don't think that's his intent. He just wants to understand what happened. And frankly, I don't think Patrick will quit too easily. He's determined to speak with the senator."

"I'll handle Mr. Kane. If he contacts you, please refer him to me."

"Of course, but I don't think he'll contact me."

"Really? It sounds like you saved his life. I'm guessing he's going to take that opportunity to say thank you."

"He already did that when I took him to the hospital."

Erica's cell phone buzzed. She glanced down at it, then said, "I need to take this."

"I'll get to work then."

As she left Erica's office, she breathed out a sigh of relief. She had trouble clicking with Erica; she'd been much closer to the previous chief of staff, Joe Gelbman, who'd been the one to give her the job in DC. Unfortunately, Joe had had health issues and had to resign. She missed his mentorship and his guidance. She knew she could learn from Erica, too; she just had to deal with the woman's colder and more ruthless approach to work.

The fact that Erica had already heard about her witness statement was a little shocking considering the incident had occurred less than twenty-four hours ago and in another state. Obviously, Erica kept close tabs on anything and anyone tied to the senator, but even so, that was fast.

When Erica had questioned her about the assault, she'd felt a little defensive, as if she'd done something wrong. But that was ridiculous. She'd saved a man's life; there was nothing wrong with that. It was Erica's job to anticipate any possible problems, but Dani couldn't see how the attack on Patrick Kane, or her involvement, would have anything to do with the senator.

Still, she had no plans to speak to Patrick again, and not just because she didn't want to get involved in whatever crusade he was on, but because he unsettled her in a much more personal way. He seemed like a man who could take over a woman's life, who could overwhelm her with his passion and his dreams, and she had her own dreams to live. So she'd focus on her job and try to put her latest Texas memories behind her.

Patrick was waiting outside her apartment building when Dani got home a little before eight o'clock Monday night. She could not believe that the man she'd decided to never see again was sitting on her steps, wearing jeans and a light-blue button-down shirt with the sleeves rolled up to the elbows.

He was sipping a large iced coffee that he'd obviously gotten at the coffeehouse on the corner, and there was a bag from her favorite sushi restaurant next to him.

"What are you doing here?" she asked with a frown.

Patrick got to his feet, and with the added height of the step, he towered over her. She didn't like that feeling at all. Well, she usually did like it with a man, but not with this man, who'd made her uncomfortable since the first moment she'd seen him.

"I wanted to talk to you, Dani. You didn't wait for me last night."

She moved up to the step next to him. That was better. Now he only had about half a foot on her. As she saw the purple bruise around his right eye and another on his left cheekbone, reminders of their last encounter, her heart beat a little faster. The bruises did little to mar his attractiveness; if anything, they made him look even more ruggedly sexy.

She drew in a breath, wondering why she couldn't find any air when he was around. "You were in the examining room a long time; I had a plane to catch."

"I didn't get a chance to say thank you."

"You did say thank-you—in the car—on the way to the hospital."

"I don't remember much about the trip."

"How are you? I can't believe you're here or that you're standing upright. I wasn't sure how serious your injuries were."

"They weren't too bad, thanks to you. The doc stitched me up and sent me home last night."

"He probably told you to rest and not to get on a plane and fly across the country."

A small smile played around Patrick's lips. "It's possible he did tell me to rest."

"Did the police catch the guy who attacked you?"

"No." His smile disappeared, and his dark-brown eyes turned grim. "I wasn't able to give the police much of a description. It happened so fast, and he jumped me from behind."

"I wasn't much help, either, I'm afraid. I'm sorry."

"Sorry?" he echoed, with a bemused shake of his head. "No. You saved my life. You have nothing to be sorry about. I am incredibly grateful to you, Dani."

"I just wish I'd gotten a better look at your attacker. I know I saw his face for a split second when the lightning flashed, but I can't bring it back up in my head. It's like it's too bright—an overexposed photograph. I can't see his features. I think he was young, maybe white, but he could have been Hispanic; I just don't know."

"The police will go through the neighborhood, see if they can drum up any other witnesses."

She had a feeling that was a long shot. The park was not in a neighborhood where people had a close relationship with the police. "I really can't believe you flew out here, Patrick." She paused, a sudden thought running through her head. "Wait a second. How did you find me? How did you know where I live?"

"I've gotten really good at finding people on the Internet. It wasn't actually that hard. You haven't been very careful. Your address came right up."

"Well, that's great to know."

"I'm sorry to ambush you like this, but I really want to talk to you, Dani. Will you give me a few minutes?" He grabbed the bag off the ground. "I picked up sushi. Are you hungry?"

She debated for one long second. She'd been told to stay away from Patrick, but the man was persistent, and she didn't feel like having an extended conversation with him in front of her apartment building. A lot of governmental staffers lived in the neighborhood, including some who worked in her office. Any one of them could recognize Patrick. While she hadn't been that aware of his celebrity, having read more about him since their first meeting, she knew a lot of people had read his book as well as the articles he'd written for publications like the *New York Times*, *Fortune* and *Forbes*.

"You can come inside for a few minutes," she said, leading the way into her building and up to her apartment on the second floor. After letting him in, she grabbed her half-empty mug off the coffee table, along with a stack of newspapers and magazines and waved him toward the couch. "Do you want something to drink?"

"I'm good with my coffee."

She got a bottle of water from the fridge and then returned to the living room, sitting down in the chair next to the couch as he pulled several trays of sushi out of the bag and set them on the table.

"This place got good reviews," he said. "I hope you like it."

"I love sushi, and Sushi Q is my favorite take-out place."

"Happy to hear it. I have to say, the name almost put me off."

His smile sent butterflies dancing through her stomach. She really should have sent him away, but it was too late for that. However, it wasn't too late to give him her bottom line.

"Before we eat, I feel like I should be up-front with you," she said. "As you know, I'm a legislative assistant to Senator Dillon. I research and review legislation, some of which will never make it to committee, much less into law. I talk to lobbyists. I talk to constituents. What I don't do very often anymore is talk to the senator. I don't handle his schedule, and I don't tell him who to call back."

"Look, I get it. You have a job to protect, but you have worked for him for a long time, and I suspect you have some relationship with him." Patrick paused. "Did he or someone in his office ask you not to talk to me?"

"You have a reputation for causing trouble. You know that. I'm sure you wouldn't be surprised to hear that politicians tend to stay away from people like you."

"I'm going to take that as a yes."

"Take it any way you want, but I can't help you."

"Okay."

His easy acceptance made her frown. "Really? That's it?"

"You made your case. And since you saved my life, I don't want to put you in a bad position with your boss."

"I appreciate that."

He held out a tray of sushi. "Help yourself."

"Thanks." She took a California roll and popped it in her mouth.

For the next few minutes, they ate in relatively friendly silence, but Dani couldn't help thinking that there was more coming. A man like Patrick didn't give up that easily.

They'd finished off about half the sushi when he sat back against the couch, grimacing as he adjusted his position.

"You're hurting," she said. "Can I get you anything?"

"No. It's not a big deal."

"A stab wound is not a big deal? You're lucky that knife didn't hit anything important."

He tipped his head. "True. But I think you were my luck, Dani. You came out of the storm like an avenging angel. I saw a knife headed straight for my heart and then you were there, swinging your handbag at the guy's head and spraying chemicals into his eyes. It was the most shocking and amazing thing I've ever seen."

"It was probably not the best idea I've ever had, but I had to do something."

"I'm very grateful to you."

"Do you have any idea why that man attacked you? Did he say anything to you?"

"Not one word. He didn't ask for anything. He didn't tell me to get out of the park. He just started hitting me."

"Maybe he was mentally ill or high or . . ."

"Or he wanted to hurt me," Patrick finished.

"Is it possible you were targeted? I read about you online, about your book," she said, meeting his gaze. "You've made a lot of enemies in the last year."

"I have, but since everything went public months ago, there's nothing to be gained by trying to warn me off now. Everything I know I've already said."

"Maybe it wasn't a warning but a punishment. It could have been revenge."

"It could have been, but most of the players in the counterfeit drug cases were in states other than Texas. I don't think the book is connected to what happened in the park."

"Why were you there alone? Why didn't you leave with everyone else?"

"I wanted some time to myself. It's been a chaotic and busy few weeks. My focus was on the ceremony and getting the final construction and landscaping details done, making sure the press would cover the event and that people would show up for it." He blew out a breath. "I just wanted a second to think about my mom and what she would have liked about the park and the day."

"What was your mother like?" she asked curiously. "I don't mean as a congresswoman—I heard all that yesterday—but as a mom."

"It's not easy to separate the two in my mind. She worked in politics my entire life. Before she got to Congress, she was on the city council and the planning commission. Her community work was extremely important to her. But she still managed to show up for the big events in my life, and my dad picked up the slack when it came to helping with homework and that kind of thing."

"Did you feel close to her or were you tighter with your dad?"

He shrugged. "I knew she loved me, but it always felt like she had a bigger purpose in life. She was making a difference in the world. That was made clear to me early on."

She thought she heard a hint of pain in his voice.

"But I was always proud of her," he added. "My father adored her. He'd never let anyone say one bad thing about her. He was her protector."

"As he should be," Dani said, thinking that her parents' relationship had not been nearly that devoted. She turned her thoughts back to Patrick. "It appears that you're following in your mother's footsteps. You might not be in office, but your investigation on the counterfeit drug industry certainly made a huge impact."

"I think she'd be proud of what I've accomplished so far, but I'm not done yet."

"What do you think the senator can tell you?" she asked, knowing that she shouldn't even be broaching the subject with him, but she couldn't help herself.

"I won't know until we talk."

"I'm sure the crash was investigated in every possible way by numerous law enforcement and aviation agencies."

"It was, but it's possible something was missed or covered up. They didn't have a lot of data to go on. There was no black box, because it was a smaller, private jet. There was no distress call. The plane just went down suddenly and abruptly, shattering into a million pieces on impact. The investigation concluded that the crash was probably the result of some type of mechanical failure, aided by the stormy conditions, and possible pilot error. The pilot was a last-minute substitute, by the way, after the assigned pilot came down with food poisoning."

She sat up a little straighter at that piece of information, her curious, sharp mind intrigued by that fact. "I didn't know that."

"He was interviewed multiple times by the FBI. His story checked out. Or at least his wife testified to the fact that he'd been in the bathroom all night."

"But?" she asked, seeing the gleam in his eyes.

"Just because his illness was real doesn't mean it occurred in an organic way."

"Are you suggesting that someone poisoned his food?"

"It's possible."

"Anything is possible, but what's probable?"

"I need to know more before I can answer that question. And I would think you, of all people, would understand my motivation. I did a little research on you, too, Dani. Your father's plane also went down in a storm, no black box, no distress call."

"And it was never found, not one small piece of it," she said. "Of course I wanted answers, just like you, but there aren't any. It was an accident. That's what I believe anyway."

"What about the rest of your family?"

"My mother feels the way I do. My brother and sister are spinning like crazy tops, chasing the same kind of answers you are."

"Have they gotten anywhere?"

She hesitated and then decided she didn't need to share the events of the last six months with Patrick. She needed him to give up and go home, and telling him her siblings were finally unraveling a ten-year-old mystery would not help that cause. "No," she said belatedly. "Not really."

His gaze searched her face, and she found herself really wanting to look away, but she couldn't seem to break the connection between them.

"You're not a very good liar, Dani."

She really wasn't. "Look, I'm sorry for your loss, for your unanswered questions, for your frustration at not being able to find anyone to talk to you."

"I don't want you to be sorry; I want you to help me."

"I can't help you. And it's not just because I'd be risking my job to go against the senator's chief of staff, but also because I think you'd be better off looking ahead instead of backwards. You've got a great life going. Why don't you just live it? Isn't that what your mom would want?"

"Everyone keeps saying that's what my mother would want, but to be honest, I'm not so sure. She was always digging for truth. I believe that she'd want me to bring justice if justice needed to be brought. She'd want press coverage and a movie made out of her life. She'd want people to talk about her legacy. She'd want to be remembered. She always talked about wanting to be remembered."

His passionate words told her that they were getting to the real heart of his desire. "That's what this is about," she murmured.

"What do you mean?" he asked warily.

"You're starting to forget her. It happens. Suddenly, her voice isn't as clear, and you can't quite remember her expressions. Some things stick but others fade away. You thought you'd always remember everything in vivid, colorful detail, but you don't, and then you feel guilty."

He drew in a rough breath at her words, his eyes blazing with anger and pain. "You're referring to yourself, not to me."

"Am I?"

He got up and walked toward her window, staring out at the view for a long moment. "You can see the top of the White House from here," he said, surprising her with the abrupt change in subject.

"Just the roof—and barely."

"My mom wanted to be in the White House. She wanted to be the first female president. She would tease my dad about being the first husband and me being the first son." A pause followed his words. "She might have made it." He turned around and then returned to the couch. "Maybe you're partly right. When we were planning for the park opening, I couldn't remember when she'd first started talking about a park in that neighborhood. Her voice had gotten hazy in my head."

"I do know that feeling," she admitted. "My siblings think I'm cold-hearted because I don't want to chase the past, but it's also because it just hurts too much. I think you're in pain, too, but I don't believe you're going to find solace from that pain by going down the path you're on."

"That's possible, but it's not just that she's starting to fade in my mind, Dani. There's more."

"What?"

"When we were planning the park opening, I contacted Senator Stuart's family, and I spoke to his daughter Rebecca. I wanted to know if we could include her or her mother in the ceremony and told her that we would certainly like to honor the senator as well as my mother." His lips drew into a hard line. "Rebecca told me that the last thing she would want to be involved in was an event to celebrate my mother. She told me that my mother was having an affair with her father and that she was glad that they were both dead."

"What?" she asked in amazement. "Had you ever heard that before?"

"Never. I told her she was crazy. There was no evidence they were having an affair. But she said they'd had numerous late-night meetings in the days before the crash, that my mother insisted he make the trip back to Texas with her despite the fact that it was her mother's birthday. She said she overheard her dad talking to my mom on the phone about keeping everything a secret and no one could know." He paused. "The longer she talked, the more truth her story seemed to hold. After she hung up on me, I couldn't stop thinking about what she'd said. That's when I started wondering if I'd missed something. Maybe she had been having an affair."

"Did you ask your father?"

"No, of course not. I wouldn't go to him with a

rumor like that. It would crush him. I've been trying to get confirmation or denial from other parties, but I'm not having much luck. My mother's chief of staff died a year after my mom, and I don't think my mother would have confided in anyone else on her staff. Senator Stuart's widow is traveling in Europe, which is why I could only reach Rebecca and not her. Stuart's former chief of staff, Craig Haller, who now works for another senator, is not returning my calls. Congressman Parker spoke to me briefly at the ribbon-cutting ceremony, but said he'd only met my mother once and didn't have any information about the crash. And, as you know, I haven't been able to speak to your boss, either. It's been my experience that the greater number of people avoiding me—the closer I am to some hidden truth."

"Or it's just that you're trying to get truth out of people who work in politics, and they're trained to spin and avoid and then spin again."

"Nice group you work with," he said dryly.

"I know the realities. Politics is a game, and you have to know how to play it."

"Which is why I need you, Dani."

Her nerves tingled at his words. She liked that he needed her but not what he needed her for. "I don't think so. You can open Pandora's box all by yourself. It's not a two-person job. As far as this whole thing is concerned, I'm Switzerland."

"I'm not asking you to take sides."

"I think you are." She got to her feet. "We should call it a night. I'm sure you're tired, and I know I am."

He gazed back at her, an emotion in his eyes she couldn't quite read. "Okay," he said finally as he slowly stood up. "But I'm not going to say good-bye, Dani."

Her pulse quickened at his words. "You should say good-bye and you should go back to Texas."

"I probably should, but I don't think you and I are done. I got a room at a hotel a couple of blocks from here—the Parkside Inn."

She couldn't believe he was setting up camp so close to her. "You're wasting your time, Patrick. You can pound all you want on some doors, but they're never going to open."

"I don't quit before I've tried."

"What about the attack last night? If you don't think it's connected to your last case, is it possible it's connected to the questions you're asking now? Who else have you spoken to about all this?"

"Not too many people. My cousin Marcus is the only one in the family I've talked to. I asked him not to share the information with his mother, who is my mom's sister. She would also be devastated to know there are rumors about my mother's fidelity."

"What about outside the family?"

"Congressman Parker, Rebecca Stuart." He

paused, thinking for a moment. "I spoke to Beverly Larson. Her husband Ned was Stuart's staffer who died in the crash. She's actually remarried now to a congressman from Louisiana. She said she knew next to nothing about the senator, that Ned had been very diligent about maintaining the privacy of his boss, but as far as she knows, nothing was going on and there's no mystery about the accident."

"You should follow her example."

"She admitted she didn't know much. Anyway, that's about it. I've left a lot of messages with various people, including Senator Dillon, but I haven't spoken to anyone else in depth. I can't imagine based on the conversations I've had that someone would feel threatened enough to send someone to attack me, unless, of course, I'm missing something important. But I've never allowed anyone to run me off, and I'm not going to start now. So, I'll see you tomorrow."

"No, you won't see me," she said forcefully and a little desperately. "You cannot come to the office, Patrick. You cannot ask for me."

"You have been told to stay away from me," he said with a knowing gleam in his eyes.

"Yes, I have."

"By who? The senator?"

"By both the senator and Erica, his chief of staff."

"Why? What's their problem?"

"He's busy, and he doesn't want to get dragged into the past. It could derail his current legislation."

"How could it do that?"

She honestly didn't know. She shrugged. "It's what they told me. Make of it what you will. Just don't involve me. I saved your life. Do me the favor of staying out of mine."

"When I contact him again, I won't ask for you. Don't worry."

"I can't help but worry. I don't have a good feeling about any of this."

"You know, Dani, there is a way to get me out of your hair faster."

"Do I want to ask what that is?"

"Help me."

"I just told you I can't force the senator to call you back."

"Then help me find someone else—someone who will talk to me, someone who might have known my mother or Senator Stuart. I'm betting you have a lot of connections. You know this world—I don't. I can figure it out, but it will take me time."

She sighed as she thought about his request. She felt as if she were caught between a rock and a hard place. But she did like the idea of getting him off her back and maybe off the senator's as well. "I might have an idea for you," she said slowly.

His eyes lit up. "What's that?"

"It might not pan out," she warned, "but I could

give Joe Gelbman a call. He was Senator Dillon's chief of staff until six months ago, and he's been in Texas politics for thirty years. I'm sure he knew your mother and Senator Stuart, at least peripherally."

"That's great. Can you set up a meeting or a call?"

"I'll try him tomorrow. He lives in Maryland, about an hour from here. Give me your number, and if he's willing to talk to you, I'll make it happen. But that's on one condition. You don't come to my office. You don't contact Senator Dillon again."

"I'll make you this promise," he countered. "I won't contact your boss or anyone in his office tomorrow. I'll reevaluate depending on whether you can get me a meeting with Gelbman. I'd rather do it in person than over the phone."

She supposed she could be satisfied with that. "All right. Deal."

He stuck out his hand, and she hesitated, remembering the last time they'd shaken hands, and how hard it had been to let go.

"Dani?"

She saw the question in his eyes. "You're trouble, Patrick."

"I think you might be, too, but that's what makes life interesting. There's a connection between us that goes beyond your job and my questions. You feel it, too."

She shook her head in denial. "No. The only interest I have in you is making you go away."

He smiled again, his hand dropping to his side, as she purposefully crossed her arms in front of her chest. "Like I said before, Dani, you're not a very good liar."

FIVE

Patrick pulled up in front of Dani's apartment building in a rented car just after five o'clock. She'd called him at noon and told him she'd set up a meeting with Joe Gelbman, Dillon's former chief of staff, for six o'clock. If he could get a car, she'd drive out there with him.

Her call had definitely perked up his day. He'd woken up tired and achy from his wounds, frustrated that he wasn't getting anywhere, and then unsure of where he was actually trying to get. Did he want to prove his mom was having an affair? Did he want to prove the plane crash wasn't an accident? Were those facts going to make anyone happy?

The problem was he couldn't un-hear what he'd heard from Stuart's daughter. Nor could he ignore it. So he'd go a little further and see where that got him.

He was thrilled to have someone new to speak to, but inwardly he knew it wasn't just the upcoming meeting that had him on edge; it was Dani. She'd gotten under his skin and she'd definitely spent a lot of time in his dreams the night before.

Images of her as his avenging angel had mixed in with images of her mouth pressed against his. He hadn't kissed her yet, but he really wanted to.

The electricity between them was palpable. Every time they were together, the air sizzled. She could deny it all she wanted, but that didn't make it false. The attraction did, however, complicate things—for both of them. It wasn't the right time to start anything. He needed to remember that.

His phone vibrated, and he pulled it out of his pocket. It was his father. He was tempted not to answer it, but after Sunday's events, he couldn't disappear on his dad. "Hey, Dad."

"How are you feeling, Patrick?"

"I'm fine. Better every day."

"Why don't you come over for dinner tonight and prove that to me in person? I can grill us some steaks. I want to show you the pictures the photographer took on Sunday. They're pretty good."

"I'd like to see them. Unfortunately, I can't make it tonight."

"Why not? What are you doing?"

"I had to go out of town."

"Out of town?" his dad asked in surprise. "You're supposed to be resting. Where are you?"

"I'm in DC. I'm doing some research for my next story." He hoped his dad wouldn't ask any more questions.

"You're a workaholic, just like your mother. Sometimes you have to take a break, let yourself breathe, heal, play some basketball, go to a baseball game—just relax."

"I plan on doing all that in a few days. I'll call you when I get back to town."

"You better. Have you heard from the police? Has there been any progress in finding out who attacked you?"

"Nothing yet. I spoke to the detective on the case this morning. They're checking surveillance video in the area to see if they can pick up anyone matching the description I gave them leaving the neighborhood or the park."

"I still can't believe what happened. It was such a great day. I thought we were turning things around for that part of town. Now everyone is talking about whether or not the park is safe."

Which might have been the sole point of his attack.

"Anyway, I'm very grateful you're all right," Harris continued. "I couldn't stand it if anything happened to you, Patrick."

"I'm okay, Dad. You don't have to worry about me."

"I hope not. But I didn't think I had to worry about your mother, either."

"I know." He saw Dani heading down the street. "I have to go. I'll be in touch."

"I'll email you some of the photos."

"Great." He slipped his phone into his pocket as Dani reached him. Today, she wore a sleeveless pale-yellow dress. Her hair was pulled back in a ponytail, her legs bare, and on her feet were a pair of strappy sandals. She looked like a summer dream and was even prettier than he remembered.

"You're right on time," he said.

"I usually am."

"Me, too. I like it when people don't keep me waiting, so I try to return the favor. How was work?"

"Busy. I should still be there. I never leave this early."

"I appreciate you doing this. I rented a car." He waved his hand toward the white Volkswagen Passat. Maybe she'd relax a little once they got away from the city. "Do you need to go upstairs first?"

"No. I'm ready."

He opened the door for her, noting her large bag filled with weighty-looking reports. "Is all that homework?"

"It is. There's never enough time to read everything I have to read."

"I didn't think anyone in Congress actually read anything."

"Well, some people do, just not always the elected officials," she said dryly.

He closed her door and then walked around to his side of the car and got behind the wheel. "Do you want to run for office someday?"

"I think so. But that's way down the road. Right now, I'm learning as much as I can and paying my dues. When I'm ready to make a move, I'll make it."

He liked that she could be both humble and ambitious at the same time. She wasn't a person who was looking for a shortcut, and that was refreshing. As a journalist, he'd spent a lot of time talking to people who wanted to make a fast buck or find a quick way up to the top of the ladder. But Dani was willing to work for what she wanted. So was he. They were a good match.

He smiled to himself, thinking that was the last thing she'd want to hear. "What are you working on?" he asked.

"I'm reviewing studies on expansion and security concerns at the port in Corpus Christi."

"Sounds fascinating."

"Not in the least," she said with a smile. "But it has to be done. It's important to our constituents, which makes it important to us." She paused. "Do you need directions?"

"I already entered the address into the GPS." For a few moments, he concentrated on getting through the congested city traffic. Once they were on the highway, he turned his attention back to Dani. "Tell me about Joe Gelbman."

"Do I need to? I'm sure you researched him last night."

"I did, and I learned a great deal about his professional career. He went to Annapolis, was in the Navy for twelve years and then got into politics. He has worked for half a dozen senators, and a couple of congressman. He's well-respected for his political savvy and his ability to keep politicians out of trouble."

"Very good, Patrick. Is that it?"

"Joe apparently has a liking for fishing, cigars, bourbon, and good seafood."

"Amazing. Did you find out whether he wears boxers or briefs?"

Patrick grinned. "I wasn't interested in that information."

"Well, I don't think there's much I can tell you that you don't already know."

"There's a lot you can tell me. Who is Joe Gelbman the man? What are his strengths, his weaknesses? What button would I need to push to get him to help me? Some people respond to flattery, others to bluntness. What's Joe's soft spot?"

"His soft spot?" She thought for a moment. "He likes underdogs. But that's not you."

"What else?"

"He's good at reading people. That's why he was so great at his job. He could figure out what someone wanted and then give it to them in a way that also benefitted his boss. He loved to come up with ways for everyone to win."

"I didn't think that was possible in politics."

"It used to be more possible. The last decade has been rough for any kind of bipartisanship. But Joe was good at working across the aisle. Oh, and he can smell bullshit from a mile away."

"Got it. No faking it with Joe."

"He'd see right through that. He's a very smart man. And he still has a lot of his Navy values: patriotism, loyalty, fidelity."

"Then maybe I can appeal to those instincts."

"He did tell me that he knew and respected your mother, which was why he was willing to talk to you."

"That helps."

"Joe is a good man. He's always been fair. He gave me my first job in the senator's office. I was green as grass, but he took a chance on me."

Patrick could understand why. He hadn't known Dani that long, but he'd bet on her, too. "I'm sure he saw your potential."

"I was scared to death at my interview. I wanted so badly to get my foot in the door. He looked at me with his piercing blue eyes, and he said, 'Do you want to work at something or do you want to be something?' " She paused. "I wasn't sure what the right answer was, but there was something about Joe that made it impossible to lie. I told him I wanted to work hard to be someone who made a difference."

"Good answer."

"It was the truth. He liked the fact that not only did I have dreams, I owned them. He hired me that day and I learned a lot from him. I wish he hadn't retired. I really liked working for him."

"What's the new chief of staff like?"

"Erica Hunt is very different from Joe. She's only thirty-eight, for one thing. She's a Harvard graduate and she's beautiful, sophisticated, brilliant, and ruthless. The senator likes the fact that she's younger and that she has relationships that Joe did not have with the younger generation of lawmakers and news media."

"I hear respect but not a lot of love in your voice," he commented.

"To be honest, I don't really know how I feel about her. I do respect her. She's very good at her job. She makes things happen, and she has a lot of influence over the senator." Dani glanced over at him. "If she doesn't want you to talk to Senator Dillon, you won't talk to him."

"I'm beginning to see that. I just don't know why everyone is so afraid of me. Don't they understand that evading my questions only makes me more curious?"

"Well, hopefully Joe will be able to help you."

"And then I can get out of your hair."

"That's the plan." She glanced out the window and let out a little sigh. "It's a beautiful day. I rarely get off work early enough to enjoy the summer weather."

"What about during the summer recess? Do you stay in DC or go back to Texas?"

"I stay in town. There's really no recess for the staff, although things do slow down a bit when the senator is in Texas. Enough about me. Let's talk about you." She shifted in her seat so she was looking at him. "Are you writing another book?"

"Not at the moment."

"So you're on vacation?"

"I wouldn't say that. I have a few projects I'm working on. There's always a lot of research at the beginning."

"I saw that you've contributed articles to just about every important news publication there is."

"I've had some good luck placing my stories," he admitted.

"But you don't work full-time for anyone but yourself? You're strictly a freelancer?"

"I am now."

"Where is your home base? Corpus Christi?"

"I have a condo there, but I spend a fair amount of time in New York and other places. I go where the research takes me."

"It must be nice to be able to call the shots and to be so free."

"It took some time to get here, but I like being my own boss."

"Not that much time. Didn't I read that you just turned thirty?"

"I did," he admitted. "Where did you read that?"

"I think it was on a celebrity news site. You were at a restaurant in Los Angeles with some actress."

"Oh, right. That was not a great night."

"Why not?" she asked curiously. "The woman was beautiful."

"A guy I went to college with lives in LA. He set me up with the friend of this woman he's dating. She was pretty, but she was boring as well. She could not talk about anything but plastic surgery and who was sleeping with who on the film set she was on."

Dani smiled. "It can't have been that bad."

"Trust me, it was. Have you ever been to LA?"

"Not LA, but I've done Disneyland and San Diego; those were pretty fun."

"How do you like living in DC? It's a big change from Corpus Christi."

"I love it. There's energy and excitement, and I feel like anything can happen."

He smiled as he glanced over at her. "My mom liked DC, too. You remind me a little of her. She was ambitious and she fought hard for what she wanted. She was always in pursuit of justice and truth, but it didn't come easy."

"It's never easy. Joe used to tell me that democracy is about compromise. To get one thing you want, sometimes you have to give up six other things that are also great. But you can't think about what you lost; only what you've gained. Otherwise, you'll lose your mind."

"Sounds like good advice, but I didn't think anyone was compromising these days."

"It's a tough climate. Did you ever consider following your mother into politics?"

"Nope. It didn't appeal to me in any way."

"But you did inherit your mother's passion for justice and truth-telling. You just do it through your writing. How did you get into journalism?"

"I studied it in college. When I left school, I got some reporting and editing jobs at various papers and online magazines, and I even worked in TV news for a while, but I really enjoy writing. Some stories just can't be told in an article or a sound bite. You need more pages."

"Will you stick with books now?"

"I'll mix it up depending on the topic. Fortunately, with the success of the book and the movie option, I have some time to work on things I really want to work on."

"Lucky guy."

He glanced over at her, curious to know more about her. "What about you, Dani? Do you take after your mother or your father?"

"Not my dad. I probably have some of my mother in me, although I hate to admit that, because she can drive me crazy. I love her, but she can be very critical."

"You mentioned siblings earlier . . ."

"Yes. I have an older brother Jake and a younger sister Alicia. I'm the middle child."

"Ah, so that's why you try harder," he said with a laugh.

She smiled, and he liked seeing the humor in her eyes, the more relaxed gleam in her eyes. It was a nice change from her constant wariness.

"It's probably part of it," she admitted. "I've always wanted to stand out."

"You definitely don't fade into the woodwork," he said, his gut clenching again as her pretty green eyes met his.

Something passed between them, that inexplicable acknowledgement of attraction. Then Dani looked away, turning her gaze on the passing scenery.

He felt a sense of loss . . . which was odd and unnerving, and he couldn't help wanting to get her attention back, so he launched into conversation again. "What was your dad like?"

"He was . . . a lot of things," she said vaguely.

"Like . . ." he pressed.

She turned her gaze back to him. "He was a pilot. He started out in the Navy. Then he flew private planes." Her eyes turned reflective and a little sad. "He was a bigger-than-life kind of man. Everyone in Corpus Christi knew him. Some thought he was nuts, especially in the last year before his death."

"Why? What happened then?"

"He claimed that he saw things in the sky—lightning bolts and dancing sprites and stuff like that. And he was obsessed with storms, especially electrical storms. Some of his family members were of Mayan descent. They lived in the Southern Yucatan in Mexico. He spent some time there as a child, and he was raised with some of their beliefs."

"That's interesting."

"My dad was caught between science and magic, because the paternal side of his family was made up of a lot of Texas engineers. So combine that with Mayan magic, and . . . well, I don't know what you get . . . but that's my family."

"What exactly do you mean by magic?"

"They don't call it that, but my great-grandmother, who we called Mamich, believed in layers within the universe. She thought there were different realms between the living and the dead. And there's some sort of spiritual journey that souls take after they die. That's why they built so many pyramids and underground caves that would take the souls on the next part of their journey."

"It sounds like you know a lot about it."

She shook her head in denial. "No. We're quickly coming to the end of what I know, but it will put into context why my dad talked about lightning so much. In the Mayan culture, lightning is a god. It has supernatural power. According to my great-grandmother, lightning shows you what you need to see. It's silly, I know. But you asked."

"I wouldn't say it's silly. Who am I to question someone's beliefs? The truth is that none of us really knows the story of the universe or what happens after death."

"That's true. Anyway, in the last year of his life, my father became obsessed with lightning. Every time he flew, he seemed to come back with a new story. And he wouldn't just tell the family; he'd talk about it all over town. The locals began to call him *lightning man.* He became a joke. My mother tried to talk sense into him, but she got nowhere. She hated that her Navy hero of a husband was now the object of ridicule. They fought a lot the last few years of his life. I don't know if they would have stayed together if he'd lived. She hasn't talked about him in years. If his name comes up at a family gathering, she'll often leave the room."

"Maybe that's from pain as much as from anger. She might have some unresolved guilt."

"If she does, she won't talk about it, but I'm sure it's complicated for her. I do remember times when I was a kid when they were happy, when he would make her laugh. I don't know if she remembers, though."

He thought about her story, one point sticking in his head. "Wait a second. Your father was called *lightning man,* and he died in a lightning storm?"

"Yes, I know. It's ironic."

"It's more than ironic—it's weird," he said bluntly.

"Which adds to the mystery of his death. Alicia

is obsessed with not only my dad's death but also with lightning. Because no one ever found my dad's plane or his body, she's never had any kind of closure. I can accept that we'll just never know, but she can't. She's channeled her desire for enlightenment into her work. She's a photographer, and she's really good at it. Her specialty is lightning storms. She chases storms wherever she can find them. In fact, she moved to Florida, just so she'd find more lightning. Apparently, there wasn't enough in Texas. She's come up with some amazing photos, but she's also gotten herself into some bad situations."

"How so?"

Dani hesitated. "It doesn't matter."

"Come on, we still have some time to go on this trip. Tell me about Alicia's trouble."

"Last year, right before I came to DC, Alicia went out to an island to take storm photos, and in a flash of lightning, she thought she saw someone getting hurt. When she got to the spot of the assault, she didn't find anyone, but she did find a military ID on the ground. That led her to a missing woman. It's a long story, but she ended up uncovering a couple of murders and a surprising link to my father."

"Your father was linked to murders in Miami?" he asked in amazement.

"No, the murders took place in Texas, and the man who was responsible for them turned out to be one of my father's friends from his Navy days. Right before he died, he told Alicia that there was more to know about our father's death. Of course, that set her off. Now she's even more convinced there's something to find."

"I can see why that would enhance the mystery." He thought for a moment. Dani's story seemed familiar to him. "Hold on. I think I read about this. Was the person you're talking about an employee at Mission Defense Technology?"

"Jerry had been an MDT employee, and, yes, he was selling classified secrets. My sister almost lost her life at his hands."

"That's quite a story." Seeing the tension in her face, he had a feeling that the tale wasn't over. "What else happened?"

"I don't know why we're talking about all this."

"Because we have a long car ride, and I'm interested. Something else occurred, didn't it?"

"Yes. A month after all the stuff with Alicia, my brother's ex-girlfriend came to him for help. Her brother, TJ, who also happened to work for MDT, had gone missing. My brother Jake is a pilot and flies charters out of Corpus Christi. He flew Katherine down to Mexico in search of her brother, and they ran into a monster storm and crash-landed. They weren't hurt, but they later ended up in the middle of more MDT trouble."

"The stolen weapons found in Mexico," he said with a nod. "It was all over the news, and my father said the FBI was investigating for months. Some of his friends were afraid they were going to lose their jobs when the bad press put a halt to some lucrative contracts that would have come their way." He paused, thinking about what else she'd said. "What happened to the guy who was missing—you said his name was TJ?"

"He was rescued by Jake and Katherine. Everyone is safe now. Everything is over—at least that's what I think."

"But your siblings don't believe that?"

"No. While Jake was in Mexico, our great-grandmother told him that my father isn't resting in peace, or something to that effect. And Jake found a medallion at the ranch where the weapons were found. He and Alicia now think that my dad was at that ranch and that maybe he didn't die in the Gulf as we thought. We don't even know if his plane actually crashed."

"Seriously? Your dad's death might be tied to the MDT problems?"

"Maybe. The FBI has been investigating, and we've had many conversations. There aren't any links between my dad and anyone at MDT, except his former friend. And my dad died ten years ago, so what could he have been involved in? All this business was recent."

"Didn't Senator Dillon get involved in the Senate hearings where the head of MDT was called to testify?"

"Yes, he's on that committee. It was a complicated situation for him, because the Packer brothers, Alan and Reid, who run MDT, are also big contributors to his campaign."

"And what about the fact that your brother and sister were responsible for revealing some of the problems at the company? Did that make your relationship with the senator more awkward? Did he talk to your family about what they knew?"

"Not really. He spent a lot of time talking to me, but they were annoyed that he wasn't interested in talking to them. But I understood it, and I gave him the information that we had. He made sure that the committee was aware of everything that had gone on. In the end, MDT was forced to make some changes to clean up their act."

"What kind of changes?"

"Well, I don't know exactly, but they've certainly been under a lot of scrutiny."

"That's a really intriguing story, Dani."

She smiled and shook her head. "Don't get any ideas. It's not a movie in the making or a book; it's just my crazy life."

"I can see why your siblings are still stuck on finding your dad. Knowing that he had to be in Mexico at some point would raise a lot of questions, since I assume he never made plans to go there."

"He didn't, although, the ranch in Mexico was not far from my great-grandmother's home. The fire there killed several members of the cartel and the ranch burned to the ground. Alicia and Jake are still hoping to find someone who was at that ranch around the time my father died and see if they can pinpoint when he was actually there. But they don't really have any clues, and the investigator we hired has come up with nothing. It's also difficult to get any cooperation from the Mexican government. So that's where we are. My siblings continue to be somewhat frustrated by my lack of involvement, but honestly I don't see what more we can do."

He could hear the desperate note in her voice, and the way she was playing with the heavy ring on her finger showed more of her tension. "Does Senator Dillon's relationship with MDT and the Packer brothers contribute to your desire to not get any further involved?"

She shot him a dark look. "That's one of the reasons, but that wouldn't stop me if I thought there was something to find."

"Maybe you need a better investigator."

"Or maybe there is nothing more to discover," she countered.

"I don't know about that. There are a lot of loose ends."

"You don't have to know. It's not your business," she said sharply. "You have your own mystery to investigate, remember? Let's get back to that."

"Yours is sounding more interesting than mine," he muttered.

"I don't think so."

"Your ring," he said. "Why is it so important to you? You came back to the park to find it. You can't seem to stop playing with it."

Her hands stilled. "It's not important; it's a nuisance. I want to take it off, but my finger is swollen, and I can't get it over my knuckle."

"It looks very old."

"It is. My great-grandmother gave it to me. I didn't want it, but Alicia and Jake insisted that she wanted me to have it. I put it on for Alicia's wedding, because she really wanted me to wear it, but it's brought me nothing but trouble since."

"Well, it brought me good luck. It might be the reason I'm still alive." He paused. "Is the ring from the Mayan side of the family?"

"Yes. Jake brought it back from Mexico. My great-grandmother said it would give me strength." She met his gaze. "And she said I was going to find the last piece of the puzzle."

"Do you believe her?" he asked, his nerves tingling at her words. He was a writer and he loved a good story. Dani had just told him an amazing one.

"I don't want to believe her," she whispered. "I want to go forward with my life, not backwards."

"Perhaps you can't really go forward until you go back."

"That's you, Patrick. You're the one who's stuck. Not me."

He had a feeling they were both a little stuck. "It's strange that we both lost our parents in airplane crashes."

"It is an odd coincidence," she agreed.

"I wonder if there's any way the two crashes are related."

"Why on earth would you think that?" she asked in astonishment.

"I don't know. It's just a feeling. I'm probably wrong," he added, but as he turned his gaze on the road, he didn't feel like he was wrong. He felt like he'd just stumbled on to something important, only he didn't quite know what it was.

SIX

She shouldn't have told Patrick her father's story. Dani mentally kicked herself for being so forthcoming. She didn't really know why she had. She'd rarely spoken about her father outside of her small family unit. Only a few of her friends even knew about her family's involvement in the MDT problems. But somehow she'd spilled her guts to Patrick.

They'd been talking about his mother, and it had seemed natural to tell him a little about her family, but she shouldn't have gone into so much detail. Patrick had been lost in thought for a good ten minutes now, and she could feel a truckload of questions coming her way.

"You know," Patrick began.

She immediately put up her hand. "If the next few words have anything to do with me, my father, my family, or MDT, then you can stop right now."

He stared back at her with his very curious brown eyes. "That's taking a lot off the table, Dani."

"Let's remember why we're in this car—we're trying to get *your* questions answered."

"I haven't forgotten. I'm looking forward to talking to your former boss. But in the mean-time—"

She let out a frustrated sigh. "You're incredibly stubborn."

"I can be. Sometimes that's how you get things done. You keep going after everyone quits."

She wished she didn't like his confidence so much or that she didn't find it so sexy and appealing. But she'd been around so many yes-men the past year that it was nice to meet someone who stood up for what he believed in. "My grandmother would have liked you," she said. "My mother's mother, not the one on the Mayan side." She stopped abruptly, realizing she'd just brought him back to her family.

"What was she like?"

"She was a no-nonsense woman, very strict, but also loving. She was around a lot after my dad died. I went a little off the rails, drank too much, stayed out too late, and dated some not-so-great men. My grades were falling. I was getting nowhere fast. I came home one night, and Grandma sat me down and said, 'Dani, here's the thing. If you don't stand up for something, you'll fall for anything. So stand up and be who you're supposed to be.'"

"Did it work?"

"It did," she admitted. "I think I needed some-one to look me in the eye and tell me to suck it up and get on with my life. My mom couldn't do it. She was too conflicted, sad and angry, and as lost as I was." She let out a breath. "That's partly why

I've been a little tough on my siblings. I feel like they need my grandmother's hard loving and she's not around anymore to give it, so maybe it's up to me."

"You can't force people to let go, Dani. They only let go when they're ready, when they want to."

"You can't force people to hang on, either."

"That's true. Basically, you can't force people to do anything they don't want to do."

"I don't know about that. I'm sitting in a car with you, and believe me, I didn't want to do that."

"Yes, but that's only because you didn't want me to come to your work, so you made a deal."

She had a feeling that the *deal* was a big mistake. She was supposed to be putting distance between herself and Patrick, but instead she was getting even closer to him.

"I think this is our exit," Patrick said suddenly.

She was glad he'd been paying attention, because she'd completely lost track of where they were and where they were going.

Joe Gelbman had retired to a town called Shady Side, located on the shores of the Chesapeake Bay and the West River in Maryland. It was a picturesque town with a small, charming down-town that offered art galleries, boutiques, and cafés. It was pretty but definitely too small for her taste. As they drove through the downtown, heading toward the water, the residential streets began to feel more rural with thick, green trees, and somewhat empty roads.

"Is Joe married?" Patrick asked.

"He was for about six or seven years when he was in his thirties. He never had any kids. He told me politics was his family. Actually, he told me his wife said politics was his family right before she asked for a divorce."

"Ouch."

"I'm sure she was right. Joe, like so many people in politics, worked very long hours and most weekends. I think he had other female relationships over the years, but he never walked down the aisle again. Now, he lives alone—as far as I know, anyway."

Patrick pulled up in front of a one-story, light-blue Cape Cod-style house with white shutters.

Dani got out of the car, happy to have arrived. The conversation had gotten a little too personal. She was ready to get back to Patrick's mystery. They walked up to the front door, and she put her finger on the bell.

Joe answered the door, wearing khakis and a white polo shirt. He was sixty-five years old with reddish-brown hair, a receding hairline and pale, freckled skin. His light-blue eyes sparkled as he gave her a friendly smile. She hadn't realized how much she'd missed him until this minute.

"Dani," he said opening up his arms.

"Hi, Joe." She gave him a hug. "Thanks for seeing us."

"As if I could ever say no to you."

"You've said no to me many times," she said with a laugh. "This is Patrick Kane, Joseph Gelbman."

"Come on in." Joe waved them inside. "As you can probably tell, my air conditioning is not working very well today, so I thought we'd sit out back. It's cool by the water. I get a nice breeze out there."

"That sounds good." They followed Joe down a narrow hallway, through a small tidy kitchen and finally out onto a brick patio. While there had been nothing special about the house, the view from the back deck of the West River flowing into the Chesapeake Bay was nothing short of magnificent.

"This is beautiful," she said, as they sat down under an umbrella at a round wooden table.

"Can I get you something to drink? Lemonade? Water? How about a cold beer? It is after five."

"I'll take a beer," Dani said.

"Make it two," Patrick added.

"Three beers coming up."

"This house and location seem like quite a change for a man who spent three decades roaming the halls of the Capitol building," Patrick mused.

"I guess he was ready for it. He definitely earned it."

Joe returned to the table with three bottles of beer and a bag of chips. "If anyone wants a glass, I can grab one," he offered.

"Bottles work for me," Patrick said.

"Yes, sit down," Dani encouraged. "We didn't come over so you could wait on us."

"Well, it's been awhile since I've had any visitors, so I don't mind the company. There's only so much bird watching and beach walking a man can do."

"Sounds like you're not as happy with retirement as you thought you would be," Dani said.

"It's been a big change, I must admit. How are things at the office? How's Raymond?"

Joe was one of the few people who called Senator Dillon by his first name. "It's busy as always. There are a lot of things to get done before the summer recess and the senator is in and out of the office with his big Fourth of July bash this weekend."

"Sure," he said with a nod. "Those were always fun. How's Erica?"

"She seems to be handling things well."

Joe gave her a knowing smile. "Very diplomatic. I know she's a little hard to warm up to, but she does know what she's doing."

"I keep telling myself that, but I miss you at the helm."

"Nice to be missed. So what can I help you with, Mr. Kane?"

"I have some questions about my mother, Jackie Kane. Dani said you knew her?"

"I actually consulted on your mother's first congressional campaign. She was a babe in the woods back then, but I could see she had a special something that voters would respond to. She was a working mom who understood her constituents, and they felt like she was one of them. It was a good match. She sailed to a surprisingly large victory. After that, I don't think she ever looked back." He paused, giving Patrick a thoughtful look. "What questions do you have about her that you can't ask your father or one of her friends?"

Patrick hesitated, then said, "It's recently been brought to my attention that there were some rumors about a possible love affair between my mother and Senator Stuart. Obviously, I don't want to ask my father about it, or any of my mother's friends. It's quite possible it's not at all true, but I haven't been able to stop thinking about it."

"I heard that rumor," Joe said slowly. "Your mother and Owen were good friends. They worked together on legislation that they wanted to get passed, and there were some late nights. But were they having an affair?" He let the question hang in the air for a moment. "No, I don't think they were sleeping together, but I believe it's possible that there was something else going on between them."

"Like what?" Patrick asked.

"Owen called me into his office a couple of days before the plane crash. He was gearing up for his next campaign, and he wanted to hire me to run it. I was working for another senator at the time, and I told Owen I wasn't sure I wanted to leave. He said I should change my mind because he was working on something big. I asked him what he meant, and he said he had some information that would make his career, establish him as a front-runner for president."

"What information?" Patrick asked.

"He wouldn't say. Frankly, it wasn't the first time Owen bragged about himself and his knowledge of something. I didn't think much of it. But after he died, I watched the investigation closely to see if anything would come out of it to give me a clue, but there was nothing."

"Do you think Patrick's mother was involved in whatever the senator was working on?" she interjected.

"They worked on a lot of joint projects," Joe replied. "If he had confided in anyone, it would have been her. Jackie was a good talker, but she was an even better listener. She made people feel like she cared about what they cared about. It was a good trait for someone in her position."

"She wasn't putting that on," Patrick said. "She did care about what people wanted. She had a big heart."

"I'm sorry for your loss, Patrick. I really am."

"Thanks. Did you know Owen's wife, Sandra?"

"Yes. She was a tightly wound, somewhat brittle, woman. She had a not-so-secret drinking problem, nothing necessitating rehab but enough of a habit for people to notice."

"Maybe she was drinking because her husband was cheating on her," she said.

Patrick shot her a dark look. "Let's not jump to conclusions."

"I didn't mean he was cheating with your mother. There could have been other women."

"Is Sandra the one who told you there was an affair?" Joe asked.

"No, it was her daughter Rebecca. My father built a park in my mother's honor, and I invited Rebecca to the opening. She was much more negative than I anticipated. In addition to the affair, she suggested that the plane crash wasn't an accident."

"Based on what?"

"I wish I knew. I've called her a half dozen times since then to follow up, but she doesn't answer, and she doesn't call back. I haven't been able to reach her mother. I've also reached out to Senator Dillon, since he and Senator Stuart were college friends. I thought perhaps they were confidantes."

"And Raymond won't call you back, either," Joe said. "I can understand that. He got into office because Stuart died. He doesn't want there to be any hint of wrongdoing connected to that plane crash. It could put him in a bad position."

"Not if he has nothing to hide," Patrick said. "The man was his friend."

"Friends are sometimes dispensable. Voters are not," Joe said cynically.

Dani frowned. "I don't believe that. I don't think you do either, Joe."

Her mentor shrugged. "I've seen too many people turn on their friends to get what they want."

"But unless Senator Dillon put the plane down himself, I don't understand what he's worried about," Patrick said. "I'm not trying to blame him for the crash. I just want to know if Stuart or my mother had enemies, if there was anyone motivated enough to take down their plane."

"If there was," Joe began, "then Senator Stuart was on to something big and probably your mother, too."

A shiver ran through Dani at Joe's words. She'd expected him to tell Patrick there was no way his mother's crash wasn't an accident, but he wasn't saying that at all.

"But Raymond won't talk to you," Joe continued. "Erica won't let him. He has nothing to gain and everything to lose. He's up for re-election next year. He has to watch every move now."

"Can you suggest someone else I should talk

to?" Patrick asked. "I'm running into a lot of walls."

Joe thought for a moment. "You need someone lower on the food chain. Have you run through your mother's staff? I know Tory Coleman died in a car crash, but maybe there's someone else . . ."

"There's not," Patrick said. "No one who my mother would confide in."

"I loved Tory. She was a pistol. Sweet Southern gal but tough as nails," Joe said. "Let's see—Rico Montalvo was Stuart's press secretary. He got out of politics after Stuart died. He owns a taco bar in Alexandria now. You could try him. He was the front man for the senator. He might know where the skeletons were buried."

Patrick straightened in his chair, a new energy in his body. "Great. He's next. Anyone else?"

"Not off the top of my head. I'll think on it. While I'm doing that, you should also consider whether you really want to go down this path," Joe said. "What you find out may not make you sleep better at night. I liked your mother, and I don't want to think she ventured onto the wrong side of the street, but I've seen it happen too many times not to consider it a possibility. Money and power are addictive and corruptive. You never know what will make someone break. Trust me, I've been around that block many, many times."

"I respect your opinion," Patrick said. "But I don't believe my mother crossed any lines. She was a patriot. And she believed in the good in people."

"But not everyone is good—even when you want them to be."

"I have to take that risk. If there's something to know, I need to know it."

Joe nodded. "Then I'll wish you good luck."

"Thank you."

Joe turned back to her. "Now that I've asked Patrick to do some thinking, I'm going to suggest you do the same. This doesn't sound like your fight, Dani, and forgive me for meddling, but I can tell you right now that getting tangled up in Patrick's problems will not endear you to the senator or to Erica. If your career is as important to you as you've always told me it is, then you should drop this right now."

She sucked in a breath at his blunt words. "I understand what you're saying. I just wanted to help Patrick because . . ." Her voice drifted away. *Why had she wanted to help Patrick?* She glanced over at him, and his handsome face, sharp brown eyes, and beautiful mouth made her heart skip a beat. She couldn't tell Joe she wanted to help Patrick because she liked him, because she wanted to kiss him . . .

"Dani knows what I'm going through," Patrick cut in. "Because she lost a parent in a plane crash."

"Oh, that's right," Joe said. "I hadn't put that together until now."

She was grateful to Patrick for giving her a reason, but while Joe might accept and respect her motivation, she knew neither the senator nor Erica would feel the same way.

"Well then," Joe said. "I'll wish you both luck."

"I am getting out of this," she told Joe, as she got to her feet. "I just wanted to give Patrick a chance to talk to someone who might be able to help."

"I get it. I'll walk you out." He led them back through the house. At the front door, he said, "I would offer to barbecue for you, but I'm pretty sure you're going for tacos."

"Good guess," Patrick said. "Thanks again for the help."

"No problem. You two watch your backs. In DC, you never know who's watching or who's listening."

SEVEN

Rico's Tacos was a trendy restaurant in downtown Alexandria, Virginia, just across the Potomac from Washington DC. When they arrived a little before eight, the small restaurant was crowded, but they were able to snag a table.

"Montalvo does a good business," Patrick said, as they settled into their seats.

She nodded in agreement. "I looked up the reviews on the way over here. They have a solid four-and-a-half star rating with over two thousand reviews." She glanced at the menu. "A lot of those reviews raved about the shrimp tacos. But look at all the other choices: pork, chicken, beef, vegetarian . . ."

"You're sounding hungry," Patrick teased.

She looked up at him and smiled. "I'm sure you heard my stomach rumbling in the car."

"I must admit I'm happy Rico owns a restaurant and not a gym or a dry-cleaner."

"A dry cleaner?" she echoed with a laugh.

"You know what I mean—any place that doesn't sell food."

"Yes, I get it, and I'm happy, too. I think we should order the assorted platter to share."

"That works for me. And maybe a margarita to wash them down."

She nodded, thinking a cool, icy margarita

would taste pretty good. "You were quiet on the drive over here."

"Just thinking about what Joe told us."

"I'm surprised that would take an hour. He didn't say that much."

"You weren't talking, either," he pointed out.

She shrugged. "I guess I had a few things to think about as well."

"Like why you're still helping me?"

"It is a concern. I don't want to lose my job, Patrick."

"I can't see why you would, but we made a deal, so I won't ask you for any more favors."

His words should have made her happy, but for some reason they didn't.

A waiter came over to take their order. "What can I get you?" he asked.

"We'd like to get the assorted taco platter to share," Dani said. "And I'll take a strawberry margarita."

"Make mine a regular margarita," Patrick put in. "No salt. Also, we were wondering if Rico Montalvo is here."

"He's in the back," the waiter said.

"Would you ask him if he has a moment to speak to us? It's important."

"Sure, I'll tell him," the waiter said, as he took their menus.

"He didn't even ask us who we were or what we wanted," Dani said.

Patrick smiled. "He doesn't care. I learned a long time ago that it's easy to lose perspective when you're deep in investigating something. You think everyone and everything around you is part of it, and you forget there's a normal world going on."

That was probably true. Since she'd rescued Patrick, she hadn't been able to think about anything or anyone else.

The waiter set down their drinks and told them that Mr. Montalvo would be with them shortly. She sipped her strawberry margarita with eager delight, happy at the fruity slide of icy liquid down her throat. "This hits the spot."

"Can you even taste the alcohol?"

"No, but that's fine. These days I need to be very aware of who I'm talking to and what I'm talking about at all times."

"Sounds a bit dull."

"But necessary. And it's not all dull. I get to go to some cool parties. There's one tomorrow night, in fact—a gala at the Dunsmuir Hotel."

"Really? Who gets to go to that?"

"All the power players."

"Senator Dillon?"

She saw the gleam in his eyes. "You're not going, Patrick."

"He's going to be there, isn't he?"

"Possibly."

"Who else? Congressman Parker?"

"I don't know. It's a big gala. There will be a mix of politicians, press, and lobbyists as well as staffers like me. It's also a fundraiser for public schools in DC, so not just a party."

"You have to get me in, Dani."

"I thought you said you weren't going to ask me for any more favors."

"One last favor, and you don't have to take me; you just have to get me a ticket."

"I don't know if I can."

"Will you try?"

He was a really hard man to say no to, especially when he looked at her with such an earnest plea in his eyes. "I'll see if there's an extra ticket, but if you go, you cannot talk to me."

"I can make my own way as long as you get me in the door. You won't regret it."

"I'm already regretting it. If Erica or the senator were to find out that I helped you ambush him—"

"I'm not going to attack him, Dani; I'll just say a friendly hello. I'll charm him, make him realize I'm no threat to his political ambitions."

"But you are a threat. And I didn't need Joe to remind me of that." She sighed. "What am I doing?"

"You're not doing anything. You're just helping a friend."

"Are we friends?"

"I'd like to think so. You did save my life. In some cultures, that makes you responsible for it."

"I've never understood that saying. It seems like once I saved you my responsibility should be over. If anything, you should be watching out for me."

He smiled. "We'll watch out for each other."

Rico Montalvo stopped by the table. A Hispanic man of medium height, Rico was an attractive forty-something-year-old man with jet-black hair and dark eyes, eyes that were already a little suspicious.

"Hello. Can I help you? Is there something wrong?" he asked.

"Not at all," Patrick replied. "We were wondering if we might speak to you for a moment. Joe Gelbman gave us your name."

Patrick's words did little to ease the tension in Montalvo's eyes.

"It will just take a minute," Dani put in, giving him a reassuring smile.

"I'm not in politics anymore," Rico said, as he sat down at the table. "And if Joe sent you, then it has to be about that."

"My name is Patrick Kane. Jackie Kane was my mother. This is my friend, Dani Monroe."

Dani was happy that Patrick had left off the fact that she worked for Senator Dillon.

"You were Senator Stuart's press secretary when he died," Patrick continued.

"I was," Rico said, not elaborating.

"Was the senator having an affair with my mother?" Patrick said bluntly.

Rico's eyes widened. "No, of course not."

"Are you sure? Because I've heard some rumors."

"They were close friends. But as far as I know, that's all they were."

"I've heard that in the weeks before their deaths, they were working on something big, that they shared a lot of late nights. Do you know what that was about?"

"Why are you asking these questions now? It's been eight years since they died," he countered. "Why not let them both rest in peace?"

"Because I need an answer and the fact that it was so long ago should make it easier for you to give me one," Patrick said. "I want to know if my mother and your old boss were working on something that might have put them in danger. I'm not getting very far with the elected officials who are currently in office, but as you said, you don't work in politics anymore, and I'm hoping that you'll understand the need of a son to find out what happened to his mother and try to help me."

Rico stared back at him for a long minute. Then he looked over his shoulder, checking the vicinity of the nearby tables and the diners at those tables. Finally, he turned his attention back to them. "They were having a lot of late-night meetings in the two weeks prior to the crash. I know that on at least one of those occasions they met with a reporter from the *Washington Tribune*—Ann Higgins."

Dani sat up straighter in her chair at that piece of information. *Was it possible they were actually getting somewhere?*

"What were they talking to her about?" Patrick demanded.

"I don't know. The senator was cagey when I asked him about it. I was the one who dealt with the press, so it was odd that they were leaving me on the sidelines when they were talking to a reporter—a reporter who wasn't always that kind to our party, either. I thought it was strange."

"Did you speak to Ann Higgins about it?" Dani asked.

"I tried. After one of my press conferences, I asked her to wait. But she evaded my questions and referred me back to my boss."

"Did you tell that to the FBI when they investigated the crash?" Patrick enquired.

"I did. I also asked Craig Haller if he knew why the senator had met with Ann Higgins. He said he didn't know anything about the meeting and seemed as surprised as I was that the senator was meeting with a reporter without keeping us in the loop. You should talk to Haller about all this. He would have a lot more information than I do."

"He's not returning my calls," Patrick said tightly.

Montalvo nodded. "That doesn't surprise me. He wouldn't want anything to come out now that he should have dealt with before. Can I ask you why you're looking into all this now? Is it just because of some rumors about a relationship between them? Because that seems like something that should be left alone. Or are you thinking that the crash wasn't an accident?"

"I'm considering all the options," Patrick said. "How did you find out about the crash?"

"I got a call from Haller in the middle of the night. We were both in DC. The senator had taken a late evening plane back to Corpus Christi. It was an unexpected trip."

"How so?" Dani asked, jumping on what she thought might be a new clue.

"It wasn't on his schedule. He told Haller he had some work to do with Jackie, and she wanted him to go back to Texas with her for a few days. He told Haller he'd fill him in when he got back." He let out a breath. "Senator Stuart was a good man. His death devastated all of the staff. He was very well-loved and well-respected, as was your mother. The two of them were becoming forces to be reckoned with in their respected areas of government."

"Why did you leave politics?" Dani asked, genuinely curious. Montalvo had risen to a prized job, one a lot of people would love to have.

"I worked for another senator for a while, but I didn't like his level of integrity. It was time for me to get away from the podium. I'd always wanted to open my own restaurant. It seemed like the right time. I've never looked back. I am sorry about your mother, Mr. Kane. But I don't know that you'll ever be able to find out what happened to her, if it wasn't an accident. The tracks would be covered by now. It's been a long time."

"Maybe long enough for someone to let down their guard, or feel more free to talk," Patrick said.

"Perhaps. I need to get back to the kitchen." He stood up, then hesitated. "The time the senator met with your mother and Ann Higgins, he used an odd word—some kind of code, I think— *hummingbird*. I don't know what it meant, but if you find Ann, she might be able to tell you. Or, you can try to corner Haller."

"Thanks for your help," Dani said, as Rico left the table.

Patrick pulled out his phone, his fingers flying as he obviously did a search for Ann Higgins. "Ann is not at the *Tribune* anymore," he said a moment later. "She runs an online political magazine—*Beltway Beat*."

"In DC?"

He nodded. "Not far from the Capitol. I need to talk to her."

"I can see why you would want to, Patrick, but can I just say that if this reporter was working on something with your mother and Senator Stuart, and they died tragically and maybe mysteriously, wouldn't she have followed up? Wouldn't she have taken what she knew and gone to the Feds? Wouldn't she have wanted the exclusive story that only she could deliver?"

Patrick's lips tightened. "All good questions that I will definitely ask her."

She was happy that his search was veering away from her boss.

"Do you know Craig Haller?"

"Only by reputation. I've never met him." She sat back as the waiter set down a platter of amazing-looking tacos in front of her. "Oh, wow. These look delicious."

"So good I'm going to have to put down my phone," he agreed. As he reached for a shrimp taco, he added, "I hope you can keep up with me."

"I can. I was the middle child, remember? I learned early on not to wait for someone to share with me. But you wouldn't know about that. The only child gets everything he wants," she teased. "That's probably why you can't believe it when people don't want to talk to you."

He laughed. "Maybe. I don't get everything, but the things I really want, Dani, I usually do get."

His gaze rested on her face for so long, her lips tingled, and she hastily put the taco in her mouth. Otherwise, she might have done something stupid, like lean across the table and kiss him.

She was pretty good at getting what she wanted, too.

• • •

"I'm stuffed," Dani announced as she got into the car and fastened her seat belt.

"You should be. You beat me by a taco," Patrick said.

"They were good, and I was hungry. I think that's my new favorite taco place. It's probably a good thing it's across the river, or I'd go more often."

"It was good. I don't usually think I can get great tacos outside of Texas, but I was proven wrong tonight."

She settled back in her seat as Patrick drove them back to the city, the lights of DC thrilling her a little, as they always did. Maybe one day she'd get tired of the city crush, the political maneuvering, the long hours, the not-so-great pay, and even the sometimes nasty lobbying and spin, but she was still green enough to want to see if she could work her way through it all and find a way to the top.

She yawned, feeling sleepy after the food and all the tension of the last few days. "I feel relaxed," she murmured.

Patrick didn't say anything, and when she glanced over at him, she did not see any sign of relaxation on his sharpened profile. His gaze darted from the rearview mirror to the sideview mirror and back again.

"What's going on?" she asked.

"Probably nothing."

"What does that mean?"

"There's a car behind us. It's been there since we left the restaurant."

"It's just going in the same direction. This is a popular route."

"Yeah, maybe." He changed lanes, then checked again.

She looked in the mirror on her side of the car. All she could see were lights. "Which car is it?"

"It's a silver SUV."

"That doesn't sound like a law enforcement car."

"Oh, I wouldn't think it was law enforcement."

Her nerves tightened as Patrick sped up, switched lanes, then took a quick exit, merging into the more crowded city streets. "Is it still there?"

"Four cars back."

Her pulse began to race. "Can you lose it?"

"I'm going to give it a shot."

He pressed the gas once again, darting in and out of traffic, turning down an alley and then across another street and into a crowded parking lot. He turned off the lights, keeping the engine on.

"Is stopping a good idea?" she asked nervously.

"I think I lost the car, but I want to make sure."

"If they come up behind us, we'll be trapped."

"I can see the only entrance to the lot from here. If they turn in, we'll move."

For several long minutes, they sat in tense, dark silence. Every time a car came near the entrance, her heart skipped a beat, but there was no sign of the SUV.

"I think we're okay," Patrick said a few minutes later.

"Are you sure?"

He nodded, putting his hand over hers. It was then she realized she'd been twisting her great-grandmother's ring around and around on her finger.

"I'm sure," he said. "I might have imagined the whole thing."

"You don't believe that, Patrick."

"I don't know what I believe." His fingers tightened around hers. "I shouldn't have involved you in this, Dani. I'll take you home now."

"We should give it a little more time, just in case."

"All right."

She drew in a deep breath and let it out. "I don't know why I feel so—scared. It was probably a soccer mom driving her kids back from a game in Alexandria."

"Could have been."

"Or it could have been someone watching us." She remembered Joe's parting words—*in DC, you never know who's watching or who's listening.* "Did you notice any cars following us back from Joe's house?"

131

"I didn't. Not on the way there or the way back. I actually looked a few times."

She wished she'd been as alert and wary as Patrick had been. She'd never considered that someone might follow them anywhere. "So why would they pick us up at the taco place?" she asked. "How would anyone know we were there?"

She didn't like the answer she saw in his eyes. "Not Joe. He wouldn't have told anyone."

"He's the only one who knew where we were going."

"He could have sent us anywhere, but he sent us to someone who gave us new information. He's trying to help. I know him, Patrick. He can be trusted."

"I have a hard time trusting anyone." He paused, his gaze clinging to hers. "But I do trust you, Dani. And I hope you can trust me."

She didn't know if she could trust Patrick. She had a lot of mixed emotions when it came to him. In her heart, she thought he was a good guy, but there was a lot about him she didn't know. Like how ruthless he could be in pursuit of the truth. How could she trust someone who might destroy her career?

Patrick's phone buzzed, and he released her hand to answer it. "It's the Corpus Christi Police Department."

Now she had another reason to be nervous.

"Hello?" Patrick asked as he put the phone on speaker.

"This is Detective Hobbs. I have some information for you. A gas station security camera half a mile from the park where you were attacked picked up a man wearing similar clothes to those you described. Unfortunately, that man was located behind the gas station with a needle in his arm. He overdosed, and he's dead."

Dani was shocked, and she could see Patrick's face pale.

"Are you sure it's the same guy?" Patrick asked.

"I believe it is."

"When did it happen?"

"We don't have an exact time of death, but it appears that it occurred several hours after your attack. We're still trying to identify him. I'll be in touch when we know more."

"All right. Thanks." Patrick blew out a breath as he ended the call. "What do you think about that?"

Her pulse was racing. "It's not good. Do you think it was suicide?"

"It sounds like it. Or someone wanted it to look that way."

"I thought I'd feel better if they found the guy," Dani said, meeting his gaze. "But I don't. Even though he's dead, it feels . . . strange. Like his death creates more questions than it answers."

Agreement showed in his eyes. "I feel exactly the same way."

She wrapped her arms around her chest, feeling suddenly cold. "I wish we knew who he was. I don't understand why someone attacked you. Why this guy was killed. Why we might have been followed. It doesn't make sense."

"There is one other person who knew where we were tonight," Patrick said, as he started the car.

"Who?"

"Rico Montalvo."

"But he gave us a lead."

"Doesn't mean he didn't tip someone else off."

"Or there was no one actually following us," she said, wishing she could believe that, but she couldn't.

EIGHT

Patrick watched the road closely on his way back to Dani's apartment building. His mind was racing a mile a minute, jumping from what Detective Hobbs had told him about his assailant, to the car he'd seen following them, to the mention of a reporter who might be able to tell them what his mom was working on. He wanted to follow up on every single thing, but it was almost ten o'clock at night, and first and foremost, he wanted to get Dani home safe.

He parked his car down the block from her apartment building, insisting on walking her upstairs. She didn't argue, so he knew she was a little spooked by the night's events.

After she let him into her apartment, he did a quick check of the bedroom, bathroom, and closets before going back into the living room. "I think I should stay on your couch tonight," he said.

She immediately shook her head. "No, I'll be fine on my own."

"You're shaken up."

"A little," she admitted, tucking a strand of blonde hair behind her ear. "But I live in a security building—"

"It's not that secure. You know how people are

135

in buildings like this; they'll ring people in without knowing who they are."

"Not usually. The tenants are pretty good, and I have a dead bolt on my door. Besides, I have a feeling I'm in more danger when I'm with you."

"That might be true," he said heavily. "So that gala that's happening tomorrow night. Can you still try to get me a ticket? It occurs to me that Craig Haller might be there as well as Senator Dillon."

"I can try."

"I appreciate it."

She stared at him, her green eyes troubled. "I've been thinking about your attacker and the way he died. It doesn't feel like a suicide."

"No, it doesn't."

"Did you tell Detective Hobbs that you're investigating your mother's death?"

"No. Sunday night, I was in shock, and since then I've debated whether or not to bring it up, but I haven't come to a conclusion. If the police can ID the man, maybe that will help me understand whether he's tied into any of this or not."

"Okay. I guess we'll just wait and see what the police come up with."

"Or what we—make that *I*—can come up with on my own."

"Are you going to get in touch with Ann Higgins?"

"I'm going to try. Maybe she'll be at the gala tomorrow night, too."

"It will get a lot of press. If I can get you a ticket, I'll call you tomorrow."

"Are you sure you won't feel better if I stay tonight, Dani? I hope you know you can trust me."

She hesitated for a split second, and then shook her head. "I'll be fine."

He felt a little disappointed in her response, but he could also understand it. "All right, but call me if you need me."

She nodded and followed him to the door. After he left, he heard the dead bolt slide into place.

He was happy about that. He could risk his own life for the truth, but he didn't want to risk hers. He knew he needed to leave her alone, to get her out of his story. But as he walked down the stairs, he wondered if it was already too late.

Dani tried to work Wednesday. She buried herself in research reports on port studies and other issues the senator needed to address before the summer recess. But more often than she would have liked, her mind drifted to Patrick, to their meeting with Joe and then with Rico, to the possibility that someone had been following them, to the knowledge that the man she'd fought with in the park was now dead.

Was the park attack related to Patrick's investigation? But why?

They hadn't really learned that much; nothing particularly incriminating, nothing worth being attacked for, or being killed over. What were they missing?

Did Patrick know more than he realized? Or was someone just worried that Patrick was going to dig up something that needed to remain buried?

As the questions buzzed around in her head, she leaned back in her office chair and stared at the computer screen in front of her. Her screensaver showed a spectacular photo of the Northern Lights, one of the items on her bucket list, and a reminder that there was a world outside DC, something that was easy to forget.

But this was her world now, and it was being threatened. If she kept helping Patrick, she could potentially risk getting in trouble with her boss and losing her dream job. Did she really need any other reason to quit?

She did feel for Patrick. She understood his motivation because his situation was so similar to hers that it had brought back all her unsettled feelings about her father and his mysterious death.

Alicia would want to know why she was willing to help Patrick but not dive into the search for her own father. Jake might even ask her the same question now. She didn't have an answer.

She told herself she had helped her siblings. She'd talked to the FBI after Jake's trip to Mexico. She'd relayed all the important information to

Senator Dillon for the Senate hearings. She'd agreed to finance the private investigator Alicia had hired, but none of that had gotten them closer to any answers. So she'd just tried to accept the fact that she'd never know what happened to her dad.

But here was Patrick, chasing his own mystery and making her wonder if she'd given up too soon on hers.

"Dani?"

She sat up abruptly, wondering how long Erica had been standing by her desk. "Sorry, I didn't see you there."

"Yes, you seemed lost in thought," Erica said. "Something wrong?"

"No, just going over the To-Do list, making sure I'm not forgetting anything."

"You're a hard worker, Dani. I respect that."

"Thanks," she said, a little surprised by Erica's comment. "Is there something I can do for you?"

"Have you spoken to Patrick Kane again?"

She hadn't been expecting the direct question. She hadn't wanted to lie to Erica. But now she was on the hot seat. She decided on a half-truth. "He did contact me again. I told him that I couldn't help him, that he'd have to speak to you."

"And his answer?"

"He wasn't happy about it, but he seemed to accept it."

"Did he say anything else?"

"About what?"

"About the senator?" Erica said impatiently.

"He reminded me that Senator Dillon was a good friend of Senator Stuart. He suggested that a conversation between them would only be helpful." She paused, licking her lips. "Maybe it would be."

"The senator is quite firm on this subject," Erica said. "I hope this is the end of your contact with Mr. Kane."

"I told him there is nothing I can do for him."

"Good. The senator wants an update on the port studies. I'd like to keep that the focus of your meeting. Do you understand?"

She understood perfectly. Erica did not want her to say anything about Patrick Kane to the senator. "Of course."

Erica nodded approvingly. "I like you, Dani. I think you'd make an excellent legislative director one day."

"I hope to continue learning and moving up," she said carefully.

"You might move up sooner than you think. Bruce has let me down a few times. He may be looking for another position. If you play your cards right, it could be yours."

She didn't know what to say. She had a feeling those cards involved Patrick.

After Erica left with that departing shot, she let out a breath. Now she had something else to think about—like whether or not Erica was offering her some sort of bribe for silence.

Bribe or not, the rest of their conversation had been quite clear—stay away from Patrick Kane.

As if on cue, her phone rang. It wasn't Patrick, but it was a woman she'd reached out to earlier on his behalf. "Hi, Fran."

"You're in luck, Dani. I found an extra ticket to the gala. Do you still want it?"

The question suddenly seemed very important. She felt as if she were standing on a precipice, and it would be really easy to fall.

Maybe she wasn't that close to the edge of the cliff, she rationalized. If Patrick showed up at the gala, no one had to know it was because of her.

"I'll take it," she said.

"Great. Do you want to swing by my office at lunch?"

"I'll be there at one," she said, glancing at her watch. "Thanks again."

"I hope he's worth trading a night of babysitting my three monsters for an extra ticket," Fran said with a laugh.

"I hope so, too."

The gala was in full swing when Dani arrived just before eight. As she walked into the stately and elegant Dunsmuir Hotel, her gaze immediately swept the lobby for any sign of Patrick. She'd left his ticket at the front desk of his hotel and sent him a text that it was there, but she'd made sure not to see him or speak to him. If she was ever going to break the connection between them, she needed to start by creating some distance.

But while she'd kept some physical space, emotional space was another story. She'd been thinking about him all day, and even now she felt a little tingly at the thought of seeing him again. She really needed to get a grip.

She walked toward the ballroom and saw some of her fellow staffers in line for one of the outside bars. She decided to join them.

"Dani, you clean up well," Kirk Robbins said with an appreciative grin.

She smiled at the twenty-six-year-old press assistant, who, like her, was living out his dream in DC. They'd both arrived in the office about the same time, and even though she had several years of experience on Kirk, they were both new to the Beltway.

"You look beautiful," Tracy Bertrand added, another legislative assistant. "You must be getting more money than me, Dani, if you could afford that dress."

The long, strapless, black designer gown would have cost her a month's salary if it hadn't had a small tear along the hem that she'd been able to sew up herself. "I got it at a discount. You look gorgeous, too."

"Thanks. Hey, there's the senator," Tracy said, tipping her head.

Dani turned to see Senator Dillon and his wife Kimberly walking down the hall. They were a stunning couple. The senator was tall and thin and looked handsome in his black suit, his brown hair showing not a speck of gray. His wife was a beautiful willowy blonde who'd had a ton of cosmetic work done and despite her sixty-plus years, there wasn't a wrinkle anywhere in sight. She wore a sequin-studded gown, with diamonds on her wrist, her fingers, and around her neck.

Erica walked behind the couple, along with Stephen Phelps, the senator's press secretary. Stephen was one of Erica's hires. She'd managed to get rid of the former press secretary about a month into her job, another reason why Dani needed to stay on her good side. There was no question that Erica was working hard to make sure that everyone on the senator's staff was loyal to her.

As the group grew near, the senator's gaze connected with hers. He paused, then smiled, and motioned for his entourage to move towards them.

"Hello, everyone," he said.

"Senator," Dani said, as Tracy and Kirk muttered rather awestruck hellos. Since they'd never worked in the Texas office, they'd had little contact with the senator.

"You remember my wife, don't you, Dani?"

"Of course. How are you, Mrs. Dillon?"

"I'm just fine," Kimberly said, with a notable Texas accent. "I miss having you at the Texas events, Dani. But I expect you're enjoying your next adventure. How are you liking the city?"

"I like it very much," she said. "I feel fortunate to be here."

"Oh, there's Laurel," Kimberly said, waving to one of her friends down the hall. "We should say hello, Ray."

"I'll be right with you," Ray told his wife. "Dani, can I have a word?"

"Yes," she said, surprised as he pulled her a few feet away from the others. They'd had a meeting earlier in the day about the port legislation, and he hadn't seemed that eager to spend extra time with her. She could see Erica giving her a not-too-happy look from afar.

"Erica tells me you're doing very good work for us," he said.

She was a little surprised at his comment, but she nodded. "I try."

"That's good. That's very good. You know how much I appreciate your loyalty over the years. It's one of the reasons I brought you to DC. I always feel like I can trust my Texas girls."

His tone was charming and a bit patronizing, but she was used to that. "I'm very happy to be working for you." She wondered if he was trying to remind her that she owed him, or if he simply wanted to make sure she knew she was valued—probably the former. She doubted if the senator wasted much time thinking about whether or not his staff members were happy.

"I'm sorry to interrupt," Erica said, not looking sorry at all. "May I steal you away, Senator? There are some very important people who'd like to speak to you."

"Of course," he said. "Dani, we should chat some time, maybe after the holiday when I'm back in town."

"Whatever works for you."

"I'll have Erica set it up."

Erica led the senator down the hall, and Dani watched him shake hands with Reid Packer, the attractive and very rich senior vice president of MDT, and then with his older brother Alan Packer, the older and more serious brother who was the president and chairman of the board. She'd met both Reid and Alan at one of the senator's Texas barbecues. Not that they'd remember meeting her.

Reid was a charming ladies' man. He'd been married, divorced, and had a long history of dating models and actresses. He'd remarried several months ago, and his much, much younger and beautiful wife now stood at his side in a slinky gown that was almost see-through and very clingy. She looked more than a little bored.

Alan was quieter and seemed more stable, with a long marriage, two college-age daughters and a wife who was very active in charity work. His wife looked very middle-aged in a matronly, conservative dress.

Both men were billionaires, thanks to a family legacy of wealth as well as the defense technology company they ran, which was the biggest in the world. MDT employed a huge number of Corpus Christi residents, making it important on so many levels.

While MDT had run into a tangled web of problems in the last year, it was still a strong company doing important work in defense technology. Alicia and Jake were a lot more negative about MDT than she was, and she didn't blame them, but she had mixed feelings. MDT employed over twenty-five thousand people, and probably more than ninety-five percent of those employees were good people, so she didn't want to just write the company off as some big bad villain.

She also needed to walk a fine line because of the senator's relationship with the Packer brothers. That relationship had taken a hit during the Senate hearings, but judging by all the smiles now, the men were getting past that.

Turning away, she got back in line for a drink, noting that Tracy and Kirk had disappeared. They'd obviously gotten their drinks and moved into the ballroom.

She was four people from the front of the line

when she felt a prickle along the back of her neck, a little shiver, as if someone had just breathed on her. Before she could turn around, she heard a husky male voice that was starting to haunt her dreams.

"I wanted to thank you for my ticket," Patrick said.

She refused to turn around to look at him. "You're not supposed to approach me, remember?"

"I'm just in line to get a drink. Besides, I passed all of your people on their way into the ballroom. The senator was with the Packer brothers."

"I know. I saw them together. Did you try to talk to him?"

"Not yet. I want to see if I can get him alone. I might have to stake out the men's restroom."

"That should make for a fun night."

He laughed. "I do what I have to do."

"Have you had any luck finding Ann Higgins?"

"As a matter of fact, I did find her—or at least her phone number. I left her a message."

"Another message?" she asked, starting to feel as frustrated as he was.

"Yes, but I think she might be here tonight. So maybe we'll get lucky."

"Maybe *you* will get lucky," she corrected. "You're flying solo, remember?"

"I do remember. I just wish you didn't look so damned beautiful," he murmured, his lips so close she could feel his warm breath on her ear.

"Patrick," she murmured, fighting the urge to turn around. "You can't say things like that."

"I try not to, but then I see you . . ."

At that, she couldn't help but turn her head. His handsome face made her stomach flutter. His dark eyes held all kinds of promises and his sexy lips were more than a little tempting. But he—he was the enemy, she reminded herself. He was persona non grata and she'd already done all she could for him.

Still . . . She let out a breath, wishing he didn't wear a black suit and tie quite so well. She'd thought he was attractive in jeans and a t-shirt, but tonight he looked sophisticated and rich and powerful, an equal match to any of the so-called movers and shakers here tonight.

"Miss?" The bartender's voice broke into her fascination with Patrick's face, and she swung back around, realizing he was waiting for her order, and there was a line of people behind her.

"A gin and tonic," she said. After she got her drink, she put cash on the bar and quickly walked away, forcing herself not to look back.

She moved into the crowded ballroom, where an orchestra played softly in the background. Two magnificent buffets were on display on both sides of the ballroom. Taking a plate, she filled it with mozzarella and tomato salad, crab puffs, a creamy lobster risotto, and thinly sliced filet mignon. Then she made her way to a table in the back of the room where Tracy and Kirk were sitting. The senator had bought two tables for the gala: one for lower-level staffers and the other for his friends, and, of course, Stephen Phelps and Erica Hunt.

Tracy and Kirk were having what appeared to be a very flirtatious conversation when she sat down, and it occurred to her that maybe they were a little more than colleagues.

When they saw her, they quickly moved apart, but there was no doubting the guilty looks on their faces.

"I don't care," she said, sitting down next to Tracy.

"What do you mean?" Tracy asked.

"The two of you are dating."

Tracy and Kirk exchanged a look.

"It's fine with me," she added.

"Well, it's not fine with Erica," Tracy said worriedly. "She's made it clear that there is to be no interoffice dating."

"I'm not going to tell her, but you might want to be a little more careful if you're worried about someone finding out."

"You're right," Kirk said with a nod. "We'll do better." He paused, giving her a thoughtful look. "I didn't realize you knew the senator's wife."

"The Texas office is a lot smaller. Everyone knows everyone there." In some ways, she missed the closeness of that office. But this is where she needed to be to grow her career, so here she would stay.

"What's Mrs. Dillon like?" Tracy asked curiously.

"She's very outgoing, friendly, has a lot of friends. She likes to throw parties. They're very social in Corpus Christi."

"But what is she really like?" Tracy pressed. "Behind closed doors."

"I haven't been behind those closed doors," she said dryly. "While they do have a social side, the Dillons also guard their family privacy."

"I think that's changing now that the kids are grown," Kirk said. "The senator never welcomed any press pieces on his family, but he just agreed to do an interview with *Lone Star Family Magazine* next month."

"Probably gearing up for a run for the White House," Tracy said. "There's been a lot of chatter the last few months. What do you think, Dani? Will he run for the top job?"

"I think he might one day, but I don't know when."

"Looks like the speeches are going to start," Kirk said, as the orchestra stopped playing, and one of the elegant women in charge of the gala stepped up to the microphone.

"With all these politicians in the room, I imagine those speeches will take awhile." Tracy raised her full wine glass. "I stocked up."

Dani laughed. "You were smart."

"You can't blame them for wanting to get

behind the microphone. No one wants to miss all the good press," Kirk said. "All these people raising money for children in need. It makes a good sound bite."

"The money is real," she reminded him. "Even if the motivation is not as idealistic as one might hope."

"It would be nice if it could be both," Tracy said.

"It would," she agreed, hating that she was getting as cynical as everyone else.

As she looked around the ballroom, she saw Patrick sitting with a group of people several tables away. He had a woman on each side, and both seemed more than a little interested in him. And why not? He looked more delicious than the gourmet food on their very expensive plates.

He caught her eye and gave her a wink.

He was so bad. He was enjoying their subterfuge.

She really needed to get him completely out of her life.

Looking back at Kirk, she said, "Do you know a journalist named Ann Higgins?"

"Sure. She runs the *Beltway Beat*, and she has a reputation for getting access to stories others cannot."

"Have you seen her tonight?"

"I saw her earlier." Kirk scoured the room. "There she is. See the table to the right of the podium? The red-head in the turquoise dress? That's her."

"Great. Thanks."

"Why do you want to talk to her?" Kirk asked curiously. "If there's a story brewing, I'd like to get in on it. It would help my resume, and get me out from under Stephen's thumb. Whenever I bring him anything, he takes credit for it."

"That's the way it is," Tracy told him. "You can't take it personally. You just have to wait for your chance."

"Could this be my chance?" Kirk asked Dani.

"No. I don't have a story," she said hastily. "Someone—a friend—was asking if I knew her. That's all."

"Well, just keep me in mind if you do get anything press-related. I think if the three of us stick together, we'll all do better," he said.

"I will," she said, because that's what he hoped to hear. But the last thing she wanted was for an ambitious press assistant to catch wind of what might be a really big story.

NINE

Patrick saw Erica Hunt slip out of the ballroom after the senator's speech. He moved quickly after her. This might be his best chance to get face-to-face with the senator's chief of staff. He thought she might be headed to the bathroom, but was happy to see her in line at the bar.

Erica was a beautiful, sophisticated woman wearing a body-hugging, dark-red dress that suggested a sexy, bold confidence. He could use that to his advantage. While his research on Erica hadn't gone much beyond her obvious job resume, he knew a few things about her. She liked a fight, and she loved to win. She changed jobs often, suggesting a tendency to get bored. Every move put her higher on the ladder. He wasn't sure what her end game was, but he doubted it was to work for a senator. Maybe she was planning to ride Dillon all the way to the White House. That he could certainly believe, but she might have picked the wrong horse.

While Dani was loyal to her boss, he found the senator's reluctance to speak with him disturbing, unless his hesitation was being fueled by Erica's counsel. It was time to find out.

As she left the bar with her drink, he stepped in front of her.

Irritation, then surprise, then calculation moved

through her gaze like a firestorm. He hadn't seen someone go through that many emotions so fast, but it was clear she'd recognized him.

"Ms. Hunt," he said. "I'm Patrick Kane."

"I know who you are." Her gaze ran down his body, unapologetically checking him out. "Your pictures don't do you justice." She sipped her drink. "I suppose I should have expected to find you here."

"I need to speak to the senator. I'm hoping you and I can come to an agreement on that."

"That's doubtful. Your reputation precedes you. You like trouble; I don't."

"Now that I find difficult to believe. My guess is that you love trouble. It makes life more exciting, more challenging."

A smile spread across her lips. "Excitement and challenges have their place, but not in my office. But I can see why you were able to turn the pharmaceutical industry upside down. Unfortunately, your charm won't work on me."

"I'm not trying to charm you. I just want to talk. I think you should listen."

Speculation entered her eyes. "Why don't we meet for lunch tomorrow? The Brady Grill on 17th Street, one o'clock."

"Perfect." He was shocked that she agreed, but he wasn't going to question it.

"Until then, I don't want to see your name on my call list."

"I can wait until one o'clock tomorrow to annoy you again."

"Excellent." She walked back into the ballroom with a decidedly sexy swagger.

He smiled to himself. She thought she was calling the shots, but he'd just gotten her to agree to meet him for lunch. That was a win in his books. What came out of that meeting, who knew? But he'd be one step closer to the senator.

As he turned his head, he saw Dani coming out of the restroom.

Erica's in-your-face sexy style had done nothing for him, but Dani's beauty gut-checked him every single time.

He'd promised to ignore her. He'd kept that promise so far . . .

Dani stopped abruptly, seeing Patrick approaching. She sent him a stern, warning look, but he ignored it and kept on coming.

"Don't worry. Erica just went back into the ballroom," he said. "I had an interesting conversation with her."

"You spoke to her?"

"She asked me to have lunch with her tomorrow."

"I can't believe it." She definitely hadn't expected Erica to make a lunch date with him.

"I think she subscribes to the idea of keeping your enemies close."

"She'll definitely grill you on your intentions."

"I can handle that. I just want a chance to plead my case."

She could see that Patrick felt good about the upcoming meeting; she did not. "I hope you know what you're doing."

He cocked his head, giving her a thoughtful look. "What does that mean?"

"Erica is a shark. Don't underestimate her."

"I won't do that."

"Okay. It's your call."

"I have to try to get her on my side. I haven't been able to get close to the senator tonight. I get body-blocked by someone every time I get within a few feet of him."

"I'm not surprised," she said. "By the way, Ann Higgins is here. I asked the press person in my office, and he pointed her out to me."

His gaze narrowed. "Will you show me where she's sitting?"

It would probably be better than hanging out in the hallway with him. "I'll point her out. Then you're on your own." She walked back into the ballroom, keeping a few feet in front of him.

The speeches had ended, and the orchestra was playing again, as couples filled the dance floor. She moved toward the front of the room. The table where Ann had been sitting was almost empty. There was one couple engaged in conversation, and Ann who was checking something on her phone. As Patrick came up behind her, she said, "The redhead."

"Got it. I'll find you later."

Before she could tell him not to find her, he was gone. As she watched him offer Ann a charming smile, she felt an odd wave of something that felt a little like jealousy, which was stupid. She should not care at all. Turning away, she stumbled straight into Stephen Phelps. "Sorry."

He grabbed her arm and gave her a smile. "No problem. I like it when a woman falls for me. It just doesn't happen often enough."

Considering he was blond, tan, and charming, she suspected it happened more often than he was saying. "Thanks for the catch. Are you having fun?"

"I am now. We never get to talk much at the office, Dani."

"Our paths do not cross that much," she agreed.

"I have to say I'm really impressed with the work you've been doing."

"I appreciate that."

"The senator considers you one of his most trusted assistants. I hope you know that," Stephen said. "He's told me that more than a few times. He said he trusts you to keep him out of trouble."

Was that another warning masked as a compliment? A reminder of how much the senator trusted her?

Damn Patrick for making her question everyone

around her. "I'm glad the senator values my work. I try to anticipate any potential problems in legislation."

"I'm sure that's not easy."

"Nothing is easy in politics. Will you excuse me—"

"Actually," he said, cutting her off. "I was hoping I could get you to dance with me."

"Uh, well, all right," she stuttered, too surprised to do anything other than say yes. Up until this minute, she hadn't even thought Stephen knew her name. "I guess we could dance."

"Don't look so worried," he said with a small laugh. "I promise not to step on your toes."

"I'm not worried. I'm just not much of a dancer." Actually, she was a really good dancer, but tonight she felt stiff and tense. She didn't know why Stephen had asked her to dance, and as they moved onto the dance floor, she saw Patrick and Ann heading there as well. Erica stood at the edge of the floor, her gaze perusing all the dancers.

She and Patrick weren't dancing together, she told herself. *Erica wouldn't know that she'd given Patrick the ticket. He could have gotten it anywhere.* But still she felt nervous.

"Are you enjoying DC?" Stephen asked, drawing her attention back to him. He held her a little closer than she would have liked.

"Yes, very much," she said.

"You don't miss the wide-open spaces of Texas that the senator loves to talk about so much?"

"Sometimes, but I like the job, and I don't have much time for anything else."

"What about a boyfriend? Are you seeing anyone?"

"No."

"Haven't met anyone or haven't had time?"

"Both. What about you?"

"Single. Concentrating on my job right now." He paused. "We should get a drink sometime, get to know each other better. I think we'd have a lot in common."

"Sure," she said, thinking that would never come to pass. He was just making gala conversation. Or maybe he had a different agenda?

Had Erica sent him to talk to her? Was Erica behind some of his probing questions?

The dance came to an end, and she was more than thrilled to say goodnight.

"I'm going to take off," she said. "I have some work to do tonight."

"Can't it wait until tomorrow?"

"It really can't. Thanks for the dance, Stephen."

"I'll be in touch about that drink."

She smiled and made her way quickly off the dance floor. When she got to the door of the ballroom, she looked over her shoulder. Stephen was dancing with Erica now, and Patrick and Ann had stayed on the floor for another dance.

She couldn't help wondering what both couples were talking about, but that wasn't as important as getting the hell out of the gala, because there was just too much stress in this room. She felt like her every move was being watched, assessed. She needed to go home—now.

But someone was calling her name.

She inwardly sighed as the senator's wife motioned her over. She had a feeling she was going to be once again reminded of how much the senator trusted her. Why on earth was everyone so worried about her? What did they think she was going to do?

"I've seen you somewhere before," Ann Higgins told Patrick.

He saw the puzzled gleam in her eyes and had a feeling she'd figure it out before too long. Maybe he could use his background as an investigative journalist to get her trust, to put her on his side. She liked a story, and he might have a really big story to tell—depending on what she had to say.

"You're not a politician . . . are you a lobbyist?" she asked.

"Why would you guess that?"

"You have a look of confidence and money," she said with a flirtatious smile. "One of my favorite combinations in a man."

With those requirements, he had a feeling Ann Higgins had a lot of fun in DC. She was in her early forties, with the kind of curves that were probably bought and paid for but definitely looked good on her. In some ways, she reminded him of Erica. They both felt like predators. He wondered how Dani would fare in a sea of such beautiful sharks. She was just as gorgeous, but she wasn't as tough or as ruthless.

"So who are you?" Ann asked, as they moved around the dance floor. "As much as I like a mysterious, handsome stranger, I have a feeling you sought me out on purpose."

"My name is Patrick Kane."

Recognition flashed through her brown eyes. "The Patrick Kane whose book is being made into a movie?"

"That's me."

"Well, you've surprised me, and that's not easy to do. What are you doing in DC?"

"I'm working on another story—a more personal one."

"And you think I can help you," she said, meeting his gaze.

"I'm hopeful."

"What is it you want to know?"

He looked around and saw no one within earshot who might be interested in their conversation—at least as far as he knew.

Gazing back at Ann, he leaned forward and whispered into her ear. "I want to know about *hummingbird*."

He felt her body stiffen, heard her take a quick, sharp breath. The word meant something to her; that was for sure.

She pulled away and looked into his eyes. "Who told you to say that?"

"Rico Montalvo."

"Rico?" she echoed. "I thought he was making tacos these days."

"He is. I was at his restaurant last night. I'm looking into what my mother was working on in the days before her death."

"You're Jackie Kane's son, of course. I didn't put that together until now."

"Can we talk?"

"Not here."

"Where?"

She hesitated, and he felt like he was about to lose her.

"Name the place—anywhere, anytime—but make it soon," he said. "It's very important that we have a conversation."

She looked around. "Not here. It can't be my place—or yours. Somewhere public, but not too public, a place we can't be overheard," she muttered.

"There's a bar not far from here."

She immediately shook her head. "No, it has to be outside where no one can hear." She thought for another moment. "Meet me at the World War II Memorial in thirty minutes." Then she let go of his hand and left the dance floor, disappearing into the crowd.

His heart thudded against his chest. He felt a wave of elation that she'd agreed to meet him. Maybe he was about to get a break.

He looked around the ballroom for Dani but he didn't see her anywhere, so he headed out of the hotel. There was a long taxi line out front, and he was more than a little happy to see Dani in the middle of it.

"I have my car," he said, stopping next to her.

"I'll just wait for a cab," she said shortly, refusing to look at him.

He dropped his voice and leaned in. "I spoke to Ann Higgins. Sure I can't give you a ride?"

She shot him a disbelieving look. "She told you something?"

"My car is in a lot around the corner on Davis Street. I'll wait five minutes." He walked away from her, hoping she would follow.

When he reached the lot, he got into his car and looked into the rearview mirror. No sign of Dani. Another two minutes passed. Then he saw her moving between the cars. She opened the passenger door and got inside.

"I feel like a spy," she said. "This is ridiculous."

"Or exciting," he suggested.

"What did Ann tell you?"

"It wasn't what she said as much as how she

reacted to the word *hummingbird*. She flinched and looked extremely nervous."

"So what is *hummingbird?* Some password for some covert operation?"

"She didn't say. She said she couldn't talk with so many people around, but she would meet me in a half hour at the World War II Memorial."

Even in the dim light, he could see the worry in Dani's eyes.

"That sounds dramatic," she said. "Why couldn't she meet you in a bar or just outside the hotel?"

He shrugged. "I don't know. She said something about not being overheard. Once she learned who I was and what I wanted to talk about, she didn't want to be seen with me. She couldn't get away fast enough. I'm starting to feel like I have the plague."

"Or you *are* the plague," Dani said dryly. "I take it you're going to meet her."

"Of course. Want to join me?"

"No."

Despite her quick denial, he sensed she was more interested than she wanted to be. "Are you sure? Aren't you curious what she has to say?"

"Do you know how many times tonight I was reminded of the senator's trust in me, his appreciation of my loyalty?"

"That alone should make you want to know what Ann knows, because the people surrounding your boss seem very intent on making sure you don't talk to me. Why? What are they so worried about?"

"I don't know, and you're right, their behavior is getting stranger by the minute. Stephen Phelps, the senator's press secretary, has never bothered to exchange more than two words with me until tonight. He danced with me, tried to charm me and ended up suggesting we meet for a drink sometime. He was smooth as silk, and I didn't believe one word that came out of his mouth. But then I wondered if it's me reading into innocent comments."

"I don't think you are reading into anything."

"Stephen is very close to Erica. He was her first hire. They're tight. I wonder if she told him to get closer to me."

"Then you should definitely come with me tonight, Dani. No one else will be there. Let's find out what Ann knows and if there's something your boss or his staff needs to be worried about."

"She might not talk to you if I'm there," Dani said.

He supposed that was a risk, but his gut told him it was important to keep Dani close, and he wasn't going to question why. "Let's risk it. I could really use your assessment of Ann, too. I think you have good instincts about people."

"All right," she said after a moment's thought.

"Good."

He didn't know why he was so relieved she'd

agreed to come with him. He was used to working alone. Most days he preferred it. But ever since Dani had come to his rescue, he'd felt like their connection was important, possibly in ways he had yet to understand.

Starting the car, he pulled out of the lot, keeping a watchful eye on the traffic behind them, but they didn't appear to have a tail.

They had to park a few blocks from the National Mall and walk in to the park. The World War II Memorial was located at the east end of the mall near the reflecting pool. There were no tourists around at just before eleven o'clock at night, for which Patrick was both relieved and worried. He didn't know if Ann had just thrown out the meeting spot off the top of her head or if she'd had a reason to pick a deserted location for their conversation, but he was going to be on his guard.

"This is one of my favorite monuments," Dani said, as they walked toward the memorial, which was set in a semicircle with a magnificent fountain in the center.

"It is impressive," he agreed. "My mother brought me here for the opening in 2004. Her father came along, too. My grandfather served in World War II, and this monument meant a lot to him."

"That must have been an emotional moment for all of you."

"Very." Patrick dug his hands in his pocket

as he looked around at the fifty-six columns representing the forty-eight states and eight federal territories unified at the end of World War II. "My grandfather was a tough guy—a stoic, silent, suffer-in-silence kind of man. He was gruff and cranky, and while he had a fierce love for family and country, he didn't express it very well. That day I saw a tear come out of his eye. It was the most shocking thing I'd ever seen. He wasn't a man who could cry, but that day he did. He didn't say anything about what he was feeling, but it was written on his face."

"My father didn't serve in that war, but he was a military man. Seeing the wall with all these stars of lost soldiers reminds me of his service. Sometimes I wish I'd known *that* man."

"Did he talk about his days in the Navy much?"

"Almost never. He got out of the Navy when I was a little kid. I knew him as the man who flew small plane charters. I guess I never asked him about his earlier life."

"Don't beat yourself up about it. I don't think most kids believe their parents even existed before they were born."

"That's probably true," she agreed, as they walked slowly around the memorial. "It's hard to be cynical here, surrounded by heroes and sacrifice. It reminds me that the job I do is supposed to support the job the soldiers do— protect our country and make it stronger."

"You're as patriotic as any of the men who fought in World War II, Dani, and I don't think you're cynical, at all. I wonder if that might change over time, though."

"I hope not. I'd like my work to matter. I'd like to do something that inspires people. I'd like to make a difference, the way you've done with your book." She paused. "I skimmed through it on my lunch hour today. It's really good. The research you must have done, the amount of investigative work, had to be staggering."

"I spent almost two years on that project."

"I can't imagine the risks you took to get to the truth. How did you even know where to start?"

"I had a source who risked his life to come to me. He'd read some of my investigative articles and thought I could give him a voice."

"You certainly did that. When is the movie coming out?"

"Who knows? It could be a year or more. Hollywood doesn't move fast."

"What were you going to work on next before you got caught up in your mom's story?"

"I hadn't decided. I was thinking about a few projects, but mostly, I was just catching my breath. It was a crazy two years. And, honestly, Dani, I was more responsible for writing up the information than discovering it all. I got more credit than I should have."

"You're being modest."

"Just honest."

She stared back at him, a thoughtful gleam in her eyes, as if she were measuring his words.

"Believe me, I'm not above bragging," he added. "But only if I have something to brag about."

"Good to know you have standards. Although, flirting with beautiful women to get information seems to be part of your arsenal."

"You mean Ann?"

"And Erica. She agreed to meet you for lunch tomorrow."

"I use what works. Ann and Erica are both women who like male attention."

"That's true. Although, I'd say in Erica's case, she likes everyone's attention. She's turned our office into her universe. She's the sun, and everyone else revolves around her, even Senator Dillon."

"What about Dillon's wife? Does she get along with Erica?"

"Funny you should ask that. Mrs. Dillon called me over to speak to her tonight. She mentioned that she misses some of the old faces on the staff, like Joe's. She asked me what I thought of Erica. She said she worried that Erica doesn't always have her husband's interests at heart and that she might have her own ambition driving some of her decisions."

"That's interesting. What did you say?"

"I was very diplomatic. I said I thought Erica was a hard worker, but beyond that I wasn't privy to what went on between her and the senator. I thought Mrs. Dillon seemed too interested in Erica and also a little worried, as if she wondered if there is something going on between Erica and her husband."

"Do you think that's possible?" he asked curiously.

"I hope not, but she does seem to have a lot of influence over him, and she is quite stunning, wouldn't you agree?"

"She's nowhere near as pretty as you, Dani."

She flushed at his words. "You don't have to flirt with me, Patrick. I'm already helping you, against my better judgment. So put the charm aside."

"I'm not flirting. I'm just being honest."

"You like that word *honest,* don't you?"

He nodded. "Yes, I do. Honesty is important to me."

"Well, if we're being honest, I should tell you that I really don't want to be part of any of this."

"But you can't seem to stay away from me," he said lightly.

"No, I can't," she said, giving him a helpless look. "And I don't know why. I want you out of my life because you're a complication I don't need, but I can't quite get there. I wasn't going to speak to you tonight, and look where we are."

His mouth felt suddenly dry at the sincerity of her words. "I can't quite get there, either, Dani. I told myself to stay away from you, but when I saw you at the gala—you took my breath away."

She swallowed hard at his words. "Everyone looks good in a dress like this."

"No, not everyone. You're beautiful, Dani. I don't think you realize just how pretty you are."

A breeze gusted, and she wrapped her arms around her waist. "Stop, you're embarrassing me."

He smiled. "Believe me, I can be more embarrassing." He stepped forward, stripping off his jacket. "You're cold."

"If you give me that, you'll be cold."

"With you standing so close, I doubt it." He placed the coat around her shoulders. The scent of her perfume wafted around him like a tantalizing dream. She was so close, and he was so tired of fighting temptation.

He leaned in and took the kiss he'd been dreaming about.

Her mouth opened under his, and he deepened the kiss, moving his hands to her head, running his fingers through the silky strands of her hair as he tasted the sweet heat of her mouth. He felt like he could lose himself in her—a minute, an hour, a week could have passed for all he knew. It was just him and Dani, and nothing else mattered.

She kissed him back with a passion that matched his, her hands roaming his back as she pressed her breasts against his chest. He wanted so much more of her than just her mouth, but he couldn't break away from her lips. He had to keep kissing her, slanting his mouth one way and then another; he couldn't get enough.

Dani finally found a way out of the madness, putting her hands against his chest, breaking free of his kiss. As she stepped away from him with ragged breaths, he could see the desire in her eyes; the tangled strands of her hair, her swollen lips, her glittering green eyes made him want to move back in.

She put up a hand in defense.

He saw the plea in her eyes. *Damn!*

"Patrick," she murmured. "Look where we are."

"I don't care," he said, meaning it with all of his heart.

"We can't do this."

"Here or . . ."

"Anywhere," she said. "The way we kiss . . . it's too much. It's too intense."

"I thought it was perfect."

She grabbed his coat off the ground. At some point in the midst of their passion, it had fallen off her shoulders and onto the cement. "You should take this back."

"You think I'm cold now?" he asked dryly.

She tipped her head in acknowledgement. "Okay. Then I'll wear it." She put the coat on and then crossed her arms in front of her, making it seem like she'd put on a suit of impenetrable armor. "We need to remember why we're here, Patrick."

"Yeah," he said, seeing the resolve in her eyes and deep down knowing it was probably a good thing she'd called a halt before Ann found them rolling around in the middle of the memorial.

"I think someone is coming," Dani said.

He turned around to see Ann stop in the shadows at the edge of the memorial. "That's her," he said, heading in her direction.

"Who's this?" Ann asked warily, as Dani came up next to him.

"Dani Monroe. She's helping me figure out what my mother was working on before she died. She was with me when Montalvo told us about *hummingbird*. Whatever you have to say, you can say in front of her."

Ann stared back at him, her expression unreadable. "The last time I talked to anyone about *hummingbird* was eight years ago, and that person ended up dead."

His gut clenched. "You're talking about my mother, aren't you?"

"Yes. And the only reason I came here tonight was to tell you to back off. Don't go down this road. You will regret it."

"It's too late for warnings. I'm already on the road, and I have no intention of stopping. So tell me what the hell is *hummingbird*?"

"It's not a what, it's a who. And I can't tell you. I've never revealed a source, and I won't start now."

"Then why did you come tonight? You must want to tell me something," he said.

She licked her lips, then said, "I've been wanting to tell someone this for a long time, but I didn't know who would be willing to listen, to really hear me."

"Tell me," he ordered. "Because I want to know."

She hesitated for a long second. "I think your mother was murdered."

TEN

He'd had doubts about his mother's death, but hearing the words *your mother was murdered* said so boldly, without doubt, without hesitation, sent him reeling.

Even though it had been a surreal possibility in his mind, he hadn't really believed it. He'd thought that in the end he'd find out it was just an accident, that Rebecca's rumors were just rumors, that there was really nothing to know.

Dani put a hand on his arm, and he savored her steadying touch. He was more than a little glad she was by his side. He turned his attention to Ann. The woman looked over her shoulder, then back at him.

"Do you have any proof of this?" he asked.

"No. If I did, I would have given it to the FBI a long time ago."

"What are you talking about?" he asked, frustrated by her vagueness. "Be specific."

"Eight years ago, someone contacted me with a story. I was a reporter for the *Washington Tribune* at the time. This person said he'd seen the tip of an iceberg, and he wanted to warn someone, but it had to be the right person, and he didn't know who he could trust. He thought he would take a chance on your mother, but he needed an introduction. I had political connections, so he chose me to make that introduction."

"Why did you choose my mother?"

"Because she was in Texas, and she had a reputation for being open-minded, honest, and tough. I had covered her work for a couple of years. I thought she was the best choice. So I made a call to your mother to ask if she would meet with my source. She agreed. She met with him once and then two more times after she brought in Senator Stuart. The last meeting was the night before the plane crash."

He drew in a breath, forcing air into his tight chest. "Who's your source?"

"I told you I can't tell you."

"You have to tell me. You should have told the FBI what you just told me."

"I wasn't sure if I could trust the FBI. More importantly, my contact wasn't willing to go public after what happened. He was too scared. He'd also given the concrete evidence he had to back up his story to your mother, so he no longer had any proof in his possession. It would have been his word against some very powerful people. He told me he'd deny everything if I tried to bring him into it. He swore he'd disappear before he talked to anyone else. I tried to get him to tell his story to me or let me set him up with another contact, but he refused. He said he'd lost and they'd won, and that was it."

"And you just dropped it? Why? If it was that big, it would have made your career, Ann, so why didn't you push harder or do your own digging?"

"I spoke to my editor at the *Tribune* about what little I knew."

"Which is what?"

"That the information concerned a defense contractor, MDT."

His gut tightened. Why did that company keep coming up? It couldn't be a coincidence.

"The owner of the *Tribune* played golf with Alan Packer," Ann continued. "I was ordered to drop the story unless I got hard, irrefutable evidence. I thought something might come up during the crash investigation, but nothing did. It was ruled an accident. The case was closed, and I had nothing except a bad feeling and a source who wouldn't talk."

"So you're saying he had something on MDT?" Dani asked, breaking into the conversation.

"I believe so. Based on the news that came out last year about their security lapses, I think my source saw similar problems eight years ago."

"Who else knew about your source?"

"No one. We used the code word *hummingbird* for the meetings."

"But Rico Montalvo knew the code word."

She nodded. "I didn't know he knew anything about it until you told me he gave you my name."

"What about my mom's chief of staff?" he asked. "Someone else must have known."

"I spoke to your mother directly. I went to the salon where she got her hair done, and I talked to her in the parking lot. I never contacted anyone on her staff. If she told them, I didn't know about it."

"When was the last time you spoke to your source?" Dani asked.

"It was probably a month after the crash. He was running scared. He gave me a number. He said if I ever found someone he could trust again, to give him a call. Otherwise, he was done trying to save the world; he was going to save himself."

"And you never found anyone else?" Dani challenged.

"No. To be honest, I stopped looking. I was scared, too. I was pretty sure whatever my source told your mother was what got her killed, and I'd already shown a bit of my hand to my boss. I was afraid I already knew too much."

"You have to call your source," Patrick said. "Tell him Jackie Kane's son wants to meet him. If he trusted my mother, he can trust me."

"I'm not sure he'll come out of hiding after this long. He still just has what he knows, no backup proof."

"You should remind him that five people died, probably because of what he knew," Dani interjected. "And now that Patrick is digging into it all again, even if you don't tell him who your source is or set up a meeting, Patrick will probably still find him. He's a very good investigative journalist."

Patrick was touched by Dani's passionate statement.

"I'm well aware of who Patrick is." Ann's gaze narrowed on Dani. "Who are you again?"

"Dani Monroe," she replied.

"Maybe a better question is—who do you work for?"

"Senator Dillon."

Ann looked shocked at Dani's answer. "Are you serious? Why the hell are you talking to me then? Talk to him."

"You think Senator Dillon knows something about this?" Patrick asked.

"I'd be shocked if he didn't. He's part of that good-ole-boy network in Texas. The Packers are his friends. They give him a lot of money." She paused, giving Dani another sharp look. "Does he know one of his staffers is looking into the crash?"

"No," Dani said.

"I didn't think so. You're walking a dangerous line. We all are. Just talking about this now is not a good idea. I shouldn't have come."

"But you did come. I think you want to help, Ann," Patrick said. "And I think you want your story—the one you would have had eight years ago if my mother hadn't died."

"I do want that story," she admitted.

Her ambition would only help them. "You can have it if you help us."

"I'm sure you're going to write it yourself."

"I'll give you an exclusive if you hook me up with your source."

She stared back at him, and he could see the temptation in her eyes. "I hate to have anyone else's blood on my hands. I felt guilty about your mother, about my part in getting her involved."

"I appreciate that. So help me now, make up for it."

She took a deep breath, then nodded. "I'll try the phone number he gave me eight years ago. There's a good chance it won't work, but if it does, I'll tell him you want to speak to him."

"Good."

"Give me your number. I'll be in touch."

He rattled off his phone number. Ann took it down and then disappeared into the shadows.

After she left, he paced around in a small circle, adrenaline rushing through his bloodstream. Ann Higgins had just delivered a bombshell. Could she back it up? Would he finally have the opportunity to speak to someone who knew what had happened and who was responsible? He wished he could do something now. He felt restless, charged up, impatient, but he was going to have to wait again, and it was frustrating as hell.

"Are you okay, Patrick?" Dani asked, as he came to a halt in front of her.

"I don't know."

"What are you thinking?"

"That this could be the big break I've been looking for, but there are parts of it that don't feel right."

She nodded, worry in her green eyes. "I know. Why did a reporter as ambitious as Ann drop this story in the first place? Why would she hold on to a phone number for eight years? Why didn't she go to the FBI, to anyone else, with the story? Was it really just fear? Was she that afraid?"

"Your questions echo mine," he said with a confused shrug.

"We should go. We can talk about it in the car." She looked over her shoulder. "I feel like it's important that we leave now."

He could see that she felt spooked and why not? He felt much the same way. He'd just been told that his mother had been murdered. An icy chill swept over him. If that was true, how had no one known? How had eight years passed without anyone digging deeper into the crash? He felt a crushing wave of guilt that he hadn't done anything before now. He was an investigative reporter, for God's sake.

"Why didn't I ask questions?" he said. "If not right after the crash, why not later, six months down the road, or a year, or three years, or last month? How did I just let my mother's death go without demanding more answers?"

"Oh, Patrick. This isn't your fault. You were what—twenty two years old when it happened? You were barely out of college, and you were heartbroken and stricken with grief."

"I still should have asked more questions. I should have made people talk. That's what I do. That's what I'm good at. But I didn't. I just accepted what I was told." He'd never felt so angry with himself as he did right now.

"We shouldn't do this here," she said. "You can berate yourself when we're in a locked car, okay?"

"Yes, sorry, let's go."

They walked quickly back to the car. Once inside, doors locked, he started the engine and pulled away, checking his rearview mirror for any followers, but the street behind him was empty.

"I'm sorry, Patrick," Dani said quietly. "To have Ann tell you your mother was murdered had to be a horrible shock."

"There was a part of me that expected it, but then I wasn't ready for it."

"How could you ever be ready for that?"

"I don't know. But it doesn't matter if I'm ready or not. I've heard Ann's theory. Now I need evidence to back it up." He turned his head to look at her. "It all comes back to MDT—your family—my mom."

"I don't think they're connected," she said quickly.

"Don't you? I do. I think everything is connected. Maybe your great-grandmother was right; maybe you are going to find the missing piece of the puzzle, not just for your father, but also for my mother."

Dani immediately shook her head. "I don't believe that. And don't forget that a lot of secrets about MDT came out this past year. Maybe the information that Alicia and Jake discovered was the same information this source had. Maybe he knew about Jerry and the other traitors at the company. The people he might have been blowing the whistle on could have been the same people who have already been caught."

"Were they caught or were they killed?" he challenged. "And you already said your siblings don't think this is over. Neither do I."

"But not everything has to be connected," she protested.

"And yet it is. You have to stop fighting it, Dani. You have to accept that we're both caught up in different parts of the same story."

"You don't have enough evidence to support that."

"Then help me find it."

She sighed. "I really should have gone home after the gala."

"Well, you're home now," he said, pulling into a parking spot not far from her building.

"You don't have to park," she said quickly. "I can walk from here."

"Not a chance. There's too much going on. I want to see you safely inside your apartment."

They walked down the block together. Dani let him in the building, and they took the stairs to her apartment. When she got to her door, she stopped abruptly, and shot him a panicked look.

"It's open," she whispered.

He stared in shock at the slightly ajar door. "I'll go in. Wait out here."

"We should go downstairs and call the police."

"You go downstairs. I want to see what we're dealing with."

"Someone could be in there, Patrick."

She had a point, but it was quiet, no sound coming from inside the apartment. "I'm going to take that chance. Go. I'll come and get you when it's clear."

He gently pushed open the door. The apartment was dark, so he flipped on the light switch. As light flooded the room, it was immediately clear that someone had searched the place. The cushions had been taken out of the sofa, drawers in the coffee table were open, jackets and coats from the hall closet had been tossed onto the floor.

He moved through the living room into the bedroom and bathroom and found the same messy chaos in each of those rooms. When he returned to

184

the living room, Dani was standing by the couch, looking dazed and confused.

"They're gone," he said. "And I told you to wait outside."

"It felt scarier out there." She let out a breath. "Who would do this? Who would break in here?"

"We should call the police."

"This is about you. Someone thinks you told me something or gave me something . . ." Her gaze swept the room. "This wasn't a robbery; it was a search."

"Yes, it was." He pulled out his phone and punched in 911. As the operator came on the line, he reported a break-in. After being told that the intruders were gone, the dispatcher told them the police would be there shortly.

Dani picked up a sofa cushion and put it back into place.

"Don't do anything else," he said. "Let the police see it as it is first." He paused. "Do you have anything of value hidden away? Money, jewelry, electronics? Do you want to check and see if anything was taken?"

"I'll look."

As she went into the bedroom, he walked back to the front door, noting that the lock had been broken.

"I don't think they took anything," she said, returning a moment later. "I had a twenty-dollar bill on my dresser. It's still there. I don't own much in the way of expensive jewelry, but the few pieces I have are in the jewelry box."

"Computer?"

"I left it at work. I had a late meeting, so I changed for the gala in the office, and I went to the hotel right after work. But there's nothing on my computer, at least nothing to do with you. This has to be about you and your questions, right?"

He met her gaze, happy to see that her green eyes were losing their haze. The shock was wearing off; she was getting back to business. "I think so. Sorry."

"But not that many people are aware that we know each other."

"Erica knows. She could have told any number of people. Joe and Rico both saw us together," he said. "Ann didn't become aware of our connection until a few minutes ago, so I think we can count her out."

"We shouldn't have called the police," she said, her eyes growing more distressed. "There's going to be a police report. Erica is not going to like that. That will be twice in one week that I've made a statement to the police."

"She may not find out. It depends on how much you want to tell the cops."

"What will they even do? Nothing was taken. No one was hurt. We have no witnesses. I can't believe they'll do anything more than take a report and file it. Do they even check for fingerprints in cases like this?"

"Doubtful. And, frankly, I don't think they'd find any. We need to call a locksmith, get your lock fixed."

"I thought I was safe here. I never felt afraid."

He was sorry that she was scared now. "I should have stayed away from you, Dani."

"It might not have mattered. I saved your life in that park. Erica knew about it when I got into the office on Monday."

He raised an eyebrow at that piece of information. "You never said that before."

"Didn't I?"

"How did she find out so fast?"

"She said she has friends in the Corpus Christi Police Department. If any staffer's name comes up, they tell her about it."

"That's odd and very creepy."

"She's thorough. The staff's behavior reflects on the senator. She's been direct about that. She's not going to like this."

Dani's security buzzer went off, and she rang the cops into the building. A few minutes later, two uniformed officers entered the apartment.

While Dani was talking to the officers, he searched on his phone for a locksmith and found one that was open twenty-four hours a day. He made a call, happy when the locksmith said he

187

could be there in ten minutes. True to his word, he arrived just as the police were leaving.

"Why don't you pack a bag and come with me to the hotel?" he suggested to Dani while the locksmith put on a new lock.

"I'll be fine once I can lock the door again," she said. "I'd rather just stay here. And who knows what's happened at your hotel? Your room could look like this one."

"You have a point. All right. I'll stay here with you then."

"Patrick, no," she said with a frown.

"I'm not leaving you alone after what happened. I'll sleep on the couch."

Dani didn't answer; her attention was drawn to the locksmith, who told them that the new lock was good to go.

"Thanks," she said, signing the receipt after providing her credit card information. "I appreciate you coming out so late."

"That's what I do," the man said. "Take care."

"I will." She shut the door and turned the new dead bolt into place.

Patrick put the couch cushions back together and sat down. He kicked off his shoes and stretched out his feet on the coffee table, making it clear he wasn't leaving.

Dani walked back to the couch. "You really can go back to your hotel."

"I'm staying. We can argue about it all night if

you want." He paused, wondering if something else was bothering her. "If you're worried that you can't trust me, Dani—"

She shook her head, cutting him off. "I'm not worried about that."

"Really? Because we were fairly combustible earlier tonight." It seemed like a very long time ago that they'd been caught up in each other's arms. But now that they were alone again, he was reminded of just how intense and amazing those few moments had been.

"We don't need to talk about it."

"We don't?"

She sat down at the far end of the couch with a frown. "Well, maybe we do."

"That was a fast turnaround."

"I feel like we should clear the air. I can't deny that there's something between us, Patrick. Obviously, there's an attraction."

"A very strong one," he agreed.

"But that said, I don't want to take it any further."

He felt enormously disappointed by her words. "I understand. Too bad, though. It's not that often I feel such a draw to someone."

Her green eyes glittered. "I know. It's kind of rare."

"Something to consider," he pointed out.

"I'm all about my job right now. And you're on a quest for the truth about your mother.

We both need to focus on what's important to us."

"I suppose. We could say we're just putting things on hold then . . ."

She sighed. "Fine. A super long hold that may last forever."

"I'll take it."

She looked around the room. "This is going to take some cleanup."

"I'll help you."

"I don't want to do it tonight."

He was happy to hear that, because he didn't want to do it, either. "Why don't you take off your shoes, sit back and relax?"

"I should go to bed."

Despite her words, he could see how amped up she was. "You're wired; so am I. Let's talk for a bit. Let the adrenaline burn off. I'm sure I'll bore you to sleep pretty fast."

She gave him a dry smile. "You've been anything but boring so far, Patrick."

"Give me a chance."

She took off her shoes and sat back on the couch, curling her legs up under her as she turned sideways to face him. "Tell me about your childhood then. What did you like to do? What were your hobbies? Were you good in school, always getting straight As, or were you a rebel, driving fast cars, cutting class, and smoking cigarettes in the parking lot?"

He smiled at the questions, happy that some of

the panic and angst had left her voice. "I was just an average kid. I got decent grades. School came fairly easy for me. I was probably a little lazy at times. If I didn't see the point to an assignment, I had a hard time doing it, and there were a lot of pointless assignments in high school."

"I bet the teachers loved that attitude."

"I eventually did the assignment, but sometimes half-assed. Dissecting the meaning of some poem just didn't matter to me. Would we ever really know if the poet meant the light to mean an actual lamp or an inner emotional brightness?"

She laughed. "Poetry is supposed to make you question things, look beyond the words to the meanings. Surely, as a writer, you can appreciate that."

"I can appreciate that poetry is not for me," he said with a grin.

She smiled back at him. "So, not the most intense high school student, which surprises me a little. I've seen how determined you can be to get to the bottom of something."

"I don't do anything that matters to me half-assed."

"Just poetry."

"And a few other things. Getting back to your other questions. I did like to drive fast in high school. Still do. I definitely was not smoking in the parking lot. However, I might have made out there a few times."

A knowing gleam appeared in her eyes. "That doesn't surprise me. With your looks and confidence, I'll bet you were very popular."

"I also played football. That came with some nice perks, like pretty blonde cheerleaders."

"Let me guess—you were the quarterback."

"I like to call the plays," he admitted.

"Did you ever get hurt?"

"I had two concussions. Back in my day, people weren't as concerned about them as they are now. I'm lucky mine were mild. Hopefully, they didn't screw up my brain too much."

"Would you let your kid play football?"

"Whoa—we're jumping to kids now?"

"Just curious," she defended. "You're the one who wanted to talk."

"Fine. I don't think I'd encourage my child to play football knowing what I know now about the sport. Unless, of course, he really wanted to. I wouldn't want to stand in the way of my kid's dream." He cocked his head to the side, studying her face. "Let's talk about you. I'm not thinking sports for you."

"Why? Do I look un-athletic?"

"I just think you'd consider running after a ball a waste of time."

"I played soccer for a while, but I didn't love it, and it took too much of my time."

"Wait a second," he said, suddenly realizing who he was talking to.

"What did I say?" she asked with an arch of her eyebrow.

"It's what you didn't say. You were a pretty blonde cheerleader, weren't you?"

A wave of pink swept her cheeks. "Possibly."

"I knew it."

"I liked to dance. It was fun. And I liked to wear the outfit," she said.

"I bet you looked good in it."

"I did," she said, cockiness in her gaze. "I had great legs."

"You still do."

"But I did more than cheerlead," she continued. "I was also class president."

"Impressive. Your love of politics started early."

"It did. I liked being in the thick of things, in a position to make things happen."

"That experience might come in handy down the road when you stop working for the senator and start working for yourself."

"I need a lot more than high school experience before I'd run for an office."

"But that's what you want, isn't it? That's the end goal?"

"I honestly don't know. I think so, but I have to admit that since I got to DC, things haven't gone exactly as I imagined. There's more maneuvering, backroom deals, political spin . . ."

"And that surprised you?"

"I was more insulated in Texas. The senator

wasn't even in the office half the year. It was easier to concentrate on the work." She stretched out her legs and stood up. "I'm going to make some tea. Do you want some?"

"Sure. Do you have any food?"

"Really?" She raised an eyebrow. "You didn't eat at the gala? There was a tremendous spread."

"That was hours ago."

She walked into the kitchen, and he could hear her foraging around in the fridge. "I can do grilled cheese with tomatoes," she said.

"I'll take it." He got up from the couch and wandered into her small kitchen. "In fact, I'll make it," he added. "I'm an expert at grilled cheese."

"I don't know if I'd be bragging about that."

He laughed. "Good point. I should save the boasting for something more important."

"Let me ask you this: is there anything you don't do well, Patrick?"

He thought for a moment. "I'm not good at walking away—even when I should."

His words stole the smile off her face. "I used to be good at that," she said. "I used to have better tunnel vision. That seems to be changing."

"Because of me?" he asked quietly.

She gave him a long look, and suddenly, the kitchen felt a lot smaller. He'd promised to behave, but that was the last thing he wanted to do.

"Maybe," she said. "But I am walking away now. You cook. I'm going to change my clothes."

As she moved past him, he caught her by the arm. "One kiss." It was an impulsive request based on the fact that his body was desperate for her touch.

She shook her head, determination in her green eyes. "It wouldn't stop at one." She slipped out of his grip. "Focus on your grilled cheese. I want to be impressed."

"All right. I won't let you down."

She met his gaze. He was talking about more than the grilled cheese, and she knew it.

But all she said was, "I hope not."

ELEVEN

An hour later, Dani was finally starting to feel sleepy. Her stomach was full after she'd eaten one of the most delicious grilled cheese sandwiches she'd ever had. Patrick had definitely backed up his boast. Now they were sitting on the couch, sipping the last of the chamomile tea. Aside from that one moment in the kitchen when he'd wanted a kiss, he'd respected the boundaries she'd set, and it had been nice to just talk to him about nothing important. It was all still simmering in the background, but it felt good to let it go for a few minutes.

She knew she should get up and go to bed, but she was a little afraid that in the dark of the night, some of the fear from the last few hours would come back. While nothing had been stolen, her private space had been invaded. Someone had gone through her things, touched her personal items, and looked in her drawers. She didn't know if she'd ever feel the same way about her apartment again.

"Stay with me, Dani," Patrick said.

She started. "What?"

"Your thoughts are taking you away, and judging by your expression, you're not going anywhere good."

"Good guess. It's late, and I have to get up in a few hours to go to work. I really should go to bed."

"You'll be safe. I'm staying right here."

"I do appreciate that," she admitted. "I don't think I'd sleep if I were here alone."

"I'll be here when you wake up."

She nodded, wishing she wasn't starting to like him so much. The physical attraction had been instant, but now there was a growing emotional attachment, too. He was sexy as hell, but he was also smart and funny. His love for his family and his pursuit of the truth in the face of danger made him even more attractive.

Another place, another time . . .

"Dani?" he questioned, his gaze searching her eyes. "Is there something you want to say?"

"No. Only goodnight," she said, forcing herself to stand up. She walked into the bedroom and shut the door firmly behind her.

Patrick got back to his hotel a little after eight on Thursday morning, wondering if he'd find it in the same condition as Dani's apartment had been in the night before, but his room looked exactly as he'd left it. Why Dani's apartment and not his hotel room? Why would she be more of a target than he was? What would she have that he wouldn't?

Was the search tied to the people who employed

her? Were they the ones who were worried? Had Joe been less of a loyal friend to Dani than she thought? Had he told Dillon's office what Dani was up to, where she was headed? Was the senator and his office more worried about what Dani was doing than what he was doing?

The questions went around and around in his head as he stripped off his clothes and got into the shower to clear his head. Hopefully things would become clearer when he heard back from Ann Higgins. He also had lunch with Erica at one. That might be more of a fact-finding mission for her than for him, but he'd take it. Erica might not be Senator Dillon, but she was the next best thing.

He'd like to get Erica on his side, make her an ally instead of an enemy. It would be better for him and even more importantly, better for Dani.

Stepping out of the shower, he dried off and got dressed. He'd just finished buttoning his shirt when his phone rang. His heart jumped.

"Hello?"

"It's Ann."

"What do you have?"

"A place to go for further instructions."

"What are you talking about? Did you speak to your source?"

"I spoke to an intermediary. He answered the number I had. He gave me the address of a con-venience store and said you should go there at six o'clock tonight. Tell the man at the counter you'd like to borrow his phone."

"Why?"

"Just do it."

He jotted down the address she gave him. "What else can you tell me, Ann? You've got to give me something more than this. Why are you being so mysterious?"

"Because I don't want to die," she said bluntly.

A chill ran through him. "You're being dramatic, Ann."

"I'm not. The year after your mother died, I felt like someone was watching me, following me. My apartment was broken into twice. My desk at work was searched; someone hacked into my computer and someone else threw a brick through the windshield of my car. Look, I want to help you. I'd love to break this story after all these years, but I have to be careful, and so does my source. So you'll play it this way or you won't play it at all."

"Fine. I'll go to the store."

She ended the call before he could ask her any more questions. He sat down at the desk and opened his computer. Plugging the address in, he pulled up a map of DC. The address she gave him was down the street from Union Station. Did that mean anything? Was the source coming in by train from somewhere?

He hated having to wait all day to find out. But in the meantime, he was going to do some research on Erica. If he could find her weakness, her insecurity, maybe he could play off it.

"I need to speak to you," Dani told Erica a little before one. She'd been thinking about the report she'd given to the police all morning, and she'd decided to be up-front with Erica, rather than let her find out about it on her own. Unfortunately, Erica had been tied up in meetings most of the day. Now, she was on her way out to meet Patrick, not that Dani was supposed to know anything about that.

"Can it wait?" Erica asked, as she turned off her computer.

"It will just take a second. When I got home from the gala last night, I discovered that my apartment had been broken into. I called the police, and they came over and took a report."

Erica's eyes widened. "Oh, my God! You were robbed?"

She wasn't quite sure how to answer that. She also wasn't quite sure Erica's reaction was genuine. But maybe she was overthinking everything.

"What did they take?" Erica asked. "Did you have work from the office at home?"

"I don't think they took anything, and my work computer was here. I had some printed reports on the Corpus Christi port at home, but that's about it."

"So, nothing confidential?"

"No. I don't take those things out of the office."

"Good. But I still don't like the sound of this. Who would break in and then take nothing?"

"I honestly don't know."

"Well, I'm glad you're all right. Did you have the locks changed?"

"I did."

"We'll talk later. I do have to run."

"Of course." She headed back to her office, but as she went around the corner, she barreled straight into Stephen Phelps. "Sorry, I seem to be making a habit of running into you."

He smiled. "That's a habit I could like. Where are you headed?"

"My office."

"Have you had lunch yet?"

"No, but I have a lot to do."

"You still need to eat. Let's go to the café downstairs. I was just about to grab a bite."

She hesitated, then realized the only reason she hadn't already said yes was Patrick. But she had to stop thinking that every conversation would be about him. Stephen was an important person for her to get to know. "Sure," she said. "Let's go."

Patrick had his lunch date, and she had hers.

Erica Hunt was late. Patrick checked his watch with irritation. He hated when people didn't show up on time, but he wasn't surprised. Erica would be exactly the kind of person to keep someone waiting. It was part of her power. She was the important one, not him, and she wanted him to know that. Unfortunately, as much as he wanted to bail and show her she wasn't that important, he couldn't do it. This wasn't about him. This was about his mother.

She arrived five minutes later, wearing a tight brown skirt and a silky top, her brown hair pulled back in a clip at the back of her neck. She slid into the seat across from him.

"Mr. Kane."

"Ms. Hunt," he said. "Thanks for meeting me."

"You're welcome." She paused as the waiter came by to ask if they'd like a drink. "I'll have an iced tea," she said.

"Water is good for me," he told the waiter.

"They have a very good steak here," Erica said. "If you're a meat lover, and I'm guessing that's true since you're a Texas man."

"That would be a good guess—for a California girl."

"I haven't been a California girl since I was twelve."

"That's right. You moved to Connecticut with your father after your parents divorced. You went to prep school there. Eventually, you made your way to Harvard. You have a very impressive resume. No left turns, no set backs—just one straight drive to success. At least, that's what the public records say."

"Your path hasn't been nearly as clean," Erica

returned. "You've jumped around in jobs ever since you graduated from Northwestern. Your focus seems to change every few years. You don't appear to have a very long attention span, and while you hit huge success with your book, you haven't done anything new in months. Maybe you're just enjoying all the lovely money your movie deal must have brought in. Tell me, who's going to play you in the movie?"

He smiled at her smugness, not at all rattled by the fact that she'd read up on him as well. He would have expected no less. "I have no idea if anyone will actually make a movie, but I'm sure they'll find someone good if they do."

She sat back in her seat. "Maybe you could play yourself."

"I don't act."

"Don't you? I'm betting you've done quite a bit of acting in your investigative work."

"It's more like politics than acting. You find out what someone wants and then figure out how to give it to them while making sure it works in your benefit as well."

She nodded. "What do you think I want?"

"A promise that I won't hurt the senator's reputation, that I won't cause problems for him or for you."

"See, the problem with promises is that they're just words. And people break promises all the time."

"I don't."

"What do you think Senator Dillon would know that you couldn't learn in the accident reports?"

"He was Senator Stuart's friend. I want to know if the senator told him what he was working on before the accident."

"As in legislation?"

"As in whatever. And I want to know if my mother was involved."

"I heard rumors that your mother and Senator Stuart were more than colleagues," Erica said. "Is that true?"

"Something else I'd like to ask the senator," he said evenly. "I only have a few questions for him. I won't take up much of his time."

"Is that all you want to know?"

"It's a start. Not as scary as you imagined?"

"I'm not scared of you, Mr. Kane, but it is my job to protect the senator from pointless conversations that distract him from his work. I can tell him what you told me, and I'll see what he says."

"What has he said so far?" Patrick challenged. Dani had already told him that the senator was aware of his interest.

"Nothing really." She paused, studying him for a long moment. "Do you have some doubts about the crash itself? Is that why you want to know what your mother and Senator Stuart were working on?"

"Yes, that's exactly why."

"Aren't there people who worked with your mother who could answer those questions?"

"Not so far."

"Senator Dillon wasn't in office when Senator Stuart died. I seriously doubt he has any idea what Senator Stuart was working on. He might be able to tell you his typical golf score or whether or not he liked his steak rare or well done, but I doubt they were sharing legislative ideas."

They were getting nowhere fast. Erica was as good at saying nothing as anyone he'd met. Time to shake her up a little.

"Here's what I think, Ms. Hunt. I believe Senator Stuart was working on a case involving MDT. I think he had some potentially damaging information on the company."

"Based on what?"

"Based on what I've heard. I also think that Senator Dillon is avoiding me because of his relationship with the MDT top brass. And that would be a mistake. They've already had a lot of problems at that company in the past six months. There may be more to come. He might want to give himself some distance."

Erica didn't even blink while he was talking, but that alone told him he was getting her attention.

"If Senator Dillon's desire is to avoid problems, especially with one of his largest donors, he might want to get out in front of what's coming," he added. "I think he'd prefer to have me as an ally, not an enemy. I think you would, too."

She cleared her throat, but she still had a steely-eyed gaze. "That sounds like a threat."

"Don't be ridiculous. I wouldn't threaten a US senator. I want to help Senator Dillon. In fact, I think we can help each other. We can both win, and isn't that always the best outcome?" He pushed back his chair and stood up. "I've asked the waiter to charge your lunch to my card."

"You're leaving?" For the first time, she looked truly surprised.

"I have work to do. Tell the senator to call me back. Enjoy your lunch."

Her stunned expression made his day. Erica had just learned she wasn't calling the shots. She'd worry her way through lunch, if she stayed, although he doubted she would. On the other hand, she might enjoy charging a very large and expensive meal to his credit card.

He walked out of the restaurant and paused a moment to put on his sunglasses. He hoped his calculated move was enough to make Erica think he had more than he was saying and that she'd advise the senator to join forces with him. It could backfire. She might decide that he was too much of a dangerous risk for the senator to take. If that happened, he'd deal with it. He'd learned a long time ago that there were a lot of ways to the truth.

He was tired of waiting for the senator to decide whether or not to get in the game. If he didn't want to play, Patrick would find someone who would, and that might not only put the senator on the sidelines but possibly also in a very tenuous position.

"Erica is worried about you," Stephen told Dani as they finished their salads in the café located in the basement of their building.

She almost choked on a carrot. Lunch up to this point had been easy, and they'd talked about movies and DC gossip. She'd started to relax. That had obviously been a mistake. She swallowed hard and took a sip of her water. "Why would she be worried about me?"

"She told me yesterday that you were involved in an altercation when you were in Texas and that you hadn't been yourself since you got back."

"I'm fine. I'm a little tired. My weekend was busy with my sister's wedding and then the problem at the park, but I'm good. No one needs to worry."

"Did you really break up a fight?"

"It wasn't that big of a deal. And I wasn't hurt. The person ran away."

"Lucky and brave. When Erica told me the story, I was a little surprised. You don't seem the type."

"What type do I seem like?" she asked.

"Well, you're very studious and quiet, at least when you're in the office."

"I'm surprised you have any idea what I'm like in the office. We haven't had much interaction. In fact, I think this is the most we've ever talked."

He looked taken aback by her candor. "That's true, but I've noticed you. You're a beautiful woman."

"And you're an attractive man who has more dates than he can count, so why are you suddenly so interested in charming me?"

Maybe it wasn't smart to confront him, but she was getting a little weary of being on the defensive. She wasn't a pushover, even though some of the people in the office seemed to think she was. Maybe she'd been a little quieter, a little more introspective since she'd gotten to DC, but that was just because she was trying to fit in, find her way.

"I'm not trying to charm you, just get to know you," he said.

"I don't believe you. I think Erica sent you to talk to me."

"Why would she do that?"

"Because you just said she was worried about me. Since you know about the incident in the park, I'm sure you're also aware that I became friendly with Patrick Kane, someone the senator is apparently determined to avoid. So, can we cut the charade and you just ask me what you want to know?"

A glint of admiration appeared in his eyes. "Are you involved with Patrick Kane?"

"I've spoken to him a few times. He's trying to find out more about his mother's plane crash. I don't know why that's an issue for anyone in the office or for the senator." She paused. "I lost a parent in a plane crash, too. It was a couple of years before the one Patrick is looking into. I know what it's like to search for answers, and I have compassion for his desire to know everything he can about his mother's death."

"That death was a long time ago. Why question everything now?"

"Because someone suggested that he didn't know everything."

"Who?"

"You'd have to ask him that."

"The senator can't get involved in anything that looks like a cover-up, Dani. You know that wouldn't be good for his political ambitions, and it wouldn't be good for yours, either. Our fortunes are tied to his. If he has a job, we have a job. So, maybe think about that when you decide how much you want to help Patrick Kane."

"Erica already said as much to me."

"But it didn't sway you. You left the gala with him last night."

"How would you know that?" she asked in surprise.

"I saw you walking down the street. I was going

to offer you a ride home, so I tried to catch up with you. Before I could, you got into a car with a man at the wheel. You drove right by me. I could see it was Patrick Kane."

"He offered me a ride."

"But you walked to the parking lot by yourself, as if you didn't want anyone to see you together."

She sighed. "Because Erica had ordered me not to talk to him."

"You should have followed that order."

"You told her you saw me with him, didn't you?"

"Actually, I didn't. I wanted to speak to you first."

She didn't know if she believed him. "Why?"

"Because I didn't want her to fire you. You may not believe a word I'm saying, but I do actually like you, Dani. I think you do good work, and I know Erica can be vengeful. I don't want you to lose your job."

"Well, I appreciate that."

"You need to cut your ties with Kane." He put up a hand as she started to speak. "Don't tell me if you're going to or not; just think about it. If you are going to help him, be careful." He got to his feet. "And just for the record, if I have to choose a side between you and Erica, I'll choose Erica. I like my job, and something tells me you don't like me quite as much as I like you."

"I don't know you, Stephen."

"Well, maybe someday we can change that—if you want to. The ball is in your court." He tossed a tip down on the table. "I'll see you back in the office."

After he left, she let out a breath and wondered what the hell had just happened. She had no idea what to think about Stephen Phelps. Had he been trying to be a friend? Or was he playing her? It had been a lot easier in Texas to figure out who the bad guys were.

TWELVE

Dani was happy to get back to work after lunch, and for the next few hours she concentrated on pending legislative reports. But she kept her phone handy, expecting to hear from Patrick at some point. His call came just after three. "Hello?"

"Can you talk?" he asked.

"Not really." She had little privacy in the office.

"Then listen. I've got two leads. I found the pilot who was supposed to fly the plane before he got sick. He lives here in DC, and I have his address."

Her pulse picked up at his words. "Are you going to talk to him?"

"Yes. I'm hoping you'll come with me. Ann also set up a meet at six near Union Station in regards to her source. I think we should go by the pilot's house first, maybe four thirty, then go to the meet."

She wanted to go. She was getting as caught up in the mystery as he was. She also wanted to know what he and Erica had talked about at lunch, but she couldn't ask him about that now. Still, leaving the office that early could raise some suspicion. *Oh, what the hell—they were suspicious already.*

"I'll go with you," she said, giving in to probably a really bad impulse.

"I can pick you up at work."

"I'd rather meet you. Text me the address."

"It's coming now. See you soon."

She set down her phone and tried to finish up some work, but she couldn't concentrate. She was too tense and now having second and third thoughts about going with Patrick.

Finally, the hands on the clock made it to four. She left her cubicle and managed to get out of the office without anyone stopping her. She took the metro across town, then walked four blocks to the address of the home that Patrick had given her. The house was a modest two-story home near Rock Creek Park. Patrick got out of his car as she walked down the street.

"Hi," she said, wondering if she'd ever stop getting butterflies in her stomach when she saw him. Today, he wore jeans and a short-sleeved shirt, a pair of sexy aviator glasses. It was ridiculous how attractive he was.

"Thanks for coming," Patrick said.

"Is he here?"

"There's a man inside. I saw him go into the house about fifteen minutes ago. I got here early to check things out. His name is Matt Walker. He's fifty-three years old and ex-Navy, like your dad. He still flies for the same charter service that my mother used."

"Do you know what you want to ask him?"

"Somewhat," Patrick said. "Let's see where it goes."

"You like to wing it, don't you?"

"Sometimes the best information comes from the most unexpected moment, comment, or question. I try to remember that when it doesn't feel like I'm getting anywhere."

They walked up to the front door and rang the bell. A moment later, a man answered. His gray hair was cut very short. He had a square face, a strong jaw, and sharp eyes. He looked ex-military, Dani thought. He also looked annoyed.

"I'm not buying anything and I'm not interested in changing my religion," he said.

"We're not selling or preaching," Patrick said quickly. "Are you Matt Walker?"

"Who wants to know?"

"My name is Patrick Kane. My mother was Jackie Kane. She died on a plane that you were supposed to pilot eight years ago."

The man tensed, the blood draining out of his face. "I told the investigators everything I knew."

"I know," Patrick said. "I'm not here in any official capacity. I just want to understand what happened to my mom's plane, and I haven't been able to get many people to talk to me about it."

"I wasn't there. I don't know any more than the investigators, who had far more access than I did to all the data."

"Could we come in for a minute?" Patrick asked.

Matt hesitated a long minute, then said, "I suppose."

"This is Dani Monroe," Patrick added, as they walked into the house. "She's a friend."

He gave a nod and led them into his living room.

As they settled into their seats, Matt said, "What is it you think I can tell you?"

Patrick leaned forward, clasping his hands together. "You were sick the day of the flight. What happened? When did you know you weren't well enough to go to work?"

"I got ill a little after midnight—stomach flu. The flight was scheduled for ten a.m. I called the dispatcher around two in the morning and said I couldn't do it."

"Did you know the pilot who took the flight?" Dani interjected.

"No, I had never met him. He had recently joined the company. He'd only flown one or two charters before that, but he did have a lot of experience. He was former Air Force."

"Did you read through all of the investigative findings?" Patrick asked.

"The ones that were made available to me," Matt said. "I was stunned when the aircraft went down. I'd flown that plane and that route a dozen times. However, the storm conditions were difficult, and it appeared that there was a power outage that took out several important navigational systems." He paused. "I'm very sorry about your mother. I had flown her several times, and she was a very nice woman, very kind to all the people who worked for her and with her."

"I appreciate you saying that," Patrick said.

When Patrick seemed at a loss for words after Matt's comment, she jumped in. "You said you had the stomach flu—but I thought there was speculation that it was food poisoning."

"I had eaten take-out from my favorite Vietnamese restaurant that evening, so it was possible, but I'd eaten there many times before that without any problems. Not that that matters, I guess. You can pick up a bug anywhere." He paused. "It sounds like you think I had a reason for not getting on the flight, that I had some knowledge of what was to come. It's not the first time that's been suggested to me. The FBI agents who spoke to me surfaced that theory as well. But it's not true. I was sick and that's the only reason I didn't get on that flight."

There was not a hint of evasion or insincerity in his eyes. She didn't know if he was a practiced liar or completely innocent, but it was difficult to doubt him. "You said you ordered take-out from this restaurant quite frequently."

"Yes, several times a week. My wife worked a lot and I was never good in the kitchen. But I was very good at calling out for food."

"Did you call the restaurant directly or did you use a service?"

"I used a meal delivery service—Kincaid's. The FBI also spoke to them. The delivery person had delivered food to my house many times in the past. They couldn't find any evidence that someone poisoned my food." He gave them a tired, sad smile. "I don't know what you're looking for or why you're looking now, but the FBI did their job. I think it was just random luck that left me at home and put Carruthers in the cockpit."

"There were a lot of conspiracy theories about the crash," Patrick put in. "Did you think any of them had merit?"

"There wasn't as much hard data as I would have liked to have seen," Matt admitted. "Carruthers shouldn't have had problems with that storm. The plane shouldn't have lost power. Whenever we flew high-level passengers, there were extra layers of security. Do I have questions? Sure. But I also don't see anything I can disagree with. I wasn't on the plane. So I don't know what they were facing, and that's the problem for all the investigators." He paused. "What do you think happened?"

"I don't think it was an accident," Patrick said.

"But you don't have any proof it was anything else?"

"Not yet. But I'm not done looking."

"I wish you luck then. If there's something to be found, I hope you find it. That crash has haunted me for years. I've wondered a million times if I'd been the one at the controls, would I have found a way to change the outcome. But who knows? I might be dead, too."

"Thanks for your time," Patrick said, standing up.

"We appreciate it," Dani added, shaking Matt's hand, before leaving the house.

They walked out to the car and got inside before uttering a word to each other.

"I don't think it was just random luck Matt wasn't on that plane," Patrick said to her.

"Really? He seemed pretty confident in his answers, and he definitely knew why we were asking the questions."

"That did make him seem honest," Patrick agreed. "He was very smooth, very charming, disarming."

She frowned. "I think he was telling the truth."

"Well, you might be right."

"What do you know about the replacement pilot?"

"Not much. Sean Carruthers flew for the Air Force and had recently gotten into commercial aviation. As Matt said, Carruthers had a lot of experience. He was certainly well-trained."

"But he was new to the company," she pointed out, that little fact sticking in her head. "And here's something else to consider. MDT has a history of hiring military-trained pilots to test their products. My father's former friend, who almost killed my sister, was one of their test pilots after he left the Navy." She paused. "I wonder if we should try to figure out if Jerry had any connection to Matt or to Carruthers."

A gleam entered Patrick's eyes. "That's an excellent idea. Maybe there's a link to your father, too," he suggested.

She didn't like that idea. "I doubt that."

"Why? Your dad was in the military and in private aviation, same as these guys."

"I think I'm going to regret what I just said. Actually, I already regret it."

He gave her a compassionate smile. "Too late to take it back, Dani." He started the car. "We'll have to work on this later. We need to get to the convenience store where Ann is apparently leaving me some sort of message."

"She's not going to be there?"

"She said I should see the man at the counter and ask if I can borrow his phone."

"I think Ann has seen too many spy movies."

"Or her source has. But I'm going to play it out, see where it takes us."

"Let's do it," she said, fastening her seat belt.

As he drove across town, Patrick thought about Dani's suggestion that the pilot could be a link to MDT. As soon as they were done with the next meet, he intended to do more research on the man who had been in the cockpit.

Although, there was an obvious question: Why

would the pilot, who had gotten the job only a few hours before the flight, be willing to die himself? If he was going to sabotage the plane, why hadn't he saved himself?

Unless he hadn't known what was coming. Maybe he'd been duped himself—a double cross. Something else to think about.

When they entered the convenience store near Union Station, there were a bunch of teenagers at the counter, so they moved down the aisle to wait until the line cleared out.

He grabbed two bottles of water out of the refrigerator section. When the counter cleared, he approached the clerk. The man tending the register appeared to be in his late thirties, with thinning brown hair and a notable scar across one eyebrow. He looked like the kind of man who knew how to fight and might even enjoy it.

Setting the water bottles down, he pulled out a twenty-dollar bill. "Is there any chance I could borrow your phone?" he asked.

The man's gaze sharpened. He looked around the store, then pulled a phone out from under the counter. "You can take it. I don't need it."

"Thanks."

As they walked out of the store, he took Dani's hand so he wouldn't lose her in the crowded pedestrian traffic. He wanted to see what was on the phone, but he also wanted to get back to the car and a little more privacy.

As they moved down the block, he felt like someone was watching him. He cast a glance over his shoulder more than once, but no one stood out. Maybe he was just being paranoid.

"Everything okay?" Dani asked quietly, also casting a look over her shoulder.

"I hope so," he muttered.

"Sometimes you're a little too honest, Patrick. A better answer would be *everything is fine*."

"Everything is fine," he said, trying to take the worry out of her eyes.

But clearly she didn't believe him. They finally reached the car. They got inside and flipped the locks. He gazed down the street they'd parked on. He didn't see anyone sitting in a car or looking out of place. He opened the phone. "There's one number in the contacts." He connected the call and put the phone on speaker.

A man answered a moment later. "Hello?" he said in a deep voice.

"This is Patrick Kane. Who's this?"

"That doesn't matter. You're looking for information on your mother's death?"

"I am. Do you have any?"

"The last people I spoke to about this are dead."

"Was that my mother?"

"And the senator."

"You met them the night before they got on the plane," Patrick said, feeling a sense of excitement that he was getting close to something.

"Yes, and I gave them all the information I had. They assured me they'd protect me. And then they were dead."

"Why didn't you go to someone else after the crash?" he asked.

"Because I'd given them all my proof, and because I didn't want to die, too. I didn't know who to trust. The police, the FBI—they could have all been involved, so I went underground. I changed my name, my appearance, and my life. I'm risking all of it now just to talk to you."

"You may not have proof anymore, but you do know what you told my mother and what you gave her, so tell me what it was."

"It was information on security leaks at MDT."

"Like the ones discovered last year?"

The man snickered. "Those leaks were just a small ripple in an ocean of deceit. The disappearing weapons and stolen technology have been going on for more than a decade. There's an entire faction of the company that runs outside the law. They've been siphoning off money, weapons, technology, everything . . . This shadow company is leaner, more powerful, and it operates on the black market, providing weapons for anyone who wants them."

Patrick sucked in a breath at the scope of what was being suggested.

"Some of the smartest people in the company work both for MDT and for the shadow company," the man continued. "The new weapons that are coming out are going to be duplicated and sold to the highest bidders. Or worse, they'll be used on our own soil. Nothing drives profit more than terror. The more turmoil in the world, the more money MDT gets."

"What kind of proof did you have?"

"I had financial reports that showed a constant stream of anomalies regarding government money being funneled through the company divisions. I had photos of key MDT executives meeting outside the company, sometimes with individuals who were known to play on the black market. I had a person who could testify to working at an off-site location on a weapon that was exactly like the one MDT was building."

"What kind of weapon was that?"

"The railgun, similar to the ones that went missing last year and ended up at a ranch in Mexico."

"Was that the offsite location?"

"I don't know. It might have been. But my gut tells me they were also using a location in Texas."

"Where is that person now?" Patrick asked.

"Dead. He died of carbon monoxide poisoning the day before the plane crash. I didn't know about it until a week after the crash. He'd gone underground while I was trying to get the information to your mother. He's another reason I gave up on all this. I don't believe his death was an accident any more than I believe your mother's plane crashed in a storm."

Patrick's stomach twisted. He felt sick. "I still don't know why you didn't go to the accident investigators and tell them what you knew."

"I watched the investigation closely. I figured if someone had sabotaged the plane, they'd get there eventually, and then I'd talk. But they never came to that conclusion. And I had nothing left to show anyone. I could talk, but who was going to believe me without proof?"

He was beginning to see why the man had gone underground. "What did my mother say when you showed her what you had and told her all this?"

"She was shocked, but she was open-minded. So was Senator Stuart. He told me he'd thought there were problems with that company for years, but they were so heavily involved in politics, it would be difficult to get anyone to stand against them. He felt he finally had the proof he might need. It was a good talk. I came away thinking that they were going to get to the bottom of everything. But you know how that ended."

"Yeah," he said heavily.

"When Ann called the number I gave her years ago, I couldn't believe it. But when she said it was Jackie Kane's son who wanted to talk, I took a risk, because while the FBI and Congress may think the holes at MDT have been plugged, I know otherwise. The shadow company might have taken a hit in Mexico, but they're still in existence."

"Who do you think is at the top?"

"I don't know if it's one of the Packer brothers or both, or it could even be their father, although that's less likely now since he retired. It has to be someone who has the power to move money, technology, and weapons and then cover their tracks. If you want to get into this, you're going to need top-level connections. Ann said you were with a woman who works for Senator Dillon. Can she help?"

"You think the senator might be involved?" he asked, glancing at Dani, who looked less than thrilled with the man's suggestion.

"I'm sure he knows something, and he's in tight with the Packers. After your mother and Senator Stuart died, money to MDT increased by threefold. Look through the budgets; you'll see I'm right. They didn't just take out two people who were about to blow the whistle; they replaced them with two other people who were pro private defense contracts."

He already knew that to be true. "We need to meet in person. We need to talk more. You have to lay out everything you know."

"No, I can't do that. You have to do the rest on your own. I'll give you one more lead. Tania Vaile."

"Who's that?"

"She's a senior financial manager at MDT. She moves a lot of money around the company, and she's very close to the Packer brothers and their father. A few years ago, I would have said she'd never go against them, but that might have changed. The men aren't as tight with her anymore. They've all moved on to younger women. She might be angry. You could use that."

"You've got to give me more," Patrick said, sensing the man was about to hang up.

"I've given you all I can. If you can get enough proof, I'll come in as a witness, but until then I'm staying in the dark where it's safe."

Before Patrick could say another word, the call disconnected.

"Dammit," he said in annoyance. He looked over at Dani. "What do you think?"

"I think I found Tania Vaile," she said, turning her phone to face him. "She's with both Packer brothers, Reid and Alan, at a Texas fundraiser at the Ashton Hotel in Dallas. She's a beautiful, busty blonde."

He could see that. "It looks like she is tight with the Packers."

"Who knows? It's a fundraiser, and she's standing in front of them. No one has their arm around her."

"True."

"I also pulled up another page while you were talking on the phone," Dani continued. "I found her business profile. It says she's a senior financial manager, and that she's been at the company for twelve years." She looked back at Patrick. "If Tania is on the financial side, maybe she was or is the one moving around the money."

"It's hard to believe that no one would have found evidence of any of this during the FBI investigation," he muttered. "Someone at MDT is operating a shadow company and the guys in charge don't know about it? Are they stupid? Are they complicit in some way?"

"I don't find it so difficult to believe that this side group exists, not after what my brother saw in Mexico. Those weapons were taken out of the company by someone, and it seems like more than a one- or two-person job, yet they've never been able to figure out who was responsible."

"I'd like to talk to the FBI about it."

"Good luck. From my experience, they like you to talk while they say nothing."

"From your experience?" he echoed.

"They came to my apartment when Jake and Katherine brought TJ back into the country. The FBI met them there. I heard a few things, and they asked me a few questions. Obviously, I didn't know anything. So, what do you want to do now?"

"Hell if I know."

"Maybe I should go back to work," she suggested.

"Or we could go back to my hotel and regroup,"

he said. "It's almost seven. Isn't your workday over?"

"I often work later than seven."

"We need to talk about everything, Dani. I would really appreciate your insight."

"All right. I'll check my work email when we get to the hotel and make sure there's nothing important I'm missing. I really don't want to believe that Senator Dillon knows about any of this, but it is true that MDT has gotten a lot of contracts over the last eight years. They went through a bad couple of months with the congressional hearings, but they seem to have repaired their reputation and are getting back in business." She let out a sigh. "That company is huge and the people who run it are very powerful, with a lot of contacts and a lot of money. It won't be easy to bring a case against them."

"I like to take things one step at a time. Seeing a huge mountain in front of you can defeat you before you even start climbing, but if you just look down and keep moving forward, it's amazing how far you can go."

She smiled. "Is that your philosophy for life?"

He tipped his head. "It is."

"Not bad. But even taking it one step at a time, this mountain could be too big for us. Maybe we should go to the FBI."

"Not yet. We need proof, Dani. A random call from a nameless guy won't take us too far, and our conversation with the pilot who missed the trip was inconclusive. It's too early. We need more evidence, and we need to be sure who we can trust. This isn't just about me and my mother anymore; it's also about your family and maybe your boss. We need to keep digging."

"I can't help thinking we may dig ourselves into a hole we can't get out of."

She might be right, but he hoped not.

THIRTEEN

"So was this the way your room looked when you came back here this morning?" Dani asked as she walked around Patrick's hotel room. Everything was neat and organized, not a pillow out of place.

"Yes. It didn't appear anyone had been inside," he replied.

"That's so odd. Why search my apartment but not your hotel room?"

"Maybe they didn't know where I was staying."

"Whoever *they* is," she said with a sigh, as she sat down at the round table by the window. "Before we get too deep into research, what are your thoughts about food?"

He smiled. "I'm in favor of it."

"Me, too. There's an Indian restaurant down the street. They have a really good chicken curry, and they deliver."

"Sounds perfect."

"If you want to look at the menu, I can pull it up on my computer," she said, taking her computer out of her bag and setting it on the table across from him.

"Just order whatever you like, and we'll share."

As Patrick got on his computer, she ordered dinner. Once that was done, she checked her work email, happy to see no pressing emergencies. She gazed over at Patrick, who was frowning at his computer.

"What are you working on?"

"Our source. He's sending us down a particular path, and we don't know anything about him."

"How are we going to find out? We don't know his name, his age, his location . . ."

"True, but I think he knows the guy who gave us the phone."

"That makes sense. Or the cashier at the store could have been Ann's contact. She's the one who sent you there."

"No, I think our whistleblower would only be willing to give his phone number to someone he trusted implicitly. He's clearly paranoid. That's why he didn't have Ann give us the phone. He must not trust her, either. In fact, maybe he wonders if she's the one who blew the whole story up eight years ago."

"But then he wouldn't have given her a number that she could contact him at. I don't think he mistrusts her."

"Maybe not. The store where we got the phone is owned by the Cammerata family." He turned his computer around so she could see the screen. "This is their website. Recognize the guy in the middle?"

"That's the clerk."

"Vincent Cammerata. The other two men are his father George and his brother David."

"You think one of them is the source?"

"No, but I think that Vince knows our source. He's either a best friend or a relative or both."

"I'll look on social media, see who pops up in Vince's friend feed. I've researched a few dates over the years, so I have an idea what to look for."

"Proactively or after you went out with them?"

"Both. You can't tell me you haven't done the same thing," she said dryly.

"Never. I prefer to get my information first-hand."

"Well, it's different for guys." She paused. "I've got his profile page. He has three hundred plus friends."

"You can exclude the females. Concentrate only on the men and those in his age range, which appeared to be late thirties."

"He's divorced," she said, reading through some of the posts. "Looks like it's recent, about a year ago. He has a seven-year-old daughter."

"Does Cammerata have any Texas friends?"

"Not that are obvious. It would take some work to figure that out. Shall I focus on that?"

"If you don't mind. I'll get into Tania Vaile."

"Deal." She actually liked having something specific to work on. It helped keep her mind off Patrick and the fact that they were alone in his hotel room with a comfortable-looking, king-sized bed not too far away. They'd been so busy chasing down leads that it had been easy to keep her attraction at bay, but any time she looked at him too long her brain turned to mush, and she started thinking about other things—like touching him, kissing him, maybe taking off his clothes, seeing what muscles lay beneath the shirt and the jeans, because it was clear that Patrick was fit. He might not play football anymore, but he still moved like an athlete.

"So have you done any dating here in DC?" Patrick asked.

His question startled her out of her distracted reverie, which was good. "I've gone out with a couple of guys, but no more than a few dates with any of them."

"Why not?" he asked, interest in his eyes.

"There wasn't any chemistry," she said with a shrug.

"Well, it's important to have that."

"We also either didn't have anything in common or too much. One guy worked for another senator. Even though his boss and mine are in the same party, it felt too close. I was never sure if we were just talking, or if he was looking for information."

"What about the other guys?"

"One was a cyber geek. He was fascinated by technology, and he talked a lot about it. My eyes glazed over by the end of the night. The other man was a dentist. Nice guy, but he was looking to move to the suburbs, open his own practice, and have a bunch of kids really, really soon."

"I thought women liked a man who was ready to get married," Patrick teased.

"That's a myth perpetuated by men who think every woman wants the same thing."

"So you don't want a husband and kids?"

"I do—someday. But not right now. What about you?"

"I'd like to have a family—someday," he said, repeating her word with a smile. "But I'm not in a rush. Doing what I do, it's nice to have the freedom to be flexible and to work long hours if I need to."

"Exactly," she agreed.

"I will say that after my mom died, the holidays have been depressing," Patrick said. "Our family was always small, but losing my mom created a huge void. My father has never really recovered from the loss. I worry now that the park is done that he won't have anything positive to focus on. It's been his goal for so long; it's what he's lived for."

"He'll find something else. And he has his job, which he enjoys, right?"

"Yes, he likes teaching."

"Does he know what happened to you in the park?"

Patrick nodded. "He came to the hospital that night with my aunt and my cousin, and he's called me a few times since then, but I haven't returned his calls. I should do that. I just don't want to get into details."

"Like the fact that your attacker overdosed behind a gas station under suspicious circumstances."

"Exactly."

"When are you going to tell him that you're investigating your mother's death?"

"When I have something specific to tell, but not before then. I don't want him to worry or to try to stop me."

"Would he do that?" she asked curiously.

"I'm not sure. To protect me—maybe."

She looked down as her cell phone buzzed with an incoming text. "The food is downstairs in the lobby."

"I'll get it," he said, getting to his feet.

"I already put it on my credit card, including the tip."

"You didn't have to do that."

She shrugged. "Not a big deal." After Patrick left, she turned her attention back to the computer. She checked out several other social media sites to see if Vincent Cammerata was more active online somewhere else. He seemed to have a fondness for boating and fishing on Chesapeake Bay. He was a Washington Redskins fan during football season and followed the Nationals for baseball. But what tie did he have to MDT? Or even to Texas?

She couldn't see an obvious link.

She jumped onto another site and saw photos of Vincent at a bar for a St. Patrick's Day pub crawl. She was about to move on to the next picture when a familiar face caught her eye.

Her heart leapt into her throat at the picture of Stephen Phelps standing just to the right of Vincent. *Were they together? Was it a coincidence?*

Her lunch conversation with Stephen earlier in the day returned to her head. He'd known an awful lot about her movements and about what had happened in Texas. She'd thought it was because Erica had filled him in. But did Stephen have some other connection to everything that was going on?

But that was crazy. Wasn't it?

Vincent Cammerata had just handed them a phone. What did he have to do with anything?

The door opened, and she jumped, her nerves on edge.

"What's wrong?" Patrick asked quickly, as he strode across the room.

"I found a picture of Vincent in a bar. Stephen Phelps, the senator's press secretary, is in the shot."

Patrick gave the screen a closer look.

"It's hard to say if they're even together," she muttered. "But it seems weird."

"It does." Patrick set the bag of food on the table. "Phelps was at the gala last night. I saw him with Erica."

"Yes, and I had a conversation with him earlier today. I was going to tell you about that. He asked me to go to lunch and then as we were eating he made sure I knew that he'd seen you and me together last night. He said he was going to offer me a ride home when he saw me walking down the street, so he followed me. He saw me get into your car. It felt very creepy to know he was watching me like that. And why go to all that trouble? Up until last night, I hadn't exchanged two words with him. Suddenly, he wants to dance and give me a ride home and take me to lunch?"

Patrick's troubled gaze didn't make her feel any better. "I wonder if he had anything to do with the break-in at your apartment last night."

"How would he have known we weren't going straight to my apartment, though?" she asked.

"Good point."

"And he's a press secretary. Would he break into my home? That seems like a stretch."

"He wouldn't do the dirty work himself. Where did Phelps come from? Is he a Texas boy?"

"No, he's from New York, and he's been in DC for at least ten years. He's been around politics for a while, but he didn't start working with the senator until Erica came on board. They're tight with each other. Anyway, it could all just be a coincidence and perfectly harmless behavior."

"You like coincidences, Dani, but I don't. It's too easy to say something is just fate or luck or a random event, but that's rarely the case."

She frowned, his statement echoing words her sister and brother had said many times before. She closed her computer. "Fine."

"I didn't mean that as an insult, Dani."

"Sure you did. I've heard it before from my siblings. *I'm in denial. I don't like to face the truth. I dismiss anything that doesn't fit with my life. I'm selfish and I don't care about my father's death.*"

"Whoa," he said, putting up a hand. "I didn't say any of that, and if they did, I'm sorry, because the last thing you are is selfish. I know you loved your father."

She felt somewhat better by his vehement response. "I did love him. And sometimes I distance myself from that whole situation. It's been ten years. How long do I have to live in grief? How long do I have to ask questions that can't be answered?"

"You don't have to live in grief. Believe it or not, I understand how you feel."

"I don't see how you could. You're just like Jake and Alicia in your drive to get to the truth about your family mystery."

"But I understand the emotional cost of that pursuit. It can be extremely high, with no reward."

She felt a little better. "Thank you."

"Don't leave, Dani."

"I'm not leaving. I'm too hungry to go." She

offered him a little smile, and he smiled back.

"Good," he said, relief filling his eyes. He opened the bag as she put her computer on the bed. "It smells great."

"It is great. I love all the food choices in this city. One week, I had a different ethnic dish each night. It was like a world tour of cuisine: China, Thailand, India, Vietnam, Germany, Japan, and France."

"That's quite a week. What was your favorite?"

"I liked it all."

"I noticed you left off Mexican," he commented as he removed the lids on two containers.

"You can't beat Texas for Mexican food," she replied.

"Very true. I've never found anything better than Maria's Cantina on Forrester Street."

"I love that place. It's one of my favorites. I probably ate there once a week last year. I'm surprised we never ran into each other. Or maybe we did, and we just didn't know it."

"I don't think so. If I'd seen you, Dani, I would have remembered you."

She probably would have remembered him, too.

"So what did you get?" he asked.

"There's butter chicken and shrimp curry. Which do you want?"

"You pick. I'll take the other."

"Then I'll go for the chicken. But I think we should each eat half and then switch."

"Deal," he said with a laugh. "See, you're not selfish at all."

She liked that they could tease each other and that they could take a break and just be normal for a few minutes.

As they ate, Dani decided to get a little more information on the man sitting across from her. "I told you about my adventures in dating—what about yours?" she asked.

"I wouldn't call any of my dates adventures."

"When was the last time you had a serious relationship?"

"Years."

"Can you be more specific?"

"Let's see. I had a girlfriend in college and for most of the year after that. We were together about two and a half years."

"You were with her when your mother died?"

"Technically yes, but we hadn't been getting along that well. We were both twenty-two, just out of college, trying to figure out what we wanted to do with our lives and whether we could do them with each other or in the same place. Amanda was actually on a job interview in Los Angeles when my mother's plane crashed. I was working in Chicago at a local newspaper. I went to Corpus Christi as soon as I got the news. At first, there was some hope that there would be survivors, but that didn't last long. Amanda flew back from LA to be with me. She stayed through the funeral. But when it was over, she told me that she'd gotten the job, and she wanted to move to Los Angeles."

"Did you consider going with her?" she asked curiously.

"I did, but Amanda said she wanted to settle in first, concentrate on her job. I didn't fight her. I was in such a shocked state that I felt numb about everything. As you can probably guess, I never did move out to LA. In fact, we never saw each other again. She broke up with me in a text a few weeks later."

"That's cold. She had to understand you were grieving for your mother."

"I was partly to blame. I wasn't much fun anymore, and Amanda didn't want to be dragged down into my darkness. Who would? I can't blame her. She was young, and I suddenly felt a million years old."

She understood that. "I was eighteen when my father died. I was living in a dorm on campus. I'd been at a party that night, and I was actually a little drunk when Jake called me to tell me my father's plane was missing. I sobered up really fast. He picked me up, and we went home. Alicia and my mom were hysterically crying when we got there. It was a really long night and an even longer few days. Our hope went on, because no one found the plane. In some ways, that just made it worse, because when do you give up?"

She paused, swallowing back a knot in her

throat. Patrick reached across the table and put his hand over hers, his fingers warming her all the way through.

"You don't have to keep going if you don't want to," he said.

"It's fine." She drew in a breath and let it out. "We all wanted to give up at different times, and it split the family apart. Sometimes tragedy brings you together, but for us it did the opposite. We were all so angry, I think we took it out on each other. We drifted apart for a long time. It's kind of ironic that Alicia's lightning strike last year brought her back into the family."

"My dad and I had a hard time connecting after my mom's death, too. I did have one person I could talk to—my cousin Marcus. But we didn't actually talk much; we just shot a lot of baskets and drank a lot of beer."

"How long did you stay in Texas?"

"About three weeks. Then I went back to Chicago and my job, but I was still so distracted, I eventually quit, probably right before they fired me. I jumped over to another newspaper and then an online magazine. After that, I did some freelance work. I couldn't settle in anywhere. But eventually I started to find some subjects that really interested me. I came up with some hard-hitting pieces, which eventually led to the big idea that turned into a book and maybe a movie one day."

"Your mom would be proud that you got yourself together and moved on."

"I hope so. What about you? What were those first years like after your dad died?"

"I had school to finish, so that was my focus. After I graduated, I got the job in Senator Dillon's office. He was new at the time, and the staff was young and fun. We had a good time together."

"But you were itching to get to DC."

"It only took me seven years," she said dryly. "I wasn't sure it was ever going to happen, but finally it did." She paused for a moment. "You should let go of my hand, Patrick."

His fingers tightened around hers, and he gave her an endearingly sheepish smile. "I always have a hard time letting you go. The day we met—when we shook hands—it was like an electrical current shot between us. It was unlike anything I'd ever felt before. I felt like I'd been waiting my whole life for you to show up."

She drew in a quick breath, remembering that moment in vivid detail, and how strong the connection between them had been. "But you did let go, Patrick, and you should do that now."

He slowly released her hand. "I wish we could spend time just getting to know each other, Dani."

"Why? What would be the point?"

His brows furrowed at her question. "We can find out what's going on between us."

"It doesn't matter what's going on. My life is

here, Patrick. I'm finally where I want to be after so many years of waiting. I'm not leaving DC. I'm not quitting my job. There's a chance I'll get fired, but until that happens, I'm going to stick it out. Your life is—somewhere else."

"My life could be anywhere. Don't use my job as an excuse. I can write from any city in the world. If you don't want to see where this goes, then own it. But you can't say that, can you? You can't deny the insane attraction between us. I know you're as intrigued as I am."

She couldn't deny it, but she really wanted to. "I'm going to go home, Patrick."

"No, not yet. We're just talking."

"I'm done talking. There's no point. I know what I want—and it's not you. I'm owning it, okay?" She got to her feet and put her napkin on the table.

"What are you so afraid of, Dani?" he challenged, as he stood up. "Why do I scare you so much?"

"You don't," she protested, wishing she had a stronger defense.

"I told you before you're a terrible liar."

He had a way of seeing right through her. And she knew he wasn't going to let her go until she told him how she really felt.

"All right. Here it is. I'm afraid of caring about someone so much that I'm willing to change my life for them. I'm afraid of loving and losing, because that hurts like hell. And I know I'm jumping the gun by talking about love when all we're really talking about is sex."

"That's not all we're talking about," he said angrily.

"Isn't it?"

"No. If this were just about sex, we'd already be in bed together. I want more from you. I think you want more from me. That's what's so scary."

"That's the thing. You want too much. I'm afraid that you're someone who could make me want to throw all my ambition out the window just to be with you. Then where would I be?"

"With me?" he suggested.

"We don't even know each other."

"I feel like I've known you a very long time, Dani. But I want to know more. We don't have to decide anything right this second."

"You're making this too hard," she said with a sigh.

"Good. It should be hard. I understand your fear. I had second thoughts about coming here, tracking you down, and every time I say good-bye to you, I think this should really be good-bye. Then I wake up in the morning and all I can think about is when I'll see you next."

She put up a hand. "Stop. You cannot say things like that."

"It's the truth."

"If it's the truth, then let's say good-bye now and mean it."

"I can't. I need you."

"You don't need me to figure out anything. You can do this yourself."

"I do need you, Dani," he said, the husky note in his voice weakening her resolve.

When he stepped forward and put his arm around her, she told herself to push him away. But his mouth was so close, she could feel his breath on her lips, and her body was reminding her how great the last kiss had been.

If this really were good-bye, then what was the harm in one last kiss?

The question had barely formed when Patrick's lips touched hers, and just like before, the slightest touch of his mouth launched a firestorm of feeling and emotion and need. She wrapped her arms around his neck and leaned into the kiss. If it were the last one, she'd make it count.

Patrick did so many things well, but kissing was definitely at the top of the list. His commanding, passionate tenderness was intoxicating. She felt heady and off balance, and so, so ready to tumble into bed with him.

But she'd just gotten done telling him it was over. She was going back to her life. He was on his own.

How could she change her mind now?

She had to say no.

It took every ounce of strength she had to end the kiss, to step away from him, to grab her bag and walk—not run—to the door.

"Dani," he said. "How can you walk away from this? Do you know how rare it is to feel the way we feel?"

Of course she knew how rare it was to feel so strongly about a man. That's why she was leaving. "Don't follow me, Patrick."

She slipped into the hall, letting the door bang shut behind her. Then she ran to the elevator, happy when the doors opened right away.

She needed to get out of the hotel, put some distance between herself and Patrick, and breathe a little.

Patrick swore under his breath. *How the hell could she run away from him after that kiss?*

He understood that she was scared, because he felt shaken himself. But he didn't want her to leave like this. He wanted to at least talk to her some more.

What could he do? She'd made her choice.

He turned back toward the table, and that's when he saw her computer on the bed, where she'd put it when they started to eat.

He grabbed it and ran out of the room, almost ridiculously happy to have an excuse to go after her. She couldn't fault him for bringing her back her computer.

When he got to the ground floor, he jogged through the lobby and out the front door.

Dani's apartment was only two blocks away. She'd walk there, and he couldn't be too far behind her.

His heart sped up as he saw her getting to the next corner. He sprinted down the block.

He was a dozen feet away from the intersection that Dani had just stepped into when a car came racing down the street. He heard the roar of the engine before he saw it. Then everything seemed to happen in slow motion.

He saw the car . . . he saw Dani . . . and he knew in that instant that the vehicle wasn't going to stop.

Dani froze, the headlights pinning her in place.

He rushed forward with as much desperate speed as he could muster, knocking her out of the way just as the car bore down on her. He could feel the heat of the engine as they hit the pavement hard and rolled toward the curb. Luckily, the car kept going, missing them by inches.

A couple walking their dog rushed toward them, the older woman asking if they were all right.

He thought he was okay, but Dani was staring at him in shock. He got up, then helped her to her feet. She leaned on him, still shaky.

"What just happened?" She looked from him to the couple.

The woman said, "That car almost ran you down. You're bleeding, dear."

Dani looked down at her scraped knees in bemusement.

"You want me to call 911?" the man asked. "I wish I'd gotten the license plate of that car. He must have been drunk, speeding down this road like that."

"I'll call the police," Patrick said, helping Dani up onto the sidewalk. "Thanks for stopping."

"You two take care," the man said, then he and his wife continued down the street.

Patrick grabbed Dani's hand. He wanted to check her out, see where she was hurt, but he didn't want to stand on this street corner. They were too vulnerable. "We need to get to your apartment. It's closer than the hotel."

"All right," she said, licking her lips, as she looked down the street. "Where did the car go?"

"I don't know, but I don't want to be here if they come back."

She stared at him in bemusement. "What— what are you doing here, Patrick? You weren't supposed to follow me."

He suddenly realized her computer had flown out of his grip when he tackled Dani. He let go of her hand long enough to grab it off the ground. "You left this in the room. I thought you might need it for work tomorrow, so I came after you. It's a good thing I did."

"Did you see who was driving? Did they just run the stop sign?"

He knew she was hoping for a yes answer to that question. "It's possible it's one of those coincidences that seem to follow us around."

"The ones you don't believe in," she said, her eyes still wide and panicked. "Someone just tried to kill me, didn't they?"

FOURTEEN

L et's discuss this when we're inside." He put
his arm around her shoulders as they walked
quickly down the street.

Once inside the apartment, he locked the door
while Dani walked around in circles, obviously
still shocked. Her face was white. Her green
eyes were huge, and she was not at all steady
on her feet; there was too much adrenaline
running through her body to allow her to sit
down and take a breath. There was also blood on
her legs from where she'd hit the pavement. He
couldn't solve all her problems, but he could take
care of that.

"I'll get a towel," he said, moving toward the
bathroom. He ran some cold water on a hand
towel, found some antibiotic ointment in the
medicine cabinet and took both back into the
living room.

Dani was now staring out the window, her arms
wrapped around her body as if she were freezing
cold.

"Why don't you sit down?" he suggested.

She didn't move; he wasn't sure she'd heard
him.

"Dani?" he pressed.

She took in a deep breath, then turned away

from the window, walked to the couch and sat down.

He tended to her knees as gently as he could, but he had a feeling she wasn't feeling much of anything right now. Tomorrow would be a different story. She'd landed hard, and so had he, but he'd had jeans to protect his legs; she hadn't.

"I hope I'm not hurting you," he told her.

"It's fine," she said in a dull voice.

She wasn't anywhere close to fine. "Do you hurt anywhere besides your knees? What about your hands? Your wrists?"

"I'm okay—I think. I can't really feel anything."

He didn't see any other obvious injuries; hopefully, her knees had taken the worst of the fall. He wished he could do more than just fix her scrapes. This whole situation was his fault. He never should have gotten on the plane and come to DC. He never should have involved Dani. He never should have kissed her so hard tonight that she wanted to run away from him.

But all that said, he couldn't walk away from her now so she'd be safe. It was too late for that. Someone knew they were together. Maybe they thought Dani already knew too much. Or maybe it wasn't what she knew; perhaps it was just their relationship. Hurting Dani, someone he was obviously working with, might be a warning to him.

He shuddered at the thought of how deadly that warning would have been if he hadn't gone after her. He set the towel on the coffee table and sat down next to her.

Her breath wasn't as ragged now, but her eyes were still a little cloudy. He took her hand in his. Her skin was ice-cold, so different from the last time they'd touched.

"I froze," she said, her gaze meeting his. "I saw the headlights, and I heard the engine, and I didn't know which way to go."

"You would have moved in time."

"I don't know," she said doubtfully.

"I do. I've seen you in action before—when you saved my life in the park. Today, I got to return the favor." He squeezed her fingers, happy to feel a little more heat coming into her hand. She was coming back to him. "You're all right, Dani. That's what's important."

"Why would someone try to run me over?"

"It could have just been a drunk driver." Right now he was more interested in reassuring her than speaking the truth, but Dani wasn't having it.

"No, you were right when you said there aren't any coincidences, at least not about this kind of stuff. What do we do now?"

He hadn't had enough time to think of their next move. He wished it could be *his* move and not *theirs,* but he didn't think that was possible anymore.

He let go of her hand and ran his fingers through his hair as his thoughts raced around in a maddening circle. Finally, they slowed down long enough to settle on one thought. "I think we need to get out of town."

She met his gaze in confusion.

"And go where? I have a job, Patrick."

"It would just be for a few days—let things settle down. We'll have a chance to figure out what we know, because someone obviously thinks we know something."

"What would we do? Hide out somewhere? That doesn't sound like you. And it's not me, either. I don't want to let someone stop me from living my life."

He could see the fight coming back into her eyes, and he liked it. "Trust me, we're not going to stop living or stay in hiding for long. Just a few days, and those few days could be put to good use. The people we need to talk to are not here in DC—at least not all of them. I think you know where we need to go."

"Texas," she breathed.

He nodded. "It's where MDT is. It's probably where Tania Vaile is. The plane crashed in Texas. If we're going to find any witnesses to that, they'll be in Corpus Christi. And didn't I hear that the senator is going back this weekend for his annual Fourth of July bash? I'm betting his top level Texas contributors like the Packer brothers have an invitation to that party."

"Yes, you're right. Senator Dillon and the

senior staff will be in Texas this weekend and the Packer brothers and their families are invited to the barbecue along with other notable Texans. The mayor goes to the party. Usually, the president of Texas A&M is there as well."

"So it's a big deal."

"Huge. I met the Packer brothers at one of those barbecues a few years ago."

"There you go."

"But I can't go to the barbecue. I'm not invited this year. Erica limited the invitations to senior staff only."

"We'll find a way around that or we won't go to the barbecue. But it looks like the show is moving to Texas, and I think we should get there before they do. I'm tired of being behind. I want to run from the front. I want to be unpredictable. I'll look into flights."

"Wait. I don't know . . ."

He saw the worry in her gaze. "You don't have to commit to anything right now except getting out of town. Tomorrow is Friday. Call in sick. Make it a three-day weekend. You can do that, can't you?"

She slowly nodded. "I can do that. I would feel better getting away and having a chance to catch my breath."

"Good." He pulled out his phone.

"Let's go tonight, if we can. I don't think I'll sleep at all if I stay here."

"I'll see what I can do."

She picked up her computer from the coffee table. "I wonder if this will still work." She opened it up and then blew out a breath of relief as it turned on. "Thank goodness. I didn't back up the paper I was working on earlier. I really didn't want to lose it." She shook her head. "Silly to worry about losing a paper when I should be thinking about how close I came to losing my life."

"You're trying to maintain a sense of normalcy. There's nothing wrong with that."

"Who do you think was driving that car, Patrick?"

He paused in what he was doing to look up and meet her gaze. "It could have been anyone, Dani. I doubt it was someone we'd recognize. The people we're dealing with don't do their own dirty work."

"That's true; like the man who attacked you in the park. I wonder if he was killed because he failed to take you out. I wonder what happens to the person who didn't run me over tonight. Does he or she end up dead in an alley somewhere?"

He frowned, not liking the dark route her thoughts were taking. He'd wanted her to see that not everything was a coincidence, but now she'd gone to the other extreme. "I doubt that."

"But you don't know. You have no idea what's going on."

There was a note in her voice that told him she

was reliving the fear again. He set his phone down and put his hands on her shoulders. "You're okay, Dani. And we will figure this out. We're as smart as anyone, maybe even smarter. They've had the advantage up until now, but we're going to change that. We have leads to follow. We have people to talk to. This isn't over, but when it is, we're coming out on top."

She stared back at him. "You're so confident, Patrick. I want to believe you."

"Believe me."

She took several deep breaths. "Okay."

"Okay," he echoed, happy to see the panic receding from her eyes. He grabbed his phone again and searched the airline schedules. "No flights tonight, but there's a six a.m. flight tomorrow."

"Let's do it. I'll pack a bag and then we can go back to your hotel and get your things. After that—I don't know . . . maybe just go sit at the airport? I really don't want to stay here, and I'm not sure your hotel is safer."

"We can stay at an airport hotel and get a few hours' sleep. What's your birthdate? I'll make the reservations."

She gave him her personal information and then went to pack a bag.

After making their reservations, he got up and walked back to the window, peering through the shutters at the street below. Everything looked fine, but it didn't feel that way. He didn't even know if they would be safe walking the two blocks back to his hotel.

He wondered if they should call the police, report what happened. Maybe the cops could pull surveillance video off the traffic cameras. They might be able to find the driver of the car, or at the very least, the owner of the vehicle. But that would mean wasting a lot of time talking to the police, making a report, and it would probably yield nothing. Even if they found a license plate, he suspected that car would be long gone or hidden away and the person driving it would be even harder to find.

Dani returned to the room with a roller suitcase. Seeing him at the window, she asked, "Is there anyone out there?"

"It's quiet."

"Should we call the police?" she asked, her thoughts echoing his.

"If you want."

"You don't think it will accomplish anything."

"Not really, but it's your decision."

"I don't want to wait around for the police to come and take another worthless report. I think you're right. We have to try to get out in front of this. No more denial for me. I have been a little too fond of calling everything a coincidence, not just with you, but also with my siblings. I have been trying to ignore the prophecy my great-grandmother left me along with this ring." She twisted the gold ring around her finger. "This ring led me back to the park, and the lightning showed me where you were. I think that was important. If I'm going to find the last piece of the puzzle, then I need to start looking. I don't know if the circumstances surrounding our parents' deaths are tied together, but if they are, then if we solve one mystery, we might just solve the other."

He saw the new resolve in her eyes, the strength, and the courage, and he'd never liked her more. "So you're in?"

"I'm in. Let's go to Texas."

They arrived in Corpus Christi at ten a.m. on Friday morning. They'd spent a tense night at a hotel near the airport where they'd tried to do a little research but they hadn't accomplished much. Dani had felt too shaken by her near-death encounter to concentrate, and Patrick also seemed too distracted to focus.

Patrick had insisted on sharing a room, although they had gotten two beds, and they'd both studiously avoided any personal contact, sometimes to the point of ridiculousness. She'd never felt so awkward in her life. But she had the terrible feeling that if her hand even brushed his, her resolve would go out the window, so she'd kept her distance, and so had he.

They'd ended up turning on the television and

watching late-night comedy until they'd fallen asleep. At four a.m., the clock had woken them out of their fitful sleep, and they'd headed to the airport.

Now, she was tired and achy from her fall, but actually happy to be out of DC, a sentiment she'd never thought she'd experience.

"So, where do you want to go?" Patrick asked as they walked out of the airport. "My place? Your place—do you even have a place?"

"Not anymore. I gave up my apartment when I moved to DC. When I was in town for the wedding, I stayed at my mother's house, but I don't want to bring her into this."

"My condo then."

"I'm not sure that's safe," she said with a frown. "Maybe a hotel?"

"We'd have to register. That might be too easy to trace."

"We could use a fake name."

"True." He thought for a moment. "I have an idea. My dad owns a cabin outside of town. We could stay there."

"It could still be traced to you, couldn't it?"

"That would take time, as it's part of the Raleigh family trust set up by my grandfather on my mother's side years ago. Someone would have to track all that down, and we're only going to be in town a few days. I think we'll be safe there. Let's go to my dad's house and get the key."

"Your dad's house?" she echoed in dismay. "I'm not up for talking to your father. I think we should leave our families out of this, Patrick."

"We don't have to tell him anything. You can just be my new girlfriend. My dad will like that I want to take you to the cabin. The first time he told my mother he loved her was at that cabin. It's a special place for him."

"I can't be your new girlfriend. I met your dad at the ribbon-cutting ceremony last weekend. He'll know we only met last week."

"He also knows you saved my life," Patrick said with a smile. "I'll tell him I went to say thank you, and one thing led to another."

"That doesn't make me sound slutty at all."

He laughed. "I didn't mean it like that. He's going to think it was love at first sight, and he's not going to ask that many questions. If you have a better idea, I'm open."

She really wished she had a better idea. "I guess not."

"Then let's get a cab."

A few moments later, they were on the way to Harris Kane's house. It felt strange to be back in Corpus Christi and not be going home, not talking to any of her friends, not driving down the familiar streets. For the first time in forever, she felt like a visitor and not a resident. It was odd to feel that way about the city she'd lived in her entire life.

"Does your father know you were in DC this week?" Dani asked, turning her gaze away from the view and back to Patrick.

"I told him I was out of town, but I didn't give him any details. We're very used to living our own lives. There's nothing to worry about, Dani. He's not going to grill you on what you know about me and what I know about you. He'll probably be happy I have a woman in my life. I can't remember the last woman I introduced him to. It might have been Amanda." Patrick shook his head in bemusement. "Time moves fast."

"What about your father? Does he date?"

"I don't think so. He may have taken a few women out to dinner or to coffee, but as far as I know, he hasn't gotten involved with anyone. But, like I said, we don't ask each other personal questions. He could be seeing someone, and I don't know about it."

"Would it bother you if he was seeing another woman?"

"No, it would be great. It's been a long time. Life goes on. I want him to be happy. What about your mother? Does she date?"

"I have no idea. She asks me a lot of questions, but she's not good at answering mine. I do worry about her being alone. Alicia is in Miami. Jake is in town, but he's a guy, and now that he's madly in love with Katherine, he doesn't get over to see my mother that often."

"What does your mother think about what Alicia and Jake discovered about MDT?" he asked curiously.

"She's trying to pretend it's not there. She's even better than me at denial," she said dryly. "She keeps telling them to be happy they're alive and to move on. She would not like to see me going down the same path they just took."

"I'd like to meet Alicia and Jake. It might be helpful for us all to put our heads together, line up the clues and the players and see where we are."

She had a feeling that Alicia and Jake would like to do that, too. "Alicia will be back from her honeymoon tomorrow. Until then, let's work on this ourselves."

The cab pulled up in front of Harris Kane's home a few minutes later.

The stately two-story house on an acre of land was impressive. "It's beautiful," she murmured as she got out of the taxi. "This is where you grew up?"

"This is it."

"There must be money in your family some-where, because your dad is a teacher, and I don't think your mom made that much as a congress-woman."

"My grandfather on my mother's side, the soldier I told you about, was also in the oil business. He didn't get super rich, but he did well. He passed away a few years ago."

"I'm sorry for asking such a personal question; it's really none of my business. You've just gotten me into a questioning mood."

"I don't mind. I have nothing to hide."

"You seem to be one of the few people in our world right now who can say that."

"Let's stay honest with each other, Dani. If we do that, we'll always have trust between us."

The look in his eyes brought the damned butterflies in her stomach back to life. "I can do that."

"Me, too." His gaze lingered on hers for another moment, then he led the way into the house.

They found his father in a large combined family room and kitchen. Harris sat in the middle of a massive brown leather couch, a baseball game playing on the flat-screen television hanging over the stone fireplace.

Harris jumped to his feet, surprise in his face as he saw his son. "Patrick. I didn't know you were coming over today."

Harris wore a navy-blue t-shirt and jeans with loafers on his feet. He looked a lot younger and a lot more casual than the last time she'd seen him.

"It's a surprise," Patrick said lightly, as he hugged his father. "Do you remember Dani Monroe?"

"Of course. It's nice to see you again. I've wanted to say thank you for saving my son's life, but Patrick was not inclined to give me your phone number." He sent his son a pointed look. "I assume you got all my texts and just ignored them."

"I brought her here, which is even better," Patrick replied.

"Well, sit down. Can I get you something?" Harris asked. "I just made a pot of coffee. Your aunt Jill dropped off one of her frittatas yesterday if you're hungry."

"That sounds good to me," Patrick replied. "Dani?"

"I would love both coffee and frittata. Can I help you with it?"

"Don't be silly. Sit down. Make yourself comfortable."

"How are the Rangers doing?" Patrick asked as his father moved into the kitchen.

"Game just started," Harris said. "What do you take with your coffee, Dani?"

"Just black."

"Same as Patrick. You two are easy." He brought over two mugs of coffee and sat down. "It will just take a few minutes for the frittata to heat up. So what brings you two here today?"

"I wanted to ask you if anyone is renting out the cabin right now," Patrick said.

"No, I don't have anyone coming in until the middle of the month. Why? Do you want to use it?"

"I thought I'd show it to Dani."

"Really?" Harris gave them both a speculative

look. "I take it the two of you have been talking since last weekend."

"We have," Patrick said with a smile. "Dani is an amazing woman."

"Well, I already knew that," Harris replied.

She felt a little uncomfortable by the male scrutiny, even though it was positive. "Can I use your restroom?" she asked, getting to her feet.

"It's down the hall, first door on the left," Harris replied.

"Thanks." She got up from the couch, hoping Harris would quiz Patrick while she was out of the room, and then she wouldn't have to lie about why they were really together.

"What's going on?" Harris asked Patrick as soon as Dani was out of the room. "You never take anyone to the cabin. Is this love at first sight or is something else going on, something related to what happened in the park?"

Seeing the sharp gleam in his dad's eyes, he realized he would have to come up with a better story. "It could be related to the attack in the park. The bottom line is that Dani and I need to lay low for a few days, and I think the cabin would be a good place for us to do that."

"You're going to have to come up with a few more details, Patrick. The police told me that the man who attacked you was found dead of a drug overdose."

"I didn't realize you were keeping in touch with the police."

"I have friends in the department, and you're my son. I wanted to know that you were out of danger. It sounds like you don't think you are. So what's going on? What are you investigating this time?"

"I'd prefer to discuss it when I have more information."

"This has to do with your mother, doesn't it?"

He tensed at the question. "What do you mean?"

"Congressman Parker told me that you were asking questions about the plane crash. I couldn't figure out why you'd do that now—after all these years. I thought maybe you were just thinking about your mother because of the park finally getting done. We spent a lot of time talking about Jackie the past few months."

"That's part of it," he admitted.

"What's the other part?"

"I just have some questions, and when I've tried to ask them, I've gotten the runaround. It makes me wonder why."

"I asked a lot of questions when your mother died. I talked at great length with all the investigators. Did I miss something, Patrick?"

He met his father's worried gaze and wished he could say no, but he couldn't. "I hope not. I need a few days to think, to put some things together, and I thought the cabin would be a good place to do that."

"I want to help."

"If you can help, I'll let you know."

"Patrick, what aren't you telling me?"

He couldn't tell his dad there were rumors of his mother having an affair, especially since he didn't believe those rumors were true. And he couldn't tell his father his mother had been murdered when he had no proof. It would only hurt him. "Can you give me a few days to figure some things out, then we'll talk?"

His father frowned. "If you're in the middle of something dangerous because of your mother's death, I should be involved. I may not be an investigative reporter, but I have a brain. I can help. And I know more about this than you do."

"I don't believe the crash was an accident," he said finally. "I think that mom and Senator Stuart were working on something that got them killed. But I haven't figured it all out yet, and I could be off base."

Harris let out a heavy breath. "Well, I can't say that the thought didn't cross my mind a dozen times after she died. But there was no proof, Patrick. The FBI agents were thorough. I don't see how they could have missed anything."

"And yet someone seems determined to shut me up," he said.

"That's why you were attacked in the park?"

"I'm almost certain that's why, and the fact that my assailant died under those particular circumstances doesn't make me feel better."

"How does Dani figure into all this?"

"I went to DC to thank her for helping me and also to ask her to get me in to see Senator Dillon, because he's avoiding me. She wasn't able to do that, but she's been helping me try to figure out some other things." He really didn't want to get into the MDT connection yet. His father had friends who worked at the company. If he let anything slip, they'd be in more trouble. "Can you give me some time, Dad? I promise to fill you in when I know more."

His father gave him a long, speculative look. "I can do that. But if I can help . . ."

"I'll let you know."

"In the meantime, you'd appreciate it if I didn't say anything," Harris finished.

"Yes. And I'd like to borrow your truck, too. My car is at my condo, and I've decided to give my house some distance for the moment."

His father frowned. "I really don't like the idea of you being on your own and in danger."

"I don't think I'm necessarily in danger. I just need to stay under the radar." He wasn't about to tell his father that someone had almost run Dani over the night before.

"All right. The key is by the front door. I have one more question, though."

"What's that?"

"Is Dani just business or is she personal?"

"She's everything, and she's important to me," he admitted.

"Really?" Surprise ran through his father's gaze. "That's the first time you've said that about any woman in a long time."

"It's the first time I've felt it."

"Then you better keep her safe."

"I intend to."

FIFTEEN

W hen you said a cabin, I pictured an A-frame with maybe one bedroom, a kitchen with a hot plate, a microwave and furniture from another era," Dani said, as she looked around the spacious, luxuriously decorated house with the ten-foot ceilings in the living room, the long oak table in the dining room, the gourmet kitchen, and the staircase leading up to the second floor. "This is bigger than any house I've lived in, and more luxurious too."

"I told you my grandfather made some money in oil. He always called it the cabin, and the name stuck."

She set her bag down on the dining room table and said, "Well, I think this will do."

He smiled. "I'm glad. Do you want to take a nap? A shower?"

"No, I'm tired but I think I'll feel worse later. We need to figure out our plan of attack."

"I agree. I put together a list on the plane." He grabbed his computer out of its case and took it over to the dining room table.

She sat down across from him. "I saw you tapping away on the keys during the flight. I wondered what you were doing."

"It helps me to lay out everything I know." He

read through his list. "We have our whistleblower, who apparently told my mother facts similar to what he told us—that there's a secret faction run out of MDT that is funneling money from the legitimate side of the business to fund this shadow company. This group is run by someone high up in the company, possibly one of the Packer brothers or their father or some other highly valued employee."

"Someone with enough power to make things happen," she agreed.

"Yes. Then we have Ann Higgins, the reporter, who probably doesn't know any more than what the whistleblower has already told us. If she had more concrete evidence, she would have used it already. So, while talking to her again might be helpful, I'm putting her farther down the list."

"Okay."

"Then there's the military connection between the pilots—the one who died on the plane, the one who missed the flight, the traitor at MDT who was your father's best friend, and even your dad."

She frowned at that. "My dad should not be on the list. We can't connect him to MDT."

"He's connected to Jerry, so, yes, he is connected to MDT."

"Only through friendship. More than half of the people in Corpus Christi are connected by friends to the company."

"I agree, but he's also a former military pilot and

he died in a mysterious crash, so he's staying on my list."

"Fine. Go on."

"Tania Vaile. We don't know what her connection is, but the whistleblower wants us to talk to her, so we need to find out more about her and set up a meeting." He glanced up from his computer. "The rest of the people on my list are tied to your group: Senator Dillon, Erica Hunt, his trusted chief of staff, and Stephen Phelps, his press secretary."

"What about Congressman Parker? Let's not forget that he replaced your mother, just as Dillon replaced Stuart. We can't leave him out of this."

"Good point. He also told my father I was asking questions, and I'm not sure why he did that, so he's still on the list. Who else? What am I missing?"

She thought about his question. "There's the cashier at the convenience store. We saw him in a photo with Stephen, but that's it, and we don't even know if they just happened to be at the same bar." As soon as she said the words, she realized she was going back to coincidence again. "But it probably wasn't random."

"It's definitely worth figuring out if there's any other link between them," Patrick said. "But we should start with Tania Vaile. I've done a little research on her. When she's not working at MDT, she's an avid and experienced equestrian. She participates in horse shows at Barclay's Barn and Equestrian Center, not far from here. And when I say *barn,* you should know that I'm referring to a very sophisticated equestrian center that also offers a spa to relax your tired muscles after riding."

She smiled. "I already knew that. I'm familiar with Barclay Barn. I've ridden there a few times."

He raised an eyebrow. "You ride?"

"Of course I ride. I'm a Texas girl. Don't you ride?"

"Not since I was about twelve."

"Until I went to DC, I rode probably once a week—not anywhere as fancy as Barclay's Barn, though."

"Maybe you'll get another chance. Tania Vaile is featured on the Barclay's Barn website. Apparently, she won one of the events in their horse show last weekend, which has put her into the event finals this weekend." He turned the computer around so she could see the photo of Tania astride a black horse, a blue ribbon around the horse's neck. "I'm thinking we should try to catch her there. It will be easier to talk to her outside of MDT."

"But how will we know when she'll be at the barn? Are we going to stake it out all weekend?"

"We might have to. Or . . ."

"Yes?" she prodded when he remained lost in thought for a moment.

"We need a ruse."

"What kind of a ruse?"

"I'm thinking."

She could see that. She could also see that Patrick thrived on impossible challenges. Most people would have quit by now or just gone to the police and asked them to figure things out. But Patrick wasn't most people, which was probably why she liked him so much.

"Why don't you pretend to be an employee with Barclay Barn?" he suggested. "Call her office and ask her assistant, or her, if by any chance she comes to the phone, to confirm her next riding session?" he suggested. "Tell her there's been a glitch in the computer and the reservations got screwed up and with the event finals this weekend, you want to make sure she has her practice time . . . or something like that."

"That's clever, assuming that they use a computer for reservations and that she actually reserves riding time before the show."

"It's a gamble," he agreed.

"Why me? Why not you?"

"As a woman, I think you'll be less threatening."

"I feel like I should tell you that's sexist. Do you think only women take reservations?"

"No, but a soft, friendly female voice can sometimes disarm people more than a man."

He had a point. "All right. I'll do it."

As she reached for her cell phone, he stopped

her. "Not from your phone. Use the one our whistleblower gave to us. It won't be traced to us."

"You are one step ahead of me."

"Not my first go at this kind of thing."

"If your writing gig doesn't work out, the CIA or the FBI might be interested in you."

He grinned. "I'm too much of a loose cannon for those agencies."

"Probably true." She took the phone. "I suppose you have her number handy."

"I have the main company number. I'm sure they'll transfer you." He rattled off the number.

She punched it in, then hit the speaker as she set the phone down on the table between them. After working her way through the central operator, she reached Tania's assistant.

"I'm calling from Barclay's Barn about Ms. Vaile's reservation for this weekend's horse show," she said. "Is she available?"

"No, she's not. Can I help you?"

"We had a little problem with our reservation system today, and I'm calling everyone personally to confirm their next riding time. Can you check with Ms. Vaile or perhaps she has it down on her calendar?"

"Just a moment."

Dani gave him an excited look. "I think this might work," she muttered. "Her assistant doesn't seem suspicious."

"You were convincing," he said with an approving nod. "You have a talent for subterfuge."

The woman came back on the line. "She'll be in at three o'clock this afternoon."

"That's what I have down, too. Excellent. Thanks so much." Dani disconnected the call. "She's going to be there today. How lucky is that? I can't believe it. I feel like we're actually making some real progress."

"Almost. We know where she's going to be. Now, we need to figure out how to approach her."

"And what we want to say," Dani added. "The whistleblower said Tania might be in the mood to help us because she's not as tight with the Packer men anymore. That implies she had a personal relationship with one or more than one of them. Is she married?"

"I don't believe so. I haven't seen her linked with any men on social media except the Packer brothers. And if I had to guess which one, I'd pick Reid. He's been divorced and single for most of the past decade."

"But he recently got married to a young, beautiful swimsuit model. I saw her at the gala. She's stunning. Maybe Tania is a scorned woman."

"That could be good for us," Patrick replied.

"I'm going to look her up, too."

For a few moments, they both worked in silence. Dani found out a few more details about Tania. The woman had grown up in the San Francisco

Bay Area and had graduated from Stanford University with a master's in economics. She traveled frequently and had made several trips to Cancun in the past year. That gave her pause. "Interesting," she muttered.

Patrick gave her a questioning look. "What did you find?"

"Trips to Cancun."

"Why is that important?"

"Katherine's brother TJ was kidnapped from a conference in Cancun, and the ranch in Mexico where TJ and the stolen weapons from MDT were found is not far from there."

He sat back in his chair. "Tell me more about that."

"It was a ranch in the Southern Yucatan owned by the Calderon family, a long-time trafficker in drugs and weapons. The Calderon family ran that territory. The police were in their pockets. They terrorized the local villages, including the one where my great-grandmother lived. The ranch was as luxurious as this cabin, every modern amenity, and the barns didn't house horses but rather weaponry."

"What kind of weapons?"

"There were two railguns at the ranch."

"Our whistleblower mentioned the railgun," he said with a nod.

"It's the newest weaponry in the MDT arsenal. It fires projectiles using electricity instead of chemical propellants, which increases its velocity, range, and striking capability. I learned a lot about it during the Senate hearings. MDT is still testing the guns. They're not in use yet, at least not from the legitimate side of the company. Apparently, there have been some problems. TJ was actually kidnapped because he had some technical knowledge that was needed to fix a problem with the weapons at the ranch. Luckily, he was rescued before he did that, and the weapons were destroyed in a massive fire. In the subsequent investigation, MDT claimed that those were the only two weapons that were missing from inventory. But there are a lot of people who don't believe that, including my siblings."

"That is interesting. So Tania's vacations to Cancun could have been tied to the ranch in Mexico."

"Yes."

"Can you find out who she went with?"

Dani turned her attention back to the computer. A moment later, she said, "Tania was at the conference that TJ attended before he was kidnapped. I don't know if that matters . . ."

"I'd like to talk to TJ. He might be able to tell us more about Tania. Does he still work at MDT?"

"No, he left the company after he got back from Mexico. He works in the health industry now. He didn't think he'd ever feel safe at MDT again, although he told the FBI everything he knew, so he hoped there would be no reason for anyone to come after him. I'm sure he's not going to want to get roped into all this stuff again."

"But he owes your brother his life, and he may have information we can use."

She knew he was right. She also knew that sooner or later she was going to have to bring Alicia and Jake in, too. "I'll call him," she said, pulling out her phone. She looked up TJ's number, then punched it into the other phone to connect the call.

TJ answered on the second ring. "TJ Barrett."

"Hi TJ, it's Dani," she said, putting the phone on speaker.

"Dani. This is a surprise. Is everything all right? Is Katherine okay?"

Of course his mind would race to the worst possible scenario. After all the events of the past year, she couldn't blame him. "Katherine is fine. I just have a question for you. Do you have a minute?"

"Sure. What's up?"

"Do you know Tania Vaile?"

Silence met her question. Then he said, "Dani, what are you doing? I thought of all the Monroes, you were the least interested in pursuing the past."

"I was, but sometimes the past drags you back. Someone contacted me suggesting that the problems at MDT go back farther and deeper than anyone knows. They think Tania might be someone who is ready to blow the whistle."

"Why would she do that?" TJ challenged. "She's been at the company for more than a decade, and she's very high up on the financial side. She's also tight with the Packers and lives a big lifestyle."

"It sounds like you know her pretty well."

"Not at all. We did not move in the same circles, but Tania was one of the few women at MDT in a top-level executive position, so she stood out."

"You said she was tight with the Packers? Do you think there was a personal relationship between Tania and one of the brothers?"

"Probably. There was a rumor that she was sleeping with one of them, but I don't know which one." TJ paused. "Who is this person who suggested that Tania might be ready to talk? Because from what I heard during the recent FBI investigations, Tania went along with the party line."

"Well, they might be wrong," she said, choosing not to say that the whistleblower they had was a blind source. "I saw that Tania was in Mexico at the conference you were at before you were kidnapped."

"I forgot about that," TJ said slowly. "But there were at least two dozen other executives there as well, so I'm not sure that matters."

"Did you have any contact with her there?"

"You know, I did," TJ said, surprise lacing his voice. "I forgot about that. She bought me a drink. I thought she was unusually friendly. Like I said, we didn't travel in the same social circle. But then again, we were in Mexico, and everyone was more relaxed. However, I don't recall her saying anything of interest."

Dani paused as Patrick typed something on his computer then showed it to her. It was a question for TJ.

"Were either of the Packer brothers at the conference in Mexico?" she asked.

"They both were there for the first night, then they left. I told the FBI all this, Dani, and I think you need to back away from whatever you're doing. It's too dangerous."

"I'm being careful."

"That may not be enough."

"Thanks for your help, TJ."

"I don't know that I have helped, but you're welcome."

She ended the call and looked across the table at Patrick. "What do you think?"

"That TJ is right, that this could be dangerous," he said seriously. "I keep thinking I need to get you out of this, Dani."

"It's not your decision, Patrick. And I'm already in too deep. We are where we are. Someone, or more than one person, knows we're investigating your mother's crash and asking questions about

MDT. We've shown ourselves. I think the only way we're going to be safe is to figure out what happened and who's responsible."

"You left out one thing," he said.

"What's that?"

"It's not just about solving the mysteries of the past. We need to figure out what's going on now . . . is there a bigger plan? Are there weapons somewhere else besides Mexico, and if there are, what's the end game? What's the long-term goal of this shadow company?"

His questions sent a shiver down her spine. She'd been so focused on the past, she hadn't considered the present or the future, but Patrick was right. If they kept looking back, they might not see what was right in front of them.

"But first things first," he continued. "We'll go to the stables this afternoon and see if we can make contact with Tania. Depending on that encounter, we'll figure out our next move."

"I need to think about how we should approach Tania." She sat back in her seat. "I think I'll do that in the shower. The night is starting to catch up with me. I need to wake up. Do you think there's any coffee in the house?"

"I'll check," he said, getting to his feet. "My father keeps this place well-stocked. In the summer, he comes down here quite often. If I find some, I'll make it, or I can run down to the market and get some."

"Don't do that," she said, feeling a little panicked at the thought of him leaving.

He must have seen the sudden fear in her eyes. "Okay. You're right. We'll stick together for now. In fact, if you want me to join you in the shower . . ."

His teasing, light smile took her stress away.

"Just being in the same house is close enough," she said dryly.

"I seriously doubt that, but for now we'll play it your way."

SIXTEEN

After Dani went upstairs to take a shower, Patrick found some coffee and made a large pot. He was tired as well. It had been a long night, and they still had a long day ahead of them.

He checked the cupboards to see what other snacks he could find and came up with a box of granola bars. He unwrapped one and bit into it as he headed back into the dining room.

Clicking off the search results for Tania Vaile, he put in the pilot's name—Sean Carruthers. Most of the results had to do with the plane crash.

He skimmed through several of them, noting the same facts repeated in numerous stories. Sean Carruthers had served in the Air Force for eight years and then had gone into commercial aviation. He had only been working for Franklin Aviation for three months when he was assigned to pilot the plane carrying his mother.

He perused several more articles, searching for something beyond the basics. Unfortunately, most of the news reports had been focused on his mother and Senator Stuart, with little mention of the two staffers or the pilot who had also died in the crash.

It was difficult to see his mother's name appear over and over again with words like *deceased* and *dead* next to it. He felt like he was getting stabbed by a knife over and over again. But he forced himself to keep going. He needed to find some connection between Sean Carruthers and MDT, or one of the Packer brothers, or someone else at the company.

Finally, a familiar name popped into a news article. Sean Carruthers had been a test pilot for Vanderlane Aviation after leaving the Air Force and before moving to Franklin. More research into Vanderlane yielded another familiar name—Jerry Caldwell. Jerry had also flown for Vanderlane as a test pilot before moving to MDT's aviation division.

Had Carruthers and Caldwell known each other? Was that the connection between Carruthers and MDT that he'd been looking for? His stomach churned. He felt like he was close to a breakthrough. He was so lost in thought that he didn't realize Dani had come back into the room, until she put a hand on his shoulder. He jumped at the touch.

"Sorry. Did I startle you?" she asked, worry in her green eyes. "Is something wrong?"

"No, I was just thinking. You look—refreshed."

She actually looked more than refreshed; she looked beautiful, her skin shiny and clear, her eyes bright, a touch of pink on her lips, her hair a little damp but draped in soft and silky waves around her shoulders. She'd changed into a pair of jeans and tank top that clung to her curves, and now he got totally lost for another reason.

Dani moved away, perhaps sensing she was a little too close. By putting a table between them, she brought his thoughts back into focus.

"What were you thinking about?" she asked.

"Sean Carruthers, the pilot who died in the crash, worked for the same aviation company as Jerry Caldwell nine years ago."

"But Jerry worked for MDT," she said, sitting up a little straighter.

"It appears that he worked for at least one other firm, Vanderlane Aviation."

"Well, that's interesting. A link between Jerry and Sean Carruthers is huge. We know that Jerry was a traitor, and that he'd been stealing technology for years."

"But the one thing that doesn't make sense is Sean dying in the crash," Patrick put in. "If he was working with Jerry or anyone at MDT, and they had some responsibility for the accident, then why wouldn't Sean have known about some issue on the plane, or a bomb, or something? Unless it was an accident, and everything else is a coincidence." He ran his fingers through his hair, not really happy with that conclusion.

"No, you were right when you told me to stop thinking anything is a coincidence. Let's go the other way. Jerry Caldwell killed one of his fellow conspirators at MDT when she came to him and told him that she thought she'd been compromised. He told her he'd handle it. But what he did was kill her and the man who'd discovered her treachery, and made it look like the man's ex-wife had committed the murder."

"That's bold," he said, realizing he hadn't studied the details of Jerry's crimes but maybe he should have.

"If he could kill a woman who'd been bringing him classified information for years, then he might have been willing to kill Sean Carruthers, too."

"If he thought Sean was going to turn, he might have wanted to take him out at the same time," Patrick mused. "Maybe Jerry convinced the other pilot to call in sick. He could have put Sean on that plane on purpose."

"Or he could have had someone mess with the food from the takeout restaurant, thereby ensuring Carruthers would be on board."

He let out a sigh. "It's a hell of a theory but once again we have no proof."

"But we do have the link between Jerry and Sean. We just have to figure out how it matters, because I think it does." She gave him a smile. "Good work."

He smiled back. "Thank you. It's my turn for a shower. There's coffee in the pot and granola bars if you need a snack. After that, we'll go to Barclay's Barn."

After Patrick went upstairs, Dani poured herself a cup of coffee but instead of heading back to the computer, she walked out on the deck behind the house. The cabin had a beautiful view of thick trees, a green meadow, and a creek rippling with water. It was quiet here, peaceful. She'd almost forgotten what quiet sounded like. Not that she didn't like the big city, but she wasn't used to sirens at all hours of the night, the stink of car exhaust, and the continual blare of horns in rush-hour traffic. There were always sounds—in the apartment next door, in the office next to hers, on the crowded sidewalks when she walked to work.

Sometimes the sounds and the people and the crowds gave her energy and made her feel like she was part of something bigger, grander, but other times she felt small, alone, isolated in a huge city of strangers.

DC had been both everything she'd dreamed about and nothing like she'd expected. But that was the fun of it, she told herself. That was the adventure. There would be time in the future for quiet vistas like this. But that time was down the road. She had things to do.

Going inside, she returned to the dining room and saw her cell phone vibrating on the table. She saw she had two missed calls from Erica and one from Tracy. Tracy often asked her to get lunch, so that was no big deal, but Erica knew she'd called in sick, so why had she called twice?

She picked up her phone to call Erica back, then remembered what Patrick had said about using her cell phone. She didn't know if someone could or would try to track her phone, but since she didn't want anyone in the office to know she was in Texas, she set her phone back down on the table. Maybe she'd just see if Erica sent her a text. After all, she had said she was sick. She could be sleeping right now.

Moving on to her computer, she checked her email to see if Erica had forwarded any pressing piece of business there, but there was nothing.

Her calls couldn't have been that important.

Her phone buzzed again—this time with a text. It wasn't from Erica; it was from Stephen Phelps.

Sorry I came down on you yesterday. I hope that's not the reason you're out sick today. Let's talk.

Why would he think their lunch conversation would have bothered her enough to call in sick? She frowned, thinking maybe it would be best not to talk to anyone from the office today.

Patrick came back from his shower, looking sexy and handsome, and it was all she could do to stay in her seat. It was easier when they were focused on business, but the in-between times were tough. Her desire for him seemed to grow more intense each day. Logically, she knew she needed to resist the attraction. Patrick was a complication she didn't need. But he was also a complication she really, really wanted.

She got to her feet, needing to take some action that didn't involve throwing her arms around him. "Are you ready to go?"

"I am," he said, giving her a curious look. "Everything okay?"

"Fine. I've had some missed calls from Erica and an odd text from Stephen asking me if our conversation yesterday was what prompted my sick day."

"That's weird."

"Very, but I don't want to think about them right now. We need to focus on how to approach Tania. If we do it the wrong way, we may miss our only opportunity."

"I agree. I was thinking about that in the shower."

She was envious that he'd managed that kind of thought in the shower. When she'd been standing under the warm stream of water, she'd imagined Patrick in there with her, soaping her up with his strong hands.

She cleared her throat, feeling a wave of heat run through her. "So did you come up with any-thing?"

He gave her a quizzical look. "Did I miss something, Dani? You seem distracted."

"No. You haven't missed anything. How do you think we should pitch Tania on helping us?"

"I think there's only one way to bond with her."

"What's that?" she asked, seeing a devilish gleam in his eyes.

"You should tell her that you slept with Reid, too. You're pissed off he married the French swimsuit model Yvette. You want to get revenge, and you thought she might want in."

It was crazy and bold and perfect, she thought in amazement. It was probably the only way they could get Tania's attention.

"You work for the senator," Patrick continued. "You say you met Reid at one of the senator's parties. Let's take it a step further. Say you two hooked up and started an affair, maybe during the time Reid and Tania were together. We can figure out the details in the car." He grabbed the keys to the truck his father had lent them.

"Fine, but you do realize there's no room for you in this cover story, don't you?"

"Yes. As much as I'd like to grill her myself, I don't think she'll talk to me. She needs someone to give her a reason to give up information, and I think you're the only one who can make that happen. It's like that saying . . . *Hell hath no fury like a scorned woman.* We need Tania to get angry at the Packers."

"I just hope that we have the right Packer. Otherwise, this whole thing goes out the window."

• • •

By the time they parked in the lot at Barclay's Barn and Equestrian Center, Dani had come up with a pretty good tale to tell. She just hoped that there would be a way to get Tania alone so she could initiate a conversation.

Barclay's Barn was an impressive equestrian center. Encompassing fifty acres, there was an indoor riding arena as well as several outdoor arenas with jump courses, and a vast expanse of land for trail riding as well as a cross-country course. In addition to the riding facilities, the enormous hundred-year-old mansion that served as the operations center also housed a gourmet restaurant, a luxurious spa, gift shop, and private dining areas for groups and parties.

Being back at Barclay's reminded her of her youth. As they walked by one of the outdoor arenas, she said, "I used to come here with my dad." She paused by the fence to watch a teenage girl put her horse over a series of jumps. "That was me. I loved jumping. I was fearless back then."

"Did your father ride?"

"He did. It was actually one of the few things we both loved. He and Jake had their shared passion for flying, and he and Alicia were always talking about lightning and legends. We had our horses."

"Your mother didn't join you?"

"No. She had a bad fall when she was young.

She didn't ride after that, and she didn't like that I did, but she didn't get her way. I was too stubborn, and my dad backed me up. He told her not to let her fears become my fears. She didn't like that."

"I can understand both sides," Patrick said diplomatically. "It's probably difficult to watch your child do something that caused you pain."

"Well, she would love you for saying that."

They started walking again, checking the arenas, before heading to the stables where riders were picking up horses. Dani saw a tall, slim blonde, in tight-fitting jeans and a gauzy shirt, getting on a beautiful palomino, and her pulse quickened. "That's her, isn't it?"

"Yes," he said, a note of excitement in his voice. "We better get some horses. She's taking off on the trail."

It took about ten minutes to sign up for horses and get out of the stables. Dani hoped they wouldn't be too late to catch up with Tania.

"I thought this was my deal and you were staying out of it," she said, as Patrick rode along next to her with more than competent agility. "You've ridden before, too."

"Texas boy," he said with a smile, repeating her earlier words with a twist.

She smiled back. "I sometimes forget. Rarely does a y'all cross your lips."

"I've spent a lot of time away from Texas in the past decade, but once I'm here for a couple weeks,

I start talking like everyone else. Anyway, I'll lag behind, but I want to stay close enough to help in case you need it."

"I think we'll be safe. No one will be looking for us here."

"Probably not."

She frowned at his noncommittal response, but she was also glad that he hadn't bothered to lie to her just to make her feel better. With Patrick, she always felt like she was getting the truth.

There were several other riders on the trail, but as they got farther away from the barn, the space between horses grew larger. Patrick fell behind, and she urged her horse into a trot, wanting to catch up to Tania. The woman was on her own; this was her best chance to talk to her.

Despite the fact that she was on a mission, it felt good to be on a horse again. She'd missed the rhythm of riding, the wind in her hair, the feeling of flight, the power of the animal beneath her. Riding had always made her feel free, strong, adventurous, and she was happy for the reminder. Over the past few days, she'd been feeling unlike herself, which was probably because of all the secrets she was keeping. It had been difficult to be at work where there were so many eyes on her, where so many people were worried that she was going to do something to bring down the senator.

She didn't want to take the senator down. She

didn't want him to be guilty of anything. But it was beginning to look more and more like he had something to hide.

But first things first; she had to find Tania. She was the best lead they had.

Another twenty minutes passed before she saw Tania. The woman had paused to look at the view. There was a melancholy expression on her face, and her thoughts seemed very far away. Maybe she would be receptive to an approach. But first Dani needed to get Tania's respect and make it seem like she was no threat. She thought she knew just how to do it. They both loved horses. And she had a feeling the other woman would love a chance to compete.

Tania moved her horse back onto the path. Dani sped up, coming up next to her. She gave her a friendly smile and seeing nothing but open space in front of them, she said, "Feel like a race?"

Tania's eyes lit up. She didn't even hesitate. She kicked her horse into gear and took off. Dani did the same.

Her horse seemed just as delighted to be running as she was, and it was a joyous gallop for both of them. Tania was also an experienced horsewoman, and she knew how to ride. They flew across the flatlands, finally coming to a stop as the path narrowed by the creek.

"That was fun," Dani said, stopping alongside her.

Tania patted her horse's neck. "Brandy needed that. She hasn't had a good run in a while."

"She's beautiful. She's yours?"

"Yes. We're a team. She doesn't ever let me down."

There was something in Tania's words that told Dani this was her opening. "That's hard to find."

"Tell me about it."

"I know you," she said.

Tania stiffened. "What do you mean?"

"You're Tania Vaile. I've seen you before—with Reid Packer." It was a calculated gamble, and Dani bated her breath as she waited for Tania's reaction.

"Who are you?" Tania asked warily.

"I'm Dani Monroe. I work for Senator Dillon."

"Oh." Tania looked a little less uptight with that information. "The senator has been a good friend to the company I work for."

"Yes, he's very honored to have the Packers' support. But then, he gets millions of dollars, so it's easy to see where his gratitude comes from. I don't feel quite as generous."

"Why is that?" Tania asked, her sharp gaze raking Dani's face.

Dani looked over her shoulder. She didn't see Patrick, but she suspected he was somewhere in the trees, unless he was still trying to catch up. "I'll be honest with you," she said, turning back to Tania. "I came here today hoping to run into you."

"Why? What's going on?"

She drew in a deep breath. It was now or never. "Reid and I—we had something going on. I thought he was falling in love with me, but then he told me about you and about Yvette. He said there were others, too—that I was a fool for thinking our hook-ups were anything more than sex."

Tania's face paled. "You have no idea what kind of relationship I had with Reid."

"I know what he told me about you," she said, going all in on her story. "He said you were together for a long time, that no one knew. But he said he was never going to marry you. And he was never going to marry me. And he didn't. He married Yvette."

"Why are you telling me this?" Tania asked.

"Because I don't like being played. And I did not like the way he blew me off as if I didn't matter. I want to make Reid feel as bad as I do, but I don't think I can do it alone. I thought you might possibly feel the same way. If I'm wrong, you can forget this conversation ever happened. I just thought I'd take a shot and see if you were up for a little payback."

Tania stared back at her, but there was temptation in her eyes. "You can't hurt him. Reid is invincible. He's the most powerful man on earth."

"I know he thinks that, but do you? I know some of his secrets. And I think you do, too, because he likes to brag."

"He wouldn't tell you anything. I'm going back to the barn."

Sensing that she was about to lose Tania, she tried one last shot. "He told me that he had a US senator killed," she said boldly.

Tania's jaw dropped. "He did not tell you that."

"Then how would I know?" she challenged. "Aren't you tired of being taken for granted, Tania, dismissed for being not important enough to worry about? I know I am. If we put our heads together, we can teach Reid not to mess around with smart women."

Tania let out a sigh. "The last thing I've been with Reid is smart. But he didn't kill a senator. I know what you're talking about. He had nothing to do with that."

"Are you sure?" she challenged.

She saw the doubt in Tania's eyes.

"I'll think about it," Tania said.

She wanted to push, but she was afraid if she pressed too hard, Tania would just say no. "Can I give you my number?"

"All right." Tania took her phone out of her pocket and entered Dani's number. "But I don't know if I'll call you. I have a lot to lose."

"So do I. But more importantly, so does Reid. He can't always win, can he?"

"Up until now, I thought he could, but maybe not." Tania turned her horse and trotted back down the path.

SEVENTEEN

Dani let out the breath she'd been subconsciously holding. All things considered, her conversation with Tania had gone pretty well. She stayed where she was, certain that Patrick would show up soon. Several moments later, he came through the trees.

"Well? It looked like you had a good conversation," he said.

"I made my case that she should help me get revenge on Reid. He was obviously the one she was sleeping with. She pretty much admitted that, although she didn't say much else."

"Did you ask her any questions?"

"I thought it was more important to try to get her on my side. I did take one gamble. I told her that Reid had bragged to me about killing a senator."

Patrick raised an eyebrow. "What was her response to that?"

"She said that wasn't true, that she knew what I was talking about. I asked her if she was sure, and there was doubt in her eyes."

"So you proposed revenge?"

"Yes. I gave her my number. I told her we could take him down together. She's going to think about it."

He nodded approvingly. "You did good, Dani."

"I didn't really ask her anything, though."

"You went with your instinct; that's what I would have done. She would have never answered your questions. I think you took the right approach."

"I just hope we have enough time to play all this out before . . ." She didn't even want to venture a guess as to all the bad things that could possibly happen.

"We can only do what we can do. Today was a good day."

"At least better than yesterday," she said. "I definitely had her attention. Whether she'll reject my offer or not, I think she's going to consider it. There was anger in her eyes when she said his name, and there was pain, too. He hurt her. I just hope she wants to hit back."

"If she doesn't, she may go running to Reid, and then your whole cover story will be blown."

"It's a risk, but even if he denied everything I said, she might think he was lying. She knows he's a player. I'd bet a lot of money that he has slept his way around the Capitol. In fact, we might want to pursue that angle a little more, see if we can lure out any other ex-girlfriends or hook-ups."

"I'm impressed, Dani. You've got a lot of ideas going on in your head right now."

"Like you, I'm tired of being one step behind. I want to get out in front. But we'll see if Tania gets in touch." She paused. "Do you feel like riding a little longer? It's a beautiful afternoon, and I'm not quite ready to go back."

"Sure. You do look happy on that horse," he said, as they continued down the trail. "I watched you race Tania. You had a lot of fun, didn't you?"

"I did. She was a good competitor. I have a feeling you would be, too."

He smiled. "You're up for another race?"

"We've got more flatland coming up," she said, as they left the narrow part of the trail.

"You're on," he said, taking off a split second before she did.

She wasn't worried. Patrick might beat her at a lot of things, but not this.

Patrick didn't mind losing the race to Dani, because watching her ride past him had been totally worth it. Her blonde hair had flown back in the breeze and her joyous smile had sparkled in the sunlight. He felt like he was seeing the real her: the fearless, adventurous girl with big dreams, and the willingness to make them happen.

They had a lot in common. He liked to dream big, too. But right now his biggest dream had a lot to do with her.

She wouldn't believe that. She thought all of his focus was on his mother's plane crash, but in truth, he couldn't stop thinking about Dani, couldn't stop wanting to be with her, and not just as her friend, but as much, much more.

As their thundering pace slowed down, Dani glanced back at him with a smile, and whatever ice he'd put around his heart a long time ago began to crack. He hadn't even realized the ice was there until now, until he felt the warm, unsettling heat run through him. It was desire but it was also something else, something he hadn't allowed himself to feel in a long time.

He shouldn't let those feelings in now. As soon as all this was over, they'd probably go their separate ways. But right now it was difficult to imagine a day without Dani in it, much less a lifetime.

Dani turned and rode back to him as they came to the end of the trail.

"That was fun," she said. "I beat you, even though you took a head start."

"I had to. You have a better horse."

"Or is it that I'm a better rider?" she challenged.

He grinned, liking her cocky attitude as much as he liked everything else about her. "I would never admit that."

"Well, we both know the truth."

Their horses fell into a slower walk as they made their way back to the barn.

"Sometimes, I forget how beautiful it is here," she said. "I guess it took being away for a few months for me to appreciate Texas more."

"I feel the same way when I come back into town, although this is a really nice day, not as hot or as humid as it can be this time of year. We got lucky."

"We did. You said you live some of the year in New York. Do you ever think of making that your permanent address?"

"I love the city, the energy, the great restaurants, the feeling that a lot of important things are happening all around me, but the crush of traffic, the stink of trash, the constant noise wears on me. I guess that's why I like living there only part of the year."

"If you weren't working on the plane crash, what would you be doing now?"

"I have a few subjects I've been researching."

"Like what?"

"I've been fascinated by the cluster of earthquakes related to fracking in Oklahoma. I've also been looking into the new swarm of killer bees that are coming up from South America. And then there's insurance fraud, identity theft, and phony high-yield investment programs, which are draining a lot of people's bank accounts. Since my book came out, I've been contacted by a lot of people eager to tell me their personal story with the hope that I can give them a voice."

"That's cool. You've become the megaphone for the whistleblower. How do you decide what case to pursue?"

"It's getting more difficult. There are a lot of stories to tell, and I'm only one person."

"Maybe you'll have to become more than one person."

"I don't think cloning is an option," he said with a grin.

"You could start your own publication—digital, print or both, and you could hire other researchers and writers to work on a wider breadth of stories."

"I've had that thought," he conceded. "I just don't know if I'm that much of a manager-type person. I like working alone, not having to answer to anyone, and if I want to take a few days off, there's no one depending on me to make sure there's enough work for them."

"It would be a change, but you'd still be the boss. And just think of all the good you could do. You've created this amazing platform for yourself; you should use it."

"I might do that. After I figure out what happened to my mom."

She nodded, her gaze more serious now. "I hope we can get you the answers you want, but if we can't, I don't want you to waste the rest of your life looking for them. You have so much more to do, Patrick."

He was touched by her words. "Thanks," he said, holding her gaze for a long minute.

She gave him a sweet smile. "You're welcome. Shall we pick up the pace?"

He almost said no. He was having such a good time with her, he didn't really want the day to end, but Dani was already giving her horse a nudge, and he had no choice but to follow.

"I'm hungry," Dani said, after they turned their horses in at the stable. "I remember the restaurant here as being very good."

"Let's do it. There's not much at the cabin to eat."

They walked down the path to the mansion. The restaurant inside was designed to look like someone's living room, with dark wood paneling, bookshelves, comfortable chairs around small round tables, with lamps on each table providing a cozy, warmly lit environment. Some might even call it romantic, but Patrick was trying not to be one of those people.

After perusing the menu, they both ordered steak and salad, and Dani nodded happily at his suggestion that they split a bottle of red wine.

"This almost feels normal," she said, as they sipped their wine and waited for their food. "What happened last night seems like a bad dream." She frowned. "And now I wish I hadn't brought up last night because I just ruined the mood, didn't I?"

"You didn't ruin anything. But we don't need to think about all that now. It is nice to take a break."

She settled back in her seat. "So where are your friends, Patrick? Why aren't any of them involved in this search?"

"Uh, well . . . I don't usually involve my friends in my business."

"But this isn't just business; it's your mother. You really haven't talked to anyone about your worries?"

"I told my cousin Marcus after I talked to Senator Stuart's daughter. He advised me to drop it."

"What about your aunt? Isn't it possible your mother would have confided in her?"

"My mother would not have spoken to my aunt about politics. And I no longer believe she was having an affair. I think whatever was going on between her and Senator Stuart was all business related."

"I would agree." She paused. "I wish I could have met your mom. I think I would have liked her."

"She would have liked you," he said, feeling the ache in his heart that never quite went away. He wished he could introduce Dani to his mother, but he couldn't. He drank the rest of his wine in one long swallow, happy to see their steaks arriving.

There was no more talk of mystery or family as they ate. They stayed on neutral topics like books and movies, horseback riding and Texas football. By the time dinner was over, he felt more relaxed.

But as they drove back to the cabin, his relaxation slowly evaporated, replaced by a tension that was not about the case but all about Dani.

They were returning to an empty house, to a big

bedroom with a king bed, to a two-person spa in the master bathroom, to so many opportunities . . .

By the time he parked the car in the driveway, he felt completely wound up. He didn't speak to Dani as they entered the house. They made their way through the rooms together, making sure all the doors and windows were locked, and there was no sign that anyone had been in the house while they'd been gone.

They eventually ended up in the master bedroom.

Probably the very worst place to finish their tour.

Dani was on one side of the bed; he was on the other.

He wasn't drunk, but he felt lightheaded. He wasn't crazy, but he felt incredibly reckless. He wasn't going to make a move, but then she did.

She came around to his side of the bed.

He licked his lips, wondering what she might say . . . what she might do.

His chest tightened, making it hard to breathe.

What the hell was he doing? He should move. He should walk away. He should say . . . something.

"Patrick?" Dani spoke first, a conflicting mix of uncertainty in her voice, as if she were fighting her own internal battle.

"Dani?" It was all he could come up with.

"I know I should leave."

"Or I should."

"There are three other bedrooms," she said, a slightly desperate note in her voice.

"All comfortable," he agreed. "Plenty of room for us to spread out . . . if we want to."

She stared back at him with her beautiful green eyes that were now glittering with desire, and he felt an answering rush of need. He dug his hands into his pockets, trying as hard as he could not to touch her.

"I don't want to," she said. "Spread out. I don't want to spread out."

Her words made his heart skip a beat. He couldn't remember a time when he'd felt so conflicted, so torn, so filled with want.

She was important—maybe too important. He tried not to do important.

"Are you sure?" he asked.

She put her hands on his waist and looked up at him. "If I weren't sure, I wouldn't do this."

"If we start this, we're going to finish it," he warned. Because there was no way one kiss was going to be enough for him.

"I certainly hope so," she said, a smile playing about her lips. "I want you, Patrick. I don't know what's going to happen tomorrow or next week or a month from now, but tonight, this moment—I want you. And maybe that's all that matters."

"Works for me." Her words sent any lingering doubts right out of his head. He pulled her up against his chest and ran his fingers through her silky soft hair as she opened her mouth and invited him inside. His tongue tasted hers, and he could have lingered in the wet heat of her mouth for hours. On the other hand, there were other places he wanted to go, too . . .

Her hands pulled at his shirt, unbuttoning it with needy, urgent fingers. And when she pulled the shirt off him and pressed her fingers against his chest, he felt like he couldn't breathe.

"Oh, Patrick," she murmured, tracing the scar from his stab wound. "This was bad."

"It doesn't hurt anymore."

"An inch or two—"

"Sh-sh, don't think about that." He pulled her in for another kiss, and then his mouth took a hot path down the side of her neck.

She let out a little sigh of pleasure and his body hardened.

He wanted to go slow. He wanted to go fast. He wanted it all.

Luckily, so did she.

They stripped off each other's clothes in a passionate flurry, stopping every now and then to go back in for another kiss, another touch. Her body was soft and curvy, and he liked that she was bold and passionate and a little shy, all at the same time.

When they tumbled onto the bed, he pushed her onto her back and licked his way down her neck, collarbone, and around her breasts and nipples as his hand explored the heat between her legs.

She gasped with each touch, and he felt his own tension rising to an impossible height.

And then Dani pushed him onto his back and threw her leg over his. She sank down on him as her mouth met his. They moved in perfect rhythm, finishing what had started days earlier—when he'd first taken her hand . . .

She'd never seen stars exploding before her eyes, never lost herself so completely in another person, never felt so terrified and exhilarated and satisfied all at the same time.

Dani rolled onto her back, her breathing still coming hard and fast.

Patrick turned on to his side and gave her the sexy smile that always sent butterflies through her stomach.

Those butterflies should be exhausted now, but they were still there, still thinking that maybe it would be time to dance again soon.

"That was amazing," he said.

She smiled back. "It was good."

"Damn good."

She drew in another breath and let it out. "I guess it was silly to think we wouldn't end up here together."

"We've been heading here for a while," he agreed.

He put his hand on her stomach and leaned over

and kissed her. His kiss was tender, loving, and this time there weren't just butterflies in her stomach: there were tears gathering in her eyes.

What the hell was wrong with her? She couldn't cry. But she felt suddenly overwhelmed with emotion, and she didn't know why.

Actually, she did know why.

It was Patrick. He'd gotten past her guard, and she didn't quite know what to do about it. In fact, it was probably too late to do anything about it.

She wouldn't regret what had happened; she'd wanted to be with him as much as he wanted to be with her.

"Are you okay, Dani?"

Like always, he saw too much.

"I'm fine."

"You looked a little more than fine a few minutes ago."

"Let's not analyze each other," she said lightly. "We had fun. Let's leave it at that."

A mix of emotions ran across his face. On one hand, he looked a little relieved. On the other hand, he seemed like he had more he wanted to say. In the end, he said, "All right. But if you want to talk, Dani, you can. I'm here."

"I'm here, too," she said, as his fingers caressed her stomach, bringing back all the heat they'd just tried to dispel.

"So we could have a little more fun . . ."

She smiled back. "I'm counting on that."

Hours later, Dani woke up to the sun streaming through the windows and a buzzing sound coming from her purse. She got out of bed and grabbed the phone, sliding back under the sheets as she answered. "Hello?"

At the sound of her voice, Patrick turned over, giving her a sleepy, questioning look. When he realized she was holding the phone their whistle-blower had given them, he came all the way awake and sat up.

"Hello?" she said again.

"Is this Dani?" a woman asked.

"Yes. Tania?"

"I don't know why I'm calling you. This is a mistake."

"It's not," she said quickly, hearing the hesitation in Tania's voice. "At least let's talk. We don't have to do anything."

Silence followed her words.

"You called me, Tania. I think you want to have a conversation."

"I'll meet you at the Waffle House on Collins Road—in an hour."

"I'll be there."

Tania didn't reply. She'd already hung up.

"That was Tania," she told Patrick. "She wants to meet me at the Waffle House on Collins Road in an hour. She sounded conflicted. I don't know how much she'll say, but she's willing to talk to me."

Excitement entered his eyes. "This is great. Your plan worked."

"But now we have to figure out what my plan is. I came to her with some idea for revenge. If she asks me what that is, I better know."

"We'll come up with something. We have an hour."

"More like forty-five minutes. It will take me fifteen minutes to get there."

"It's enough time."

"You can't come with me, Patrick. If she sees anyone with me, she'll never talk."

He frowned at that, but she could see that he knew she was right. "I hate to send you there alone."

"I'll be fine. It's a restaurant at nine o'clock in the morning. It will be filled with people. I'm more concerned with my revenge plan." She paused. "I'm going to get in the shower while you start thinking."

"We could think together under a warm spray."

She was so tempted to say yes, because Patrick looked even more irresistibly sexy in the morning with his tangled dark hair, and his beautiful brown eyes, and the shadow of beard along his jaw. Flashes of memory swept through her. Their passionate night together had been one she'd always remember. It would have been really nice to stay together a little longer. But they were back to reality, and maybe it was better that way.

Because if she stayed too long with Patrick, she didn't think she'd ever want to leave.

An hour later, Dani drove into the parking lot of the Waffle House. After taking a quick shower, she and Patrick had decided that she'd keep her plan as simple as possible and try to let Tania do most of the talking. If she needed to reveal anything, she would focus on the theories about the plane crash, and Reid's alleged boast about being involved.

Getting out of the car, she walked into the restaurant, spotting Tania at a booth in the back. She slid into the seat across from her, noting the woman's weary eyes and dark shadows. It didn't look like Tania had gotten much sleep.

She didn't quite know what to say, how to start. Fortunately, she had a second to think as the waitress came over to pour her a cup of coffee.

"Are you ready to order?" the waitress asked.

"Not yet," she said.

"Take your time," the waitress replied.

When the woman left, she gave Tania what she hoped was a friendly smile. "I'm glad you called."

"I don't know why I did. I don't even know you."

"I'm sure you looked me up online."

"Of course."

"Then you know I've been working for Senator Dillon for seven years."

"Where did you meet Reid?"

"At one of the senator's parties two years ago. I thought it was a one-night stand at first, but then he called again a few weeks later."

"Was that here in Corpus Christi?"

"It started here. Then it moved on to DC. We were together a few days before the news about his engagement to Yvette came out. I was so stupid. I'd heard about her, but I never thought he would actually marry her. But he did." She drew in a breath, trying to get into the character she was playing. "He used to talk about us being together forever. It was all lies. I wasted two years on him. I was a fool to think I wasn't just one of many."

Tania stared back at her with a bleak expression. "I wasted more years than you."

She had to fight not to react to Tania's words. Finally, she had confirmation of something. "How did it start for you?"

"It was at work."

She wished Tania would elaborate, but she left it at that.

"What do you want to do?" Tania asked.

She licked her lips, knowing she had to be even more convincing now. "I want to take Reid down. I know some things about him, things he's been doing on the side that would get him in a lot of trouble, but I need more concrete proof than I have, more than just what he let slip when we were together."

"Reid doesn't let things slip," Tania said sharply, doubt appearing in her eyes.

"That was the wrong word. You're right. He didn't let anything slip. He deliberately told me that he had the power to make people disappear, including a senator. I said I wasn't aware of any senators who were missing, and he told me that I wasn't counting those who died in mysterious circumstances."

"Why would he tell you that?"

"Probably because I was fighting with him. I made the mistake of threatening to tell people about our relationship, and he suggested I'd be very sorry if I ever went against him. He wanted to scare me. He wanted me to think that he could hurt me, and the truth is—he did scare me. He had a wild light in his eyes. He said one day everyone was going to know how powerful he was, that no one had any idea what he was capable of doing. After he married Yvette, I started trying to find out what he was talking about, what he'd been hinting at. When the news came out last year about stolen classified information, I was pretty sure he was involved, but after all the Senate hearings, he came out unscathed. I know he's guilty of something, and I want to prove it. I want to take him down. But I need help. Will you help me, Tania?"

Before Tania could answer, the waitress came back, and Dani inwardly seethed with frustration.

"I'll have a short stack," she said, picking the first thing on the menu, so she could get back to her conversation with Tania.

"Nothing for me," Tania said.

"You're not going to eat?" she asked in surprise. "I don't have to eat, either."

"It's fine. I have to go. I wanted to hear what you had to say."

"Well, don't go yet. Can you at least tell me what you're thinking—if I'm completely wasting my time hoping you'll help me?"

Tania stared back at her for a long moment, her gaze unreadable. "I'm not sure yet. You haven't been honest with me, Dani."

"What do you mean?" she asked, trying not to look guilty at the accusation.

"Your sister and brother have been part of the problems at MDT. I find it difficult to believe that you were sleeping with Reid while all that was going on."

"Our relationship ended just before all that happened. But when the news came out, I thought about the things Reid had told me. I watched him testify before the Senate committee, and I knew he was lying. But he got away with it. MDT is back in business, like nothing ever happened."

"I wouldn't say that. We lost a lot of contracts last year." Tania's gaze narrowed. "Did Reid really tell you about the senator? Or did one of your siblings tell you that?"

"Neither one of them knew anything about the senator's plane crash," she said, able to be honest for the first time. "The only reason my brother was involved in the problems in Mexico was because he was trying to help his high school girlfriend's brother. Jake isn't political; he's a pilot and Katherine is a doctor. They just wanted to save her brother, who had been kidnapped. I'm not lying. You have to believe me. I was shocked when I found out people at MDT were involved. I had no idea."

She didn't know if her earnest defense worked, but it did seem to ease Tania's tension.

After a moment, Tania said, "I don't know what to believe. Your sister Alicia also stirred things up. Why should I think you're after anything but more trouble for the company?"

"I don't want trouble for the company; I want it for Reid," she said, trying to hang on to her cover story that was quickly being torn apart. "I'm sure he would have dumped me after my siblings got involved with his company, but it happened before that, and when it did, it hurt. Can't you relate to that?"

Tania let out a sigh. "Yes. I really did love Reid, you know. He's a complicated man. He has so much charm and charisma, it's easy to forget that there's another side."

"A dark side," she murmured.

"I knew he wasn't faithful to me. How could I

think otherwise? He was with me when he was married to his first wife."

"That was a long time ago."

"Our affair was the reason he got divorced, or so I thought. He told me every year that next year would be our time. He just didn't want to rush back into marriage. He didn't want his daughter to have to deal with a stepmother; he always had a reason." Her lips tightened. "I could bury him if I wanted to. The things that have come out in the press are not the whole story. There is so much more."

Dani's pulse sped up. "Then help me tell it."

"I don't know if I can trust you. I don't know if you slept with Reid for sex or love or a hidden agenda. Your family hates MDT. Why would you feel differently?"

"Because I work for Senator Dillon. I've seen more sides of the story than my family has. I know that thousands of people rely on the company for their livelihood. I'm not out to take the company down. It's Reid I want to destroy." She drew in a breath, feeling like she was fighting for her life. "You don't have to trust me, Tania. I don't have to trust you. But we can use each other to get what we both want." She could see that Tania was thinking about what she'd said, that she was tempted, so she pressed forward. "If you don't want to be on the front line, I'll put myself there. Reid can't fire me. He can't hurt me again. All I need is some proof that I can take to the press. He won't have to know where it came from."

"He would know," she said flatly. "And you're a fool to think he can't hurt you."

"If I go public, he won't be able to touch me."

"Don't underestimate him."

Dani didn't reply as the waitress set down her pancakes. Then she said, "If you get me information, I won't say where I got it."

"I'll think about it."

Dani was disappointed that she'd gotten very little out of Tania. "Are you sure you can't tell me anything now? How did Reid sabotage the senator's plane? If you can't tell me specifics, can you tell me where to look? And if not that crash, can you point me in the direction of something else, something I could use?"

Tania hesitated, then she said, "There's a ranch about twenty miles from here. It belonged to the Carmichael family. But it hasn't been used as a ranch in a long time. You should take a look. That's all I can say for now."

"Can we talk again?"

"We'll see."

And with that, Tania got up and left the booth.

Dani stared after her in amazement. She'd gotten a clue of sorts, but what the hell did an old ranch have to do with anything? It had to be something. Tania wouldn't have given her nothing, unless—was Tania sending her on a wild-goose chase? Maybe the woman had come fishing for information. Perhaps she was as loyal to Reid now as she had ever been.

Her heart jumped as a man slid into the seat Tania had just vacated. "Patrick, where did you come from? How did you get here? I took the truck."

"And I took a cab. I didn't like the idea of you being here alone. I waited in the smoke shop across the street until I saw Tania leave." He coughed at the end of his sentence. "I may have cut five years off my life by inhaling some very potent cigar smoke, but I wanted to be close in case you needed me."

She was touched by that thought. "I appreciate that."

"What did you learn?"

"Not much. She asked me a lot of questions. She looked me up, and she tied me to Jake and Alicia and their involvement in the problems at MDT. I should have thought about that when I was making up my story. I think I covered well enough, saying that Reid broke up with me before all that happened, and that it was just coincidence."

His lips tightened. "We should have thought of that."

"I told her she didn't have to trust me; she just had to use me. She thought about it. At the very end, I begged her to give me something. She said there was a ranch that belonged to the Carmichael family that hadn't been used as a ranch in a very long time. She wants me to go there. I know it's not much, but it's something."

"It could be a good lead," he said thoughtfully. "Or not."

"I know," she said, seeing the same unease in his eyes. "I thought I was setting her up. But what if it's the other way around?"

EIGHTEEN

Dani made a good point. *Was Tania playing them?*

"Only one way to find out," he said, meeting Dani's worried gaze. "We'll go to the ranch."

"I've never heard of it. Have you?"

"No, but I'm sure we can find it. Are you going to eat those pancakes?"

She stared down at her plate as if she were surprised the food was there. "I forgot all about them. Want to share?"

"I'll order my own."

"Well, if you're ordering, get some bacon. I didn't want to go all out when Tania was sitting here."

He liked her sheepish smile. "You've got it." He motioned for the waitress and added an omelet to Dani's request for bacon as well as coffee and orange juice.

"Did Tania say anything else?" he asked, as Dani made her way through her stack of pancakes.

"She admitted to being involved with Reid. She said she loved him. She knew he wasn't faithful, because apparently they'd been together when he was married the first time around. She said she knew a lot of his secrets, but that she was afraid of him. She told me not to underestimate him."

"Probably good advice," he said, thanking the waitress as she set down his breakfast. He made fast work of his omelet and shared the stack of bacon with Dani, who gave him a guilty smile when she grabbed her second slab. "Don't worry; I'm not judging," he told her.

"Good. I don't usually eat bacon, but when I'm out for breakfast, there's nothing better."

"I like it, too. We'll be able to concentrate better with full stomachs."

"And if we stay in public places," she said with a teasing smile. "Where we can't be alone. Where we can't be distracted."

"You distract me wherever we are," he said, as they exchanged a look of remembered intimacy.

"I could say the same about you. How is it you don't have a girlfriend, Patrick?"

"I was waiting for you."

"That's a good line."

He'd said it teasingly, but in truth it really wasn't a line; it was the way he felt. There were so many things he wanted to say to Dani, but now wasn't the time. He pulled out his phone and searched for Carmichael Ranch. "I've got an address. It looks like it will take us about forty minutes to get out there."

"I think we should go now."

"Me, too." He took out his wallet and put cash down next to the bill. Then they made their way outside. Dani tossed him the car keys and he slid behind the wheel.

They were about fifteen minutes into the drive when Dani pointed to a small airfield. "That's where my dad worked," she said. "And where my brother Jake works now."

"Looks like they fly a lot of small jets."

"Yes, and before you ask—they do fly MDT executives around the country."

"You read my mind. Has your brother been the pilot on one of those trips?"

"He's only flown lower-level management. The executives have their own planes and their own pilots."

"That makes sense. I'm surprised you didn't want to be a pilot, Dani. You ride like the wind on the back of a horse."

"And that horse is on the ground," she said pointedly.

He grinned. "My point is that you're not particularly fearful. Or did your feelings about flying change after your father died?"

"I'm not afraid to fly. It's just not something I want to do as my job. Jake loves it, though. He never wanted to do anything else."

"We're going to meet him and Alicia today, right?"

She didn't look too happy about his words. "We'll see. I don't want to dump all this on Alicia the second she walks in the door."

"What bothers you about telling your siblings?" he asked, certain he hadn't heard her real reason.

"It will just get them hyped up, and although we've heard some stories, we don't have any real evidence. I'd like to go to them with more than a theory."

"I would think they'd be happy about your involvement. You said they've been angry that you haven't wanted to get into it. Now you have." His gaze dropped to her hand, where she was twisting the gold band around her finger. "And as often as you've told me you hate that ring, you still haven't taken it off."

"I can't get it off," she said with annoyance. "It won't go over my knuckle."

"But it fell off your hand in the park last week."

"I can't explain it. Sometimes it feels loose, but most of the time it's tight."

"It was your great-grandmother's wedding ring?"

"Yes. And she seemed to think it would protect me in some way. But so far it's just led me into trouble."

"Well, it saved me, so I say you keep it on."

"At this point, I don't seem to have a choice."

As they got closer to the ranch, his nerves tightened. He wondered if Tania was setting them up. The area they were in now was farmland; miles between houses, empty roads—the perfect place to get rid of someone. As he turned off the highway, he found himself on a dusty one-lane road, and his tension increased. He pulled over, turning to Dani. "I don't like this."

"I don't, either," she admitted. "But we can't not check it out. We have to trust Tania isn't sending us into an ambush."

"Why on earth would you think we could trust her?"

"I'm not sure. I just have a gut instinct. If you were alone, I think you'd keep going, so don't stop for me."

She was right about that. He would keep going, but while he was willing to risk his own life, he didn't want to risk hers. "I don't want anything to happen to you."

"I feel the same way about you, Patrick. But I think we're stronger together. And I've got my lucky ring."

"You don't believe in it," he reminded her.

"Sometimes I kind of do," she admitted, giving him a helpless smile. "But don't tell anyone else I said that. Now, let's go, before I lose my nerve."

Against his better judgment, he said, "All right." Several minutes later, he drove between two old posts and past a broken-down gate. The road led to a large, sprawling, shuttered-up ranch house and barn. There were no cars anywhere to be seen. No sign of life. They parked in front of the house and walked up to the door. It was locked and no one answered the door.

"I don't think anyone is here," Dani said, staying close to Patrick.

"Let's check the barn."

They walked across the open space and entered the horse barn.

He'd been expecting to see stalls, hay—all the usual items found in a barn—but the building resembled something more like an airplane hangar: a large open space and then an area with desks, at least twenty. Near the desks were electrical outlets and extension cords. There were filing cabinets along one wall but most of the drawers were open and empty.

A jolt of awareness ran through him. "This must be where the shadow company was conducting business."

Dani nodded. "But there's nothing here now. Why? Did they move their operations to Mexico, or did this recently shut down? And why would Tania send us out here?"

"All good questions." He looked around, and his gaze came to rest on one desk at the far end of the building. There was a folder lying on top of it. He walked quickly across the room.

The folder wasn't dusty or dirty. It didn't look like it had been left behind but rather that it had been purposefully placed on the desk.

When he saw the name on the file folder, his heart jumped against his chest.

"What is it?" Dani asked.

He really didn't want to tell her.

"Patrick?" she pressed, trying to peer over his shoulder. "Is it about your mother?"

"No." He swung around to face her. "It's about your father."

"What?" she gasped.

He held up the folder so she could see the name written on it: Wyatt Monroe.

Dani put a hand to her mouth as her stomach turned over and nausea ran through her. "Why would there be a folder on my father here?" she muttered, the letters of his name blurring in front of her eyes as she felt dizzy and short of breath.

"Dani." Patrick put a steadying hand on her shoulder. "Are you all right?"

"I don't think so," she whispered. "Could you open it and tell me what's inside?"

He nodded, a grim expression in his eyes. He opened the folder and she could see several pieces of paper, including a photograph. Even from a few feet away, she knew it was a picture of her father. She couldn't hold back. She grabbed the photo from the file. It had been taken through a fence at the airfield. Her father could be seen standing by a plane. He was talking to one of the airfield managers.

Her heart ached at the sight of the tall, handsome man, who had always been bigger than life. He wore his favorite jeans and black jacket, his aviator glasses on top of his head as he looked at some sort of clipboard.

"Oh, God," she said, feeling an intense wave of pain. "This is exactly how I remember him. Just like this—those clothes, those glasses." She bit down on her bottom lip, trying to breathe through the heartache. Missing her father hurt so much. She'd thought she'd gotten past it, but one photo and it had all come back.

She lifted her gaze from the photo. "Patrick, why would there be a photo of my father here?" she asked in confusion.

"It looks like someone was following your dad."

"Why?"

"I think this might be part of the reason." He handed her a paper.

She stared at the typed page for a long moment. "This is a police report. My dad went to the police and told them he had seen lights in the sky that looked like gunfire on his last flight. That was a couple of weeks before he died." She looked back at Patrick. "I told you he talked about seeing weird lights when he flew at night. He thought it was lightning, but sometimes there weren't any storms in the area. That's when he started to get the nickname of *lightning man*. Why would this report be here? Why would anyone care what he saw in the sky?"

She saw the answer in Patrick's eyes.

"Because he wasn't seeing lightning; he was

seeing gunfire," she said, answering her own question.

"It was probably from a gun they were testing. This ranch isn't far from the airfield. If it was an early version of a railgun, that operates on electromagnetic energy, it's possible it looked like lightning."

"Everyone thought my father was crazy. My own mother was convinced of it, and I kind of thought so, too, at times." She moved around the desk and sat down in a chair, feeling like she might fall over from the overwhelming force of her emotions. She didn't just feel sad now; she also felt guilty. "Alicia defended him all the time, but I never did."

"You didn't have the information you have now."

"I should have had more faith."

He frowned. "Dani, you told me that something of your father's was found at the ranch in Mexico, right? It was a medallion or something . . ."

She nodded. "It was a medallion on a chain that he always wore around his neck, and we were sure he was wearing it the night his plane went down. But we have no idea how the medallion would have gotten to Mexico. Unless, of course, his plane didn't go down in the Gulf, but crashed in Mexico."

"Maybe it didn't even crash," Patrick suggested.

"Why would you say that?"

"Because there's a note from your father's friend, Jerry," he said, handing her another piece of paper. "He doesn't address any one person, but read what it says."

"*Wyatt is becoming a nuisance,*" she read out loud. "*He's talking to too many people. There are going to be more questions. Even if we move operations, he could be a problem. He told me he took photos on his last flight. I'm going to have him meet me—you know where. You do the rest.*"

She sucked in a quick breath as the reality of what she'd just read sank in. "Jerry must have lured him to Mexico."

"That would make sense since that's where your brother found the medallion," Patrick said. "It's possible his plane didn't crash, Dani."

"But he was flying that night. He was coming back from Florida. He had a flight plan to return home. Wouldn't someone have known if he changed it?"

"Maybe he didn't tell anyone. He had no reason to distrust his friend Jerry, did he?"

"I don't think so." She paused, holding Patrick's gaze. "How do you think they killed him?"

His lips tightened, his gaze filling with compassion. "I don't know, and I don't think you need to know."

"Says the man who wants to know everything." She thought for a moment. "My great-grandmother told Jake, in her very dramatic Mayan way, that my dad's bones weren't where they were supposed to be. She must have sensed he wasn't in the Gulf. He must have been killed and buried in Mexico. Alicia and Jake both think that. I was holding on to the other story."

"I'm surprised they didn't tear up the land around that ranch in Mexico."

"We couldn't get the authorities to do that. Alicia tried, but the Mexican government wasn't willing to cooperate, based on our lack of evidence. But maybe I have more now." She stood up. "Why do you think Tania left this file for me?"

"She probably knew that your real goal was to find out about your father."

"So you don't think she believed me when I said I slept with Reid?"

"I'm not sure. Maybe she thought you slept with him because you believed he had information on your dad. Your cover story might have held up, just not your original motivation. As to why she left you the file here and now . . . I have no idea. She must have come out here before she met you for breakfast. There's no way this file was actually here. She put it here for you to find. She wanted you to see this ranch. I think she's giving you what you asked for—ammunition to use against Reid."

"It's not enough. Unless there's more here to be found."

"I don't think so. I'm betting this ranch hasn't been used in a while. That's why Tania felt safe enough to use it. Probably no one comes out here anymore." He paused. "I think we should get out of here, Dani. This place is really remote."

She could see the tension in his body, and she suddenly became aware of how vulnerable they might be. As they walked out of the barn, she felt a prickle of uneasiness, but they made it to the truck without any problems. Her tension didn't decrease until they left the narrow roads behind and returned to the highway.

"I'm going to call Tania," she said. "Maybe she'll talk to me more about the file."

"Give it a shot."

She connected to Tania's number. It rang four times, and she thought it was about to go to voice mail when Tania finally answered.

"Hello?" she said.

"It's Dani. I was just at the ranch," she said, putting the phone on speaker. "Why did you leave me the file on my father?"

"I knew that's what you really wanted to know. You might want revenge on Reid for his part in it, but what you want is the truth about your dad. I knew that as soon as you told me your last name. Reid thought that once they'd taken care of your father, no one would ever find out about the ranch or the tests or your dad. For years, it seemed that they were right. Then your sister started poking around last year, and Jerry made a huge mistake by going after her. Then your brother went to Mexico and blew up that operation. Now, it's you. I don't think you hooked up with Reid. He wouldn't be stupid enough to sleep with you after being responsible for your father's death. But I know why you want to get back at him."

"It was Reid?" she asked. "He killed my dad?"

"He ordered it. He doesn't actually do anything himself. He's too smart for that. And you'll never be able to pin it on him. I'm telling you so you can sleep at night."

"I don't think that's why you're telling me," she said. "What's the real reason? You've been tight with Reid for years. Why betray him now?"

"Because I'm tired, Dani. Tired of the lies and the pretense. Tired of believing things will change. Tired of looking at the calendar and realizing how many years have passed and how long I've been waiting. I don't know how you knew I was the one to approach; I'm not sure I want to know." She took a breath, then continued. "This whole thing has become so much bigger, so much more dangerous than I ever imagined it would. When it first started, I was just a small player, and I understood Reid's motivation. It's hard to be passed up for someone else. It's hard to be second best or not recognized by your own father. But I had no idea the level of insanity that was actually driving everything. So many people have died. And there are so many more to come.

You have no idea of the magnitude of destruction that could happen."

"Help me stop him, Tania. I can take the file to the police and to the press, but I need more."

"I can't give you any more. I told you about your father so you could have closure, but I have blood on my hands, too. I'll go down with them. Or they'll sell me out."

"Sell them out instead. You might be able to get immunity in exchange for information," she said, wildly grabbing at anything to get Tania's trust. "Reid is the most important player, not you. You can use that."

"If we had more time—maybe. But it's too late. I won't be able to escape my part in this, not after tomorrow."

"What's happening tomorrow?" she asked worriedly, hearing both resignation and fear in Tania's voice.

"You'll find out then. Be grateful that I gave you this. I know it won't prove anything. If you take it to the police, it will be scandalous, and there will be rumors, but there's no one mentioned by name except Jerry, and he's dead," Tania said. "Your father knew too much, and he paid with his life. Don't make the same mistake he did. Don't waste your life trying to shut this down. You can't do it."

"I want to bring the people who killed my father to justice. I want to know exactly how it happened—where it happened. Was it in Mexico?"

"I don't know the details. I only know that he was taken care of. You need to move on, Dani. You'll never end this. It's too big. It's too complicated. Men tell so many lies. They never end. Even the good ones turn out to be bad. If you can learn anything from me, Dani, it's don't trust anyone. Everyone has an agenda, even the people you think care about you. Everyone has a price. Everyone is weak. Greed and ambition take down even the best men."

"What do you mean?" she asked, her pulse speeding up. "Are you talking about Reid? Or about someone else? Who else is involved in this? I know Reid couldn't be managing an operation of this size without help."

Tania didn't answer.

"What about the plane crash?" she asked, changing tactics. "You said Reid didn't kill the senator, but he did, didn't he?"

"He did everything you imagined he did," Tania said. "Oh, God."

"What? Tania, are you there? We need to meet again. We need to talk more."

"Someone is following me," Tania said, terror in her voice. "I thought I was careful. But they know what I did. They know I went to the ranch. I was such a fool. I tried to help you. I knew I shouldn't have done it. I just felt so bad, because I saw you at the funeral. You and your siblings were crying so hard. It was that day that I realized exactly what

I'd gotten myself into. I never thought people were going to die. You have to believe me. I thought it was just about making money. I knew that day I could never leave. If I tried, I'd be dead, too."

"You were at the funeral?" she asked in shock. Now that Tania had brought it up, she remembered that Jerry had been there as well. In fact, there had been a large crowd at the church. She'd thought at the time that she never knew her father had that many friends. "Tania," she said, when the woman didn't answer.

"I have to go. I have to get away," Tania said, desperation in her voice.

"Who's following you? Where are you? I can help you. I'll come to you."

There was a clatter, as if the phone had been dropped, and then the call cut off.

Dani swallowed hard and looked over at Patrick. By the hard profile of his jaw, she could see that he was thinking the same thing she was—Tania was in bad trouble.

She punched in the number again. It rang until it went to voice mail. "She's not answering. Do you think something has happened to her?"

"I hope not," he said heavily, giving her a bleak look. "But I think so."

NINETEEN

Dani tried Tania's number a dozen more times on the way back to the cabin, but there was no answer. On her last try, the phone didn't even ring or go to voice mail—an even worse sign.

She thought about everything Tania had told her, realizing that the other woman might have just risked her life to give her the truth about her father. She hoped Tania was okay, but she had a sinking feeling in the pit of her stomach that she couldn't get past.

She went over the rest of their conversation in her head, one point sticking out. "What do you think she meant when she said something was going to happen tomorrow?" she asked Patrick.

"Tomorrow is the Fourth of July. Could they be making some sort of a statement?"

"Like what?"

"I don't know, Dani, but it's time we bring a few more people into the conversation—your family, for one, maybe the FBI or the police . . ."

As much as she didn't want to involve her family, she knew he was right. There was no way she could just sit on the information she'd gotten about her father. "I agree. I need to show them this file. I think my great-grandmother was right. I may have just gotten the last piece of the puzzle."

"You did well, Dani. You got Tania to trust you enough to share a piece of vital information."

"She didn't really trust me. She knew I was lying the whole time. I just caught her at the right moment. The whistleblower was right. She was ripe for an approach." Dani paused. "I know she's probably done some really bad things, but I hope she escapes. I think she could help us if she does."

"That's a big *if,* Dani."

"I know. I'm going to use my real phone to text Alicia. I'm not sure my presence in Texas is a big secret anymore."

"No," he said tersely.

She frowned at his tone. "Why not? What aren't you saying?"

"I'm just wondering when Tania was first followed. Was it when she met you for breakfast? Was it when she went to the ranch beforehand? Was it later?"

"She thought someone saw her leave the file, which means . . ." Her voice drifted away as she realized exactly what it meant. "They could have seen her with me at the Waffle House."

"That's what I'm concerned about."

"But no one followed us to the ranch. No one is behind us now." She looked in her sideview mirror. There wasn't another car for miles.

"I haven't seen anyone, so maybe we're fine. It's possible they were tracking Tania long before you met up with her."

She hoped that was the case. Pulling out the phone from the whistleblower, she texted Alicia: *It's me, Dani. Are you and Michael back in Texas yet?*

Her sister replied almost immediately: *Yes. Had a great time. What happened to your phone?*

She replied: *Long story. I'm in Corpus Christi today. Got info on Dad. Can you meet me away from house? Don't want to talk to Mom yet.*

Alicia said: *Are you serious? Yes! Mom isn't home. She's at a wedding, so come to the house. She won't be back til 6. Should I call Jake?*

She said: *Yes, super important. Be there in 20.*

Dani set down the phone. "Alicia will meet us at the house. My mom is at a wedding, so we don't need to deal with her yet."

"You don't think she'll want to hear this?"

"I'm sure she won't want to hear it, but we will speak to her, just not yet. I want to tell my brother and sister first. My mom is still convinced it was an accident, and she hates talking about my dad. She'll be a distraction."

"Whatever you want."

"Patrick—I feel like we've gotten a little away from your mom's death. I should have asked Tania more about the crash."

"You tried. She told you that Reid did everything we imagine he did."

"But that's not good enough. I just want you to

know that I'm still very invested in helping you find out the truth."

"Thanks. I think I knew from the beginning that their deaths were tied together."

"It's a morbid connection we have."

"Well, that's only a small part of our connection," he said with a smile.

He extended his hand to her, and she took it, feeling the instant heat between them when their fingers touched. Patrick was right; there was so much more between them than the mystery of their parents' deaths.

They drove the last few miles holding hands, because just like every other time they touched, they both had a hard time letting go.

Patrick finally released her hand when he parked the truck in front of her mother's house. But when she saw her sister fly out the front door, she wished she was still hanging on to him; what she was about to do was going to be difficult.

Alicia hugged her and then gave Patrick a curious look. "Hello. I'm Alicia, Dani's sister."

"Patrick Kane," he said, shaking Alicia's hand.

As Michael came down the stairs, Alicia introduced her husband to Patrick.

"Nice to meet both of you," Patrick said. "I've heard a lot about you."

"That's interesting, because we've heard nothing

about you," Alicia said with a speculative gleam in her eyes.

"It's quite a story, but I'm going to let Dani tell it."

"Are Jake and Katherine on their way?" she asked as they walked up to the house.

"They should be here soon," Alicia replied.

"Great." She was relieved that she'd be able to tell them both what she'd learned at the same time. "How was the honeymoon?"

"It was amazing," Alicia said, sending Michael a beaming smile. "Everything I imagined and more."

"Same for me," Michael said.

"It's good to see you both so happy," Dani commented, thinking that marriage certainly agreed with her sister. She was as glowingly pretty today as she'd been at her wedding last weekend. It was difficult to believe only a week had passed; so much had happened since then.

"Where did you go for your honeymoon?" Patrick asked.

"We went to Maui," Alicia replied. "We had incredible weather. We snorkeled, sat in the sun, and did next to nothing. It was heaven." Alicia paused, giving Dani a questioning look. "I know Jake said for you to wait until he got here to tell us what's going on, but I'm super curious. Can you give me a hint?"

"I'd rather just say it once. Sorry."

"All right," Alicia said with a sigh. "I was just making some sandwiches in the kitchen. I'll finish them up and bring them in, all right?"

"I'll help you," Michael said, leaving Dani and Patrick alone in the living room.

"They're in such a good mood. I'm going to change all that," she said regretfully.

His eyes filled with empathy. "You are going to change that, but your sister has been haunted by the mystery. In the long run, this is what she wants."

"I suppose, but it's one thing to believe something is true and another to know it's true."

He put his arms around her and looked into her eyes. "All the pain is coming back, isn't it?"

"It's why I didn't go down this road," she admitted.

"It's hard to open the old wounds. You think they're scarred over and too tough to break, but then someone says something and you remember, and it's like it happened yesterday."

"Will we ever get past it?"

"Past it—no. Accepting, remembering the good times more than the bad—definitely yes. We've both tried to move on. In my case it was easier. I didn't think there was a mystery involving my mother until a few weeks ago, but you've been living with uncertainty for a long time."

"We're going to find out what really happened to your mom's plane, too."

"I have no doubt. We're getting closer every day." He let go of her as he looked around the room. "So this is the house where you grew up?"

"This is it. It's small, but it's always been home. As you can tell, my mother loves neutral colors—everything is beige or cream or tan, with the occasional gray thrown in. She says they're calming colors. When my father was alive, the wall behind the couch was painted maroon. There were colorful crocheted or knitted blankets on chairs and paintings from Mexico on the walls; it was chaotic and loud but also warm and vibrant. And when my dad was here, everyone noticed. He filled a room." She paused. "Alicia takes after him. She's definitely got his passion and imagination and creative tendencies. I'm really more like my mom."

"You're not beige, Dani. And you've got a lot of passion, trust me."

She flushed at his intimate look. "I wasn't talking about that kind of passion."

He smiled. "You might not be colorful and loud, but you're beautiful, intelligent, interesting, and courageous as hell. I've never met anyone like you. Every day you surprise me—in a good way. You wear a bit of a mask, and you have your guard up, but once you take off the mask and let down the guard, you're something else."

She felt a little overwhelmed by his statement, not just by the compliments but how well he could read her. "Thanks. But you should save that cheesy stuff for when you want to get me into bed," she said lightly.

"Since that's just about every second of every day—"

"Stop," she said, putting up a hand.

"You started it."

"And I'm finishing it. I don't need my family to hear any of this. There will be way too many questions to follow."

"I understand. Just for the record: I meant every word, cheesy or otherwise." He let that sink in, then walked over to the mantel to look at the assorted family pictures. "You were a cute kid."

"Better after I got the braces off," she said with a self-deprecating smile.

"This was your high school graduation?" He pointed to one of several family group shots.

"Yes. We had a big barbecue here at the house afterwards. My dad grilled up steaks. Half the neighborhood came. It was a family tradition to celebrate big events like that with barbecues. But we didn't have one for Alicia. My dad was gone by then." She drew in a deep breath and let it out. Before she could say another word, the front door opened and Jake and Katherine walked into the living room.

She introduced them both to Patrick, as Alicia and Michael came out of the kitchen with platters of food and cans of soda.

"We actually met before," Katherine said to Patrick. "In the examining room at the hospital."

"Right. I remember you. That seems like a long time ago now," he said.

"You look better today."

"Thanks. I feel better."

"What's going on?" Jake asked, giving her an expectant look.

"Let's all sit down." After everyone settled into the couches and chairs around the coffee table, she reached into her bag and pulled out the file folder she'd gotten at the ranch. She set it on her lap but didn't open it.

"What's that?" Alicia asked.

"It's a file on Dad."

"What?" Alicia gasped. "Whose file?"

"Where did you get it?" Jake asked tensely.

She looked around at their expectant faces and almost didn't know where to start. Patrick put a hand on her thigh and said, "You better give them a little history here, Dani."

He was right. "Let me back up a few days," she said. "I met Patrick last Sunday at a ribbon-cutting ceremony for the park honoring his late mother, Congresswoman Jackie Kane. As some of you know, Patrick was attacked at the park, and I came to his rescue."

"You did what?" Alicia asked in shock.

"That part isn't important," she said. "What matters is that over the last week, Patrick and I have discovered that we have a connection that goes back to both of our parents. We believe that Patrick's mother's plane was sabotaged, and that the crash wasn't an accident. We also know that Dad didn't crash his plane into the Gulf. It appears that both events are tied to MDT. In researching and asking questions, we came upon some information this morning, and this particular piece is about Dad."

"Don't stop there," Alicia said. "Someone from MDT killed Dad, didn't they? Was it Jerry?"

"It might have been," she replied. "In this file I'm going to share with you, it says that Dad went to the local police and reported seeing flashes of what he thought was gunfire, along with jagged lightning strikes that didn't seem to make sense. We know that that is what started the rumors about his sanity and his obsession with lightning. But what we didn't know is that someone at MDT had created a shadow company. They were using classified information and money funneled through MDT to make the same weapons to sell on the black market. They were testing those weapons out of a ranch about twenty miles from here—Carmichael Ranch. It's no longer in operation. I don't know when it closed—if they moved everything to Mexico, or only part of it. But the ranch was completely cleaned out when we went there this morning. There was only one thing left behind—this file."

"Who left you the file?" Jake asked.

"The same person who sent me to the ranch, Tania Vaile. She works in finance for MDT, and I'm not sure what exactly she knows. She hinted that she knew a lot and said that Reid Packer is the one behind the shadow company and behind Dad's death." She handed the file to Alicia. "There's a note from Jerry in there, saying that Dad needs to be taken care of, that he's becoming a problem."

"Oh, God," Alicia said, putting a hand to her chest as she pulled out the photo of their father. "He looks just like I remember him here."

"You're saying some woman gave you this file?" Jake asked, his lips tight, his eyes filled with shadows. "Out of the blue?"

"Not exactly out of the blue. I approached her, trying to get more information on the Packer brothers. We had two short conversations. Then she sent me to the ranch where I found the file."

"That's crazy," Jake muttered. "I want to talk to her directly. I'm sure Alicia does, too."

"I don't know if that will be possible. After I got the file, I called her. She was in her car, and in the middle of our conversation, she said someone was following her. She got scared and panicky, and then that was it—the phone went dead. I've called her number a dozen times, but there's no answer. I'm really worried about her."

"We think it's time to bring in the police or the FBI," Patrick interjected. "Dani said you had a contact with a special agent after your trip to Mexico."

"Agent Damon Wolfe," Jake said with a nod. "He questioned us several times. I still have his number. I'll call him. But I'd like to know more first. Putting my father's death aside for the moment, you said your mother died in the plane crash that killed Senator Stuart?"

"Yes," Patrick said. "Eight years ago."

"I remember that crash. I thought it was ruled mechanical failure with a storm as a contributing factor. I know it was investigated for months."

"That doesn't appear to be the whole story now," Patrick said. "Dani and I discovered that my mother and Senator Stuart were talking to an MDT whistleblower the night before the plane crash. He told us he went underground after it happened, that all the evidence he'd given them had been destroyed in the crash, and that he was sure the crash was not an accident."

"Who was that?" Jake asked.

"He wouldn't give us his name, but he's the one who sent us to Tania. We still don't know what happened to the plane," Patrick added. "But in light of everything we've learned, I'm certain it was sabotaged."

"If MDT is running a side operation off the books, that would explain the ranch in Mexico," Jake said, glancing at Katherine. "We always wondered how those guns got there."

"TJ said he believed that someone very high up in the company knew about the leaks," Katherine put in. "He thought it went all the way to the top, and he wasn't convinced that all the bad guys were caught after Mexico."

"It looks like Reid Packer is definitely involved; I don't know who else," Dani said.

"This is so shocking and terrible," Alicia said, holding up the note Jerry had written. "Jerry talks about killing one of his best friends as if it's nothing."

"I know," she said, wishing she hadn't brought her sister so much pain.

"Jerry came to his funeral. We called him Uncle Jerry, and he killed Dad." Alicia shook her head in bemusement. "I don't know if I'll ever understand that."

"Jerry was insane," Michael put in, putting his arm around Alicia. "You know that."

"I do know that, and I'm glad he's dead. I just want to make sure whoever else was involved also pays." She turned to Dani. "I can't believe you got this. It's just like Mamich said—you were going to find the last piece of the puzzle."

"I know it's weird," she admitted. "And that damn ring is what led me to Patrick. It fell off my hand in the park, Alicia. I knew you would kill me if I lost it, so I went back to look for it. There was a storm, and lightning was flashing, and I saw Patrick fighting for his life."

"That's amazing. There was lightning, too?" Alicia asked, her eyes widening.

"Yes."

"So the ring led you to Patrick, and he led you here."

"With some stops along the way," she said. "I don't know if this is the last piece of the puzzle. It might be in regards to Dad, but Tania said something big is coming, and it's coming tomorrow. We need to get the FBI involved now."

"I'll call Agent Wolfe. It's the weekend, but I'll tell him it's urgent," Jake said.

"I—I need a minute," Alicia said, getting to her feet.

"Do you want me to come with you?" Michael asked with concern.

She shook her head and walked out of the living room, heading toward the kitchen.

"I'll go," Dani said, getting to her feet.

"I might need you for this call," Jake said.

"Patrick can talk to Agent Wolfe with you. He knows what I know."

She found Alicia in the backyard, standing in front of the cement waterfall their father had built a long time ago, a water feature that had never been used since his death.

"Are you all right?" she asked.

Alicia shook her head, her shoulders shaking. Then she turned and threw her arms around Dani.

Holding her younger sister as she cried made Dani feel like she was going to lose it, too. But she was the big sister. She had to stay strong. "It's going to be okay," she said, when Alicia's sudden burst of sobs began to slow down.

Alicia pulled away, her face streaked with tears, so much pain in her eyes it was hard to look at her. In some ways, she envied her sister's release of tension.

She felt like a million emotions were building up inside her, but she couldn't let them go—not quite yet. There were still things she needed to figure out.

"I've known forever that Dad didn't crash his plane," Alicia said. "No one would believe me."

"I know." She felt guilty that she'd been one of those people. "You were right all along. I'm sorry I ever doubted you."

"Everyone did. But I just had this feeling, and after what happened last year, it got even stronger. That's why I couldn't let it go." She sniffed and wiped her eyes. "You figured it out, Dani. I still don't really know how you did it, but I'm glad you did."

"I got lucky. I was actually trying to find out if someone at MDT was responsible for Patrick's mother's death, but he thought all along that his mom and my dad were tied together in some way, and he was right." She paused. "I took too long to get on board."

"You're here now, and you came with answers, with actual proof."

"I don't know if it's much in the way of proof."

"It's enough to get the FBI looking again. We are going to take down that company if it's the last thing we do. They keep coasting by, telling lies, getting people in power to back them. But one day they are going to get caught, and I think that day is soon."

"Things do seem to be unraveling," she said, her thoughts turning to Senator Dillon as Alicia's words reminded her that her own boss might be part of this.

"They were running a secret operation," Alicia said in bemusement. "So everything was being doubled, weapons and technology?"

"Apparently. But we're going to need someone to talk who really knows what's going on. Unfortunately, the people who want to talk seem to keep dying." She thought about Tania again and really hoped the woman was all right. "We're going to unravel the layers, Alicia."

"I know we are. Sorry for the meltdown. I'm okay now. Let's go back inside."

When they returned to the living room, Jake was just getting off the phone.

"Agent Wolfe said he will be here tomorrow morning," Jake said. "Patrick and I filled him in on what we know. He's going to check with the local police and have someone do a welfare check on Tania Vaile to make sure she's all right."

"That's good," Dani said, relieved that they were going to have help.

"I hope it's good," Jake said.

She wondered why her brother didn't seem that happy. "Why wouldn't it be?"

"I just can't help thinking that Agent Wolfe just ran a six-month investigation into MDT and found nothing. Was he stupid? Was he not trying to find anything? Were the people at MDT just too smart for him? Or is he involved in some way? Are we trusting the wrong person?"

"Whoever is running this show is good at covering things up," Patrick put in. "Look how long they've been in business—more than a decade. And there has to have been more than one FBI agent looking into the company over the years. We're just going to have to trust that Agent Wolfe is not under their control."

"That's a big leap of faith," Dani said, not sure she could trust anyone anymore. "So what now?"

"Now we eat," Katherine said. "There's nothing more we can do at the moment, and we're all going to need energy for whatever is to come."

"I agree," Alicia said, picking up the platter of sandwiches. She grabbed one and passed it to Dani.

For the next couple of hours they ate, drank, and rehashed what they'd learned so far. Then they moved on to more personal topics. Dani had to admit she liked watching Patrick interact with her family. He was a man who was comfortable in any group, the kind of man both women and men wanted to hang out with. She knew that had a lot to do with the fact that he was genuinely interested in whoever he was talking to.

At some point, when Patrick went to use the bathroom, and the others were engaged in conversation, Alicia leaned over and whispered to her. "I like him. He's sexy and interesting."

She smiled. "Yes, he is."

"So, there's more going on than just solving a mystery?"

"Yes, but that's all I'm going to say for now."

"You can't stop there."

"I have to. He'll be back in a second."

"You should give him a chance."

"We'll see."

"One of these days, you're going to have to let someone into your heart, Dani," Alicia said. "Even if it's scary."

"How do you know I haven't done that?" she asked defensively.

"Because you haven't," Alicia said, meeting her gaze. "I was the same way until I met Michael. Losing Dad did a number on all of us. Love got really terrifying."

"You might be right," she conceded.

"I want you to be happy, Dani. I know you love your career, but isn't there room for love?"

"It's way too early to talk about love." She was relieved when Patrick came back into the room. She got to her feet. "We're going to go now," she told the group. "Mom will be back soon, and no one needs to mention that I'm in town."

"Hold on," Jake said. "Speaking of Mom, we need to decide what we're going to tell her."

"Nothing," Dani and Alicia echoed at the same time.

Jake sighed. "I know you two want to leave her out of this, but it's not fair to her, and it's getting complicated. We have FBI agents coming tomorrow."

"To your apartment," Dani said pointedly. "Right?"

"Yes, but still, she's going to find out, and she's going to be angry that we didn't tell her."

Her brother had a point. She looked over at Alicia. "What do you think?"

"Let's wait until after we meet with Agent Wolfe."

"I can do that," Dani said. "I'll bring the file to our meeting tomorrow. Then we can all come back here and fill Mom in. I don't want her to be part of the FBI conversation." There were things about her job and the senator that she didn't really need her mother to be involved in, either. "So no one says anything tonight or before the meeting—are we agreed?"

Jake gave a reluctant nod. "Fine. Katherine

and I are following you out the door anyway."

"And Michael and I will just talk about the wedding and the honeymoon, which is what she wants to talk about anyway," Alicia said. "We also have some presents here we haven't opened yet. She likes to be a part of that."

"Great. We'll see you guys in the morning," Dani said. "Text me when you hear from Agent Wolfe about what time he's coming."

They all exchanged hugs and then headed out to the car. As she and Patrick drove away from the house, she said, "So what do you think?"

"I think we're putting together a good team."

"A team I was reluctant to join," she said dryly.

"And now you're the leader," he said with a smile. "Funny how that worked out."

"I'm not sure about leader, but I'm definitely in the middle of everything. Alicia had a meltdown in the backyard."

"I figured. Her eyes looked red when you both came back."

"She's always been the most emotional person in the family. She has a lot of heart."

"So do you, Dani. You just don't show it as much or as often. Were you always like that, or did you pull back after your dad died?"

It was a good question. "Probably after he died. But even before that, I had a better understanding of what people wanted and expected of me than Alicia did. She had to go her own way and make dramatic statements and get into battles with my mom. I just didn't tell my mom stuff that I knew she wouldn't like."

"I don't see you as a bad girl."

"I had my moments, but in general, I didn't break too many rules. And my mom and I did get along better than my mother and Alicia did, so that made it easier." She paused. "What about you? Did you battle with your dad or with your mom?"

"Both of them at different times. My father was involved in my homework and after-school sports. My mom was not around as much, so I'd say my father and I had more battles, but my mom was opinionated, and sometimes I didn't agree with her thinking. She liked to argue, which served her well in politics, and I didn't mind going a few rounds either, so we'd get into it on occasion. But in general, the three of us got along well. My parents didn't really fight with each other. I think my mom was always this shining star for my dad and he was happy to orbit around her."

"It's interesting how families interact. You can't tell that much from the outside, because everyone puts on a face, but those on the inside get to see it all."

"Are you talking about your family now, or . . ."

"Actually, I was thinking about the Packers," she admitted. "About Reid having a younger brother complex. It is interesting that his older brother has always been at the helm. It's like Alan is the prince who became king and Reid was the spare heir."

"They do run a kingdom, so your analogy works for me," Patrick said.

"They seem like they're a tight family unit, but maybe they're not. How could Alan not know what Reid has been up to all these years?"

"When companies get as big as MDT, a global leader in defense technology with over twenty-five thousand employees around the world, there are a lot of places to hide money and people and everything else."

"They've certainly been successful at it so far," she agreed.

"So back to the cabin, Dani?"

She hesitated, thinking that back at the cabin it wouldn't be as easy to ignore the bed they'd spent the night in together. It had been easier to keep the memories at bay while meeting with Tania, chasing down the file, and then filling her family in on what was happening. But now, it was just her and Patrick again. Sometimes she thought he might be the biggest danger of all.

But in the end, all she said was, "Sure, let's go back to the cabin." It was starting to feel like home. Actually, that wasn't true. It wasn't the building that felt like home; it was Patrick.

TWENTY

It was half past six when they got back to the cabin. Patrick couldn't believe how fast the day had gone. It seemed only a short time ago that Dani had left to meet Tania for breakfast. A lot had happened since then. He wondered if Dani had really processed it all yet. It had been easier when they'd been with her family, when they'd been going over everything that they knew. Since they'd left her mother's house, Dani had been quiet, and he was a little worried about her. But he reminded himself that she was a strong woman. She'd been dealt a big blow, but she was handling it, and he would do everything he could to make things easier for her.

The sun was drifting behind the trees as they entered the house. Patrick turned on the air conditioning while Dani headed into the kitchen, muttering something about getting some water.

While he knew he should get to work, he was feeling a little overloaded on information, so he walked into the living room, sat down on the couch and turned on the television. It seemed like a million years since he'd done something normal. Flipping through the channels, he saw the usual reruns of sitcoms and old movies, cable news and sports.

The Texas Rangers were in the tenth inning of a tied game against the San Diego Padres. It was bottom of the tenth with Texas at bat, one out, two strikes. The next ball came in high, and the batter took a look: ball two. Then came a curve ball that the batter looped just over the second baseman's head. It was a lucky hit, but the home crowd was thrilled.

"Who's winning?" Dani asked, taking a seat on the couch next to him. She handed him a glass of water.

"Thanks," he said, as he took a sip. "It's tied. But we just got on base, so we have a chance. We just need another hit." He groaned as the next batter watched two strikes go by.

"He's going to have to swing if he wants to get a hit," Dani said lightly.

"No kidding." Fortunately, the next pitch was a ball. The one after that, the batter hit deep into left field. For a moment, he thought it might get out of the park, but the outfielder made a great catch. "Damn."

"It's only two outs. A hit will win the game."

"I'm sure the pitcher is thinking three strikes, and he'll win this game," he replied.

"It's all about perspective," she agreed. "Kind of like our investigation. Someone keeps trying to strike us out, but we keep on swinging."

"Yes, we do," he said with a smile. "How are you holding up, Dani?"

"I'm trying not to feel too much right now. I don't want to get overwhelmed with emotion. I need to be able to think."

"You got some devastating news today. Anyone would be overwhelmed."

"I'm going to deal with the emotional part of all that later."

He had a feeling Dani was very good at keeping her emotions in check. In this circumstance, it was probably a good thing.

He watched the next batter foul off a dozen plus pitches.

"He's battling," Dani commented.

"Hopefully, he wins the battle."

Finally, the batter connected dead center on a ball, and this time there was no doubt that the ball was going into the stands for a two-run homer. The announcers went wild.

"Yay," Dani said with a smile. "They pulled it out."

"My father will be very happy." He changed the channel, not needing to hear the recap of the game. He paused on a game show. "My cousin Marcus is so good at these game shows. He has an amazing amount of trivia in his head."

"I bet you're good, too."

"Only at sports and current events. Anything having to do with art or dance or fashion—not my thing."

"Me, either. I'm also really bad at scientific

questions. But I could probably match you in current events and pop culture."

"Let's see, shall we?"

"You're on."

They played along with the game show for the next thirty minutes. Dani knew far more than she'd given herself credit for, and the competition between them grew a little intense. Then again, everything they did was intense. He could feel heat rising between them even while they were playing the game. Of course, the game was really just a distraction so they wouldn't fall into each other's arms and make love on the couch. He knew that as well as she did.

Although, why would that be a bad thing? As he considered that question, he completely lost track of the game, and Dani took the final round.

"Beat you," she said with a cocky smile.

"You're such a gracious winner," he replied with a laugh.

"You should say congratulations, or does that word stick in your throat? No one beats Patrick Kane, right?"

"It wasn't a fair contest."

"What? Why?"

"I started thinking about kissing you, and I didn't hear the question."

Her eyes glittered at his words. "That's just an excuse."

"It's the truth. I've been thinking about it all day."

"Really? You've been thinking about kissing me while I was meeting with Tania, while we were trying to find the ranch, while we were talking to my family?"

"Yes, yes, and yes. It never crossed your mind? Last night was good, Dani; I want to do it again."

She drew in a breath and let it out. "That was a one-night thing, Patrick."

"Why?"

"Because . . ." She couldn't seem to finish her statement.

"That's not an answer," he said.

"We have a lot to do right now. We shouldn't even be taking this break. We should be on our computers, researching the Packers and everything else we've learned."

"We'll get there. We've taken in a lot of information today. Sometimes it needs to settle a bit. We need time to think."

"Think," she said, jumping on the word. "Not kiss, not have sex—no matter how good it would be. We need to think."

"I can multitask." He leaned over and stole a quick kiss. "You taste so damn good."

"Patrick, no." She put a hand on his chest. "If we start this now, we'll lose the whole night."

"So, you're not saying no—you're saying later?"

"Let's talk about what Tania said instead."

He sat back against the couch. "We already rehashed that with your family."

"Not the part about my dad—the other things she mentioned. She made a point of saying that men lie, that you can't trust anyone, even the people you think care about you. Was she talking about Reid? About their love affair gone bad? Or was she referring to someone else?"

He thought back to that phone conversation. "Actually, her words seemed pointed to you, Dani. I wondered if she was talking about your relationship with the senator."

"The senator?" she echoed doubtfully. "I don't know. She never mentioned him by name, well, at least not today. She did say something about him when we were riding yesterday. She told me that he knew a lot more than I thought he did. I hate to think he's involved in this. I know all politicians spin and probably lie, but I've always felt he was a good person down deep, you know? I wouldn't imagine that he could be involved in murder."

"Maybe his involvement didn't go that far. We need to find a way to talk to him. Perhaps we'll have better luck here in Texas—at his Fourth of July party tomorrow."

"I told you I'm not invited. It's his friends, high-level donors, and top staff only. If I show up there, Erica will probably fire me."

"I wonder if the Packers will be there tomorrow," he mused.

"They're always invited, so I think there's a good chance. Unless we can convince Agent Wolfe to bring Reid Packer in for questioning before then."

"I doubt he'll do that with the minuscule amount of evidence and hearsay information we have."

"You're probably right."

"Dani, I think we should go to the senator's house before the party starts. He's not going to throw you out."

"I wouldn't be so sure of that."

"You can tell him what Tania said. We can act like we're doing him a favor by warning him of a potential problem, which, in fact, we are doing. If he's not involved, he'll be grateful for the tip. And if he is involved, he'll be nervous. Either way, we'll get a reaction. And I don't think Erica will fire you if we play it that way. We'll make it clear we're looking out for the senator's best interests."

"That might work," she said slowly. "It's risky, though. And what about Tania? We'll be revealing her desire to help us."

"That might not matter anymore," he said heavily.

"I wish I didn't think that might be true," she said, her brows furrowed with worry.

"There's nothing we can do about it. Getting back to the senator, Dillon might thank you for the information you're sharing with him. It may give him the opportunity to play the hero. He can distance himself from MDT and perhaps even turn on them. This could make his career—if he's innocent."

"You're very persuasive, Patrick."

He smiled, thinking he was nowhere near as persuasive as he'd like to be. "I don't know about that. We're a long way from the bedroom, Dani."

She shook her head. "You have a one-track mind."

"Only since I met you." He paused, getting back to the business at hand. "So FBI in the morning, then Senator Dillon in the afternoon?"

"Sounds like an awesome day," she said with a cynical sigh.

"We can find some fun in there somewhere," he said suggestively. "Is it *later* yet?"

"No," she said, grabbing the remote out of his hand. She moved through the channels, stopping on a re-run of *Saturday Night Live*.

Patrick kicked his feet up on the coffee table as they watched the show. By the time it was over, it was dark outside, so he turned on a lamp by the couch while Dani decided to see what else was on.

As she paused on a local news show, a breaking headline ran across the bottom of the screen, and he sat up abruptly. He almost didn't hear Dani gasp through the thundering roar of blood rushing through his veins.

"Oh, my God," she said. "Is that Tania?"

He stared at the scene of a car tipped onto its

hood, headfirst into a ditch. Dani turned up the sound just in time to hear a reporter say that a female executive for MDT was killed in a solo car crash earlier in the day.

"It's Tania," he said grimly as the reporter gave her name, which obviously meant that next of kin had already been notified. The FBI and police knew as well—something else to talk about with the agent in the morning.

Dani jumped to her feet and paced back and forth in front of the television. "It's my fault. If I hadn't talked to her yesterday, if I hadn't met her today, if I hadn't convinced her to help me, she wouldn't have left that file for me at the ranch. She wouldn't be dead."

He got to his feet, grabbing her by the arm as she headed for another adrenaline-fueled walk. "Dani, stop. It's not your fault."

She stared at him with wide eyes. "How can you say that? I went after her. I got her to trust me, to talk to me."

"And I was behind you every step of the way," he reminded her.

"Then it's your fault, too."

"Look, I'm not happy about it. But the truth is Tania wasn't innocent. She told you that on the phone. She said she was tired of the lies and the game that she'd gotten involved in so many years ago. A completely innocent woman was not killed today, but other innocent people have been killed

370

by the people we're trying to stop. You have to keep your eye on the ball."

She stared back at him for a long moment, and he could see that she wanted to believe him. "Even so, Patrick. She is dead because of me, whether she was innocent or not."

"She's dead because someone killed her, and that wasn't you."

"They ran her off the road and into that ditch."

"I know. Another solo car crash, just like the one that took the life of my mother's chief-of-staff."

"And a woman that TJ worked with, the woman he thought set him up to be kidnapped—she also allegedly killed herself by crashing her car. This has to stop, Patrick. Maybe we shouldn't wait for the FBI. Maybe we should go to the local police now. We can tell them that we saw Tania earlier, that we were talking to her and that people were following her."

"No," he said firmly.

"Why not?"

"Because MDT owns this town. You know it, and so do I. We have to wait for the FBI. There's nothing we can do for Tania now. We'll tell the Feds everything we know in the morning, and they'll share whatever is important with the police."

She blew out a breath. "All right, but I can't quite believe she's dead. We just talked to her.

And I had so many more questions I wanted to ask her. She was our only real lead."

"We'll find someone else."

"Will we? You don't think Tania's death is going to make everyone even more cautious? Because I do."

"We'll use your father's file to get attention from the FBI, along with what Tania told us. We'll keep talking to people, too. We can go back to our source. We'll talk to Dillon tomorrow. I can contact Congressman Parker again; the more people who know what we know, the better. They can't kill everyone."

"I wouldn't be so sure of that," she said darkly. "They've been pretty successful so far."

"Their operation is unraveling; it has been ever since Alicia followed a lightning strike to Jerry Caldwell last year. And then the Senate investigations after Mexico took away some of their funding. People have been kidnapped. People have died. It's coming apart at the seams."

"What if I've put my family in danger?" she asked. "Should I call them? Should I tell them Tania is dead?" As the questions flew out of her mouth, she twisted her great-grandmother's ring around her finger. "I don't want them to worry, but if something happens to them . . ."

He didn't think anyone would go after her family now, but if they did, Dani would blame herself for that, too, and there would be no coming back from that guilt. "You should tell them. I don't believe they're in danger, because they're already known to MDT. Their names were in the investigations, in the Senate hearings. If something happens to them, it's going to go straight back to MDT. If they'd wanted to take them out, they would have done it before now."

"They might not care at this point."

He thought about that, wondering if the isolated house was still the best place for them to stay the night, especially after what had happened to Tania. "Why don't you call your brother and sister? I'll pack up our things and then we'll find a hotel to stay in tonight, one with lots of people around."

"Good idea."

After Patrick went upstairs, Dani called Jake. Her sister was staying with her mom, and she thought it was better to start with her brother. "Tania is dead," she said bluntly when he asked her what was wrong. "It's on the news—single person car crash. You can probably see it online."

"Damn," Jake muttered. "Hang on."

She could hear him talking to Katherine in the background, then he came back on the line.

"What do you want to do?" he asked.

"I want our family to be safe, but I don't know how to make that happen."

"I do. Katherine and I will go over to the

house. We'll just say we want to spend more time with Alicia and Michael before they go back to Florida."

"That could work."

"Michael and I will make sure everyone there is safe, but I don't think they're going to come after us. I'm more worried about you, Dani."

"Patrick and I are going to stay out of sight tonight."

"Are you staying at his place?"

"We're going to leave in a few minutes and find a hotel. I'll text you later."

"All right. By the way, I heard from Agent Wolfe; he'll be at my apartment at ten a.m. tomorrow."

"I'll see you then. Be safe, Jake."

"You, too."

As she ended the call, she got up and went into the dining room. She closed her computer and put it back in its slipcover and then into her tote bag.

Her ring finger was starting to throb. She didn't know if all the tension was making her fingers swell, but there was a definite pain in the area where the ring was. She tried to move it, but it wouldn't even budge. She felt a desperate need to get it off her finger. She felt almost panicked at the thought that she couldn't do that.

Moving into the kitchen, she decided to try to use soap and water to get it off her finger. As she flipped on the light switch and moved toward the sink, she saw a fiery orange and red light outside the house. It took her a moment to realize it wasn't light; it was fire. The woods around the cabin were ablaze.

Thunder suddenly broke the air. *Or was that the sound of the trees exploding with fire?*

Her heart raced. "Patrick," she screamed, running out of the room.

He was coming down the stairs.

"There's a fire outside," she said.

"I just saw it from the bedroom. It must have started from the lightning."

"Was there lightning?"

"I thought I heard thunder."

"Was that thunder?"

She'd no sooner finished speaking when another loud boom rocked the house. The front door blew open and flames leapt into the house.

Patrick grabbed her hand. "We'll go out the back."

They ran through the kitchen and laundry room toward the back door. And then she remembered—the file on her dad was still in her bag.

Smoke and fire was pouring through the house now. "Stop," she said, pulling her hand free from Patrick's grip. "I have to get the file. It's in the dining room."

"I'll get it." He opened the back door, and she saw more fire. They probably had about thirty seconds to get out of the house.

"I'll do it," she argued. "You go."

"No chance." He grabbed her and literally threw her outside.

She stumbled and had to grab on to the back porch railing as Patrick went back for the file. Fire surrounded the house. The heat and the tremendous amount of brush and trees surrounding the property had created a raging inferno.

She started to go back in to get Patrick when another explosion threw her off the steps and onto the ground. *Where were all the explosions coming from?* She couldn't see anything now but fire. She could feel the intense heat burning her skin. Her eyes were watering. Smoke filled her chest. She had to get away, go somewhere—but where? And how could she leave Patrick? She tried to call out to him, but she had no voice.

Blinded by ash and fire, she searched for a safe place to go, hoping against hope that Patrick would make it out. There was no way this fire was an accidental brush fire. It was too big, too deadly. Someone had tried to kill them—again.

But she was alive. Patrick had to be, too. *He had to be.* She couldn't lose him. He was more than a friend, a colleague—he was everything. He was the one who could put her heart back together. She couldn't lose him now. Life could not be that cruel.

Only she knew it could be . . .

TWENTY-ONE

Patrick didn't know how the fire got so big so fast, but it was everywhere. Holding Dani's bag under his arm, he barreled through the flames, praying that she was all right and cursing himself for putting her into danger in the first place.

When he got into the backyard, there was more fire. He heard the sound of distant sirens. Someone in one of the houses along the road must have seen the blaze and called for help.

"Dani," he yelled, dodging a flaming branch that came crashing down from the trees just a foot away from him.

And then in the midst of all the fire, he felt water.

It took him a minute to realize that it was rain—hot, summer rain.

It came out of nowhere, dousing the fire, streaming down his face, clearing some of the smoke.

Now he could see Dani. She stood twenty-five yards away in a small clearing. She had her arms wrapped around her, as if seeking some comfort from the fear. The rain was pouring down on her head. He ran the last few feet, dropped the bag at her feet and threw his arms around her.

Their kiss was filled with terror, relief, and joy.

377

He went back for another kiss and another, needing to be sure she was all right.

Finally, he pulled back, pushing the wet strands of hair off her face. "You're all right?" He searched her face for the truth.

"I'm okay," she whispered. "I wasn't sure you were. How did the fire get so huge?"

"I don't know. I didn't smell any smoke until I came down the stairs."

"I didn't, either. I went into the kitchen, because the ring was suddenly so tight. It was cutting off my circulation. I thought I could get it off with soapy water and then I saw the fire outside. I guess it could have started from lightning."

"It could have," he said, not wanting to scare her more.

Her wide-eyed gaze met his. "But that would just be one of those coincidences I can't believe in, right?"

"We'll get an answer once the fire investigators look around." He could see the gleam of lights as the fire engines came down the road in front of the house. "Let's go tell them what happened."

"Thanks for getting my bag," she said, putting the strap over her shoulder. "That file is my only link to my dad."

"I knew how important it was."

"But it wasn't worth your life. I'm sorry I sent you back. If anything had happened—"

"Don't," he said, cutting her off. "We're both all

right. That's what matters." He put his arm around her waist as they walked toward the front of the house.

For the next hour, they watched the fire department work on putting out the fire, not just in the house, but also in the surrounding brush. The rain had stopped what could have been an enormous wildfire in the making.

When the blaze was under control, they spoke to the battalion chief and then to a fire investigator and a policeman.

Patrick took the lead, choosing his words carefully. He didn't want to get too far into the case they were building against MDT so he simply said that in his business of investigative journalism, he sometimes made enemies. They asked more questions, but he was able to evade most of them. He would give the FBI agent a better story in the morning, but right now he didn't know who he could trust on the local police force.

He needed to call his father. His dad had a deep emotional attachment to the cabin. It had been a special place for his father and his mother. The loss was going to hurt, and he felt terrible that that forthcoming pain was because of his actions. He never should have used the cabin to hide out in. He should have anticipated the danger.

But right now he couldn't waste time on what he should have done. His first priority was to get

Dani to a safe place. With the truck destroyed by fire, a police officer was kind enough to drive them to a downtown hotel. As they made their way into the building, he kept an eye out for anyone watching or following, but they appeared to be alone. Still, he wanted to be extra careful.

Dani started toward the check-in desk, but he caught her by the arm and said, "I have a better idea."

"What's that?"

He led her out a back door and into a parking lot area. "There's a hotel next door. Let's go there."

"You think someone followed us from the cabin?" she asked, her gaze darting in every direction as they walked across the parking lot, through an alley and into the side door of another hotel.

"I'm not taking any chances. Why don't you wait by the elevators? I'll get us a room."

"Fine."

He ran a hand through his hair, knowing he looked like something the cat had dragged in, but he hoped that the recent and sudden rainstorm would explain his dampened look.

It took only a few minutes to get a room, and then he and Dani headed to the sixth floor. Once inside, he put out a privacy sign and bolted the locks.

As Dani went into the bathroom, he moved to the window. There was no balcony, no way to access the room from the outside. They were safe. He blew out a breath, realizing he'd been holding it for a long time.

He kicked off his waterlogged shoes and pulled off his damp socks, then sat down on the edge of the bed and took his phone out of his pocket. He'd lost the rest of his clothes in the fire, but he had his phone, his wallet, and he'd shoved his computer into Dani's bag before he'd left the house. All things considered, he was happy not to have lost anything he couldn't replace.

He punched in his dad's number. It was after eleven, and it was quite possible his dad had already gone to bed, but he couldn't let the news wait until morning.

"Patrick?" his dad asked, his voice sleepy. "What's wrong?"

"I'm all right, but there was a fire in the woods, and the cabin got caught up in it."

"What?" his dad said more sharply. "There was a fire?"

"Yes. The fire department came, and I think they're still cleaning things up there. Dani and I just left and went to a hotel."

"You could have come here," Harris said.

"I just wanted you to know that I'm fine, and I'm really sorry about the house. I'm going to do whatever it takes to get it back the way it was."

"Well, it wasn't your fault. It was the lightning, wasn't it?"

"Could have been," he said lightly. There would be time for more explanations later. "I don't want you to worry about anything."

"Should I go out there now?"

"No, the fire department is still cleaning up. Let me take care of this, okay, Dad? I really want to. We'll talk tomorrow, all right?"

"All right. I'm glad you're okay and that Dani is, too."

"Thanks."

Dani came into the room as he finished his call. She'd changed out of her smoky, wet clothes and was now wearing a hotel robe, her skin and hair smelling more like shampoo and lotion than fire.

"You look a lot better," he said.

"I feel better. My throat is still scratchy, but other than that, I'm fine. Who was on the phone?"

"My dad. He thinks lightning started the fire. I didn't tell him otherwise. He said he's glad you're all right. I think he likes you."

"I like him, too, and I feel bad about the family cabin."

"That's on me. I'm the one who wanted to stay there."

Her face was still pale, but she had a bit more color now. She looked weary but still defiant, and he appreciated that. Because he was more motivated than ever to put some people behind bars—as many as he could.

"They're not going to get away with this," she said, sitting on the bed next to him.

"No," he agreed.

"I'm getting tired of people trying to kill us."

"You and me, both, babe. I would like to turn the tables. Tomorrow, hopefully, with some reinforcements, we can do that."

"We will." She put her hand on his leg. "Patrick—I was really scared tonight."

He met her gaze. "Me, too," he said softly. "When I came out the door, and I didn't see you . . ."

"I felt the same way when you went back into the house. The fire kept popping and jumping and there were the loudest bangs. I still don't know why it was so loud."

"It was raging."

"I've never felt such intense heat."

"Never?" he asked with a teasing light in his eyes.

She grinned back at him. "You think you're as hot as a raging forest fire now?"

"Not me alone, but us together . . ."

She smiled. "We are pretty explosive. By the way, when you went back in, you threw me on the ground. I have a few more bruises now."

"I had to be forceful. Otherwise, you would have followed me."

"I would have."

"Why don't I see if I can make you feel better?"

he suggested, cupping her face with one hand, his thumb stroking the soft skin of her cheek, then drifting down to her full lip, a lip he very much wanted to kiss.

Desire sparked in her eyes. "Why don't you?" she said.

He'd been expecting a *no,* not a *yes,* and it rattled him for a second.

"We're alive," she added. "I think we should celebrate, because God knows what's coming tomorrow."

"I like the way you think, Dani."

"I like you."

"Right back at you," he said softly, then leaned over to taste her mouth. It felt like forever since he'd been able to touch her, kiss her, hold her, and he wanted to do all that and more. He wanted to take his time, but he also wanted to go fast. There was a part of him that felt like he could lose her before he was ready, or maybe he'd never be ready . . .

Dani pulled at the hem of his shirt, and helped him pull it over his head. Then she pressed her hands against his chest, her fingers drifting down to his abs, and lower still as she kissed him, sliding her tongue into his mouth.

So much for the idea of going slow. He was rock hard, and he wanted her now.

He pulled open her robe, and cupped her breasts with his hands, then tore his mouth away from hers, so he could take a hot, sweet path down her neck.

She opened his jeans.

He stripped off her robe.

Then he shimmied out of the rest of his clothes as they crawled under the covers to start their own fire.

Dani woke up just before dawn. There was a bit of light, but not much. She snuggled closer to Patrick, liking the weight of his arm across her waist, his leg over hers. Heat still warmed the air around them. With Patrick, she felt so many things: excited, teased, tormented, happy, reckless, and also safe. She could fly with him, because she knew he'd always catch her.

She'd never been with someone with whom she felt so comfortable, so free to be her real self. They'd known each other only a short time, but the intensity and quality of that time had taken their relationship into a deep, emotional space. The thought scared her. Patrick could take over her life, her thoughts, her heart . . . and definitely her body. She seemed to have little willpower when they were within touching distance of each other.

But how could she let him have so much power over her? What if this was just sex for him? Just a moment in time where they were in the same place, caught up in the same mystery—what if that's all it was?

This was why she didn't do casual flings, because she wasn't good at them. She didn't sleep with people she didn't feel emotionally connected to. Now she was bare. She was vulnerable. She was falling in love.

Her heart skipped a beat.

Well, why not? She smiled to herself as she gazed at his face, his strong male features, the growth of beard on his jaw, the sweep of his dark lashes, and the sexy mouth that could make her lose her mind. Patrick was gorgeous.

But it wasn't just his looks that undid her; it was his personality. He was intelligent and curious and interested in the world around him. He wasn't a spectator. He jumped into the action. If he saw a wrong, he wanted to right it. If he saw someone hurt, he wanted to help. And he was willing to put his life on the line for what he believed in, for the people he cared about—even for a stranger.

She'd wanted to get into politics to make a difference. But looking at what Patrick had accomplished so far with his investigative stories and where she was in her career—there was no comparison. He made her want to do better. When all this was over, she was going to do just that.

Patrick stirred, blinking his eyes open, as he said, "I can hear you thinking."

"You cannot."

"Well, then I can feel your body tensing." He gave her an intimate smile. "Morning."

"It's not really morning. It's barely light out."

"Then why are we awake?"

"I don't know. I just woke up, and then—I started thinking," she confessed.

"I knew it. What are you thinking about?" he asked, his fingers stroking her hip, reminding her that sometimes not thinking was a better choice.

She put her hand over his. "That's not helping. It's distracting."

"There's still time to be distracted. You just said it was early." He paused, giving her a more thoughtful look. "Seriously, what are you thinking about?"

"My life. My job. You know—little stuff," she said with a self-deprecating laugh. "I was thinking about all you've accomplished, and how you're way out in front of me."

"I got lucky with the drug story. I had sources who gave me the information I needed. I can't take all the credit."

"You don't have to be modest, Patrick."

"I'm not being modest. I'm a good reporter, but sometimes a breakthrough story requires a little luck, too. I bet you're good at what you do. I know you're a hard worker. You're dedicated. You're smart. And you want to make changes in the world. Maybe you just need some luck to push you the rest of the way."

"Recently, I've had a lot of bad luck."

"Now I know you're not talking about meeting me," he teased.

"Well . . ."

"Come on, Dani. We're great together."

"When we're not running for our lives."

"Even when we are."

"Hopefully we're done with that. Although, I am worried about what the day will bring. I've always loved the Fourth of July: picnics, barbecues, parades, fireworks, a sense of community and patriotism. I don't want the holiday to be ruined, and I'm afraid it will be."

"Well, we're doing all we can to prevent it from being ruined. I've always liked the holiday, too. My favorite part is the watermelon."

"Watermelon? Seriously? I would have thought you'd say shooting off rockets was your favorite part."

"That's second. There's nothing better on a hot Texas day than cold, juicy watermelon—except maybe a cold beer. Put the two together, and you've got a holiday."

"You're pretty low maintenance, Patrick."

"Simple pleasures are the best."

"Yet you're nowhere close to being a simple man. You're complicated, ambitious, driven."

"True, but I try to remember to enjoy the journey, because I know how fast everything can change. You do, too."

"Do you think we'll always be influenced by the deaths of our parents?"

"Yes, but I don't believe it's a bad thing. Life shapes you—the good stuff, the bad stuff and everything in between. I don't want to have regrets, so I'm going to live the best way I know how."

"That sounds like a good strategy."

"So I'm thinking we have a little more living we can do right now—before the sun comes all the way up."

"You're insatiable."

His sexy smile turned her stomach over. "I am. I'm glad you are, too."

"I never said I was," she countered.

"You didn't have to say it. Kiss me, Dani."

She didn't have to be asked twice, because he was right. She wanted him as much as he wanted her. It was a constant craving, and there was only one solution.

She planted a long, hot, wet kiss on his lips, then pushed him onto his back. Patrick had a lot of good ideas, but she had some as well, and she was really going to enjoy trying them out.

"We're late," Dani said, as they took a taxi to Jake's apartment a little after ten on Sunday morning.

"You can't blame that on me," he said with a laugh.

"You're the one who said *kiss me.*"

"And you're the one who said *let's take a shower together* after that," he reminded her. "Best shower of my life."

"Mine, too, but it's back to business now." She pulled the file out of her bag, happy she still had it in her possession. She could have lost it last night. Thank God she hadn't.

"Yes," Patrick agreed, his tone changing from light and happy to serious and determined. "I hope this FBI agent is good. What's he like? Young, old, by-the-book . . ."

"He's probably in his early thirties. He's attractive but aloof, kind of cold, hard to get to know. He seems intelligent and dedicated. That's pretty much all I know. I only had one conversation with him. Jake and Alicia talked to him several times. I'm sure he'll be thrilled to have another Monroe in the mix of all this."

"According to your great-grandmother, it was only a matter of time."

"Yes. Silly me, I thought I could escape the whole thing just by pretending it wasn't there. But ever since I put on this ring . . ." She held up her hand. "Not only can I not take it off, I also can't look away from the past anymore. I want to know the truth as much as Alicia and Jake do, as much as you do. And I don't want you to ever think that I've forgotten your mom in all this." It was very important for her to make sure he understood that.

"She's the reason we're where we are right now. I'm just hoping that getting to the truth about my dad will help us get to the truth about her accident."

"I'm confident it will."

The cab stopped in front of Jake's apartment. Patrick paid the fare, and then they stepped onto the sidewalk.

She gripped his hand as they walked into the building. Even though they were the ones who'd asked for the meeting, she felt nervous. She really hoped Agent Wolfe was one of the good guys. Otherwise, they were about to show all their cards.

TWENTY-TWO

A *gent Damon Wolfe was exactly as Dani had described,* Patrick thought, as he shook hands with the tall, muscularly built, dark-haired man with the sharp blue eyes. He'd brought another agent with him, a brown-eyed brunette named Abby James. In addition to the agents, Jake and Katherine were present, as well as Alicia and Michael.

He didn't feel like he'd gotten to know Michael as well as Jake, but it was clear that while he wasn't a big talker, Michael was very smart, and he was also good at keeping Alicia grounded. Katherine and Jake made a good team as well. He'd heard all about their reunion love story the day before, and he was happy they'd found their way back to each other, because clearly they were crazy in love.

But he thought he had the best partner of all. Dani was everything he'd ever wanted in a woman; not just beautiful but smart, caring, imaginative, and generous . . .

When this was all over, he intended to tell her that.

"Are you two all right?" Alicia asked, worry in her eyes. "Jake just filled us in on the fire at your father's cabin, Patrick."

"We're fine," he said. "The house was destroyed, but it can be rebuilt." He turned his attention to Damon Wolfe, as he and Dani sat next to Katherine on a couch in the living room. "Did Jake fill you in on the fire?"

"Yes," he replied. "I spoke to the fire investigator this morning, as well as the chief of police. It looks like the fire was deliberately set and that an accelerant was sprayed around the house to intensify the blaze."

"That would explain all the popping noises," Dani murmured.

He nodded, thinking again how close they'd come to not making it out of the cabin alive.

"Let's put the fire aside for the moment," Agent Wolfe suggested. "I'd like to see the file on Wyatt Monroe that you retrieved from Carmichael Ranch."

"I have it right here," Dani said, pulling out the folder. "But I want it back. It's all we have left of our father."

"We can make you a copy of the contents of the file, but we'll need it to build our case."

"What case would that be?" Patrick asked. "It's my understanding you recently closed your investigation into the security problems at MDT. Yet, from what we understand there's a shadow company being run off the books by at least one of the top executives, most likely Reid Packer."

"We found no evidence of that in our investigation, but I'll be honest with you, we had trouble getting anyone to talk beyond the party line," Agent Wolfe replied. "I never thought the case was closed, but my superiors did. The Packers have a lot of power in Washington, and everyone wanted the problems to go away, except myself and Agent James. Without proof, unfortunately, we had nothing to go on. I'm hoping you're going to change that."

Dani handed him the file. "Basically, it says that my father saw evidence of gunfire from a test site the shadow company was running at Carmichael Ranch. He thought it was lightning, but they were probably testing a railgun, which, as you know, runs on electromagnetic energy."

"Yes, I've become an expert on those guns in recent months," Agent Wolfe said, as he glanced through the file. "You said Tania Vaile sent you to the ranch. Why would she do that? Why give you this file?"

"She said she was tired of the lies," Dani explained. "That what had started out small was getting more and more dangerous. She didn't like the direction things were going. She said something big was going to happen today."

"Yes, that's what Jake told me," Agent Wolfe said grimly. "The terror alerts are already as high as they can go because it's the Fourth of July, but if we can get anything more specific, that would be helpful."

"We don't have anything else," Patrick said. "Tania took whatever she knew to the grave."

"How did you get to her in the first place?" Agent Wolfe asked.

"We had a source," Patrick said. "This whole thing actually started out as an investigation into my mother's plane crash. I got the name of a reporter who said she'd hooked my mom up with an MDT whistleblower. After the plane went down, he went underground. When Dani and I started digging around, the reporter put me in contact with the whistleblower. I don't know his name or who he is, but I do have his number."

"Why didn't the whistleblower give you the information he had?" Agent James asked, her gaze guarded but a little skeptical.

"All the evidence he had was destroyed in the plane crash. He had nothing to back up his story. He gave us Tania's name. He thought she was directly involved in funneling money from MDT to the secret operation."

"You need to call your source back," Agent Wolfe said. "Tell him we can protect him, but we need his information, even if it's only his recollection of events."

"I will call him, but he doesn't trust the FBI. He thinks MDT owns you and other law enforcement."

"Nobody owns me," Agent Wolfe said. "Or Agent James. We're going to get to the bottom of this."

"I hope so," he said. "Dani's family has been waiting awhile for that to happen."

Agent Wolfe acknowledged the jab with a nod. "Let's start at the beginning."

They spent the next seven hours with the two agents, going over every fact, every assumption, every possible scenario. They talked about his mother's crash, Dani's father's friendship with Jerry Caldwell and his mysterious death. They went over Alicia's story from the time she'd found the missing ID tag of a JAG lawyer until she'd been almost killed. Then it was Jake and Katherine's turn to rehash the Mexico trip, what they'd seen at the ranch. TJ joined them on the phone for a good hour, reminding everyone of what he knew about the company and the weapons technology.

They also called their source numerous times, but he didn't pick up, which didn't make Patrick feel too good about that connection. He really hoped the guy was all right and just in hiding. He'd probably seen the news reports on Tania Vaile and realized his lead had resulted in her death.

In the middle of their session, they ordered in Chinese food, and ate their way through a dozen containers before continuing on with more questions.

There were also calls back and forth with other agencies who were still watching key points around the country for any possible problems. So far, all was good. As the day passed without incident, he had to hope that Tania's information had been wrong, or that the plan had been called off.

The intense and exhausting session finally came to an end around five o'clock. The agents left with a ton of notes and a promise to keep them in the loop going forward.

He had a better feeling about Agents Wolfe and James after the day they'd spent together. They were smart and determined, and he thought they genuinely wanted to get to the bottom of the problems at MDT, which actually meant starting at the top. Damon Wolfe, in particular, seemed to have no fear of going after the Packers; he just hadn't had enough ammunition before. Hopefully, they'd given him something to run with.

Dani stretched her arms over her head. "Now I know what you went through, Jake," she told her brother. "You said the FBI grilled you like a cheese sandwich after Mexico, and that's exactly how I feel today."

"You did well," Jake said with a smile. "But you're not quite done."

She groaned. "No, is it really that time?"

"Yes, we need to talk about Mom."

"Why don't we wait and do that tomorrow?" she suggested. "It's late. Mom has a Fourth of July party tonight. She's probably not even home."

"She's not home," Alicia said quickly. "She was going to Marti's at four. She texted me earlier, asking me where I was. I told her I was showing Michael around town, and we'd meet her later. Let's talk to her about all this tomorrow."

"Aren't you leaving tomorrow, Alicia?" Jake asked.

"Not until afternoon. There's time in the morning."

Jake sighed. "You two are ridiculous. You can't avoid this forever."

"It's not going to be forever," Dani said. "We just want more answers."

"We have the file on Dad, or at least a copy of it," Jake said. Agent James had run out and made them copies before she left.

"That's not enough," Alicia said. "You know how stubborn Mom is. She's not going to believe any of this without hard proof. Sorry, Jake, but you're out-voted."

Jake shot Dani a dark look. "I used to be able to count on you to be the rational one."

"I know, but in this case I really don't think another day will hurt. And we're all a little talked out."

Jake threw up his hands. "I give up. We'll do it tomorrow."

"Valiant effort," Michael told Jake with a grin. "Did you ever win any battles with these two when you were kids?"

"Not many. I was always outnumbered."

Patrick smiled as the three siblings hugged out their discord. He'd always wished for a sibling to play with, to fight with, to share a lifetime with. At least, he'd had Marcus, but it wasn't quite the same.

"Do you have any sisters, Patrick?" Jake asked him as they walked toward the door of his apartment.

"Nope. Only child."

"Lucky you."

"You wouldn't trade them for anything," he said knowingly.

"They can both be a pain in the ass. Stubborn as mules, those two are."

He shook hands with Jake and then followed Dani outside. "I'll call for a cab." Before he could do that, Dani's phone rang.

"It's Erica," she said, surprise in her voice. "This can't be good."

"Hello? Erica?" she said as she put the phone on speaker.

"Dani, what's going on?" Erica asked, an irritated tone in her voice.

"What do you mean?" Dani countered.

"You're in Corpus Christi. You almost lost your life in a fire last night."

"How do you know that?"

"I told you before—I have friends in the police department."

"You seem to check in regularly with them."

"They check in with me. What are you doing in town? You're not invited to the senator's party. It's Patrick Kane, right? It was his father's house that burned to the ground. What are you up to, Dani?"

"We need to speak to Senator Dillon, Erica," Dani said, a firm note in her voice. "We need to talk to him now. It's really important. There are some things going on that he needs to know about."

"Like what?"

"MDT."

"That investigation was closed."

"It's open now. I talked to the FBI today. Senator Dillon's name came up."

"What did you say?"

"It wasn't what I said; it's what's happening with MDT. The company is in trouble, and I want to warn the senator."

"I can take care of that."

"No, this needs to come from me. I have a long history with him. I think he can give me a few minutes. Just ask him."

Silence followed Dani's request.

"I don't need to ask him; I'll set it up," Erica said. "If you have information that's going to protect him, then you're right, he needs to hear it."

"Good. I can come over to the house now. I know the party is probably already starting, but if I can just get a few minutes in a private room—"

"I might be able to break him away," Erica said slowly, then paused for a moment. "I have an idea. The senator is taking his guests out on the yacht for the fireworks show. They'll be leaving at seven-thirty. Why don't you meet him at the yacht at seven? You'll have a few minutes before the other guests arrive. Do you know which boat it is?"

"Yes, I've been on it before."

"Of course you have. I sometimes forget how long you've been with the senator. I hope you understand how loyal he is to you, Dani. You might want to return the favor."

"I'll see you soon." She disconnected the call and looked at Patrick. "What do you make of that?"

"Erica is certainly tight with the cops here in town. But we've got a meeting, so that's a good thing." He glanced at his watch. "It won't take us but ten minutes to get to the harbor. We have two hours to kill."

"There's a coffeehouse three blocks from here. Let's walk over there. We can plan out what exactly I should say to the senator. If he is innocent, I'd like to have a job at the end of this."

He gave her a grim smile. "That's a big *if*, Dani."

"I know. But he's a United States senator. Maybe he's turned a blind eye, but he's not completely involved."

"That's probably your best hope."

• • •

The harbor was crowded with boats heading out to the water for the fireworks show that would take place around nine. *It was strange to see normal people doing normal things,* Dani thought. She'd been living in a world of dark intrigue the past week. But hopefully that was going to change.

As Patrick had said, the more people who knew everything, the better. There was more danger to her when she was keeping secrets, which was why she wanted to clear her slate with the senator, too. Maybe he'd appreciate the information. Hell, he might even give her a promotion and a raise for alerting him to a situation that had the potential to blow up in his face.

If he was innocent.

If he wasn't . . . she and Patrick could be in more trouble, not less.

After two cups of coffee, she felt energized and ready to tackle whatever was coming next. She was happy not to do it alone. Patrick had given her some good advice on how to approach the senator, and she was going to take it.

"So Dillon likes to sail?" Patrick asked, as the taxi dropped them off at the harbor a few minutes before seven.

"Yes, he likes to sail and he does it in luxury. His boat is actually a magnificent yacht. It has three or four staterooms, a gourmet kitchen, an elegant salon, a sun deck, and an office. It's amazing. I've only been on it once. He took the entire local staff out for his birthday one year."

"Too bad we won't be going out on the water."

Erica was waiting at the gate leading down to the private docks. She was on the phone when they arrived. She put up her hand, turning her back on them as she finished her conversation. Then she swung back around. "The senator is on his way. He'll be here in a few minutes."

"I appreciate you giving us this time," Dani said.

"I want what's best for the senator," Erica said smoothly. "It's nice to see you again, Patrick."

"Is it?" he asked, a cynical note in his voice.

Dani liked the fact that Patrick had never been charmed by Erica, a woman who thought she could control anyone and everyone.

· "I must admit I wish it were under different circumstances," Erica said, "but we all have a job to do. I respect that. Why don't we go on board and wait for the senator in the salon?"

A steward greeted them as they got onto the boat. "Can I get you anything to drink?" the man asked as he led them downstairs into the salon, a luxurious living area with three comfortable couches, a fully stocked bar, a large-screen television, and a poker table.

"We're fine," Dani said, answering for both her and Patrick.

As the man left, Erica said, "I'm afraid I'm going to have to ask for your phones."

"Why?" Patrick demanded.

"I can't take the risk that you'll record or photograph anything. If you're not agreeable, you can leave, but this will be your last opportunity to speak to the senator," she said.

Patrick didn't look happy, but he handed over his phone, and Dani did the same.

"Thanks. I'm going to step outside; I need to make a call." She paused at the door. "I know I haven't made life easy for either of you, but I hope you can understand that I'm just looking out for my boss. Anyway, the senator will be here soon. I'm sure you have a lot to talk about."

Erica left the salon, closing the door behind her.

"That was—different," Dani said, a suspicious gleam in her eyes. "Erica and apologies don't usually go hand-in-hand."

"Maybe she's finally figured out that working with you is better than working against you."

"Maybe." She wasn't entirely convinced.

"You were right about this yacht. It's spectacular," Patrick said. He walked over to the enormous ten-foot-long, guitar-shaped coffee table in front of the couches. "What the hell is this?"

"A gift from Randy Palmer," Dani said, naming the latest Texas star in country music. "Senator Dillon has a passion for music, and Palmer had this made especially for the senator. He signed it like it was a real guitar," she added as Patrick took a closer look at the signature.

"It's quite impressive," he admitted. "The senator does have friends in high places."

"I know you don't have the best impression of Senator Dillon, but he's very well-liked. He's charming, funny, friendly and not just when he's trying to win votes. There's no doubt that he has a ruthless, ambitious side, but I've also seen a man who is a loving father and a caring friend. I'm just trying to say he's more than one thing."

"If I ever get to talk to him in person, I'll keep that in mind," Patrick said dryly. "I actually didn't realize you liked him that much."

"I liked him more before Erica came on board. Once she became his guard dog, I've had little contact with him."

"What was his reaction when he first learned your family was responsible for MDT getting called to testify before Congress? He couldn't have been happy."

"He understood that there were other factors at play, like my father's death. He didn't hold it against me. We spent quite a few hours together going over the facts I knew so that he was well-prepared for the hearings. Joe was his chief of staff when it first started. That's when we spoke the most. Once Erica came, then my contact with the senator became a lot less frequent, but by then I had already shared the information I had." She paused, seeing an odd look in Patrick's eyes. "What are you thinking?"

He shrugged. "I don't know—nothing really. I guess, I was thinking that it was odd for the senator to change his chief of staff at that particular moment in time. MDT was in trouble, and his committee was involved. Plus, he was obviously a friend of the Packers. Why shake everything up then?"

"It was because Joe got sick."

"So he actually got sick? He was out of work? He was in the hospital . . ."

She frowned, thinking back to that time. "Actually, no. Joe just came into the office one day and said he had some health issues that he needed to address. He was gone in two weeks. It was fast. I was worried about him, but he said he'd be fine." She thought about what she'd just said. "Maybe it wasn't just his health that ended his employment. He and the senator had disagreed on how to handle the MDT investigation. They'd had more arguments in the weeks before those hearings than in all the years they'd been together. We should talk to Joe again, now that we know more."

"Good idea." Patrick walked around the salon, checking out some of the senator's sailing photographs, many of which the senator had taken himself. Then he wandered back to her. "What do you think is taking so long?"

"I don't know. The senator often runs late. He's a talker."

He glanced at his watch. "It's been a half hour. The rest of the party should be arriving by now. Should I go look for Erica?"

Before she could answer, she felt the boat shift under her feet. An engine came to life, and when she looked out the window, she could see that they were moving. Shock ran through her.

"What the hell?" Patrick muttered, walking over to the window. "We're leaving the dock. What's going on?"

"I have no idea. The boat wouldn't leave the docks without the rest of the party."

"Maybe we are the party. I don't think the senator is coming."

Her heart sank. "You think Erica brought us here to . . ." She couldn't finish the statement; it was too terrifying.

Patrick left the window and strode to the door. He turned the handle. "It's locked, Dani. Erica set us up."

TWENTY-THREE

Dani looked around for another door, a way out of the salon, but there wasn't one. Patrick went back to the two big bay windows that looked out one side of the boat. Unfortunately, the view revealed little more than a walkway. They couldn't see what was happening anywhere else on the deck.

"Do the windows open?" she asked.

"Nope. There's no latch, no lock."

She moved next to him. The harbor disappeared as the yacht picked up speed. The light was fading. She glanced down at her watch. It was seven forty-five. It would be dark soon. A chilling fear ran through her at the thought of being out in the Gulf of Mexico at night.

"There are other people on board," she said somewhat desperately. "That man who helped us on board, who offered us drinks. There's a captain, probably a co-captain, maybe a chef. Senator Dillon usually has a staff on hand for sailing trips. No one will hurt us with all these witnesses."

"They took down my mother's plane with five people on it, including a pilot," Patrick reminded her.

"Okay, that didn't make me feel better," she snapped.

"Sorry, but we have to face the facts, Dani. That staff you spoke of may not be here. The man we spoke to may be working for Reid. This isn't good. We need to think of a way to defend ourselves."

"I can't imagine how we're going to do that."

"We have to find a weapon of some sort."

As he finished speaking, the door suddenly opened.

Dani's heart leapt into her throat as the senator appeared. He was dressed casually in gray slacks and a navy-blue shirt, but there were dark shadows in his eyes.

"You're here?" she said, shocked. She'd thought they were alone with Erica or that Erica had put them on the boat to die. She'd convinced herself that Senator Dillon would never actually show up.

He stared back at her through bleak eyes, his expression tense, and it was then she realized there was a gun at his back. He was shoved into the room so hard he lost his balance. The door closed behind him as he landed on his knees.

"What's going on?" she asked, as she helped him to his feet.

"Erica," he said through tight lips. "She told me you asked for a meeting and that it was highly urgent. I left my party to come down here to meet you. When I arrived, she said there was trouble."

"Is that all she said?" she asked.

"She muttered something about Reid needing a

cover story. I don't know what she was talking about."

"Have you seen Reid today? Is he at your party?"

"He was supposed to come. He hadn't shown up yet when I left." His lips drew into a tight line. "When I got on board, two men with guns grabbed me and brought me in here."

"And Erica?" she asked. "Where did she go?"

"I have no idea. I yelled for her, but she disappeared. What the hell is going on, Dani?"

She couldn't decide if he really knew nothing or if he was trying to hedge his bets. "What else did Erica tell you?"

"She said you had information on Reid Packer and what he's been doing the last ten years, and that it could put me in a bad situation. I asked her what she meant, but she didn't care to explain."

"She was right about you being in a bad situation," Patrick put in, folding his arms across his chest as he stared at the senator. "By the way, I'm Patrick Kane."

"I know who you are."

"Of course you do. Do you want to tell me why you've been avoiding me for weeks?"

"Because there's nothing I could tell you that you didn't already know. I liked your mother. I'm sorry she's dead, but I don't know anything about the plane crash."

"Then let's talk about Reid Packer," Patrick said evenly. "What do you know about the shadow company he's been running for the past decade?"

"What?" Dillon spluttered. "Shadow company? I have no idea what you're talking about."

"Then let me fill you in," Patrick continued. "Your good friend has been operating a shadow company outside of MDT and using their resources to do it. He's been funneling money from government contracts for at least ten years, maybe longer. He's killed numerous people, including Dani's father and my mother, as well as your predecessor and good friend, Senator Stuart. Now, it's your turn."

"Do you have any proof of any of that?" Dillon challenged.

"We do," Dani said. "Patrick and I had a long talk with Tania Vaile. I know you've met her a few times. Are you aware that she was killed yesterday? It happened right after she gave me a file on my father. The company was afraid that my father had seen evidence of their weapon testing out at the Carmichael Ranch, so they had him killed."

Dillon paled with each word she spoke, until his face was ashen. "I don't know anything about murder."

"But you know about everything else, don't you?" Patrick challenged. "We spoke to the FBI earlier—Agent Damon Wolfe. He's reopening the investigation into MDT."

"You shouldn't have done that," the senator

said, shaking his head. He gave Dani a disappointed and angry look. "How could you go to the FBI without talking to me? I gave you your job. I took you to DC. I made your dreams come true."

His words stung a little, but she couldn't let him get to her. "This isn't about our relationship, Senator. This is much bigger than that. Someone has tried to kill Patrick and me twice already. Forgive me if loyalty is at the bottom of my list right now. And, frankly, you're talking like you're not in as bad of a situation as we are. Erica lured you down here and locked you in. I don't know what the endgame is, but I don't think it's good."

Dillon sucked in a quick breath as if her words had finally hit home. "I don't know that much," he said slowly, making his first vague concession. "I knew Reid was doing some business on the side, but I've never known the extent of it."

"Because you didn't want to know," Patrick said.

"Sometimes it's better to have deniability," he conceded.

"Is that why you hired Erica?" she asked. "To give you more deniability?" As she watched the emotions play across his face, she was still torn as to whether he was a villain or a victim or something in between. Probably in between, she decided. Somewhere along the line, his ambition had made him look the other way.

"Erica was referred to me by Reid," he admitted. "I had no reason not to hire her. She's brilliant with an excellent resume."

"Erica was hired to make sure you didn't let the Senate hearings get out of control," she said, realizing the truth.

"How long have you been working with Reid, Senator?" Patrick asked. "Was it before Dani's father was killed? Was it before or after my mother's plane crash? When did you get into bed with him?"

"I didn't know that Reid had anything to do with the death of Dani's father," he said, sending Dani a pleading look for understanding. "Honestly, I didn't know that."

She wasn't entirely convinced. "But you don't look that surprised now. Maybe you didn't know it at the time, but at some point you did, didn't you?" she challenged.

"I didn't find out until last year when your family's name came up with the MDT problems."

She swallowed hard at the admission. "Why didn't you tell me?"

"I didn't know all the details. I wasn't even sure it was true."

"Yes, you were. You might not have wanted it to be true, but you were sure."

She'd admired the senator for a very long time. She'd always thought of him as a wise man, a visionary, a person willing to fight to better someone's life, but he wasn't like that at all. He was greedy, ambitious, and a liar. *How had she been such a fool?*

"I looked out for you, Dani," he continued, sending her a pleading look. "I gave you opportunities to rise within my staff. I've been a good boss. I think you would agree with that, wouldn't you?"

"Was that you or was that Joe?" She paused as another thought occurred to her. "Did Joe know about my father, too?" Her stomach twisted into a knot at that possibility. She could take the senator's betrayal a lot easier than she could take Joe's.

"God, no," the senator said. "Joe knew nothing. But he started to get suspicious and he worried about my ties to Reid and to MDT when all the problems came down. Even before Reid asked me to hire Erica, I knew I had to get rid of Joe. He was asking too many questions. He was starting to see too much."

"What did Reid have you do for him over the years?" Patrick asked.

"I helped him get contracts for the company. You have to understand that I was friends with both Reid and Alan long before I got into politics. Reid became angry when his father retired and left Alan in charge. He thought he should have been made an equal partner. Despite the years Reid had put in at the company, he was never going to run MDT. So he started to do a few things on the side. He told me he would one day roll his freelance business into a corporation and become a competitor for MDT. He'd eventually get all their business and show his brother and father who was the smartest Packer of all."

The senator's words reaffirmed what she'd already heard. "And what was your role in his plan?" she asked, certain there was more to it than to just help pave the way to some government contracts.

"After Senator Stuart died," Dillon continued, "Reid approached me about running for the seat. He said I'd have the full support of his family. I'd wanted to get into politics, so I said yes. Of course, I expected to do Reid and his brother a few favors once I was in office, but I thought I could manage them. Washington is all about compromise and favors. It's the way the city works. You know that, Dani."

"When did you find out what was actually going on? When did you know that Reid's real goal was to sell weapons and classified technology on the black market? When did you discover he was killing anyone who got in his way?" she challenged.

"I swear I didn't know about the violence when it happened, but a few years ago I noticed that several top people at MDT suddenly left, citing early retirements. I realized that Reid was taking

MDT's top talent for himself. I asked him about it, and he just laughed and reminded me that he'd always told me that one day he would be the most powerful man on earth, and that day was coming soon. He was always bragging; I didn't really believe him."

"Maybe you should have," she said.

"I should have," he conceded. "A few months later, he came to me with a stronger request. He wanted me to block a contract to MDT because it was going to come with too much oversight and regulation. I told him I didn't have the power or the votes to do that, and he told me to find a way or pay the consequences. I asked him if he was threatening me, and he said it's not a threat; it's a fact. He'd been drinking that night, which made him more talkative and more volatile than usual. He told me that he'd taken out Senator Stuart's plane, and he could take me down, too. I'd never heard him talk like that before. It was the first time I realized he wasn't completely sane."

"So you blocked the contract?" she asked.

"Yes, and I did whatever else he wanted, which thankfully wasn't much. But things got complicated last year. Jerry Caldwell got involved with your sister and then your brother got tangled up with the operation in Mexico. That's when I found out about your father. Reid told me your dad had been a thorn in his side years ago. He thought when he'd taken care of your father; that would be the end of his problems with your family. But then Alicia came along, followed by your brother."

"He knew that I worked for you. What did he think about me?" she asked.

"He wanted me to keep you close. Everything you told me, I told him."

She let out a breath realizing why Reid had been able to battle everything so efficiently. "Well, that's just great."

The senator's lips drew into a tight line. "I did what I had to do. Reid needed me to stall the investigation and stack the Senate hearings with senators who liked military defense contractors. I made sure two senators recused themselves by using information I had on them."

"So you blackmailed them?" she asked, surprised once again at the depth of his treachery.

"Let's just say I suggested it was in their best interests to recuse themselves. I thought it was over when the hearings ended and the FBI investigation was closed. MDT had taken a big hit on government contracts, but I figured they'd eventually win back trust and respect as they got distance from the security problems." Dillon paused, looking from Dani to Patrick. "And then you showed up with more questions, Mr. Kane. I knew you were going to be the final straw, especially when you and Dani teamed up together. Now, here we are."

"What's Erica's role in all this?" Patrick asked. "What does she do for Packer?"

"Beyond keeping me in line—I don't know."

"What about Stephen Phelps?" she asked, curious if the press secretary was also involved. "He seems tight with Erica."

"He was her hire; I have no idea what he knows."

"Is Erica romantically involved with Reid?" she asked, thinking that Reid had made a habit of hooking up with powerful women who could help him with his plans.

"She hasn't said, but there's an intimacy between them when they're in a room together. I didn't ask her, because I didn't want to know."

"How did they sabotage my mother's plane?" Patrick asked. "Was it a bomb? Was the pilot on a suicide mission? I know he was a last-minute replacement. Did he know he was going to die, too?"

"Reid told me they shot the plane down with the railgun they'd built at Carmichael Ranch."

"Oh, my God," Dani whispered, seeing the shock on Patrick's face. While they'd gone over theories that included a bomb, they'd never considered that the plane had been shot down. She moved closer to him, putting her hand on his arm.

"They shot the plane down?" Patrick echoed. "That was eight years ago. The technology isn't even ready now, is it?"

"It's close. Consistency and accuracy have been a problem with the railgun. But those are the results reported by MDT. I'm not sure about what Reid has developed in his freelance operation. MDT makes a lot of weapons, as you know. They're also involved in communications and aviation systems. The railgun is one small part of the MDT portfolio of business, but for Reid it was his main focus. He wanted to make that gun better and faster than his brother could. It's a potentially significant new advancement in weaponry. The railguns will be put on ships. They'll be able to attack from the middle of the ocean without the need for chemical propellants."

"Those weapons will be great," she said. "Unless they're used in the wrong way. Unless they're used by people intent on evil—like Reid Packer." Her stomach churned as she thought of all the possibilities. "You just said he wasn't completely sane. Didn't you think it was time to blow the whistle?"

Before the senator could reply, Patrick answered for him. "He couldn't do that. His hands were too dirty. Isn't that right?"

The senator shrugged. He still couldn't make the admission out loud.

"What about the change in pilot?" Reid asked again. "Was there some reason the other pilot was kept off the plane?"

"As far as I know, the original pilot got food

419

poisoning, and the other guy was a replacement. If that's not the truth, I don't know what is."

Patrick shook his head, pacing around the salon. "This is unbelievable. You're a United States senator; how could you stand by and do nothing?"

"Like you said, I was in too deep," the senator replied, finally conceding his involvement.

"What's happening today?" she asked. "Tania Vaile told us that something big was about to take place, but she didn't say what. Do you know?"

"I don't know. I was having my usual Fourth of July barbecue today until Erica called me away. I left a house full of people to come and meet you. They're going to wonder where I am."

She thought about that. Maybe help would be coming. On the other hand . . . "Erica probably made up a story to tell your wife and your friends. You've been called away on important business. No one will question that. You're often absent from family events."

"That's true, but not this party. My wife will be angry when I don't come back. She'll probably think something is wrong." He frowned. "At least, I hope so. It's getting dark."

She followed his gaze to window. While they'd been talking, dusk had fallen. It was after eight o'clock now. All she could see through the windows were shadows of the sea.

"I don't understand what's happening," the senator said, and for the first time there was fear in his voice. "I've always done everything Reid asked me to do."

"You think he's loyal to you?" Patrick asked in amazement. "You're nothing to him, Senator. You're a tool he uses when he wants, and when he's done, he gets rid of it."

"We're friends."

"Reid doesn't have friends," Patrick said. "He has people who are useful to him."

"Erica said you were going to be a cover story," she put in, drawing the men's attention back to her. "He's setting you up, Senator."

"For what?"

"Whatever his big plan is." She wondered how she could feel so calm when her life was on the line. "He's going to shoot something down or blow something up." She looked at Patrick. "He's going to kill us. Something terrible is going to happen. It will look like an accident, just like the plane crash and my dad's disappearance."

"Killing us isn't the big event," Patrick said, obviously following her train of thought. "It can't be. There has to be more, Dani."

He was right. There had to be more, and it all suddenly made sense. "It's the Fourth of July. We're on a boat. The railgun is made to shoot from the deck of a ship."

"Oh, God," the senator said, sinking down on the couch.

"What?" she asked. "What are you thinking?"

"When I came on board with Erica, I saw two men moving a large crate onto the upper deck. I asked her what was going on. She said she'd investigate and find out."

"I'm betting there's a railgun in that crate," Patrick said tersely.

"Is it that small?" she asked. "Can it be moved on board a boat like this?"

"There are different sizes," the senator replied, a defeated look coming into his eyes. "They have one that's huge, but others that are more transportable. So, yes, there could be a gun on the boat. It could have been in the crate that I saw."

"What would they be shooting at?" she asked. "What's the target?"

"I don't know."

She looked at Patrick; he gave her a helpless, frustrated look.

"It could be anywhere, Dani."

"Not anywhere," she corrected. "It has to be somewhere important, a place that has meaning." She paused. "What about the state capitol? Or, hell, what about the US Capitol? Could the gun shoot that far, Senator?"

"Possibly," Dillon said. "But it's after eleven o'clock there now."

"That's true," she muttered. "So it could be more local or a target on the west coast. The attack would be traced to this boat. Maybe Packer wants to tie the senator to the attack. That would tie in with Erica's mention of Packer needing a cover story."

"If they do shoot the gun from here," Patrick continued. "They'll want to take it with them before they destroy the yacht. There has to be a second boat, a way to get the gun and the people who shot it back to shore."

That made sense. "I wonder what they're waiting for," she mused. "It's been at least an hour since we left the harbor. Why haven't they done it already? Does it take time to set up the gun? Are we not far enough from shore?"

"They're waiting for cover," Patrick said, a new gleam in his eyes.

"It's already dark."

"They could be waiting for the fireworks," he added. "Think about it. With the sky lit up from fireworks, no one would notice the blast of a gun that looks like a streak of lightning."

A loud rumble echoed through the air. "Is the show starting now?" she asked, rushing to the window, but she couldn't see any fireworks. She had no idea where they were, and it was the scariest feeling in the world. And then a jagged light ripped through the night sky, revealing swirling, stormy clouds.

It wasn't fireworks; it was thunder and lightning.

A shiver ran down her spine.

It was just like all the times before, she thought, memories racing through her mind . . . her dad's plane had gone down in a lightning storm, Patrick's mother's plane had crashed in a lightning storm, Jake had rescued Katherine during a lightning storm.

And now it was happening to her.

Patrick pulled her away from the window, and said, "Stand back, I'm going to break the glass."

"Any noise will bring the men with the guns."

"We have to take that chance. We're sitting ducks in here."

As he grabbed a chair, she ran toward the bar, looking for some other weapon. There was a fire extinguisher on the wall. She grabbed it as Senator Dillon got up and opened a closet next to the bar. He pulled out a wooden broom.

"Better than nothing," he said grimly.

Patrick swung the metal chair at the window with all of his might. The glass cracked. He did it two more times, and then the window finally shattered.

Patrick went out the window first. When no one came running to investigate the broken glass, he offered his hand to Dani. She climbed out, the senator right behind her.

While she still had doubts about the senator's innocence in anything, at the moment he was on their side, and they needed him as an ally.

As they crept along the side deck, fireworks began lighting up the sky over the harbor. With the fireworks came thunder and lightning, a cacophony of sound and light surrounding them.

They headed for the stairs, stopping abruptly when a man with a gun came around the corner.

Patrick tackled him before he could get off a shot, slamming the man's head against the wall and then shoving him into a corner as he fell unconscious. She was shocked at how fast everything happened, but she'd seen the ruthless determination on Patrick's face. He was fighting for all their lives. No time now for hesitation. She had to be ready, too.

Patrick grabbed the man's gun, and they went up the stairs as quietly as they could, pausing toward the top to assess the situation.

There were three men on the deck, all dressed in jeans and dark t-shirts. Dani didn't recognize any of them. One stood at the far edge, talking on a phone. The other two were near the railgun.

She'd seen photos of the weapon during the MDT hearings, but seeing the five-foot long weapon in person was another story. Two metal rails surrounded a missile-like chamber. The gun stood about three feet off the ground.

They hadn't set it off, which meant they had a little time—not only to save themselves, but also to save the innocent people who would be killed by that gun.

Patrick whispered instructions.

"Dani—when I say go, spray the two guys by the gun. Senator—you rush the guy with the phone. I'm going to take out whoever I can with as many shots as I can get off. We have to do this all at once. We've got the element of surprise, a few seconds of time. Let's make them count."

"I'm ready," she said.

Dillon also gave a nod. "Got it."

They made their way up to the deck.

One of the men standing by the gun turned in their direction.

"Go," Patrick said.

She sprayed a sharp concentrated stream of foamy fire suppressant at the two men while the senator moved behind her.

One of the men came through the wet mist, his gun drawn. Patrick shot him in the chest, and he fell to the ground.

As her extinguisher ran out, she jumped behind a post as Patrick took cover a few feet away and exchanged gunfire with the man still standing by the railgun. Across the deck, she could see the senator fighting with a much younger man, and he did not look like he was winning.

Another man came up from the stairs on the other side of the deck. She called out a warning to Patrick. He shot the guy before he could fire off his gun.

More gunfire. Then Patrick's shot hit the man by the gun. The man stumbled and fell against the railgun, his weight sending the gun onto its side.

The railgun sparked, a magnificent shot of light

that blinded her, and then a projectile took off. It went straight up, then turned and came back toward the deck.

"Jump," Patrick yelled, shoving her toward the side of the boat.

She didn't jump. She was too terrified to leap into the inky black water, but she didn't have a choice.

As the projectile hit the deck, the boat exploded, and she was flung through the air along with wood, metal and pieces of the ship, hoping and praying that she'd survive the blast and that Patrick would, too.

It couldn't end like this, not after all they'd been through.

TWENTY-FOUR

She hit the water hard, a relentless force dragging her deep into the sea. She fought with all her strength to get back to the surface, but she wasn't sure she would make it. Her lungs were bursting. Her head was spinning. She could barely think. She needed air desperately.

Kicking and pulling at the water, she finally began to come up. When she burst through the surface, she gasped, sucking in air as quickly as she could. She was yards away from the flaming remnants of the boat, which had been completely shattered by the explosion. How quickly things had changed.

Thunder crashed over her head; lightning flashed across the sky. She swam through the darkness, using the lightning strikes to find her way. She'd never believed in the power of lightning, but now she could feel the electricity charging the air and the water around her.

You will find the last piece of the puzzle. You will know the truth. Her great-grandmother's words rang through her head.

Dani hadn't understood the prophecy.

She hadn't believed her sister when Alicia had said the lightning would show her what she needed to see.

And she'd been doubtful that her brother Jake had actually seen a vision of their dead father right before his plane crashed in the Mexican jungle.

For months, she'd maintained they were all a little crazy, that there was no conspiracy, no mystery to solve.

Now she was a believer. But had she taken too long to see the truth?

The lightning vanished. Darkness surrounded her. The rain poured down on her head, a steamy shower on a hot summer night.

She couldn't see a foot in front of her. But she had to keep going. Lives were at stake, including her own.

She swam harder, then she bumped into something hard and heavy—a body.

Her heart stopped.

Terror ran through her.

Oh, God! Was she too late?

Patrick blinked the water out of his eyes. All he could see was water and fire. The yacht had been completely destroyed by the blast. It was a miracle he'd survived. Now, he just had to find Dani.

"Dani," he yelled, as he treaded water and peered through the mix of fire and darkness.

Where was she? He needed her to be alive. He couldn't live without her. He was in love with her, and he'd never had the chance to tell her that. He had to have that chance.

He called her name until he was hoarse. His arms were getting tired. But he couldn't give up. Who knew when or if help would come?

He wondered what had happened to the others on board. And what about the second boat? There had to have been one nearby. He wished now he'd taken a look around before they'd charged onto the deck.

"Dani," he called again, realizing that if he didn't find her soon, he'd be in real trouble. The fire was burning out, and clouds covered the sky, leaving nothing but darkness and fear.

And then the air around him cracked with thunder.

He waited for the lightning to show him the way.

"I know you're coming," he yelled, looking up at the sky. "Bring it now. Show me where Dani is. I need to save her."

The black night didn't answer back. *What the hell was he thinking?* There was no magic. No miracles. He'd wished for one before when his mom's plane had crashed. He'd prayed the worst wouldn't happen, but it had.

"No," he yelled. He wasn't giving up. Dani was a fighter. She'd swim as long as she possibly could.

And then the lightning he'd wished for lit up the sky. It started high, the flash zigzagging all the way down to the water. It hit something gold.

Dani's ring!

Her hand was moving. She was swimming.

He raced toward her, crossing the distance between them in less than a minute.

"Dani," he said, as he reached her.

She stopped swimming to tread water, her beautiful face shimmering with water and probably tears, but there was relief in her eyes now.

"Patrick. Oh, my God. I thought I lost you."

He wanted to put his arms around her, but he didn't want to take them both under. He knew she had to be getting tired, too. He looked around and saw a long board floating not far away from them.

It was the magnificently large guitar-shaped coffee table from the salon, and it was intact.

"Let's get to that board," he said, swimming ahead of her.

When they reached the floating table, he pushed her up onto the top, then pulled himself out of the water.

They fell into each other's arms. He held her as tightly as he could, needing to reassure himself that she was all right. After a long hug, he said, "Are you hurt?"

"I don't think so." She brushed her wet hair away from her face. "I was so worried about you, Patrick. I was trying to find you, but I couldn't see anything."

"Neither could I, until I saw the lightning hit your ring. It was a big, beautiful spotlight." Wonder and amazement filled her eyes as the clouds above cleared and the moon and the stars came out, throwing light on her face. "And a miracle," he added. "I wasn't sure we were going to get one."

"We were due."

He kissed her wet mouth. "I completely agree."

As he pulled back, he saw someone moving a dozen feet away from them. *Was it one of the gunmen?*

"It's the senator," Dani said.

He could see the senator struggling in the water and part of him wanted to let him keep struggling. The man had stood by and done nothing while so many innocent people had been killed.

"We have to save him," Dani said.

He knew they did; he just didn't want to. But there was no way he'd let Dani get back in the water, and she would do that. "I'll get him."

He slid off the table. He swam toward the senator, who was starting to flail wearily against the current, sinking under, then coming back up spluttering.

He grabbed the senator's arm. "I've got you."

The senator gave him a dazed look. Blood was coming from a cut over his eye. He probably had a concussion.

He hooked his arm around the senator's neck and swam him over to their makeshift life raft.

It took some effort from both him and Dani to get the senator out of the water and onto the table.

The senator collapsed on the wood while Patrick pulled himself back up.

"Hang in there," Dani said, putting her hand on the senator's shoulder. "Help is coming."

Patrick looked around, wondering if she'd seen something he hadn't, but there were no boats heading their way.

When he met her gaze, she shrugged. "We have to stay positive," she said. "Someone will come looking for us, or at least for him."

"My wife," the senator mumbled. "She'll go to the harbor. She'll see the boat is gone. She'll send someone to look for me."

"I hope she does," Dani said. "Someone should come looking for you. You are a United States senator, after all."

"Is that why you saved me?" the senator asked.

"No," she said. "We saved you because it was the right thing to do. And when this is over, when we're back on land, you're going to do the right thing, too. You're going to tell the world about Reid Packer and everything he's done."

"You should have just let me die out here," he said wearily. "He'll kill me if I talk."

"He already tried to kill you," Patrick said sharply. "The only way you'll survive is to put him behind bars."

"You don't think he can kill from behind bars?"

"It will be more difficult," he replied.

"My career is over," the senator murmured.

"Yeah, but you'll live, and maybe you can do something better with the rest of your life."

The senator closed his eyes.

Dani gave Patrick a worried look. "He has a bad head injury. Should we let him fall asleep?"

"No," he said, shaking the senator's shoulder. "Come on, Dillon, don't quit on us. Just think: if you cut a deal, you can probably get immunity."

The senator blinked his eyes open. "You think so?"

"Unfortunately, yes." He wished that weren't true, but they needed the senator to get to Reid. Reid was the head of the dragon. And he'd breathed fire for the last time.

They shivered as the night grew longer and the air got colder. He tried to keep the senator awake with optimistic and hopeful chatter, even when his own spirits began to flag.

There were also other worries beginning to enter his mind. In the dark shadows, he'd seen sleek, shark-like shapes swimming not far from them, but he didn't want to scare Dani by mentioning them. She was being as brave as anyone he'd ever seen, keeping her head up, trying to stay positive. He couldn't imagine anyone else being so strong in this situation. He hadn't thought he could love her more, but he did.

The moon and the stars disappeared behind new clouds and the darkness made their position seem even more precarious. But then he saw

434

specks of light in the distance and the sound of a motor. His watch had stopped working a long time ago, but he thought it must be after midnight by now.

"Help is coming," he said.

Dani lifted her gaze to his. "Will they see us? It's so dark. I wish we had something bright."

"We do." His gaze moved to the shiny gold ring on her finger. It had saved them both more than once. "Wave your hand in the air—your ring hand."

"You think the ring is going to bring the rescuers to us?" she asked doubtfully.

"I absolutely do. Don't you?"

"I never wanted to believe in it. I never wanted to believe in my great-grandmother, in that part of my family, in my history. I feel bad that I wasn't as close to her as Jake and Alicia. I wish I could go back and hear her stories now."

"She knows you loved her."

"I don't know that I did love her," she said honestly. "I do now, because I understand her better, but when I was a kid, I thought she was crazy, like my mom did. Now, I believe that there are things in the universe we just can't explain away with logic and reason."

"Sometimes you just have to have faith," he agreed.

"I do have faith. Not just in this ring—in you," she said, meeting his gaze. "I knew you would find me, Patrick. I knew I would find you. We're connected. We always have been."

"Even before we met," he murmured. He took her hand in his, feeling like she was truly the other half of his soul.

A boat came closer, and for a split second he worried that it wasn't a rescue boat, but someone Reid had sent out to make sure they were dead. He almost told Dani not to wave for help, but then he remembered what he'd just said. They needed to have faith.

Dani waved her hand in the air; a spotlight from the boat swept over the water, illuminating their position. He saw the sign on the side of the boat. It was the Coast Guard.

"We're going to be all right," he said, letting out a breath of relief.

"Yes, we will," she said, her eyes shining with happiness. "We made it, Patrick."

"I couldn't have done it without you."

"Me, either."

The rest of the night passed in a crazy blur. Dani called Jake from the Coast Guard ship and relayed what had happened to them and the attack that had been thwarted. Jake then contacted Agent Wolfe, who met them at the hospital with a team of agents and personnel that included the local police department and Homeland Security.

The senator was alert enough to tell Agent Wolfe

that whatever they had to say was the truth and that he should listen to them. Then he gave Dani a weak smile and said, "I know I let you down, but as you said, it's time for me to do the right thing, even if it will cost me everything."

"But you'll get something back," Dani said. "Respect."

"From you?"

"From yourself," she said.

Patrick liked the fact that Dani didn't let her boss off the hook too easily. The man deserved to pay for what he'd done. Turning a blind eye to evil had put blood on his hands, too.

After being briefly examined and receiving treatment for their cuts and bruises, he and Dani were released from medical care and warmly greeted by their families waiting in the lobby of the ER. They only had a few minutes to make explanations and embrace each other before Agent Wolfe whisked them away to the local FBI office for a debriefing.

They spent the next eight hours in interviews. They were brought dry clothes and food and drinks to keep them going through the endless round of questions, but it was still a grueling night.

It was ten o'clock on Monday morning when Agent Wolfe came back from a break and told them that Reid Packer and Erica Hunt were in custody.

"Thank God," he muttered, exchanging a relieved look with Dani.

"Packer has already asked for his lawyer," Agent Wolfe said. "Ms. Hunt said she's willing to make a deal."

"Of course she is," Dani said cynically. "She's ready to play whatever side works in her favor."

"That could work in our favor, too," Patrick said. "Reid is the mastermind. He's the one we want."

"I'd still like to see her spend a few days in jail."

"I suspect you'll get your wish," Agent Wolfe said. "I also just got word from the Coast Guard that they picked up two men in a sinking boat. One has a gunshot wound, and he's also willing to talk. He said the gun's target was the White House. They were going to blow it up at the stroke of midnight under the cover of fireworks."

"I can't believe it," Dani muttered.

Patrick was also shocked at the ambitious plan.

Agent Wolfe nodded, a grim line across his mouth. "Packer is going down for everything, and his shadow company will be out of business for good. The rats are deserting the sinking ship as fast as they can."

He was happy to hear Reid's minions were going to turn on him. It would take everyone they could find to put the powerful man away for the rest of his life.

"That's it for now," Agent Wolfe said. "You're both free to leave. I think you should feel safe enough to go home. But if you could stay in town another day or two, I'd appreciate it."

Dani nodded. "Of course. I'm not even sure I have a job to go back to."

"Senator Dillon is also being investigated," the agent added. "Not only by us, but also by the Senate. He is cooperating as well. There's a good chance he'll get some sort of immunity to testify against Packer. Like you said, Mr. Kane, we want the big fish."

"I hate to see anyone go free, but we definitely want to stop the decade-long round of terror that Packer has run," he said. "Too many people have died. You have a lot of work to do, Agent Wolfe."

"Going back ten years," he admitted. "It's going to be a long investigation, and this is just the beginning."

Patrick got to his feet to shake the agent's hand. Then he put his arm around Dani, and they walked out to the street. An agent was waiting to give them a ride wherever they wanted to go. He hesitated, and then gave his address. He was going to take Dani home.

"I like it," Dani said, as she walked around his living room. "It's modern, nicely furnished, warm, and a little messy."

"When I left a week ago, I didn't know I'd be gone this long," he said, picking up an empty glass and plate from the coffee table and taking it into the kitchen.

"I wasn't judging," she said as he returned to the room. "I like apartments that looked lived in."

"Good, then we'll get along well."

"I already knew we got along well," she said with a small smile.

"Do you want to take a shower?"

"And rinse the Gulf of Mexico off me? Yes. I also want to eat and sleep and make love to you. I just can't decide in what order to do those things." She laughed at the expression on his face. "I think I know which one you'd pick."

"I think you do," he said, moving across the room to slide his arms around her waist and press his mouth against hers. "Your lips are warmer now."

"Because you saved my life."

"You saved mine first," he reminded her. "Maybe we should stick together in case either of us needs saving again."

"I'm kind of hoping we won't."

"But just in case . . ."

"Or we could stick together for another reason," she said tentatively. There were so many things she wanted to say to Patrick, but now that they were alone, now that the danger had passed, she wasn't quite sure where to start. "Like maybe we want to get to know each other better."

"I would like that. And, by the way, I could do that in DC."

"I'm not sure I'll be in DC. The senator will resign. The office will be dismantled. I'll be a legislative assistant without a legislator."

"You'll find another job, Dani. You're smart, and when the news hits, you're going to be a hero. You stopped a terrorist attack. People will be lining up to hire you."

"I'm sure you'll have a lot of offers, too." She put her hands on his shoulders and felt the tight knots in his muscles. "You're still tense."

"And you're partly responsible for that."

"I think the night's events have something to do with it, too." She paused, looking into his beautiful brown eyes. She saw relief there, but she also saw other emotions, emotions she doubted he'd had a chance to deal with yet. "Do you feel like you have closure now, Patrick? We don't have all the details, but we do know that your mother was trying to stop Reid and that she lost her life because of that pursuit. I think she'd be happy that you finished it for her."

"I think she would, too. I don't know if there's ever really closure, but it's nice not to have so many questions. It doesn't take away the fact that she's gone. I'm guessing you feel the same way about your dad."

"Yes, but I feel like today is a turning point for

my family. We've been trapped in the past for a decade. Now, we're finally free—all of us, although I do need to have a long conversation with my mother. The two minutes we had together at the hospital showed me how angry and hurt she is. Maybe it wasn't fair to leave her out of things, but on the other hand, she didn't have to deal with all the stress we did. In the end, I hope she'll be happy this is finally over."

"So, about what we're going to do next . . ." he said, leaning over to kiss her again.

"Wait, I have to say one thing first. When I was in the water, and I couldn't find you, I was terrified, Patrick. I didn't want to lose you, and I was afraid I would."

Shadows filled his eyes. "I was scared, too. All I could think about was that I hadn't had a chance to tell you that I love you. I know it's fast, and you don't have to say it back, but I need to put it on the table now, because it's how I feel."

"I love you, too, Patrick. It is fast, but it feels like forever at the same time. We were destined to meet."

"I think we were."

"I've been afraid to give my heart to anyone. Losing my dad was so painful, and then I buried myself in my career, and I thought a man would just derail that."

"I would never do that, Dani. I want us both to have what we want and to have each other, too. In other words, let's have it all," he finished with a smile.

"I like the sound of that. Okay, I know what I want to do first."

"I swear, if you say make breakfast—"

She cut him off with a kiss. "We'll eat later—much later."

EPILOGUE

Four months later

There were no storm clouds in the sky today, no echo of thunder, no flash of lightning when they arrived at the cemetery on the fifth of November to celebrate the return of her father's body. With the help of Agent Wolfe, eyewitness testimony from some workers at the ranch in Mexico, and the Mexican authorities, they'd been able to find her father's remains and bring him home.

Dani got out of the car with Patrick and waited nearby as Jake and Katherine pulled in behind them, followed by her mother Joanna and Alicia and Michael. Katherine's brother TJ and her mother Debbie came up behind them and finally Patrick's father, his aunt Jill and his cousin Marcus were in the last car.

"I really appreciate that your family is joining us," she told Patrick as they waited for the others.

"They wouldn't have missed it." Patrick gave her a smile. "In case you haven't noticed, they're as crazy about you as I am."

"They're wonderful, too. I'm glad that what we found out about your mother was all good."

"I almost forgot that my investigation started

with that stupid rumor that Senator Stuart's daughter told me about."

"She was wrong about that, but she started a small ball rolling that grew into a monster boulder."

"And almost took us out," he said with a laugh, putting his arm around her. "But we're too smart, and too tough."

"Better together," she said, smiling up at him.

They'd spent the past four months living together in Patrick's condo while the FBI and police did their jobs to piece together a case against Reid Packer and two dozen or so other individuals. The whistleblower source who had given them Tania's name had come out from hiding. The man, who had once worked in the finance department of MDT, had proven to be quite helpful, and now all of the skeletons were finally out of the closet.

As she'd predicted, Senator Dillon had had to resign from the Senate, and his office had been dismantled. Erica had cut a deal for immunity but would still spend some time in jail. Stephen Phelps turned out to be completely innocent and just had the misfortune to be friendly with Erica. He'd been shocked when the truth had come out, but another senator had already hired him, so he hadn't missed a beat. Ann Higgins had been the first journalist to report the story, and subscribers to her online magazine had quadrupled in one day.

She'd been more than a little grateful to Patrick for giving her the scoop of a lifetime.

As Patrick had predicted, Dani was already getting offers from not only other politicians but also agencies involved in counterterrorism and national defense. She'd also been encouraged by her former mentor Joe Gelbman to run for office herself, something she was definitely considering. She'd start out small, at the local level. She could see herself as a congresswoman or a senator one day, but she was willing to pay some dues.

Patrick had started the rebuild on his father's cabin, and when he wasn't overseeing the contractors, he'd begun writing a novel. He'd discovered that he could enjoy researching a fictional mystery almost as much as a real one. She doubted he'd stay out of nonfiction forever, but it was nice to see him relaxed and happy.

It was also nice to see her siblings in the same state of mind. Alicia and Michael had come back from Miami the night before, and announced that they were having a baby.

Jake and Katherine had set a wedding date for next May, and her mother was ecstatic about her first grandchild and another wedding to plan.

Life was not just back to normal; it was better than normal, because she had Patrick, too.

"Here's a small bouquet for you," Alicia said, handing her a small fistful of flowers. "I thought we'd put them on the grave."

"Great idea." Once everyone was out of their cars, they walked over to the freshly covered grave and placed their flowers. Katherine brought out a bottle of champagne and poured a dozen small cups of the sparkling wine, and then Jake made a toast.

"To the man who gave us life, who made us laugh, who taught us to look up in the sky and to dream big," he said. "The man who lived a heroic life, an example for us all to follow. Here's to you, Dad."

"Here's to you, Dad," she echoed, lifting her gaze to the sky. Then she took a sip of champagne.

"I want to say something, too," Alicia said. She turned to their mother. "I want to make a toast to you, Mom."

"To me?" her mother asked in surprise.

"Yes," Alicia said. "You were there for me after Dad died. We didn't always see eye-to-eye, but you took care of me and you loved me, and before and after Dad's death, you were a great mother. I only hope I can be half as good a mother as you."

"Oh, my," her mother said, dabbing at her eyes. "I didn't expect that."

"I feel the same way as Alicia," Dani said. "I know we came here to honor Dad, but really we want to honor you, too. So here's to you, Mom."

The rest of the group seconded her toast and they finished off the champagne.

"Before we end this, I'd also like to say something," Patrick said.

She turned to him in surprise. He gave her a smile, then fell to one knee. Her heart leapt against her chest.

"Dani, I love you more than life itself. Will you marry me?"

Her jaw dropped open in shock. "Patrick, I—yes. Yes! Of course, I'll marry you. I adore you."

He pulled out a small jewelry box. "Then can I offer you this ring to wear on your left hand?"

"You can," she said, staring in amazement at the beautiful square-cut diamond ring. She still wore her great-grandmother's ring on her right hand. It felt like it belonged there now. But this one belonged to her and to Patrick—to their love story.

Patrick slipped the ring onto her finger. Their families clapped in delight. Then she pulled him to his feet and gave him a loving kiss.

"I wasn't sure about proposing in a cemetery," he said with a grin. "In fact my father advised against it. But we're all together, and I didn't know when that would happen again. Plus, I thought you might want to be near your father, too."

"It's the perfect spot. You know me too well."

"Congratulations. I'm so happy for you," Alicia said, pulling Dani away from Patrick to give her a hug.

"You caught a good one," Jake said.

"The best," she agreed.

"I'm so happy for you, Dani," her mother said, a beaming smile on her face. "But I'm not surprised. Patrick asked me for your hand. It was very sweet."

She looked back at her husband-to-be. "When did you do that?"

"A few days ago. I wanted everyone to be on board."

In other words, he'd wanted to make sure everything about this moment would be perfect for her. She felt incredibly honored and overwhelmed with love.

Patrick's family came forward with their good wishes and congratulations, and as Dani looked around the group, she realized this was what was most important—love and family. She didn't know how she'd ever forgotten that.

"Time for lunch," Jake said. "See you all at the restaurant."

She and Patrick walked slowly back to their car as the others drove off for the second part of the celebration.

"I could have waited until the restaurant," Patrick said, putting his arms around her.

"I'm glad you didn't."

"The location is a little unusual."

"Which pretty much describes our entire relationship," she said with a laugh. "We're going to be happy."

"So happy," he agreed. "Together we can do

anything . . . maybe even get you an office in the White House someday."

"That's thinking big."

He grinned. "Always. I'd like to be the *first husband.*"

"You're going to be my first and only husband," she said, kissing him again.

"And you are going to be my first and only wife," he promised. "Forever."

"I just hope that's long enough," she whispered.

Agent Damon Wolfe thought about not intruding in on what was obviously a private moment, but as he pulled up behind Dani and Patrick's car, he decided to move ahead. He was heading on to his next assignment, and he wanted to give them an update before he left town.

They broke apart, looking at him with surprise and a bit of wariness. He couldn't blame them. He'd put them through the wringer the past few months, but he couldn't have taken down MDT and Reid Packer without their help. They hadn't always been friends but they'd always wanted the same thing—justice.

"Agent Wolfe," Dani said, as she came forward. "What are you doing here? I thought you were back in DC."

"I had to make one last trip here to finish up my report. When I spoke to Patrick the other day, he mentioned that you were going to have another ceremony now that your father is finally home. I'm sorry to interrupt. This won't take long."

"It's fine. You're not interrupting anything," she said. "We were just about to leave to meet my family for lunch, but we're not in a hurry."

"What's the latest?" Patrick asked.

"We arrested two more people in Mexico yesterday. We think we've got everyone now."

"How many does that make?" Patrick asked.

"Twenty-eight people with varying degrees of culpability. The case against Reid Packer is solid. He's going to go to prison for a very long time."

"What about his brother, Alan?" Dani asked. "We've wondered how Reid could operate for so long without his brother knowing anything."

"Alan said he let Reid handle the financials because he felt guilty at getting the company from his father. He had no idea that his brother was out for revenge and world domination. Reid's father also claims total surprise. Frankly, I'm not sure they both didn't see something, but they're finished anyway. MDT will never get another contract. Alan is already selling off divisions of the company. They'll end up in some form of bankruptcy with the massive number of lawsuits headed their way."

"I'm glad. I never want to see that company name again," she said.

"You won't. At any rate, the next year will be full of trials, in which you may be called to testify."

451

"We're ready," Patrick said.

He nodded. "The country owes you both a debt of gratitude. In case no one finds the time to say it, thank you."

Dani smiled. "You're welcome. But I really want to thank you for helping us bring my father's body home. You went above and beyond, Agent Wolfe."

"I'm glad I was successful. I'll let you get on with your day."

He shook hands with both of them and then got back into his car. He pulled out his phone and punched in a number. "I'm ready for my next assignment."

Dear Reader,

I hope you enjoyed *Summer Rain*, the third and final book in the Lightning Strikes Trilogy! I had so much fun creating this trio of romantic suspense novels.

As you may have guessed from the ending, FBI Agent Damon Wolfe will be getting his own book next year as I start a new FBI trilogy. In the meantime, if you're looking for your next book to read, I hope you'll check out The Callaways, my ongoing family series featuring love, mystery and adventure. The first book is *On a Night Like This*.

If you're looking for more romantic suspense, you might want to look into picking up my bestselling duo: *Taken* and *Played*.

Don't want to miss a single book? Sign up for my news alerts at http://www.barbarafreethy .com/newsletter/! I promise not to bother you more than once a month.

If you'd like to join my private Facebook group of super fans, please go to https://www.facebook .com/groups/BarbaraFreethyStreetTeam/. Hope to see you online.

Until next time, happy reading!

Barbara Freethy

About the Author

Barbara Freethy is a #1 *New York Times* bestselling author of 50 novels ranging from contemporary romance to romantic suspense and women's fiction. Traditionally published for many years, Barbara opened her own publishing company in 2011 and has since sold over 6 million books! Twenty of her titles have appeared on the *New York Times* and *USA Today* bestseller lists.

Known for her emotional and compelling stories of love, family, mystery and romance, Barbara enjoys writing about ordinary people caught up in extraordinary adventures. Barbara's books have won numerous awards. She is a six-time finalist for the RITA for best contemporary romance from Romance Writers of America and a two-time winner for *Daniel's Gift* and *The Way Back Home*.

Barbara has lived all over the state of California and currently resides in Northern California where she draws much of her inspiration from the beautiful bay area.

For a complete listing of books, as well as excerpts and contests, and to connect with Barbara:

For information: barbara@barbarafreethy.com

Follow Barbara on Facebook at
http://www.facebook.com/barbarafreethybooks

Sign up for Barbara's Newsletter at
http://www.barbarafreethy.com/newsletter/

Join Barbara's Private Fan Group at
https://www.facebook.com/groups
/BarbaraFreethyStreetTeam/

Visit Barbara's website at
http://www.barbarafreethy.com

Center Point Large Print
600 Brooks Road / PO Box 1
Thorndike, ME 04986-0001 USA

(207) 568-3717

US & Canada:
1 800 929-9108
www.centerpointlargeprint.com